EVA FELLNER

THE HIGHLANDERESS

Historical Novel

VOLUME 5 OUT OF 5

ENJA'S LEGACY

For additional Bonus Material
please visit

www.highlanderess.com/clan

and follow the process outlined there.

I dedicate this final volume to the future
we may shape together.

To standing shoulder to shoulder.
To overcoming obstacles without turning away.
To meeting fear with courage.
To stepping in when others are treated unjustly.
And to knowing that when you need the strength to
live your truth, you are not alone.
This final book of the saga is dedicated to
our growing Clan.

From the Heart of Eva Fellner

South Africa, February 2026

Caught in the chaos of warring lands,
Where love ignites 'midst bloodied sands,
Enja stands with fate in hand.
Duty calls; she must command.

These were the words with which I welcomed you to Enja's Voyage—the first volume of *The Highlanderess.* Do you remember?

Enja was a new kind of heroine. Bold. Uncompromising. Sharp-edged. Hard to pin down. Unpredictable.

I faced a great deal of criticism for telling her story in six-month intervals. At first, that was all I was permitted to fit into a single book. Who could have guessed that I would one day write more than 2,500 pages about Enja?

Now, the publication of the fifth—and final—volume, *this book*, is just around the corner. And I find myself writing these lines for you—my readers, Enja's loyal companions.

My thoughts keep circling the same question: why am I choosing now to bring this extraordinarily successful series to an end?

In 2021, I published the first volume of *The Highlanderess* in Germany. Since then, the series has gone on to succeed in English and Spanish. The story reached number one in Germany and Spain, and the English edition even claimed the top spot ahead of Ken Follett at the height of his reign.

I became an international bestselling novelist—and for that, I want to thank you from the bottom of my heart. Though in the beginning, it certainly did not look that way.

It sounds almost mad to me today to bring this saga to its end—and yet, everything must end eventually.

From the very beginning, so many of you wished the story would never stop. Just as I did.

I was utterly possessed by Enja—by her wild life, her trials, her blows of fate, and her fleeting moments of happiness. I lived them all. I wrote them all. And I passed them on to you—unfiltered, heart to heart.

You felt that.

Those who truly burn for books call it passion.

Thousands of hours went into research and revision. But now, I must close this circle. Everything has been told. **The rest I leave to your imagination.**

Enja has shown us how we can truly find our destination—by living with purpose, by walking righteously, perhaps guided by a dream, or simply by trusting your intuition. This is what was always meant by the motto of The Highlanderess coat of arms:

Be Fearless!
Rebel. Rise. And Reign.

Even as the saga reaches its end with this final volume, we remain a clan of extraordinary personalities—heroines and heroes—standing together to make a difference in our time.

The Highlanderess Clan lives on. Simply scan the QR code you will find in the opening pages.

And together, we can still rebel—to help you rise, to help you reign, and to step boldly into the life that was always meant to be yours.

Now the time has come to part—painfully—from characters that you and I have grown to love. But that, too, is life. Set free what you love, and it will always find its way back to you. Enja has paved an incredibly successful path for me. Now I must walk on. I want to write many more stories.

So I release the Highlanderess and turn toward new adventures. I am already working on a new series—and I can tell you this much: it will be just as gripping and intense as everything that came before. It tells the story of a strong woman who grows through her trials. Who breaks—and rises again. Who loves, and yet is not allowed to be happy.

My novels so often find their home in Scotland, because only there does nature truly mirror the soul of these women: honest, fierce, and possessed of a wildness that takes your breath away.

Look forward to the final adventure of my heroine—and to her legacy. **Now, enjoy accompanying Enja on her final great journey.**

Yours,

Eva Fellner

Chapter 1

Smithfield, England,
20 July 1328

The air above the churned sand was searing — not only from the sun that beat down without mercy upon the spectators and the tournament participants, stealing the breath from their lungs. In the arena, the climax of a long-awaited spectacle was taking shape. The vibrant crowd fanned the air and pressed into the shade beneath trees and canvas roofs that stretched along the edge of the grounds. Pennants and banners in every colour fluttered lightly in the light wind above their heads. The roar of the fighters on the sand drowned out even the shouting from the stands. The clash of metal on metal sent shivers through the watchers, whose expressions were a mix of fascination and disgust. Some craned their necks to catch a clearer view of the bloody scene. Even the wooden poles rammed into the ground, bearing the slack banners, were climbed to get an unbroken view.

The bustling air was crowned by an unseasonably dry, sun-soaked summer that drew even more curious souls from the already crowded city to the tournament at Smithfield, a suburb of London. The once-quiet town was bursting at its seams.

Upon the sand had gathered the finest knights of the western hemisphere. For days, the preparations, the group combats, and the trials of qualification had dragged on. By the final day of the tournament, only a few remained, enduring the scorching heat within their armour.

Thousands of knights from distant realms had answered the summons of the bride's mother, Isabella of Aquitaine, and her lover, Roger Mortimer. Isabella ruled England as regent, having seen her husband, Edward II, slain in his cell. Though she had wed her daughter to the son of the Scottish king, Isabella kept the reins tight in her hands until her son, Edward, was fit to bear the crown's weight.

In honour of the newly crowned child-king and his young queen, a three-day spectacle was to be held, allowing the people to share in the celebrations. Two days earlier, on the seventeenth of July in the year of our Lord 1328, the four-year-old son of the Scottish king Robert de Bruce, David II, had been wed to the English princess Joanna, three years his elder—daughter of Isabella of France and King Edward II of England. David and Joanna were not present, yet the bride's mother and her lover rejoiced in a festival unlike any other. Isabella's blue eyes gleamed beneath the silk veil that covered her hair. Eagerly, she watched the splendid horses and their armoured riders clash in perilous combat. Her hand, adorned with golden rings, clasped that of her lover, Mortimer, tightly, as though she feared to let him go. The long-awaited climax of the spectacle would begin within moments.

For the wedding festivities, Isabella had summoned the finest knights of the English crown, France, and the Holy Roman Empire to the grandest tournament ever known. Three thousand fighters had enlisted and, three weeks earlier, had marched with their retinues to the tournament field beyond the gates of London, greeted by the citizens' jubilant cheers. The magnificent event was accompanied by a host of musicians, artists, and merchants, eager for well-paying patrons, for the days of preparation and practice left all men hungry and parched. Ornaments of every kind were on offer, especially for the ladies, who had adorned themselves splendidly for the occasion. Many among the gathered used the event for their own designs; here, men might vie for the favour of noblewomen or a comely mistress, while on the sand, ambitious knights fought for glory and honour.

Highborn ladies, draped in silken gowns and glittering jewels, fluttered their fans in restless haste. Barons and princes sweated beneath their ornate doublets, dabbing at their damp faces with small linen cloths. The royal retinue suffered no less than the common folk beneath the merciless sun, although the noble lords and ladies had the comfort of a canvas canopy stretched above their heads. The thousands of lesser souls sat bare to the blinding noon heat. Those who could had found a hat or cloth for shade. Here and there, noses wrinkled at the foul air rising from the crowd, a vile blend of sweat, dung, and sour ale. Not even the ladies' perfume could conquer the stench of so many bodies pressed together in the sweltering heat.

For days, some of the victors who would ride today had already proved themselves in the group combats — the so-called buhurt. In this mass contest, the armoured knights had to keep their seat while striking at one another with maces and blunted swords, each intent on unhorsing his foe. Great skill with steed and weapon had been shown by more than eighty men who, to the delight of the crowd, endured to the end. Should a knight be felled beneath the heavy blows of his opponents, his squires would carry him from the field. Often, it was not only the body that suffered wounds but also the pride. A fall in this early stage of the tournament drew the spectators' mockery and laughter, and to add to the disgrace, the defeated man lost both his gear and his horse to the victor.

To earn their place in the gruelling, near savage mêlée, every knight had been obliged to prove his skill weeks before, mounted and under the sharp eye of a stern judge. Most trials demanded mastery of the bow and arrow or lance, each test shaping the worthy from the rest. A loyal team, well-trained horses, and the right weapons brought the knights and their squires closer to the honour they sought.

The immense expense of entering meant mostly the wealthy and nobly born claimed one of the coveted places in the buhurt, yet there were exceptions. Should an unknown man or a knight without a banner prove his skill beforehand, he might rise through the ranks and reach the final rounds.

As expected, England and France proved to be the lands of the most triumphant knights. Their warriors fought with the sharpest skill and fiercest will. Splinters flew, metal clashed, and the sand softened the fall of the defeated. To reach the mêlée, a knight had already endured hours of strain and trial. Those who survived it without losing their horse earned the right to the final test: the royal discipline of the joust.

The thrilling joust between two knights had its roots in the daily combat drills of royal warriors. Mastery of the horse and the precise aim of the lance tip towards an opponent's breast or shield had been trained since childhood and honed through relentless practice. The task was to strike, with a blunted wooden lance, against the breastplate, head, or shield of the foe, at full gallop, and to unseat him. Only a wooden barrier—the tilt—divided the two horsemen. The powerful horses would carry the heavily armoured men past one another in their charge. Often, the fighters were so skilled that they could lift their opponent clean from the saddle. More than a few knights had already met an early end to their tournament in just this way.

In the joust, a warrior's full mastery was laid bare. The noble houses loyal to Queen Isabella needed little persuasion to join, as participation itself was both honour and homage to the knightly code.

The long-awaited highlight of the day was building towards a dramatic conclusion. The victors of the first round were soon decided. Only four of the eighty knights who had passed the trial remained, men already counted among the finest of their kind, destined to be written into the annals of history.

The first two combatants faced each other astride their mounts, both man and beast clad in plates of steel to guard against flying splinters. The horses' nostrils flared with tension while foam flecked their bits. These prized destriers—broad of chest and bred for battle—had been trained for such knightly duels, to remain unshaken by the roar and restlessness around them, yet even they felt the unease draped over the field like a heavy cloak. Their hooves shifted, dancing nervously in place.

The tension was now almost tangible. As ever before, such a spectacle, a strange restlessness took hold of all who watched. Women and men alike were caught in the spell of that perilous game of triumph and defeat. Every soul present knew how fatal the slightest mistake could be.

Some among the crowd still sought an unbroken view of the field. The press of bodies seemed endless, as waves of newcomers flooded into the packed arena. Even the stable boys scrambled up the wooden frames where the horses were tied, desperate for a glimpse. Every defeated knight still able to stand pushed forward, while the less fortunate—those with no access to the field—relied on swift-footed lads to bring them word of the fight.

The herald had just announced the name of a famed knight who was to face another finalist. The crowd erupted. Beneath the blazing sun and upon the sands of Smithfield, history was about to be made; that much was clear to all. Fingers pointed, whispers and chatter rose in a frenzy, while the two opponents entered the arena with their horses and squires.

The women craned their necks, fanning themselves in frantic motion. A few swayed on the brink of fainting—whether from the heat or the rising tension, none could tell. Some men rose from their seats to steal a better view, drawing sharp protests from those sitting behind.

The two fighters who had drawn the greatest attention now faced each other across the tilt. The drums began to beat. When they ceased, the horses would break into their charge. At once, silence fell among the spectators, as if thousands of people held their breath as one.

The tension among the crowd owed not only to the promise of the joust itself, but to the fame of the two knights now facing each other. Clad in the white and blue of the Douglas line, Sir James Douglas had fought his way into the final four. The Scottish king's general had been knighted by Robert de Bruce himself on the eve of Bannockburn, and with the triumph that followed, he had carved his name deep into the hearts of king and country alike.

James was among the eldest in this tournament. He relied less on strength than experience to keep his foes at bay. The bearded face of the famed general—who had never left his king's side in the struggle for the Scottish throne—shone red beneath his helmet. The visor was lifted to let the air in.

The hard gaze from dark eyes measured his foe over the steel plates guarding his horse's neck. James Douglas felt no fear for the fight ahead. His steed was swift, and with the weight of countless battles behind him, he had crushed every previous rival. Yet one thing unsettled the Scotsman; his opponent bore neither name nor banner. The stranger rode with uncanny skill, sure of hand and seat. Something about him felt amiss, though Douglas could not name it.

He wore black armour, his appearance bearing neither crest nor colours of any land. The herald spoke no name, nor offered the slightest hint of the rider's origin. Even during the buhurt, the darkly clad warrior had drawn notice from fighters and spectators alike. The brutal way he wielded his weapons and guided his horse against his foes had already stirred lively debate among the knights present. He seemed a master of fighting and skilled in holding off the pounding and pulling of his adversaries with blunt, unshaken composure.

It was not James Douglas alone who wondered whence this formidable foe had come. None had taken note of him in the skill trials a week before; an easy thing among three thousand men-at-arms. Yet now, the black knight stood among the final four, and all eyes turned his way. The sight set Douglas, and more than a few others, to pondering who he was.

From Douglas' experience, such resolute fighters usually hailed from the lower guilds, men eager to measure themselves against the nobility. Yet the costly armour and the quality of the horses the knight brought forth with his many squires spoke against that. The stranger's plain tent had been raised not far from that of the Scottish lord of Dumfries. Behind the canvas, he had remained shielded from prying eyes.

Rumour was already boiling fiercely. That morning, Sir Douglas' squires had whispered behind their hands as they laced his padded doublet. Thoughtful and silent, he had listened to the lads' talk. One claimed the stranger was a king from the north, come to claim victory in disguise, for only men of those lands grew to such height. A single sharp look from James ended their chatter. He loathed careless tongues and twisted truths.

In fact, the attention the stranger drew irked him. Knights of rank, repute, and long service had entered this tournament.

It was an honour to be announced by the herald with one's full title, yet this foreigner seemed untouched by any notion of reverence. Even the curiosity of the ladies in the stands left him unmoved. How hardened must a man be to rely solely on his skill in combat and deny both his name and origin?

James let no shadow of his thoughts cross his face. His mind was fixed on the duel ahead. The squires' chatter meant nothing to him. To his eyes, the stranger was but another foe to be felled, be he king or common knight. He had ridden into every battle thus; honour to whom honour is due.

A tall squire from his retinue stood beside his horse and placed the wooden lance into his hand. Lord Douglas' gauntlet of iron links creaked as he gripped it firmly. The weapon, nearly twice his height, was heavy in his grasp. It had been perfectly balanced by the master of arms and inspected by the tournament judge, as the rules required. The blunt end would strike past the shield, crash against his opponent's chestplate, and lever him from the saddle with full force. That was the plan. Until now, James Douglas had remained unbeaten, having cast aside every rival. The Black Knight before him, as the crowd had begun to call him, also had yet to fall. Douglas hoped to learn the man's name at last when he lay before him in the dust. His confidence was unbroken; a Douglas feared no foe.

The drums fell silent in a signal for both rivals to drive their spurs and charge.

James slid the visor down before his eyes, and it locked into place with a sharp click. Then, he drove his heels into the horse's flanks. From stillness, the dappled steed leapt forward, carrying him into the field at full gallop. The soft ground muffled the thunder of iron-shod hooves. Sand sprayed high. In that instant, Sir Douglas was cut off from the world. His pulse raced, and his gaze fixed upon the target through the narrow slit of his visor. His advantage lay in the swiftness with which his lance would strike the opponent's chest. He had to keep it utterly steady. The force of impact would lift the stranger from the saddle. His hand clenched hard around the wooden shaft. The lance shifted almost imperceptibly. He was certain of himself; he had no doubts.

It took but seconds for the two weapons to strike. Their blunted tips crashed near-simultaneously against the opposing shields. With a harsh crack, the treated wood splintered apart. Sir Douglas felt the jolt through the hand that held his shield and, at the same instant, against his breastplate. His rival's lance had glanced off his guard and pierced his defence.

Tense as a drawn bow, James Douglas barely felt the pain of impact; he sensed only the brutal force that tore him from the saddle. Mid-fall, he heard the startled cry of the crowd through a daze, and then came the thud as his body struck the sand of the arena. The soft ground at least tempered the blow. With a clang and a crash, his helm flew free, followed by a boot that had been caught in a stirrup. Helpless to move, the Scottish knight lay where he fell.

James became aware of his defeat. As though he had just lost a battle, he suddenly felt the full weight of pain and frustration over what had been lost.

With sheer will alone, the seasoned warrior raised his head. He saw the horror written across the crowd, their faces pale and their mouths covered, their eyes fixed upon him, the fallen Scottish hero. If he rose now, his foe might strike again. He turned his gaze to the opponent still astride his mount. James' lance had aimed for the breast, yet the mighty man had not been unseated. Had the tip slipped off his shield?

The Black Knight reined in his horse on the far side and turned it, ready for another round. James's vision blurred. Should he make a fool of himself and suffer humiliation at the hands of a mightier foe, or yield with dignity?

With effort, he lifted himself with the help of a squire who rushed to his side. Pain burned through his chest, and each breath came hard. Never had defeat found him, neither in tournament nor war, and now, of all places, at the grandest tourney of the age, his skill had failed him.

James' disbelieving gaze flickered towards the stranger who waited, shield raised. He sought the barely visible eyes of his opponent. Behind the slit of the iron helm, there was no movement; the knight's hand rested upon the pommel of his sword. The gesture needed no words. The knight was ready to press his victory.

James drew a sharp breath, pain lancing through his ribs. His squire had him beneath the arms and struggled to haul him to his feet. How he longed to rise once more and face his foe on foot, to finish what honour demanded, but his legs betrayed him. What shame, to endure such humiliation before all eyes! He stayed upon the ground and raised his right hand in surrender. Too weak for a second round, James Douglas yielded, acknowledging, with the last of his pride, the triumph of his mightier foe.

A murmur of astonishment swept through the stands. The noble ladies gasped in dismay. None could fathom how the mysterious Black Knight had unseated the until-then undefeated Sir James Douglas.

Still on the sand, James cast a helpless glance towards the dais, his face twisted into an embarrassed grimace as he recognised the figure emerging from the crowd. His wife was hurrying to his aid. She had watched the scene with growing concern. Lady Enja Douglas had not even bothered to wear a gown for the occasion. As ever, she was dressed in leather riding trousers and a tunic, having forgone only the weapons usually strapped to her jerkin. Enja's boots stirred the sand as she ran towards him.

James forced a wavering smile to ease her worry, though he could not quite escape her discerning gaze. Perhaps he had indeed cracked a rib or several, but she needn't know that. He bit down on his lip as several men rushed in to lift him, armour and all, from the field. His condition would be plain to a healer like Enja, yet she held her tongue. And as he met her eyes, with shame burning through him, something else struck him—a truth that unsettled him to the core.

The gaze from his wife's crystal-blue eyes was not fixed on him; she was looking past him. When he turned his head in the same direction, he saw what had caught her attention. The unknown victor rode from the arena to a chorus of cheers, yet the excitement surrounding him seemed to leave him unmoved. The Black Knight saluted neither the queen nor the highborn ladies. He appeared to care for nothing but winning this tournament. In truth, he was well on his way with only one foe left to face: the victor of the next duel.

James closed his eyes, wounded in pride as much as flesh. His whole body throbbed with pain. When, at last, he turned his head towards Enja, their eyes met. She looked as though guilt shadowed her face, or was it only his imagining? Could she know who the Black Knight truly was? A new ache crept through him then, deeper than the bruises of battle; this time, it struck his heart.

I had never seen a tournament on such a scale. Thousands of noble men with their retinues had gathered to test one another's pride and strength. Since our arrival three weeks past, my husband James Douglas had lived as if in his own glory, basking in honour and acclaim. Many kindred spirits did the same, and to me it all seemed a grand fair of vanity. I must admit, I had never felt such a charge of battle spirit as here in Smithfield, a place otherwise quaint and still, with a church, a single main street, and now and then a tourney held upon its field.

My husband could display his full prowess at this tourney beneath the admiring eyes of knights and, most significantly, noble ladies. James was a master of his craft, his reputation untarnished even among the haughty Frenchmen.

King Philip IV had spared no expense, bringing an entire contingent of his finest warriors to distant London. Grand weddings had ever been a welcome occasion for rulers to display the prowess of their cavalry in a setting of peace. Isabella, too, had followed that tradition, offering the arena as hostess of the games.

Naturally, the marriage between the young royals, David and Joanna, was a political move rather than love. Through it, Robert de Bruce had won the formal recognition of the English crown as Scotland's sovereign king. To bind the occasion to a grand tournament suited him well, not only to honour his son's wedding with triumph, but also to strengthen ties between the English and French courts.

Indeed, in rare accord, King Philip IV of France and his wife sat beside Isabella and Roger Mortimer on the royal stand, conversing animatedly in French.

However, the mighty figure of Robert de Bruce was absent. He had excused himself for reasons of health, and the news had troubled me deeply. This marriage—so vital to his cause—had been his design since David's birth. It was meant to secure Scotland's standing against her old enemy, England, vanquished at Bannockburn. Such had been Robert's will, and I knew how dearly he cared for the legacy he hoped to leave behind.

That he could not be present now was most strange. I shared my concern with James, who was very aware of the Scottish king's failing health, yet my husband remained silent, even towards me, about the sovereign's condition.

The rumour clung stubbornly that the King of Scots was stricken with an incurable illness. Perhaps he simply suffered the wrong physician? I had held my tongue so as not to seem forward, yet before my return to Caerlaverock Castle, I would likely have to pay him a visit as a healer. In time, James would come to the same thought.

My gaze drifted over the heads of the crowd that had gathered in the scorching heat. With caps, cloths, or fans, they shielded themselves as best they could from the blazing sun. The scent of sweat, cider, and sweet essences wafted to my nose. The sand before us shimmered. I sat at the far right of the royal stand, and the stretched canvas above cast just enough shade to spare me the worst of it. Still, I sweated beneath the leather of my trousers. Instead of my thick riding jacket, I had chosen my black doublet for the occasion. It was a fine piece of cloth, though the sweat ran down my back just as it did the men in their armour.

I stood out in my man's attire among the silk-draped ladies of high society. The critical glances no longer unsettled me, yet I would far rather have been clad in armour upon the field than sitting here beneath the curious eyes of a mostly female crowd as though these preening knights were of greater worth than a woman in breeches!

I fixed my gaze on the fighters in the arena. From up here, I had a clear view of the two knights now facing each other in the joust. Down on the sand, James was challenging the Black Knight.

My husband was now thirty-nine, one of the oldest men to ride in the lists. His body was still forged hard by daily training, and as I had watched him dress this morning, I was reminded again how well-shaped it remained—well enough to make our wedded duties a pleasure still.

Even in the morning hours, I could feel his energy, the same fierce force he had carried within him since his youth. But his black hair was now streaked with grey, and his full beard gleamed in every shade of silver. James was a fighter through and through, and the sight of him in the tournament saddle filled me with pride to be his wife.

Unlike him, I knew how this battle would end. I clenched my teeth to stop myself from making the mistake of warning

James. Gladly would I have spared him this moment of humiliation, but it would have done his pride no good.

Together with a few trusted souls, I knew who hid beneath the black armour. There in the arena, James faced one of the finest warriors of the Western world. Even my husband would stand no chance against him …

I swallowed hard as the herald proclaimed James' name and title. Then came the sound of the musicians' drums. The heat made the air above the lists shimmer. I shaded my brow with my hand to see more clearly. The sunlight was sheer torment for my pale eyes.

When the lances struck the shields, my stomach clenched, despite all my experience. Gooseflesh rose along my arms. I was utterly captivated by the mastery of combat unfolding before my eyes.

The Black Knight wavered slightly in the saddle, yet his foe was no longer where he'd sat moments before. James had been hurled from his horse as though struck by an unseen fist. My heart faltered. God, grant he had come to no grave harm!

James lay with his face turned away from his opponent. His fallen helmet had clattered and rolled across the sand. His horse wandered aimlessly through the arena before it was caught, and then came silence. My breath—and that of the thousands watching—faltered for a heartbeat. For a moment, I feared the worst, but then James moved his head, and I felt a surge of quiet relief. He was alive.

My heart began to steady. The hope that his wounds were no graver than to his pride set my feet in motion; nothing could keep me on the stands now. Glad to escape the whispering women, I hurried down into the arena. Dark thoughts swarmed my mind. Why had I not stopped the meeting of these two men when I still could have?

I dared not betray myself. The answer to my question was plain. How could I have known that James would face the Black Knight of all men in the round before the final? No one had foreseen it. I cursed myself a fool. James was a knight driven by ambition, and even from his deathbed, he would have entered the joust. My knowledge of subtle poisons would have been of no use.

I straightened my shoulders a little, preparing myself for what was to come. James would be furious if he ever learned what I had done. My conscience wrestled with the truth. After all, he need never know who the Black Knight truly was. I had accepted my husband's certain defeat to clear the path for the Black Knight's battle against a greater foe: Nicholas de Verdun.

In that moment, I was reminded why I had come. I sought justice. A man who had dealt great suffering to others must die, and for that end, I would gladly pass over awkward questions. For that, I would endure my husband's anger.

I was close to my goal. The arena was to be the stage for the death of an English nobleman who had chosen the wrong side in the war for Ireland. Sir Nicholas de Verdun, that knight, had long ago trapped my friend Sir Cathal O'Conchobhar, the provincial prince of Connacht, in an ambush upon Irish soil. Cathal, many comrades, and Ihad fallen captive to the Englishman. Some of our most loyal men were executed before our eyes. I had escaped that grim fate by the narrowest margin, slipping my bonds and plunging into the lake. Cathal, though, had been forced to march in chains towards the harbour. Had my escape failed, I could never have saved him, yet through a daring capture of his own ship, I had won him his freedom and the passage home to Ireland. I almost smiled at the memory of Cathal's face that night when I had freed him under the cloak of darkness and mist.

Nicholas de Verdun had stood in Cathal's black book for years. Now, of all places, the despised English commander had resurfaced here, at the tournament in London. What a fortunate coincidence that I had obtained the list of participating knights through my loyal husband!

I reached James at the far end of the arena and took in the scene with a measuring glance. His squire struggled to raise him, but the weight of his armour made it hopeless. James was too dazed to fight on. The defeat cut deep; I could see it plainly. He tried to mask his shame and pain with a forced smile, yet he would not meet my eyes; his gaze stayed fixed, stubbornly, on the stands, on the place where the queen sat. Was her regard worth more to him than mine?

My gaze drifted from James' iron shoulder guard to the Black Knight on the far side of the arena. With one hand, he had reined in his stallion, while the other rested, poised for battle, on the hilt of his sword. Cathal trusted the moment no more than I did; I could feel it. The first charge had left him unscathed. He had likely not even felt the strike of James' lance beneath his thick armour. It had splintered instead, the shards still scattered in the sand. My Irish friend's green eyes gleamed with delight behind the slit of his helm. Even the black plume upon his crest bobbed merrily with each movement of the horse.

It dawned on me that Cathal had taken true delight in casting the famed James Douglas into the sand. He had waited all his life for this moment. My face stayed solemn, though I did not begrudge him his triumph. In the joust, Cathal had yet to be defeated.

I let none of my thoughts show as I met James' gaze again. He looked unsettled, having noticed that my eyes had passed over him. I had merely seized the moment when shame kept him from meeting mine. At first glance, nothing seemed broken. His ribs might have taken a blow, which would explain his dizziness. He was surely in pain. Instinctively, I drew my hands back when I realised I was aiming to help him. It would have been too much for him to be touched by his wife before all eyes. I left it at that. Later, in the tent, I would examine him more closely.

James, carried from the arena by his squire, was no longer a contender. With a single motion of his hand, he had signalled the judges his acceptance of defeat. That, no doubt, wounded him more deeply than damage to his ribs ever could.

I could not help but smile a little.

Nicholas de Verdun had dispatched the Frenchman in the second round before the final more swiftly than the latter would have liked. The young knight was a worthy foe, yet his horsemanship lacked the mastery to best a seasoned fighter like Verdun. Even his deft swerve in the saddle, just before the lances met, failed to serve him. The move cost him speed, and with it, the force needed for a decisive strike.

Verdun's trick, however, won him victory on the second charge. His weapon struck the Frenchman squarely on the shield, which shattered, and Sir Nicholas de Verdun drove the splintered end of his lance beneath his opponent's arm where the breastplate lay open. The thrust, though with a blunted tip, not only wounded the young Frenchman but hurled him sideways from the saddle.

That wound meant the tournament was over for him. Verdun's follow-through with a splintered lance might not have been knightly, but it had done its work. Nicholas de

Verdun was not a man of delicate scruples. The eyes of the queen and her court were upon him. He alone remained of England's chivalry in the lists. With the Frenchman fallen, only one rival stood between him and victory, and Verdun was certain he would claim this last bout as a home triumph for the English crown.

The ruthless English knight cast a measuring glance at his next opponent, the victor of the previous duel against James Douglas. Even to Sir Nicholas, the fallen Scottish knight was a hero, for he had won every great battle against King Edward. He was a man of great honour and spotless repute.

Of all men, it was a knight without banner or name who had unseated him. Just like that, out of nowhere, he had hurled one of the mightiest contenders from the saddle. Now, the Black Knight sought to face Verdun in the final. Admittedly, he was a towering, broad-shouldered fighter who had carved his path through the brutal games with purpose. Verdun would rather have ridden against James Douglas, yet fate had chosen otherwise, and he would not make the mistake of underestimating this nameless foe.

Afternoon had come. A light breeze had chased away the burning heat, yet the heavy air beneath his armour still stole his breath. It was as though a storm were gathering, though no cloud darkened the sky. Perhaps it was only the tension that made his breathing so laboured. Beneath the iron of his helm, he could hear his hurried breaths.

After the Frenchman's defeat, the musicians had played a while longer. The crowd took the chance to stretch, eat, and drink. The guests were to want for nothing. Now, the herald's voice rang out once more, proclaiming Verdun's name and titles, but when it came to the Black Knight, he, as before, remained silent.

Verdun watched intently from his place as the attendants prepared the arena once more for the coming clash. Thus far, his participation had paid off handsomely. He had won fine horses and gleaming armour on his way to this final duel. Now he was already gloating over his next opponent's magnificent steed.

It was strange that no one had the faintest notion who the mysterious fighter was. Though watchers had kept a close eye on the unknown knight's plain tourney tent, he had given them no cause for suspicion. Perhaps the whispers were true, after all?

It might be a lord or even a king from some foreign land who now stood before him. But would such a man truly seek to test himself against the finest knights while keeping his face hidden? Rumour had it that Ludwig IV, King of the Romans, liked to mingle in such tournaments to bolster his renown. Would he reveal himself, if indeed it were so? The excellence of his skill and the costliness of his armour spoke in favour of it. Even if he were a king, Verdun meant to hand him defeat. His confidence was fed by his past triumphs; he had never lost a duel. Yet a strange unease stirred in his gut.

The closer he drew to claiming this tournament for himself and his queen, the more that unknown knight troubled him. The man's prowess had been proven in his deft dispatch of one of the greatest fighters. Could this become Verdun's first defeat?

His place in the tourney was his best chance to win back the court's favour. Edward II, in whose reign he had fought the Scots, had once promised him a future at court. His victory on the Irish field of Faughart, where he struck down Edward de Bruce, had earned him the king's esteem. Lord John de Bermingham himself had sent the young Verdun to London in 1318 with a letter of commendation. Yet his career as a loyal knight within Edward's elite circle had ended abruptly, four years later, with England's disgraceful defeat at the Battle of Byland.

That damned Robert de Bruce had, once again, defended Scotland's right to stand as its own with his army and wrested a 13-year peace from England's King Edward II. Nicholas de Verdun's fondness for the Scots had never run deep, but since then, it had curdled altogether. He had not been at Byland, yet Scotland's growing authority was a thorn in his side.

Not only that, but the second—and most shameful—blow to Nicholas de Verdun's career had been Queen Isabella's open affair with the vile Roger Mortimer of Wigmore. The debased pair had driven the weak Edward from London before the eyes of his own people. As a loyal knight, Verdun had fought to keep his place at court. If he had held fast to his fleeing king, he would have fallen from favour, yet he had sworn his oath of fealty. A curse slipped from his lips.

The effeminate conduct of England's sovereign had become intolerable even in the eyes of his supporters, more so when he yielded to his lover's wish and stripped magnates and powerful nobles of their titles as punishment for rebellion. Enraged, many withdrew their loyalty from the despised king. Queen Isabella had turned against her husband and taken the wealthy nobility's side.

With the aid of her lover, Roger Mortimer, the shrewd Isabella seized the moment's advantage. She hunted her husband across half of England with Mortimer's troops and the backing of sympathetic barons. After Edward's capture in late November 1326, the Queen brought charges against her king. Through her allies among the nobility, she forced the fallen ruler to abdicate in favour of his son. By the end of January 1327, young Edward III had replaced his father on the throne, and Nicholas de Verdun had lost his place among the favoured few.

He cursed and perspired beneath his coif. Streams of sweat ran from his brow down his cheeks and gathered on his chest, yet he no longer felt it. Excitement surged through his blood. Again, his stomach stirred with a restless churn. With deep breaths, he fought the unease. His helmet was still open, letting him draw what air he could, but it would soon be closed.

The sandy floor of the Smithfield arena stirred in the growing breeze, dust whirling across its surface. Countless helpers had smoothed the ground churned up by so many hooves. Horse and rider alike suffered beneath the weight of their armour on this sweltering day. Verdun squinted towards the crowd pressing close around him and thus, saw them rise as one, as if struck by lightning. A roar of fevered applause erupted when his opponent was led into the field.

A stranger, a nobody, was the thought that flared angrily through Verdun's mind. His searing gaze fixed on the knight astride the great black horse now emerging from the passage between the stands. Only the four dark legs showed from beneath the heavy armour, thick with coarse hair about the fetlocks. Proudly, the beast lifted its head, as did its rider, whose silhouette struck Verdun as immense and almost otherworldly. Like a demon, he thought; a demon clad in black armour.

He faced the silent and menacing figure across the field. The ladies shrieked and cheered. Hatred coiled in the Englishman's gut, while jealousy raged in his chest. His gaze darkened as he watched the women clamour for the stranger's favour. After the final bout, he would have his pick of them all. Nicholas de Verdun would show this pompous fool his rightful place: face-down in the sand at his feet.

With full intent, Verdun set his horse in motion and trotted towards the grandstand. Applause of approval followed his bows to the nobility and the queen. At least he had the support of his own people, he thought with satisfaction. No Englishman had come as far as he in this tournament. Today, an English knight would claim victory for his queen. For that, he meant to earn a token from her; it was his due. His ambitious gaze fixed on Isabella, who sat laughing and jesting with her lover in the shade of the stand.

A murmur rippled through the crowd. Only now did the queen seem to grasp Verdun's intent. It was bold—unseemly even—for a common knight to court the queen's favour, yet he cared little for propriety. He would see to it that his name stirred memories in her heart.

With the courage of a true knight, he brought his horse to a halt directly before the queen's dais. She smiled, faintly abashed. He removed his helmet and bowed his head. Her companion, Sir Mortimer, was struck silent for a moment by the boldness of the gesture, yet Isabella seemed pleased by his audacity, for she slipped one of her rings from her finger and had it passed to the daring knight. Not only that, but she wished him a steady hand for the fight ahead, studying the athletic warrior closely from behind her fan.

Nicholas de Verdun exulted inwardly. Outwardly, he met his queen's gaze with a courteous smile, as though humbled by her favour. With that ring, he had opened a door into the highest circles of courtly grace. Perhaps Isabella would at last recognise his worth and grant him land and standing. With his free hand, he slipped the ring onto his little finger and drew the glove back over it.

With renewed confidence, he turned his horse, set his helmet back in place, and rode towards the starting line. His opponent already stood there, lance lowered and waiting with calm patience. Now, there were only the two of them. The tournament was reaching its height and its final reckoning.

A murmur swept through the crowd. All could feel the sudden tension settling over them. Cathal, provincial king of Connacht, dared not lift his visor despite the stifling heat. The black war paint upon his face and scalp would betray him at once, and he could not risk such notice here. He longed for the moment he might face his mortal foe, Nicholas de Verdun, and take his life in fair combat. That and nothing else was his intent, and it must appear that the noble knight had fallen at the hands of a nameless stranger.

Today was his day, at last. Nicholas de Verdun would meet his rightful punishment. More than ten years ago, he had led Cathal and his men into a trap near the ruins of Mag Lurgh Castle at Loch Key. Many of his friends and comrades had perished miserably at English hands, not in battle, but executed by Verdun like sheep upon the slaughtering block. Bitterness lodged like a thorn in Cathal's flesh. Verdun had robbed him not only of good men but also of his honour.

Cathal owed his freedom solely to Enja, who had risked everything to snatch him and the pitiful remnants of his men from the ship that was to carry him to his final reckoning before the English king. He bit his lip. She had risked her life then to save his. Now it lay in his hands to avenge what had been done, to atone for the sacrilegious deaths of his companions.

The black stallion beneath Cathal was a steadfast beast, strong and patient. He had borne him across the tourney sands more than once and feared not the flutter of banners, the roar of the crowd, or the clash of steel upon steel.

Silence fell. None among the spectators wished to miss the final fight. Even the flies that drifted about went unnoticed.

The herald gave the signal—a roll of drums—and Cathal loosed the reins. His black steed needed no spurs to leap from stillness into a gallop. A triumphant roar escaped him as he surged forward, certain of victory. Through the narrow slit of his visor, he saw his foe charging, clad in the gold and crimson of the king. Sand sparkled as it flew. Cathal's breath came in sharp bursts as his powerful arm tensed around the lance. The heavy shield stood like a wall before his chest. He braced for the strike, and it came. The tip of Verdun's lance punched through his shield like a stone and slammed into his side, high at the ribs. The blow stole his breath, and his wooden lance fell from his grasp. Cathal reeled, yet he did not fall. He fought for air, his lungs frozen tight. Only when he began to draw shallow breaths did he grasp what had happened.

The tip of his weapon had struck Verdun squarely through the slit of his visor. His lance had been specially prepared for this one duel. Normally, the wooden weapons splintered on impact, but not this one. On the contrary, it became sharp and deadly the moment its outer edges broke away. The judges had neither noticed nor suspected the deceit.

Cathal had aimed for the visor's slit. Under the force of impact, his opponent should have lost his helm or his senses, but with a hardened core hidden within the otherwise soft wood, the lance tip had driven clean through the narrow gap and pierced Verdun's eye. Cathal had rehearsed the killing strike with Enja many times. It was meant to look like an accident—a splinter breaking loose and striking the head. In truth, it was a deliberate move, executed with the precision and cold resolve of a man who knew his strength and who possessed the deepest reason to use it.

Nicholas de Verdun fell from his horse without ever regaining consciousness. The armoured body struck the ground hard and lay twisted in an unnatural heap. One glance at the blood seeping from the helm was enough for Cathal to know he was dead. His lance had found its purpose.

The squires hastened to spare the crowd another glimpse of the corpse, carrying the heavy body and its armour from the field. Only then did the spectators grasp that the duel was done, and they hailed the victor with thunderous applause. Nicholas de Verdun was already forgotten. Cathal O'Conchobhar, the nameless knight, remained in their minds. His face stayed hidden behind the visor, leaving a trail of questions in his wake. He gave only a brief nod to the queen and her retinue; no more was needed to show that he was dedicating his triumph to the young bridal pair.

Cathal's name was as feared among the knights of this land as that of James Douglas. He need not add this victory to his tally; it belonged to the death of his greatest foe. A wave of gratitude swept through him; the commotion and the cheers surrounding him barely reached his senses. His gaze turned towards the stands, towards Enja. The one person to whom he would have gladly dedicated his triumph was not there. His friend, the one whose meticulous planning had made this victory—and Verdun's death by his hand—possible. She had likely left the grounds after her husband's injury to tend to him. No doubt she had known Cathal would prevail. She had told him so again and again. And, as so often before, Enja's brilliant plan had come to fruition.

Chapter 2

Ireland, Castle Dunguaire, 1328, a few months before the Smithfield tournament

I confess the years have not passed without leaving their marks. Wars, conflicts, and a childhood torn to pieces shaped my life. Losses and cares steeled my soul as a smith tempers his iron. After forty-five years, my body bore the signs of ageing. Life in the saddle, the hardness of those days, and, above all, the fighting had left their traces. Unwittingly, I touched my right ear, of which only half remained. The lower part had been severed many years ago by the assassin Rabia, may she roast in Hell.

A scar ran down my cheek, once a gaping wound from being struck by Nicholas de Verdun's iron glove. It had never healed cleanly and now marked the left side of my face as a raised ridge of flesh. I bore the signs of my past with pride, for no warrior's face was ever smooth as a boy's. James used to say that scars were the lasting memory of courage and pride. For once, I agreed with him.

Against all odds, our children had grown, and now, they were parents themselves. As much as I longed to see them safe and sound, I knew they, too, would one day walk their own path. All I could do was shape them into souls strong enough to face whatever fates lay before them. At times, my words sufficed. At others, it was steel, not softness, that forged their strength.

In my youth, the future felt distant and untouchable. Now, I could feel time slipping through my fingers. Some things had come to mean more to me than before, others far less. Life had taught me the worth of love, friendship, and humility. As a child, I swore never to surrender my freedom. I lived, and bled, by that vow. I killed. But through the long years, I changed. The dead I left behind grew fewer. Rarely now did I claim the right to take another's life. I found far greater joy in preserving it; in healing instead of harming.

My gaze fell upon the rise, a plateau-shaped hill I had long known. A narrow path led us gently upward onto the wooded crown that granted us a breath of shade for our combat drills. The sunrise was a spectacle of violet clouds sweeping across the heavens, promising a fair spring day. We would not wait for the noon heat to descend, so we had set out after the morning prayer, at the fifth hour.

The hill was so small it bore no name. It lay not far from the Irish stronghold of Dunguaire, ancestral seat of the O'Conchobhar line. From afar, the great tower rose proud and solemn through the morning mist, keeping silent watch over Scotland's northern coast. Dunguaire belonged to my friend and provincial king, Cathal O'Conchobhar, bound to me since our shared youth in the Orient. With him at my side, I had journeyed to Scotland as a young assassin.

For him—more even than for James—I would have walked through fire.

My gaze drifted to him riding silently beside me on a striking black stallion. His eyes were fixed ahead, his mind adrift in thoughts as deep as mine. Perhaps he, too, was haunted by memories bound to the two of us, or maybe his thoughts strayed towards the future, that uncertain horizon in Ireland, where fate seemed even less predictable than in my homeland, Scotland.

I loved Cathal as one may love a dearest friend. Our bond was as singular as he was. His towering frame was hewn from years of swordplay, his shoulders so broad he could scarce pass through an ordinary door. His powerful legs lent him the bearing of a fearsome warrior, and the markings upon his skin drew every eye. Yet for all his might, his great heart mattered most to me. That heart he had given to Moira—my finest student and closest friend—and he kept a small piece of it for me.

As if he had felt my thoughts, he turned his face towards me and his eyes, gleaming green as the Irish lochs, met mine. That, truly, was Cathal's finest trait: his eyes. They were the mirror of his soul, and for that, I was weak. In all else, Cathal was no beauty. A broad nose ruled his rugged face, near entirely masked in black war paint. He was the perfect warrior, and that mattered far more to me than looks ever could. Yet I saw change in him. Of late, he wore a trimmed white beard, stark against the dark paint upon his skin.

His scalp, as ever, was shaven smooth; his hair had likely left him long ago. Like me, he bore a scar where half his right earlobe once had been.

After Cathal noticed my gaze lingered on him, a faint smile touched his lips. Love and trust needed no words between us. It had ever been so, and we had no need to speak it aloud. The gentle giant favoured such quiet understanding, and I smiled back.

Our morning combat drills were a long tradition. Through them, and through a tincture known only to me, I had shaped him into the man he had become. Cathal had once been a young eunuch, drawn into the ranks of Hassan I'Shabbah's assassins. With my guidance, he had made peace with his body and forged his rage into strength. His secret was known to but a handful of trusted souls. His heart, to even fewer.

Wordlessly, we tied the horses to the gnarled oak that had cast its shade over this hill for decades. Then, we followed the same ritual that had bound us since the dawn of our friendship. We checked our weapons, shed our cloaks, and woke our muscles with some warming exercises. Stretching and preparing had grown ever more vital to me with age. Cathal's strength had also begun to wane in mass; he had to train all the harder to keep the power that once came to him so easily.

Cathal meant to train the fury from his body that morning, and in that, he was a master. I could feel it, the tremor in him, the weight of cares he could not command. Unlike his wife, he was no man of words when it came to his heart. My friend preferred to let his broadsword speak for him, and I was glad to meet him as an equal on the field.

Cathal had summoned me to Ireland for Moira's sake. A messenger had brought word that his wife was unwell. Moira was more than Cathal's wife; she was my old friend who walked the path of healing I had once shown her. Naturally, I had answered his anxious call without delay and sailed for Ireland. It had been eight long years since last we met at Dunguaire, eight years since I had set foot on Irish soil. In that moment, I rued the distance, for our friendship had ever been dear to me.

The sight of Moira after only a few months of illness shook me deeply. Her shoulders had sunken, her face was lined with furrows, and her hands looked like those of an old woman who had toiled all her life—which, indeed, she had. Yet her spirit and beauty had always taken my breath away. I never knew her true age; she was surely far older than I, but lying there before me, she might have been a crone. How could a body wither so swiftly?

After my arrival in Dunguaire, I had seated myself in the dim chamber beside her bed and taken her cold hand in mine. It had once been the couple's room, yet Cathal no longer seemed to sleep there. Moira lay adrift in the vast bed, made up for one alone. A single candle burned upon the bedside table, the only thing in that room that still held a spark of life.

In my memory, Cathal's wife had always brimmed with strength and vigour. Despite her rank as provincial queen, she had laboured tirelessly for the sick and the weak. She had brought children into the world, tended the plague-stricken, and seen wars and too many deaths. Now, the light of life was gone from her eyes; the spark I had always felt, no matter how dark the times. Her irises, once the colour of ripe honey, had grown dull and pale.

Moira's skin was as pale as the sheet she lay upon, and wrinkled flesh clung to her arms and legs. She had once been a woman of full and graceful form, with curves in all the right places. Now, but half of that woman remained.

For a while, silence hung between us while I found the right words. She listened with patient calm as I told her how we had first met, how she had fought for her child's life in a well with water that rose to her chin. The story had long inspired my entire clan. With sheer, unyielding strength, she had saved her child—and herself—until we heard her cries for help and drew her from the depths.

In that moment, I could feel her spirit stirring again. Moira returned once more, slipping back into the body she had meant to leave behind. Warmth flowed back into her hands, and her eyes regained the colour of honey. A lump rose in my throat as her fingers tightened around mine.

Only then, in a frail voice, did Moira ask the question I had been waiting for.

"How fares Catriona?"

Her lips had trembled, and her frail body lifted slightly. I gave her one of my rare, warm smiles.

Moira's daughter, Catriona, had found her home with me at Caerlaverock Castle. The young woman now led my infirmary, as her mother had before her. She was wed to our foreman, Lachlan McKay, and had borne two healthy children. I told her proud mother of the grandchildren and of my life in Dumfries. As in days past, we warmed ourselves with old tales from Caerlaverock. Now and then, a faint smile stole across her wrinkled face, and for a fleeting moment, I saw the Moira I remembered, the one who had once laughed beside me.

When, after a few conversations, she began to recover a little, my closer examinations revealed fluid in her lungs. Most likely, her heart had grown weak with age and could no longer bear the work of keeping her lungs clear.

I had the kitchen-maid set a nettle decoction to boil, to draw the water from her limbs and lungs. I also massaged her chest and the lymphatic swellings to encourage the drainage. It would be a long travail, but I was resolute to drive her from that wasting bed and have her stand and walk of her own accord.

After two weeks, I had brought her that far. My old friend rose and, with my help, managed a few halting steps. The motion stirred her strength, and her body began once more to rid itself of the fluids through kidneys and skin.

She cursed me more than once in those days, yet I cared not. I had thought I'd heard the finest curses in all of Ireland from Cathal, but I was sorely mistaken. Moira knew a few rousing words I'd never heard before, but the way she spat them sounded as though they were meant not for me, but for herself and the life she'd lived.

During her treatment, I urged Moira to speak of her years in Dunguaire, of her children and of Sophie, who had passed a few years before. It kept her mind from the pain of my tapping and the firm pressure I put upon her chest and limbs.

With each passing day, I drew nearer to the root of what fed her sorrow. I sensed something gnawed at her deep within, a wound unseen, and I feared it was to do with the man we both loved so fiercely.

The problem was not her adopted son, David, who was meant to inherit Cathal's throne. As a eunuch, Cathal could sire no children of his own, so he had taken in Moira's daughters by birth, along with several others. Together, they had raised twelve sons and daughters. Moira deemed her eldest too weak to bear the rule of Connacht. The times were unsettled, and she wished to wait until the others came of age before naming an heir, but the law allowed no such delay.

That was not the trouble, nor was it the small worries that kept Moira's mind uneasy. It had to be her husband, the man who had left his wife to face her frailty alone when she needed him most.

Moira hinted that Cathal had grown scarce of late. When I asked after their marriage, she dodged the question, offering flimsy excuses and how the burdens of a kingdom consumed all his time. Perhaps even she could not truly explain his distance. Something was amiss, and Moira, in her quiet way, took the blame upon herself.

The next day, I drew her from her chamber into the open air. Moira wrapped a cloak around her narrow shoulders and took my arm. We walked a little within the castle grounds, careful not to weary her. The fresh air did her good, and I could see colour bloom upon her hollow cheeks. The spring day was brisk, and though dark clouds loomed above, the rain held off. Around the castle, the trees were budding, heralding the coming summer. The first lilies-of-the-valley bloomed, banishing the grey sameness of winter. Cows, horses, and sheep rejoiced in their newfound freedom, tugging at the tender green tufts of early grass. Man and beast alike greeted the lengthening days with quiet joy, awaiting the approaching solstice.

"How are Winnie and Padraig?" I asked at last, turning our talk to the two dwarves who had met and fallen in love here at Dunguaire. The question weighed heavy on my heart, for I had not seen them once since arriving at the castle. The warriors Winnie and Kalay had stood beside me through every storm and battle; we had been a fierce and loyal trio. After Kalay's brutal death, my finest archer, Winnie, had settled here with Padraig.

Moira laughed aloud for the first time as though it had been years since she last thought of the two of them. She had always gotten along with Winnie, though that venomous little imp never missed a chance to mock her. Perhaps Dunguaire's former court jester, Padraig, had been her antidote. In any case, the sharp-tongued woman had softened under his influence, becoming a kinder version of herself.

"Winnie has married Padraig," Moira told me as I poured her a fresh cup of nettle brew, the remedy that did her so much good. I added a spoonful of honey, which was precious stuff in those times, but she knew its healing worth. A spark of mischief lit her eyes once more.

"Winnie was with child, so Padraig had little choice but to make her his wife."

I stared at her in astonishment. I could scarcely imagine how Padraig had ever managed to get close enough to fiery Winnie to bed her, let alone leave her with child.

Yet the news did not surprise me. That little bundle of fire had found her twin in Padraig in body and spirit. Both were small of stature and sharp of tongue. It seemed his raven-dark humour had somehow reconciled his fierce wife with life itself, for I could find no other reason to explain such a love.

"Where are they now?" I asked, surprised, for Padraig had been Cathal's castle's court jester.

"They've had a healthy child," Moira told me softly. "A son."

"And?"

My friend looked at me strangely, as though she could not believe I truly failed to grasp her meaning.

"They thought it best to raise their boy, Cailean, away from the settlement," she explained gently. "They've withdrawn to a hut in the forest. One day, they'll return to Dunguaire, but not until Cailean is old enough to work in our household. The life they endured because of their size—the mockery and exclusion—they would spare their son."

Silence lingered between us for a long while. With my free hand, I toyed awkwardly with a blade of meadow grass between my teeth. I vowed to visit Cailean one day. I was curious to see which of them the boy favoured. I prayed he might take after Padraig.

"How old is he now?" I asked thoughtfully, turning with Moira to make our way back across the courtyard.

She paused in thought. "Cailean must be eight years old by now."

It had been so long since I last saw Moira, and the sight of her had struck a pang through my heart. I missed my friends dearly, yet returning to Dunguaire would have torn open an old wound I had long tried to seal. Here, the memory of my lost son still lived, sharp and near. The thought of his laughter, of the place where I had brought him into the world, hurt in my very flesh. At once, I turned my thoughts—and our steps—another way.

I reckoned Winnie must have rethought her life after Kalay's death. I had always kept a small place in my heart for that spirited fighter. Perhaps I would visit her someday, wherever she had made her home. But Moira only shook her head in quiet sorrow. Winnie had told no one where she'd gone. Her wish for chosen solitude was no passing whim; it was sacred to her, as it ever had been to my former warrior.

With each passing day, Moira grew stronger. Her spirit had returned, and as her heart regained its strength, so, too, did her old energy. With the help of a maid, we washed her silver-grey hair and pinned it up with a needle, just as she had done in the old days, then she wrapped a cloth around it to tame the last rebellious strands.

I had thought we might take a longer walk together, but Moira had other plans. Our next outing led us straight into the "witch's kitchen," as she fondly called her place of work.

Naturally, I helped her return order to the neglected herbs. She allowed only me into her domain, fearing they might truly take her for a witch. We made lists and sent kitchen boys into the gardens and woods to gather what was missing. With Moira's renewed strength, life returned to Dunguaire's infirmary. Countless helpers swept and mended the long-empty chambers, and the first sick began to come forth with their needs.

It seemed as if Moira's wasting had stilled all life within the courtyard. With the coming summer and her newfound will, everything stirred and bloomed anew. Only one thing remained to be done, to rid us of the cause that had driven her to relinquish her life. I was resolved to seize that rotten root of all ill and wrench it out.

The gratitude I saw in Cathal's face was as true as our friendship. After Moira's recovery, he had embraced me warmly, and I felt a single tear trace its way down his cheek. As ever, he found no words to voice his thanks.

"Come with me to the morning drills," he had rasped, just like in the old days. For him, that was near enough to a declaration of love. And I'll admit, the thought of crossing blades with Cathal again after so many years stirred a spark of excitement in me.

Now that Moira was on the mend, I found time to return to my training, and there Cathal stood on the flat rise before me. At first glance, he seemed invincible. No warrior in his right mind would choose to face him, yet with my chosen weapon, a Japanese katana, I was swifter, more fluid, and more precise. In the past, our sparrings had always ended the same way, with one of us yielding, breathless and grinning. There was always fire between us, but seldom did Cathal manage to break my force. I welcomed this fight, for at last,

I could test the steel beneath his charm, and I was set on settling what still smouldered between him and Moira.

With wild roars, we charged at each other, our battle cries meant to rouse the warrior spirits within. Yet somehow, we could not keep our solemnity. Between every clash of blades, we grinned like fools. This was our element, it was where we belonged. The good humour returned to our faces, born of the sheer joy that came from doing what our souls still loved best.

Cathal's shirt was drenched in no time, with sweat dripping from his nose. I felt each fierce blow reverberate deep into my bones. Not every strike still carried the full force of my youth, but for an aged Cathal, it was enough. I puffed and gasped, my muscles warming, and it felt good. I gave him no room to score, until something strange happened. At first, I did not notice, but after the second mistake, my senses sharpened with unease. I had known my friend for many years; his sword tricks and sequences of strikes were etched into my very flesh. Yet, after these years of pause, he was no longer the man I remembered. My friend had once been a master of the blade, with every stroke driven by precision and long-forged instinct. Now, I saw mistimed swings and mislaid blows. Cathal should have mastered blindfolded, but he was making errors. Surely, this could not be age alone? My suspicion deepened when he failed to parry altogether. I had shifted my stance in a flash. His eyes darted, unfocused, before they fixed on me again, and in that moment, I knew what it meant.

I lowered my weapon. Cathal had already taken his stance and looked at me in surprise. Questioning, he let his broadsword fall and straightened to his full height.

I saw his Adam's apple leap in his throat. Until that moment, we had exchanged barely a word, and we needed none. The sword spoke its own tongue.

His green eyes fixed on me as his lips pressed tight in unease. He knew well enough he could hide nothing from me. Shaken to the core, I cast my katana to the ground before me in a gesture that once meant surrender, but not today. Today was no fight for victory; it was for my friend.

With both hands, Cathal drove his broadsword into the earth, the blade quivering where it stood. His resistance broke, and he sighed in surrender as his arms fell limp. I had seen through him.

Cathal should have known better. Enja's healer's eye had not missed the hesitation in his movements. She had studied his swordplay for years and could foresee each strike before it came. How could he have been so foolish as to think she would not notice? He cursed himself for a fool, for giving her the chance to see through him.

Enja and Cathal stood facing each other. Her arms were folded across her chest, her gaze steady and expectant. She was still breathing hard from the gruelling swordplay. Cathal noticed she had grown leaner with the years, and in that leanness her woman's grace revealed itself more clearly. Her body remained strong and trained, though the thick shoulder and arm muscles that had once carried her through the brutal hours of battle had softened. She no longer had to prove herself in a fight, yet she still held that alert gaze and self-assured smile, and in her crystal-blue eyes flickered a hint of suspicion. Cathal weighed his choices. Should he confess?

The corners of her gently curved lips twitched faintly. Her brow—marked with the inverted cross tattooed in black when she was a child—furrowed in thought. Her silken, silver-shining hair danced in the wind. The graceful warrior had hardly aged, save for fine lines around her eyes. Even the scars upon her face and the half-lost earlobe did nothing to mar her. Unlike his wife, Enja had never let the harshness of life defeat her. Cathal held deep admiration for his friend, though he knew she was about to make his life difficult. He could already sense what was coming.

"Is there something you wish to tell me?" she asked. Cathal drew in a sharp breath through his teeth. That was quick and straight to the point.

"What do you mean?" He tried to buy time. Perhaps she was still in the dark after all. Folding his powerful arms across his chest, he tilted his head to one side. He'd be damned if he made it that easy for her.

Now she smiled and pointed with one finger at the broadsword still quivering before him. "If I recall correctly," she began, "that blade of yours has never failed you."

He held his tongue.

"Cathal," her tone grew edged with impatience. "The sword is still the same, but you are not."

For a few heartbeats, silence hung between them. Then, impatience broke from her like a storm.

"Your eyes have grown weak. Do you see anything at all anymore?"

Her voice trembled slightly as she finished the sentence. At least she still cared what was happening to him, and that was reason enough for him to speak plainly at last. His head bowed a little, and he nudged a pebble with his boot in quiet embarrassment.

"It's my right eye," he reluctantly grumbled at last. "Something's ... off with it."

His gaze met hers. She held it, unwavering, and waited. Aye, when Enja wanted to know something, she could be stubborn as stone.

"Well ..." he mumbled, his eyes wandering everywhere but her face. "I haven't seen properly for weeks. Truth is, I can hardly see at all. Everything's just ... grey."

He heard Enja draw a sharp breath through her nose.

"Why in heaven's name didn't you tell me sooner?" she exclaimed. "I've been tending to Moira for weeks, and not once did you mention your failing eye!"

Cathal felt like a chastised schoolboy. "Moira mattered more to me, Enja. She is my life; my love."

Enja let out a loud breath, as though bracing herself for a tirade. She had no answer to that. Shaking her head, she tightened her jaw; her beautiful face tensed. Her dark brows drew together above the bridge of her nose, carving two sharp lines between them.

"And you truly thought I wouldn't notice in the midst of battle?"

Once more, a tense, heavy silence fell between them that was sharp enough to cut.

"A man of lesser skill might still fall to you, but if you face a seasoned fighter, he'll see your blind spot in a heartbeat, and he'll use it. You must do something about it, my friend." Then, softer than she'd meant to, she added, "Before someone else does."

Cathal sighed. He knew all too well that she was right. Who besides Enja could possibly help him? He cursed himself for not speaking to her sooner. Perhaps she might even have stopped his failing sight from worsening.

"Can you still help me?" Cathal asked, his voice subdued. Despite everything, shame flickered in him at the thought of accepting her aid.

"It depends on what caused the blindness and how far it has gone. If it's only the lens that's clouded, I can remove it, but if the nerve is damaged, the outlook is grim."

She spoke in that calm, assured tone she always took when it came to matters of illness. Cathal knew it well from Moira. Instinct told him to stay silent. He had made a mistake, and it might be too late. Enja had struck straight to the heart of it.

"Well then, now that Moira's on the mend, I can tend to your eye," she declared without hesitation, pointing towards the weathered wooden bench beneath the great oak's sprawling boughs.

"The sun falls just right there this morning. That light will serve me well for looking at your lens. Sit down, my dear. You won't even have to undress for this."

That was the Enja he knew, pragmatic without fuss or ceremony. She would have pulled a tooth right there if he'd been in pain. As instructed, he sat on the wooden bench, which creaked beneath his weight. Obediently, he turned his face to the right, towards the rising sun. The fiery orb cast its orange-red glow straight across his face.

With a healer's precision, Enja examined his right eye. Her face came close beside his, and he could see the keen focus in her gaze as it traced the curve of the orb. She had him look upward and roll his eyes as she studied every movement. So near was she that he noticed the black lashes framing the blue of her irises like a painted portrait. A fine crease lay beneath her lower lids—one he had never seen before—lending her face a quiet sorrow.

Turning his face slightly towards the sun, she studied his eyes for a long, silent moment. Cathal caught her scent, as notes of leather, smoke, and myrrh weaved together into a heady, irresistible blend.

Her expression stayed grave as she turned his face this way and that. He felt the urge to close his eyes and pretend it was Moira's touch upon his skin. He longed to taste her kiss again. He missed her fiercely, yet it would have been his wife, above all others, who'd have first noticed the weakness in his sight. He had turned from her, unwilling to seem a man beset by frailty. Cathal O'Conchobhar was Provincial King of Connacht. A man in such a station did not show weakness.

At some point, Moira had fallen ill. That had been the reason he'd called for Enja, and it had become his undoing. Now, his friend knew of his failing eye. Still, better her than Moira, he thought as Enja finished her examination and sat beside him in silence.

Cathal kept his gaze fixed ahead, waiting for her to speak. The stillness of this place struck him. It was profound after the noise and bustle of the castle. Only the birds offered a small concert for the two of them, and far away, he caught the faint murmur of the sea. Otherwise, all was utterly still.

With a sidelong glance, he made sure Enja was still there. She had straightened her back and was staring silently towards where Cathal guessed the sea lay. Was she waiting for a sign?

Enja sighed, lowered her head, then met his gaze. Her voice took on that familiar professional steadiness once more as she said, "The lens of your right eye is badly clouded. You'll lose sight there completely within a short time. Your left eye isn't yet as damaged, but I've already seen signs it will follow the same path."

Cathal swallowed hard. A blind warrior was no warrior. No one could be allowed to know how near his sight was to failing. Until one of his sons had taken the throne, he had to remain strong for his realm, his people, and his family.

Cathal drew a deep breath. It still did not come easy to ask Enja for help. "Can you help me save my sight?" he pleaded at last, desperation breaking through his pride.

Enja met his gaze, her eyes clear and a gentle curve softening her lips. She nodded, hesitant. "I can heal your right eye enough for you to see shapes, light, and shadow, and perhaps even your Moira's face. But I cannot stop the darkness from advancing."

A silence fell between them, each lost in their thoughts. For Cathal, Enja's words struck like a blow. He must have pushed the truth aside these past months, driven by his despair over his failing sight. Enja, in contrast, had spoken her words without mercy, as any healer would, yet she was visibly shaken, and her lips were pressed into a tight, pained line.

"You were to sail back to Caerlaverock tomorrow?" Cathal asked, breaking the silence he usually cherished. Her voice, once more, felt comforting, regardless of what else she might say.

Enja met his gaze with solemn eyes and nodded slowly. "Aye," she said, "but if I'm to treat you, I'll stay until I can see the outcome, which means you'll have me on your neck for at least another week."

A twitch crossed Cathal's face, as though he could not decide whether to laugh or weep.

"Then let's get to it," he said at last, urging for action with firm resolve. "Blindness seems my certain fate, but if I can wrest a few more days of sight from it, I'll leave no path untaken."

Cathal heaved himself up from the wooden bench, his bones cracking in protest. A little stiff, he strode to his black stallion and mounted with Enja's help. No girth strap could have borne Cathal's weight; the saddle would have slipped the moment he swung himself up.

"Are you certain? Now?" Enja asked, looking up at him. There was an edge to her voice, as though she did not quite believe him.

Silently, Cathal took the reins from her hand and guided his horse back towards the castle. As he crossed the hill's plateau, he drew his broadsword from the earth with one hand and slid it, by long habit, into the scabbard strapped across his back.

"What are you waiting for?" he called over his shoulder to Enja, although he was damned sure she'd be right behind him. She'd been eager to begin the treatment; he had seen it plain in her eyes. That she would have to stay another week seemed to trouble her not at all.

The sound of approaching hooves behind him drew a faint, contented smile to his face. Enja would find a way, of that he was certain. As she always did.

I found myself unexpectedly tense. I had performed such eye treatments before, yet never on someone so close to me. The risk of complete blindness after the procedure was grave, given how far the affliction had advanced, but I bit back the words; Cathal had pinned all his hope on this operation. What worried me far more was the threat of infection. I set about brewing a chamomile infusion at once, to ease the swelling and soothe the flesh.

Moira took the grim news without a single bitter word. Bravely, she faced the shadow of her husband's blindness. She wisely held back any comment, for Cathal already bore a heavy guilt before me. She had only embraced him in silence in a gesture of pure love. For a long while, they held each other without speaking, and I struggled to keep my relief from showing. From now, they would face their trials together again.

By then, I was certain it was Cathal's pride—that cursed, hollow pride—that had nearly undone their marriage. Moira had taken his withdrawal as a loss of love, and it had made her ill. One truth my years as a healer taught me was that the body must live in harmony with its feelings. When the soul falls out of balance, sickness takes hold. In some, it strikes the mind; in others, the flesh.

Moira assisted me in treating Cathal, almost as she once had in Caerlaverock when she was still learning from me. She had already boiled the dried chamomile blossoms and now strained the brew through a cloth. Fortunately, she had witnessed several eye treatments before and knew exactly what to do. The sickroom she had offered us smelled of uisge beatha. Cathal insisted on a generous cup; it was his cure-all for every ailment, inside or out. That was fine by me; the more relaxed he was, the better. Soon, I would heat my instruments and dip them to keep them clean. The scent of alcohol was already thick in the air.

Cathal sat opposite me on a chair. I performed the treatment with him seated, for it made it easier to press the clouded lens downward. We talked for a while, until he had drained his cup of strong spirit. At such moments, I always sought to distract my patients before the procedure, offering a morsel of knowledge that would seize their thoughts. This time, it was a matter of politics—information I had, of course, from my husband, and shared with a clear conscience. It amazed me that Cathal, ruler of Connacht, did not yet know the full story. He listened intently, forgetting even his uisge as I spoke.

"Through the mediation of Pope John XXII, Robert de Bruce concluded a peace treaty with Edward III on the first of March this year, called the Treaty of Edinburgh and Northampton. Since then, Scotland and England stand united, and the English king has renounced all claims upon Scotland."

I cast Cathal a sharp look while cleansing my needle in the alcohol. He gave a short belch and wiped his mouth with the back of his hand, then had Moira refill his cup. He took another swig of the vile brew, the stench alone being enough to turn my stomach.

Cathal pondered a moment before replying, "The Pope has taken King Robert de Bruce back under his wing as a Christian after excommunicating him in 1306 for the murder of John Balliol."

A belch followed. Cathal was, indeed, aware of this political turn made by the Pope.

"As a gesture of peace, Robert now intends to marry his four-year-old son to the seven-year-old daughter of Isabella and Edward III," I added before Cathal's focus faded. This news seemed to surprise him little. I heard only the familiar low hum that passed for Scottish approval, and then another hearty swallow of the sharp spirit slid down Cathal's throat.

"On the seventeenth of July this year, the two are to be wed in a grand ceremony."

My words drew no further reaction. The cup was empty now, and Cathal handed it back to Moira, who did not refill it this time; she must have deemed he'd had enough. Before he could grumble at the lack, I pressed on. "In honour of the young bridal pair, a tournament is to be held in London, one the world has never seen before. Three thousand knights from every corner of the realm are expected."

Now I had his full attention. Even the empty cup no longer troubled him.

"In London?" he croaked.

"Aye," I said, "Queen Isabella, the bride's mother, and her lover Roger Mortimer have invited every soul of rank and name, including knights from the Holy Roman Empire, Castile, Portugal, Scotland, and, of course, the royal house of France. They say King Philip VI himself has accepted the invitation."

Cathal's green eyes studied me keenly. One would have to look closely to observe the clouded lens. I smiled knowingly, for what was to come next, not even my old friend would have foreseen. I had kept the most important news for last.

"A certain Sir Nicholas de Verdun is also among them," I said almost casually, adjusting my stool. The fingers of my left hand brushed the scar upon my cheek. "James saw the guest list himself, laid out on Robert de Bruce's desk."

We were ready to begin the treatment. I gave Moira a sign, and she steadied her husband's head from behind with both hands. Yet I could see something seeming to weigh suddenly upon him. Cathal leaned forward once more, fixing me with a sharp, searching gaze. I froze, tense with expectation. Had he changed his mind?

"Nicholas de Verdun, eh?" His tone had turned to steel, sharp enough to raise the hairs on the back of my neck.

Nicholas de Verdun was his arch-enemy. I blamed the strength of the whisky for the time it took Cathal to grasp what I'd said. He leaned back and fell silent. As always, he needed time to digest such truths and preferred to do so wordlessly. My eyes turned to Moira. Her complexion had grown rosier these past days, a sign that her blood flowed well again and her heart was strong. Her lips were slightly pursed. She met my gaze and gave a single, steady nod. She, too, was ready. Moira knew the risks. She had seen often enough how even the cured had not regained their sight. Together, we sent a brief prayer to our God, who, in the end, would judge the outcome according to how well my skill might please Him.

Cathal's pupils, wide and dulled by drink, stared at me as I lifted the cleansed needle. Then, while steadying his chin, I guided the point beside the iris and into the eye. He did not flinch. I moved the sharp tip from the anterior chamber through the pupil, angling it upward. There, I severed the tiny bands that held the lens suspended. With the blunt edge, I pressed the clouded, useless lens down to the base of the vitreous body and held it there for a time. Then I withdrew the needle. Why the lens clouded in some and not in others, even my master Isaak had never known. I had long suspected it to be an inherited affliction, for those stricken often came from the same bloodline.

Moira took care to bandage the eye, keeping it still. Cathal, meanwhile, sat motionless as a statue, still fixing me with his remaining eye. It had a faint glassy sheen, whether from pain or the uisge, I could not tell. I gave him an encouraging nod and placed a steady, familiar hand upon his shoulder.

"It's done," I said softly. "Now all we can do is wait—and pray."

His shoulders slumped forward at last, and he ran a hand over his scalp, wiping away the sweat that had gathered there. Cathal spoke no more of the ordeal, though it had been more than merely unpleasant.

"I think I need a uisge now. I mean—" he must have caught the lift of my questioning brow "—a whole bottle, not that dainty glass like before."

I could not fault him for it, neither as his healer nor as his friend.

The next day, we devised a daring plan. Cathal meant to take part in that tournament to slay Verdun openly, before all eyes. However, it could only be done if he matched Nicholas de Verdun as an equal, and therein lay the problem. The English knight was skilled and renowned in the lists, but Cathal would win the joust itself blindfolded, of that there was no doubt. But no matter how much sight returned to his eye, it would never be sharp enough for the tournament trials. Catching a ring or striking a mark with a bow from a galloping horse demanded perfect aim, and Cathal was far from that now.

Our plan struck us as risky, yet perfectly doable. Disguised as a knight in black, he would blend unseen among the colourful throng of contestants. At first, no one would give him a second glance. I would take his place beneath the black armour for the entry trials. Equestrian skill drills posed no challenge to me. Who would ride in the ensuing buhurt, we would decide only once Cathal's eye had healed. Close combat atop a horse was Cathal's domain; the one-on-one tilt with lance we agreed belonged to him alone. I was no use in that field, never having practised it. For the rest, his sight should be more than enough.

The next days flew by, for our plan demanded careful preparation. Again and again, we went over every detail. In the end, we had to craft a disguise. How fortunate I was not to perform my training in Cathal's heavy armour. A padded surcoat with his helm drawn low over my face would serve just as well. At the opening of the games, no one would pay heed to a knight without armour or banner. Only at the very end would the crowd look closely and, by then, with luck, Cathal himself would be inside that black armour.

During our preparations, we conceived the notion of a "hidden edge," a razor concealed within a wooden lance. The act must appear an accident. I feared too greatly that Cathal might otherwise find himself marched off to the Tower for wilful murder, condemned for breaking the lists' laws. I had been within those stones once, and I would see none of my friends swallowed by them. Cathal must cast away the planted weapon at once, flinging it to the earth. In the chaos that followed, a confederate squire would lift the lance and free the hidden blade. Thus, we would leave no trace of a tampered tourney-lance, which would be a plain breach of the rules.

At week's end, Moira unwrapped the bandage from Cathal's head. We watched his face in tense expectation as he looked from one of us to the other. Then, at last, his features twisted into a disbelieving grimace.

"Could it be," he chuckled, "that you two women have grown old?"

Moira scolded him as though he were a naughty child, but I couldn't help laughing. For all he'd endured, Cathal had not lost his sense of humour. I clapped him on the shoulder, sharing in his coarse jest; however, his laughter would not last for long.

“Mind yourself, my friend,” I warned, leaning in with confidant menace, “or I may well reconsider tending that other eye of yours. I could blind you outright, and then we’d have our peace!”

Even Moira laughed now. For an instant, the faded beauty of the woman flared to life. Her sensuality was plain as day, and again, my breath caught. Cathal seized the moment and pressed a fervent kiss to her lips. She pulled his head close, holding him there. They had found each other again. A wave of unspeakable joy rose within me and swept me along.

How fascinating—and vital—personal happiness seems to be to a woman’s beauty. We humans must all depart this world one day, sooner or later, yet with true love, our days burn brighter, deeper, and more fiercely alive.

Dear God … do not let me die alone.

Chapter 3

Caerlaverock, Dumfries, Scotland, December 1328

Caerlaverock rose in quiet majesty above the loch into which the great water castle had been built. The sun had just fought its way over the hills and was bathing the four towering bastions and trapezoid walls in a golden glow. Another bright day was dawning, far too mild for a Scottish winter. It was as though the calm air and gentle warmth mocked me, here in the fortress that was my heart's own, my beloved Caerlaverock.

I had pulled on my riding boots and stormed down the stair from the upper chambers, anger burning through every step. Fuming, I strode through the entrance to the great hall and out onto the steps, only to find Mass had just ended. The church door gaped wide, and the bells clanged louder than ever, as if mocking me for good measure.

All within the castle rejoiced in the unseasonable warmth, venturing out with their families, still dressed in their Sunday finery, to celebrate the Lord's day upon the meadows and fields. None knew what storm raged within me. The shock and the truth were only just beginning to carve their way into my mind. Reason refused to grasp what my heart had already understood. What I had just heard had shaken me to the core. My Sunday was lost, and though it was my own daughter, Fionna, who had soured my spirit, I could not bring myself to forgive her.

In my fury, I had seized the first horse I found saddled in the yard. A young mare, green and wilful, baulked beneath my hand and fought against my leg. Her defiance mattered little to me then. With a hard rein, I forced her out of the courtyard and onto open ground. Out there, at last, was the only cure for us both, the release we craved. Jaw set, I loosed her head and drove her on, across tracks, meadows, and fields, until at last, she slowed of her own accord, spent and trembling.

My heart pounded as wildly as hers. Like the sweat and foam that flecked her neck, my tears were also spent. I fought to steady my breath until I found the rhythm of the mare, and we inhaled and exhaled as one, the slower gait soothing my mind. I reached for her spirit and felt her soften beneath me; her neck relaxed, and she mouthed the bit and snorted in a sign of calm contentment. I did not even know this mare's name, yet I trusted she would make a fine companion. Gently, I patted her neck, but my thoughts refused to stray. At least now, my mind had settled enough to face Fionna's words from the morning. Never had I imagined a choice of hers could shake me so deeply, nor that Fionna—my daughter, our child, mine and James'—could wound me with such disappointment.

My Fionna. She was a rare creature. With her silvery-blond hair, milk-white skin, and those eyes clear as glacier water, she might have been carved from my likeness. She'd also taken her stubborn streak from me. Yet her spirit was nothing like mine. Where I'd wield my will with steel and defiance, she'd weave hers through words. Where my patience ended, hers began.

She was born on the first of December 1314, a few months after the Scots' hard-won victory at Bannockburn. Now, she was fourteen, and by all measure, it was time she be wed.

Fionna's frame was like mine, tall and slender. No doubt, I might have looked the same, had I not become a warrior.

All of James' and my attempts to find her a suitable husband had failed. Each was too stout, too plain, or too simple for her liking. She had led us all by the nose for far too long, yet she was the very image of womanly grace. Men would twist their necks just to glimpse her face. She matched the age's vision of an angel made flesh, yet she used her quick mind for every trick imaginable to escape a match. That, perhaps, I could have forgiven, but she had gone further.

She was a mischief-maker wherever she deemed it right. Her foul moods sometimes struck even the dogs that crossed her path in search of affection. The only visible joy she knew was found in her books. Even Latin posed her no challenge. In her few young years, she had read more than I ever had, and at times her knowledge unnerved me. Were men to see how effortlessly she wove history, philosophy, and science into new ideas, they'd abandon any thought of courting her. Her grasp of things was remarkable, and Fionna never yielded. When she'd had enough of someone, she simply walked away or locked herself in with her books for days on end. In her quiet nature, she was entirely her own company.

She was not a cruel soul. Quite the opposite; her heart was vast and tender, and she loved the siblings I had taken in as her own. She shared a bond deep as blood with her brother Thorvil, a deaf, mute boy. They spoke in signs, and I often suspected they had woven their own silent language that I would never truly fathom.

With a sigh, I drew the mare to a halt. Gratefully, she lowered her neck and began to graze. Why could life not be as simple as it had been with Rachel? Longing stirred in me at the thought of my adopted daughter, the infant my late friend, Jasemin, had entrusted to me from the Orient. Rachel was nothing like Fionna. She had honoured her father's wish and was happily wed to Liam McLeod, chieftain of the Western Isles. Now, she was mother to three sons and a daughter. Perhaps it was only my heart's wish that Fionna might know such joy, but she wanted none of it. My daughter resisted every path we set before her.

And now this. Without thinking, I bit a nail, spat it out in disgust, and wondered at the anger twisting in me over Fionna's ways. She was, after all, nothing but a mirror of myself.

My gaze wandered across the gentle hills and tilled meadows. The peasants had laid down their tools, for on the Lord's day, rest was their due. On such a sunlit day, folk strolled to the waters or up the slopes as laughter carried on the wind. My vassals greeted me with cheerful smiles, yet my mood allowed no pleasant reply; I only nodded, dour and distant. Goats bleated amiably, tugging at grass and leaves. No one seemed to notice the storm that raged within my heart.

I let the mare fall into a slow trot. There was no use running from it; I had to face the truth. And, above all, I had to tell James. He was in Edinburgh these days, standing at King Robert de Bruce's side. I did not expect him back for at least three days. Until then, I could forge a way to tell him what Fionna had revealed to me that morning. Weary, I brushed a hand across my face, her words echoing in my mind once more.

"I will not marry," my daughter had told me in that resolute tone of hers. "I could never bow to a man, nor do I wish for children. You are family enough for me, and I want you to understand why I must leave this place."

That single statement was enough to make me sweat. I could well understand why Fionna had no wish to marry.

"But why will you not stay with us? Here, we can care for you." My voice had turned hoarse with emotion. Fionna's beautiful face was pale as chalk, a mask of resolve. I could tell it cost her dearly to speak to me that way.

"I want to learn, to study. I want to shape my own life, but not as a warrior. Out there ..." she faltered, searching for words "... out there lies so much I've yet to understand. I want to be free to think."

Her voice was steady, each word sounding as though she had rehearsed it long before. My mouth fell open in disbelief. Where did she find such certainty? Of course, she had learned it from me.

"To live a life of your own as a woman, Fionna, can only be done with a weapon in hand, as the wife of a clan chief, or ..." I could not bring myself to finish the thought.

"I want to enter a convent ..." the words burst from Fionna as though she had carried them within her for a long time.

My jaw dropped, and my thoughts scattered into nothingness.

Fionna stood before me with quiet confidence. She looked lovely in her plain gown of grey linen. She had never cared for adornment and chose her garments for sense, not show. Hidden behind her books, she was seldom seen by anyone.

"A convent ...?" I stammered. The mere thought left a bitter taste on my tongue. All my life, I had wrestled with the Christian faith, converting only for my husband's sake. And now, of all things, I was to lose my only blood daughter to a cloistered life.

"You're not losing me," the impish girl had countered, catching my thought before I could speak it. "I'm only to wed God, not some husband."

"But convent life is harsh," I replied. Would you trade your freedom for a life bound by endless rules, merely for the sake of learning?"

Fionna's face remained calm, yet her eyes shone with fervour. She was a young, naïve girl, driven by an unquenchable hunger for knowledge. I knew then she would not be swayed from her resolve. The more I resisted, the more defiantly she clung to it.

My arguments had failed me. In truth, she had chosen the only path left to an unmarried woman unwilling to remain with her kin. Life in a convent offered safety and the chance to learn, yet her decision struck me like one of Cathal's axes: it was clean and merciless.

When I said nothing, she continued nervously. Perhaps Fionna thought her rush of words might persuade me to her cause. "Your library inspired me, Mother. Those shelves hold books of science I barely comprehend, no more and no less than what is written there. It isn't enough. I want to meet learned minds who speak other tongues and follow other faiths."

I had fled the brutal life of the Orient for the desolate peace of Scotland, yet this child could not get enough of the world's boundless variety.

"I can share what I know within the sisters' community and use it for others. You're a healer, Mother; your knowledge has saved lives. I wish to do the same."

Her words had struck home. Had she learned nothing of the dangers I had faced or the losses my knowledge had cost me? Perhaps I had shielded Fionna too well from the world's brutality, and now, she was walking straight towards the very fate I had always warned her away from.

Slowly, I leaned forward, bracing my hands on the dark wooden table. The room felt too small and the air too tight around my chest as I met her gaze in those crystal eyes so like my own. She held me with that steady look, her mouth drawn tight with the courage it had taken to speak her mind. She must have carried this resolve for a long time. I knew then there was no turning her from it. I had learned that lesson before.

"May I ask—" I rasped, "—may I ask where you mean to go, my dear daughter?"

Her slender chin lifted, and a faint, triumphant smile flickered across her pale face. She believed she had already won.

"France."

I fixed my gaze on her, yet unlike most men, who would have buckled beneath that look, she held her ground.

"France …" I had repeated in disbelief. Of course. She spoke fluent French, Gaelic, and Latin. She could read, write, and reckon with ease. All this she had learned from our priest, Armand, a monk ordained in France. The young man of God oversaw our children's education, and it seemed he had told Fionna a touch too much about his cloistered world.

"England is at war with the French!" The words burst from me before I could hold them back. King Edward III of England had claimed vast parts of France, and the struggle between the two realms had already turned fierce. Perhaps I could still frighten her from this foolish notion with the shadow of war.

Of course, no road would be too far for her purpose, for in her mind, God Himself stood behind her choice. I should have known better. A strange emptiness spread through me in a hollow certainty that I could not shake. I had nothing—nothing at all—to set against her resolve; only my husband might help me now. It would take a hefty dowry to place our daughter in a convent of her choosing, and beyond the silver it would cost, James would rage at Fionna's decision. The House of Douglas would gain no power from a nun in France.

I sat bent forward, my head buried in my hands. Since that morning, all the pieces had fallen into place into an image I had been shaping of Fionna for years. Her refusal to marry, her vision of a world she might heal with her learning, and her turning away from worldly life. In truth, she had long been planning to leave us.

My thoughts hummed like a beehive in my skull, so I didn't notice when Fionna slipped quietly from the room. Anger flared, and I stormed after her, out of the chamber and towards the stables.

The ride had done me good. My horse plodded calmly along the path back to Caerlaverock Castle, my thoughts were once again in order, and my heart beat once more in rhythm with my daughter's. I was resolved to honour Fionna's wish; that much I owed her, as I would have wished of my own mother. Yet I would not let her stride blindly into an adventure that had depths neither she nor I could see. Armand would answer to me. No doubt he could tell me more of the cloistered life and my daughter's future. He was half my age and a poor liar; it would be an interesting conversation indeed.

Thorvil stood a little uneasily by the stable door, regarding me with a weary glance. Only minutes before, he had seen me ride off in a state of turmoil. The young man took the sweating mare from me, not without casting a critical eye over her hooves, but they had withstood the wild ride unscathed, with all shoes still firm. I tried to appear composed, not wishing to unsettle him further. His senses were keen, attuned to the smallest tremor. Without waiting for a signal, he turned and led the steaming horse away.

Thorvil had chosen his path. He wished to work with the horses, creatures who understood him without words. He had only his hands and an uncanny sense for the clever beasts. In their company, he turned his silence into strength. He did his work with quiet mastery. Thoughtful, I watched him disappear into the stable's dim light.

A sorrowful thought struck me. Had he known of Fionna's plans? Likely so. Those two had ever been of one heart and mind. On reflection, perhaps I ought to bless her wish. If she found peace within a convent's walls, it would be more than any cursed marriage could give her, provided Armand had not filled her head with falsehoods.

My children had grown and gone their ways, so why did I struggle so? Perhaps it was the thought of losing my daughter to a God who had, all my life, remained a stranger I could never quite trust.

James had not returned to his castle as expected. Instead, he had sent a messenger bearing an urgent plea that I follow him to Edinburgh and bring my healer's satchel. No further details were given, which unsettled me deeply. James had been eager to see the family and me again. Only one matter could have kept him from coming home, and it filled me with dread. Could it be the king's health? Was it to be kept secret how Robert de Bruce truly fared? His healers were well known for using every art known to keep him alive. Grim tales of obstinate miracle-workers came back to me, and I shuddered at the thought of once more standing against those arrogant learned men. Yet in my rank and with my experience, I had no need to prove myself to any of them.

I went to the infirmary, which had seen unusually few visitors these past days. The province of Dumfries and its surrounding villages were blessedly free of illness. Perhaps the nearness of Hogmanay—the Scots' New Year—meant no one wished to find themselves abed with sickness when the year turned.

Driven by resolve, I paced the small chamber, ever kept fresh by an open window. The cold air chased away the staleness and sickly vapours of the infirm. Two wooden cots stood within; a third could be added if needed. Shivering, I drew a deep breath of chill air before closing the window to keep out the draft. My gaze fell upon the leather satchel leaning against my worktable, my faithful healer's bag, still carrying the scent of tanned camel hide. It was a fragrance I had known since childhood from my old master Isaak—mingled in my memory with the aroma of brewed mocha and sweet dates. Even now, I still delighted in the taste of that bitter drink and those exotic fruits. They were among the goods we traded in plenty with the far Orient, bartering them for our Scottish uisge beatha, furs, and forged steel. The flavour of those delicacies lingered on my tongue from the afternoon's brief respite.

The physician's satchel was in good order, though it bore the patina of long journeys. It never failed to stir memories of older days. What tales that satchel could tell!

In my infirmary, I found not only that old relic but also a wealth of freshly rolled beads in every hue. Each colour held a different power, which I used to ease folks' sufferings. Through my studies, I had refined Isaak's ancient recipes, tested new compounds, and built a vast store of remedies, now a full array of healing craft born of years of trial and faith.

I thought of Fionna. She had the makings of a scholar, yet to study at the scale I had known in the Orient, she would find no easy path among the nuns. She would need to enter a true school of medicine. In Salerno, women were admitted to the faculty, I recalled. Francesca Romana had earned her surgeon's licence in 1321. Among my collection of medical writings lay the *De curis mulierum—"On Treatments for Women"*—by the healer Trota, one of the few treasures I had coaxed from Isaak. Under the protection of a greater circle, women could study and teach beyond the walls of cathedral schools.

With the breadth of my knowledge, I could aid, calm, or rouse the human body, but above all, I could ease its afflictions. Most of my remedies drew their strength from nature itself, from plants and beasts alike. Even Cathal's manhood had I restored through the means within my reach. Only a few rare ingredients came from the distant East by the sea trade; even frog venom or powdered ape organ could be procured, should I deem them useful or required. Yet Fionna wished not to study under me, nor to journey to Salerno. She longed for the convent.

With my lips pressed tight, I checked that all my instruments were packed and slipped in a little more of the opiates I liked to experiment with. My last self-trial had ended, regrettably, in a state I could no longer put into words. Even now, I could not quite summon the details of that strange lapse of consciousness.

I was rifling through the drawers when I suddenly paused as a sharp stench caught my nose, foul and putrid, an insult to my refined senses. It came clearly from the right side of the room, and I took a few steps towards the back corner. The smell grew stronger, and then something grey shot towards me in a blur of matted fur and paws. With surprising force, the cat pressed itself against my leg and began to purr. I bent to stroke the familiar creature, our castle tom, no doubt standing guard over his prize that had clearly been dead for some time. My searching eyes found it beneath a shelf. It was the half-decayed corpse of a rat. Annoyance flared in me; such things had no place in a sickroom. I would have a word with Catriona about the matter of cleanliness.

With a fair amount of fury in my gut, I stomped across the courtyard, seized a shovel, and flung the decayed rodent in a wide arc over the castle wall. The act gave rise to a strange impulse that drove me back to my worktable. I tucked a small pouch of aloe and mugwort—good against parasites and worms—into my old satchel. It was now so full I could scarcely fasten it.

I did not know what awaited me at the sickbed of the ageing king, and I meant to be prepared for anything. It had been long since last we met. I vaguely recalled he had once suffered from scaly skin, but that was more than ten years past. Surely his healers had managed that by now. Still, I slipped the ointment of onion and honey into my already bursting satchel. Everything else I could find in the king's herb kitchen, if, indeed, there was any cure for what ailed him.

Thoughtfully, I drew the leather ties of the satchel closed. It was all that remained to me from the Orient, along with the vast knowledge my late master had left behind. I was deeply grateful for his teaching. Isaak had been stern, yet his heart was kind. Why he came to my mind so vividly now, I could not tell. Perhaps because I had reached the very age he'd been when he took me from the streets of Baghdad.

I stared at my hands, feeling uncertain. They had grown rough and calloused from years of swordplay, the fingers strong and bronzed by the sun. They were a worker's hands, not those of a noble lady of the keep. Scars and thick veins traced their way across the backs in the markings of my life and of my years.

"I regret nothing, Isaak," I murmured, as though I still owed him an explanation. "But I cannot promise that one day I won't."

Resolutely, I gathered my instruments and heaved the heavy satchel out of the infirmary. I nudged the purring tomcat out with my boot, then locked the door with the key I meant to hand later to Lachlan McKay, who would oversee Caerlaverock in James' and my absence. Not, of course, without a stern word to his wife, Catriona, the healer charged with keeping the infirmary clean.

It was too late in the day to depart, but come morning, I would set out for Edinburgh with my mare, Bela. She was the right beast for the near eighty-mile journey to the Scottish royal city, a swift two-day ride from my keep. We would need only to arrange for one night's rest. Bela had been my steadfast companion on many a road, and she was sure-footed and loyal in every trial.

I took the physician's satchel straight to the stables so the lads could fasten it to my saddle. My maid packed my clothes and provisions, for I expected a longer stay at the king's court. I would see to the medicines and weapons myself.

I reached the stone-built stable in a few strides. Dusk had already settled, and the servants had replaced the fading daylight with small oil lamps that cast flickering shadows along the walls. Their warm glow lit the building, which some of the stable lads also used as a place to sleep. It was warmer there than in any chamber, thanks to the beasts' body heat.

Inside, I let the satchel drop before the wooden door of the right stall. The head of my loyal mare, Bela, shot over the half-door at once to greet me. With my right hand, I stroked the soft hollow behind her ear and let her breathe in my scent from the left, though this time, I had no fruit to offer. In the dim light of the stable, her shape was little more than a shadow. She seemed well enough; the lads would have told me otherwise. Bela was newly shod and ready for the road.

My gaze drifted down the stable aisle and caught on an empty stall. As always, when I looked that way, a sharp ache pierced my chest. That had been Taycan's place, the horse gifted to me by Sheikh Hassan I'Shabbah, the one who had carried me from the Orient to Scotland. The faithful stallion had been my companion for near twenty-five years, siring countless foals and strengthening the bloodline of my war and riding steeds. His passing, peaceful as it was, had left a hollow in me as though I had lost a child.

Into that memory crept, with painful clarity, the face of my son, Conor. He had turned twelve that year. Since parting from him when he was a small child in Ragnar's arms, I had never seen him again. His last image was seared into my mind like iron to flesh. I would never forget how he'd stood upon the ship's deck, waving that tiny hand in farewell. Conor likely never even knew I was his mother. I swallowed hard, as I always did when that thought returned, and held back the tears. It had been a farewell for life.

Conor was the child born of my affair with Ragnar Sigurdsson. The Icelander had slipped into my life and, before I knew it, my heart. I could swear I had never truly loved him, and yet I had never been able to forget him. In Conor's face, I saw his father's; they were one and the same.

How vexing, I thought, twisting my face into a grimace. How could I even picture my son when I had not laid eyes on him for eleven years? The only face that came to me was Ragnar's, scarred and fierce. I shuddered.

James knew nothing of what my affair with Ragnar had brought forth. Only Rachel and Fionna knew of their half-brother and, of course, Cathal, Moira, and Winnie, who had helped me keep the pregnancy hidden. They had taken little Conor into their home at Dunguaire and raised him as their own. A strange tenderness stirred in me at the thought of how richly God had blessed me with true friendship. I made a quiet note to myself to remember it at my next service.

In that instant, I realised, startled, that I must have missed the last two Masses in our new chapel. My eyes flicked nervously towards the farthest corner of the stable, as if God Himself might be lurking there to scold me. But I was alone; no voice stirred my guilty conscience. With a wistful glance at Taycan's name, still carved upon the board above the stall door, I turned away, yet my thoughts slipped, unbidden, back into the past.

In a moment of painful resolve at the harbour of Galway, I had made the heart-wrenching decision to let my son depart with Ragnar to the land of our birth. The striking wooden ship had set sail for Iceland at the end of 1318, bearing them both away. With each passing year, the hope of seeing him again drifted ever further beyond my reach.

In a moment of sudden tenderness, I closed my eyes. I pictured Conor running across the dark cliffs of my homeland, fur boots flying over jagged stone and his young hands steady on the bow, ready to hunt ... what? I knew not. In Iceland lay the ruins of my childhood; all that remained were scattered images and shards of memory.

Unconsciously, my fingers sought the gemstone I had worn since my unwilling parting from my mother. My hand found the pendant, warm from my skin. The leather cord had been replaced more than once, yet the stone remained the same. It was a black onyx, shaped like an oval teardrop and set in ornate silver. Tiny loops with dragon heads clasped the stone at either end, as though guarding it.

My mother had pressed it into my hands in the moment of her certain death. We had been adrift, helpless, after our ship went down. Seconds later, she vanished beneath the freezing waves. She had meant to accompany me on my journey to Mount Hekla. My mother had been proud of me then; it must have been deemed an honour for our family to offer me, at six years old, to the god of the volcano, to be cast alive into his fiery maw. The thought of it still made me shudder. Love for one's child, I had since learned, wears a different face.

Bela snorted in protest. I had forgotten to keep stroking her. I patted her neck, feeling the steady pulse of her strong, loyal heart beneath my palm.

"Tomorrow, you and I shall take a little ride, Bela," I whispered to her, and she pricked her ears at once. Her bright eyes fixed keenly on me. "We'll have ourselves a fine time," I promised, for she rejoiced in every chance to move.

I remembered little of my childhood in Iceland. It had been cold and full of wind. We had warmed our hands on hot stones my father had carried from a cave. They kept the goats and us from freezing. Were we rich? I could not say, only that we had never gone hungry. My sister, Jalla, and I would huddle together beneath a bed of furs. Beyond that, my memories were few, and mostly grey and black. Was Iceland truly so dark, or was it only how I remembered it?

I closed my eyes in irritation. The tales from my childhood in the Orient were so much clearer, more vivid, and more alive. True, I had been a beggar child, yet after fleeing slavery, I had known freedom there, and we had never gone hungry, until Isaak entered my life and took me as his assistant. As his pupil, I was bound to him by fate and fortune alike, and I had been fortunate indeed. The old physician shared his vast learning with me, teaching me all a healer must know. If only he had not been so stubborn!

It was for that very stubbornness and his blind religious zeal that Hassan I'Shabbah's men had struck him down. A Shiite would not serve a Sunni. Foolish man! Gold has no scent, and Hassan would have paid him handsomely. At twelve years of age, I was forced to take his place. Disguised as a boy, I rose within the fortress of that infamous sect leader, trained to perfection as an assassin. I was good, but my disguise was undone by the return of my old friend Jasemin, heavy with Rachel in her womb. She died bringing her child into the world.

Hassan's trust did nothing to unravel my disguise. The leader of the famed Assassins had charged me with securing half his fortune from the Seljuks' reach. That meant riding west, far into the lands of the setting sun and straight into the heart of the Scottish War of Independence. Perhaps it had been fate's design, for it was there that I met James Douglas, Fionna's father.

At once, my mood darkened as though a black cloud hung over Fionna's name. No, I would not let my anger at her plans take hold of me again. I would deal with her when I returned from Edinburgh with James. I told myself no decision had yet been made, but deep down, I already knew the truth.

Unlike Conor, Fionna was here with me, and that was what mattered. I could speak with her, laugh with her, and quarrel with her. I would bid her farewell that evening so as not to wake her come morning. She would wait for me. She was here. Conor, by contrast, was so far away. My son, who seemed no longer to exist, as though he had died long ago. Unbidden, I sent a prayer to the God I now served, asking Him to guard my son's life. According to Brother Armand, the Holy Trinity was far mightier than any of the countless gods of my former homeland.

"Protect my son Conor, Lord," I whispered, "and grant that one day he be returned to me."

My late friend, Brother Brian, had once given me a precious truth: "Souls that are forgotten die a second death."

That prayer was true for every soul in the Lord's realm. The words had come from one who should have known, the cleric who had chosen to fight with the sword rather than the Word of God. He had fallen in battle upon the road we once walked together. God keep all their souls in His mercy.

It was a bright day with a brisk wind and the promise of a touch of snow in the days ahead. That troubled me little, so long as we reached Edinburgh dry. The road was fair, broad and well-worn, and wound through woods, meadows, and streams. Though winter had turned the grasses more brown than green, I took pleasure in the gurgling water that seemed to spring from every hill. Gentle rocky rises gave way to ploughed autumn fields, soon to bear summer's bounty again. Here and there, a farmhouse appeared. Folk waved as we passed. Stone walls overgrown with evergreen shrubs enclosed goats, cattle, and sheep, each searching for what forage they could find. Often, a bundle of hay lay within the pen to see them through the lean season.

On my journey to Edinburgh, I was accompanied by one who had been at my side for as long as I had been parted from the Scottish king. Mina was now sixteen years of age, or so I reckoned. When she had come to me as a six-year-old foundling, without parents or kin, she had known only her name. She had just crossed the threshold of womanhood and smiled at me with easy cheer. Her brown curls lifted in the brisk wind that nipped our faces, and the flush on her cheeks lent her a look of health and youth. Her blue eyes shone bright upon me.

Mina admired and revered me, not only as her mistress but with fierce devotion as a warrior, striving to follow in my every step. She even mimicked the tilt of my head, the smallest of habits, with uncanny grace. The clever girl helped herself freely to my precious dates, too. Mina saw herself not as a woman, but as a warrior, and that suited me fine, for she showed remarkable skill with the bow. She had seen to our lodgings, horses, and baggage, never hesitating to grant me the comfort of a chamber and a warm meal while she slept in the stable, softening dry bread in hot water. A smile never left the face of that ever-willing girl.

The next day, I could not resist stealing a closer glance at my eager pupil. Seeing Mina ride so boldly beside me, her bow across her back and her knife at her belt, I had to admit that, at her age, I had also taken pride in besting men.

Where might she have come from, I often wondered? I never did find out; she had been a foundling from the harbour of Galway.

At that moment, the first signs appeared along the roadside as proof that we were nearing Edinburgh. Wayside crosses and inns lined the unpaved road. Carriages and riders, wanderers and farmers all moved towards the city. It had been long since I had last come this way. Since the end of the wars for independence against the English, the great Scottish towns had swelled and spread. Edinburgh's borders had stretched outwards, and the lands around it had been tamed and tilled. How times had changed!

After Robert de Bruce's victory at Bannockburn in 1314, peace had returned to Edinburgh. The walls and royal fortress, once shattered by war, had been rebuilt by the proud Scots. In the calm that followed came prosperity, and with it, the city's trade flourished anew.

Our horses kept an easy trot past low cottages and roadside inns until, at last, the grim fortress loomed before us. Mina and I reined in, struck silent with awe. The low winter sun of a fading December evening bathed the outer walls in gold, setting the stone aglow. Wordless, we sat side by side in our saddles, caught in the spell of the structure's dominion. Robert de Bruce's castle rose in full majesty, its massive towers and sweeping roofs proclaiming the breadth of his power. One glance was enough to feel it. That, after all, was the very purpose of its making.

In that very moment, I understood why Bruce's royal seat had been built upon that towering rock above the heads of men. The crag was deemed unassailable save for one legendary exception. The mad Scotsman Thomas Randolph had taken the castle on the fourteenth of March 1314, only months before Bannockburn, leading fifty men in a daring night assault. Until then, it had lain in English hands. Robert de Bruce, in honour of such valour, later made his bold nephew, the first Earl of Moray, his co-regent.

As I drew closer to the fortress, I had to commend Robert's men for their audacious work. The walls, patched and mended in many places, would grant no foothold to an intruder. And yet, I remembered, I had scaled more than one such wall myself during a siege, just as Sir Randolph had with his band of fearless Scots.

The road into the city grew ever more crowded. We could not ride straight up to the castle; had we been able, we might have spared ourselves the crush of people. We women, in our martial attire, drew glances but no challenge; the townsfolk, it seemed, were used to strange sights. At last, we found the turn that led towards the royal stronghold, and from there, we rode alone. The horses snorted and stamped as they climbed the steep slope to the gate. Iron shoes rang against the heavy cobblestones that paved the entire ascent, which was broad enough for whole garrisons with siege carts to pass. Bela was blowing hard now; the old lady was no longer accustomed to such strain, and she felt the weight of the long day's ride. With steaming flanks and the clatter of iron on stone echoing around us, we passed through the open gate into the courtyard. The sound rebounded from the walls, doubling the din. By the noise alone, one might have thought an entire troop of riders had entered.

We had reached the inner bailey, beyond the storehouses and chapel. Only at the second gate were we halted and inspected by the guards. In times of peace, the king's retinue had little fear of the fortress being taken. From the watchtower, a soldier called down our names before granting us passage into the keep.

There stood someone already, and the joy upon his face at seeing me was unmistakable. A warm smile lit the man's features, and at the sight of him, my heart gave a sudden leap.

Chapter 4

Edinburgh Castle, Scotland, January 1329

James Douglas was beside himself with worry. Robert de Bruce's illness was growing worse by the day. Even without a scholar's training, the king's general sensed that his sovereign's end was drawing near. His suggestion to summon Enja as an additional healer had met with fierce opposition among the royal counsellors, but Robert's own request for her had stilled the uproar. With the king's quiet but unmistakable command, a messenger had ridden for Caerlaverock before the day was out.

His king's strange affliction weighed heavily on James, and with it, God had placed a cruel burden upon him. Even the finest healers in the land had given up. None could name the source of the curious skin sores. The ageing monarch's itching and pain worsened, yet the brave man bore them with patience. James had been driven to grasp his final hope: Enja.

As his wife rode through the archway with her warrior, Mina, his chest swelled with pride. He had not seen her since the joust at Smithfield. She had tended his broken ribs, but left after a week, bidding him to rest while he was still too pained to mount a horse. Fate had not allowed James to return to Caerlaverock. The Scottish court had summoned him straight from Smithfield. Robert had required his counsel and, above all, his healer's aid.

Enja had returned to and remained at their castle, bringing back the prized gear and horses from the tournament to Scotland. Lady Douglas of Caerlaverock—despite her years—was not only one of the most striking women he had ever known, but she had altered the course of his life entirely. It had been a change for the better, though at the start of their marriage, there had been many storms he would rather forget. He had made his share of mistakes, yet Enja was no ordinary woman, as he had painfully learned. Their love had been like a river in flood. At first, he had been swept away by it, then both had crawled to shore to breathe, only to plunge back into the current again. Now, at last, they had reached calmer waters, drawing strength from a deep and steadfast trust.

James had long ceased to see her merely as his wife; she was far more than that. She was his companion, his kindred soul, his fate. The moment he had parted from her and ridden through the gates of Caerlaverock, he had felt her absence keenly. To see her face again stole his breath still, after all these years. His longing for Enja only deepened as the years grew upon him.

His wife rode straight towards him without a moment's hesitation. A shy smile touched her even features, which was a rare and striking sight. She seldom let her joy show, but this time, she seemed scarcely able to wait before finding herself in his arms.

James all but lifted her from the saddle and drew her tightly to his chest. Her embrace went straight through him. She nestled against him like a cat, and he held that wondrous body—which he knew as well as his own—close against him. The scent of her journey enveloped him in horse and sweat, fire and resin. The perfume of Enja.

James took his wife's face in his rough, calloused hands and kissed her softly. All his longing was poured into that single kiss. Enja lingered for a heartbeat, perhaps weighing how much passion a public kiss might bear. At last, she slipped free of his tender hold. The chill air had brushed a rosy hue upon her pale skin, and a smile touched with mystery played on her face.

"I can see you've missed me," she whispered, her voice a lure, and a shiver sparked at the nape of James' neck.

"Indeed. And I am not ashamed of it. I cannot shake the feeling that it was the same for you, was it not?"

Her face was so close to his. The faint scar on her cheek quivered, and her eyes gleamed with light.

"Without you, my bed has been cold. I had to lay hot bricks in your place, though I must confess, you feel far better than they ever did."

Despite the long journey, she was in good spirits, which gave him hope. A grave task lay ahead, and as he had expected, her humour did not last long. She must have felt his tension, for at once a shadow of seriousness crossed her face.

"He is unwell, then?"

James inclined his head almost imperceptibly. With a glance at the guards surrounding the guests, he discreetly guided his wife and Mina towards the royal chambers. He kept a guest room here that he always occupied during his longer stays at court. He led his wife there, that she might ready herself for supper. Mina followed, carrying the satchel holding her medicines and instruments that Enja guarded with her very life.

"Will Robert join us for supper?"

Enja was no doubt eager to see him again after so long, yet she would have to wait until dawn. Robert was too unwell.

"My lord has already retired for the night. He will receive you at first light." James cast his wife a warning glance, then nodded towards Mina, who was busy unpacking her mistress' travel gear. The signal was clear: say no more than needed about the king's true condition. Then, he turned towards Robert's chambers to announce her arrival. James knew Enja would take all the time required; the king's ailment had become her personal cause.

Robert de Bruce had always stood, in my memory, as a tall and noble man. His life's energy seemed to flow into all who surrounded him, including his subjects, friends, and even his kin. Where he drew such strength from had ever been a mystery to me, for fate had not treated him kindly. As the sole survivor of four brothers, he had borne the loss of his first and second wives and his daughter. Another man would have broken beneath such weight, but Robert de Bruce did not bow to fate. I believed he loved his people as fiercely as they loved him. Perhaps that was what kept him standing; it was his life's purpose.

Another of his blood was his illegitimate son, Archibald William de Bruce. The boy had grown up with us at Caerlaverock and now served as squire to the McLeods in the northern reaches of Scotland. At eighteen, he would return to his father's court, hopefully as a knight who had earned his spurs.

Robert's one bright light was his son, David. Only a few months earlier, the young man had been wed to the daughter of Isabella, Queen of England, in a political move of rare cunning, for it had drawn the final line beneath the long feud between Scotland and England. With that union, his youngest had also left the family seat behind.

Robert de Bruce had been left alone in his royal palace, and I secretly feared that loneliness would claim him sooner than any sickness. I was not far wrong in that thought; his symptoms had worsened since David's wedding and his lingering stay at the English court.

When I saw Robert that morning for the first time, I was struck with shock. As with Moira, I wondered if a body could truly wither so much in just a few years. Robert, standing before me in his chamber, was but half the man he had been fourteen years before. His once-black hair had turned silver-white, and coarse stubble shadowed his furrowed face.

His dark eyes studied me as I stepped into the shadowed bedchamber. They said he had grown averse to light. It was a trait I could well understand, for my eyes burned and smarted when the brightness grew too fierce.

It took only a moment for my eyes to grow used to the gloom, and I was able to meet his gaze. Robert stood beside his bedframe of dark, carved wood. The heavy canopy above it cast nearly the whole chamber into shadow. Beyond it, I saw a few more furnishings, including a chess table and perhaps a desk. They were plain, functional pieces. There were no ornaments or useless trinkets to gather dust.

Behind the bed, a hearth spat bright tongues of flame, giving off a faint warmth, yet I felt little of it, for the terrace doors stood wide open and the chill breath of January swept through the room. Before I could take a seat on one of the visitors' chairs, Robert asked me to follow him outside. I did so gladly, grateful for the chance to escape the stifling air within.

Robert greeted me with his old charm as one welcomes a long-lost friend, resting a hand on my forearm as he led me out. At least I escaped the strange scent that clung to his chamber—a sweetness laced with something I could not quite name. It sat unpleasantly in my nose, as though someone had tried to mask another, fouler odour beneath.

Outside, the sun had already fought its way above the horizon, as it bathed us in its pale light. Even the birds chirped cheerfully, as though it were the most natural thing in the world for folk to be sitting outdoors at this time of year. Gratefully, I took my seat on a fur-lined bench beside a table inlaid with marble. The servants had placed hot bricks beneath its surface, and with relief, I set my boots upon them, warming my chilled toes.

I gathered my focus and turned my full attention to Robert, who had settled into a deep, winged chair across from me. He wore a long robe, richly embroidered with silk, with its hem trimmed in pale fur. The garment reminded me faintly of a bishop's cassock; it must have been Robert's dressing gown, or perhaps his night attire.

I was unsettled as I met his gaze. His dark eyes studied me as openly as mine did him. He had brought full-grown men to their knees with that very look. I swallowed hard. In truth, Robert was one of the few men in my life for whom I held a profound respect. Even in a plain nightshirt, his authority was immense and his presence undiminished. It had been many years since I had seen him, and now he was a man of great power. Could I, a woman, dare address the king directly?

My thoughts drifted back to the days of war, to his simple tent, which any of his captains might enter without summons. He had always been more general than king. More than once, he had felled his enemies with the axe in his own hands. He was no god, but a man of great courage, I recalled, and I cleared my throat before I began to speak.

"My lord, I thank you for summoning me and for placing your trust in my craft," I began, knowing full well Robert himself had called me here. James had told me as much. My eyes, traitorous things, flicked towards my husband standing a short distance away. His face remained almost unreadable.

The king tried to smile, but his effort faltered. Instead, he merely nodded in weary surrender, and I saw his Adam's apple rise and fall.

"Dearest Lady Enja." His once-mighty voice that had thundered across battlefields was now but a whisper. "I am most grateful for your presence. Thank you for coming."

Robert paused between sentences; speech, it seemed, cost him great effort.

"God has granted me little time to see my wishes fulfilled. I fear I shall never hold a grandchild in my arms. The physicians have given me but half a year …" his voice broke on the words.

The moment pierced me to the core. To know one's death was near—what must that feel like? My hand moved of its own accord across the table towards this iron-willed man who had never granted himself more mercy than he demanded of others. My fingers found his right hand, which was strangely cold, the dry, scaly skin rasping against mine. I gripped it firmly, and he accepted the gesture with quiet gratitude.

"Wherever I may be of aid, Sire, I shall be. My knowledge is yours, and I would give my life to preserve yours."

The words came from my heart, and he felt it. His gaze dropped, and I thought I saw a wave of pain pass through him. Before me sat a man at the end of his life. Though he had done and achieved so much, time itself had not been enough for him.

"The Lord will aid us," I whispered, steadying him with my gaze. "If it be God's will, He shall grant me the grace to heal you or guide you to your end. Let me begin my work. 'Tis a duty I owe to our people and, most of all, to my husband."

Robert's thoughts returned to his loyal general, and he looked to him with quiet command. James had not wished to leave us, yet neither would he intrude upon the private moment between his king and me. For James, the loss of this man—to whom he owed all—would be a heavy blow.

The monarch had restored to him his name, honour, and power, the very things the English king Edward, the Hammer of the Scots, had once torn from his father William and from their bloodline. Robert had redeemed James, binding him as one of his closest allies. Never had he forgotten the loyal souls who would have followed him into death itself; those who stood by him still, even when he had hidden like a hunted beast in the caves of the Outer Hebrides.

James stood silent, his head bowed, arms folded across his chest. He had placed his hope in me, and I felt the weight of it pressing down. It was likely thanks to him that our king received me with such ease. No counsellor, no charlatan dared to interfere. Only the three of us were here to make one final attempt at saving the king's life.

Robert de Bruce was, in truth, a picture of misery. His skin and eyes bore a yellowed hue as signs of a liver ailment or, at the very least, of its failing strength.

I asked him for a sample of his urine, and the deep yellow hue stirred my concern. His organs seemed to be granting him no more time. A glance into his eyes revealed grave trouble with his kidneys, and the pain in his back confirmed the failing of what lay within. But what had brought him to this state?

Ordinarily, I would have urged a patient to drink plenty of water, but Robert had long done so. Neither a sweating cure nor letting of blood had brought him any relief. His frailty had grown plain even to strangers; thus, it mattered to him to withdraw from sight; he was no longer fit to govern his realm, and James had stepped in to bear the burden in his stead.

It dawned on me how crucial it had been that my husband had come rushing here straight from Smithfield. Though

James still suffered from fierce pain in his ribs, he had taken over Robert's affairs together with the royal secretary. He discussed the greater decisions with Robert, depending on how much strength remained in him. To my mind, a little more rest would have served the ailing man far better.

What astonished me most was that neither Robert's heart nor his lungs had suffered harm. His bones and muscles remained sound, remarkably so for a man of five and fifty, given all he had endured. It was his organs and skin that troubled me, though I could not tell cause from cruel consequence.

Conspicuous to every eye, white scabs flaked from the dry eruptions upon his hands, arms, and feet, while crimson welts stood out stark against the rest of his skin. A closer look revealed that they covered near his whole body. Robert confessed they itched terribly, and that in the past months, they had spread without restraint. It was a sign of his body's waning defence, worn thin by its battle against Robert's vices. His habits and restless ways did little to aid my efforts. Against his reckless indulgence in wine and uisge beatha, and his fevered work-fury, my gentle herbs stood powerless. Still, I left no remedy untried.

Compresses of sour milk and chamomile eased the swelling and itching, yet the afflicted skin refused to heal despite all my efforts. I suspected a bond between the ailing dermis and the exhaustion of his organs; thus, I set myself to treating the skin with all the care and fervour I could summon.

Indeed, my treatment brought a brief easing of his torment. The welts faded, and the itching subsided, until, after near four weeks, both returned with full and merciless force.

It was near two months later when I struck my fist upon the table. That morning, I had found Robert senseless in his study, reeking of strong drink. He had slumped over a letter he'd near drowned with a bottle of uisge beatha. His grief and gnawing burdens drove him ever deeper into the brown devil's grasp. As a human soul, I could fathom his torment, but as a healer, it was bitterly disheartening.

I had now been within the royal palace since January of our Lord's year 1329. My patience and, more so, my knowledge were wearing thin. None of my remedies had taken hold, and I feared that a new plague might have swept through Scotland. Yet no other case of such an affliction had been reported to me. During the brief spell of Robert's recovery, I made good use of the time, seeking counsel on the symptoms and, most of all, the strange aspect of those welts.

Through all the weeks in which I tried remedy after remedy, what perplexed me most was that Robert suffered neither fever nor skin heat, for any inflammation should bring warmth with it as a natural defence, the body's own uprising against disease.

The scaly surface of his skin felt cool beneath my hand. Even through the magnifying lens, the crust showed no sign of mites or other parasites. My precautionary cure against worms also failed. It vexed me deeply for more than Robert's sake; I longed for his healing, but above all for James' peace of mind.

My husband grew disheartened by my lack of success, yet I dared not stand against God's decree; such defiance would be sacrilege. I reminded James of his faith before he lost faith in me. I bore him no grudge; the love he held for his king was tearing him apart.

For a few weeks, my ban on spirits had stirred Robert's failing body back to life, yet by May 1329, he suffered a grave relapse, once more after days of abusing the Scottish brew. Fierce itching, restless longing, and bitter self-reproach seized him. Still, he would not yield to reason. Robert de Bruce reached more readily for the uisge when his strength failed than for the silken thread of life. His organs, above all his kidneys, were too burdened to keep his waning body alive much longer.

At the end of May in the year 1329, the Scottish king sank into a slumber so deep that not even my vial of smelling salts could rouse him. From that moment, I knew, as only long experience teaches, that it would not be long before his heart could no longer feed his ailing organs. His death was now but a matter of time. My throat tightened as I beheld the great man lying in peaceful sleep upon his bed. No remedy on earth would bring him back. Perhaps, at the end of his days, Robert de Bruce simply longed to return to the family he had so sorely missed, to his wife and the beloved daughter of his heart. Aye, the uisge had surely eased his passing.

I made my peace with him and steeled myself for what was now to come. There were precise instructions for his final days. From the first, it had been his wish that King Robert de Bruce should not die in his seat of rule at Edinburgh. Many servants and companions lent their hands as I oversaw his removal. His last royal journey, though he slept through it, was taken in a black carriage, unmarked by any banner. The rickety vehicle bore the dying king to the small castle of Cardross near the village of that name in the shire of Argyll and Bute.

The idyllic Cardross, the haven Robert had chosen to soothe his weary soul, lay upon the banks of the Firth of Clyde some four miles northwest of Dumbarton and southeast of Helensburgh. Here, he had hoped to find his peace.

The dying man's wishes were plain and without artifice. Robert would pass only in the company of his closest friends and confidants. He had known for some time that his end had come, and no physician in this world could have kept it at bay. The priests of Cardross had already laid out his Last

Anointing, awaiting the hour of his swift departure. For my part, there remained but one duty: to make his leaving easier.

James Douglas kept vigil at his king's bedside as a son would over his father. He was ten years younger than the man he revered above all others, yet unlike Robert, he still had his family, his clan and, most dearly, his wife beside him. All this lent him strength and faith, but Robert had been stripped of everything. His political legacy was vast, but as a man, he had paid a fearsome price.

James' gaze lingered on the sunken face of the monarch, who, though unconscious, still tossed restlessly in his bed. His body must have been racked with unspeakable pain. Sweat gleamed upon his brow. The servants repeatedly wiped away the traces of his dying struggle and changed the sheets. Even the potent pearls of the medicus brought no relief now; the damage within was too grave, so his wife had told him, taking from him all hope of recovery, yet he stood steadfast beside the dying king. He could see in Enja's eyes how Robert's death was striking her to the core and making her feel helpless.

"His kidneys are failing, his blood is poisoned, and his heart has grown too weak to endure."

Enja's few words had struck the truth clean and sharp. Robert de Bruce would be dead within hours. James pressed his lips tightly together, finding what comfort he could in the thought that none but Enja could ever have saved the king.

James Douglas had driven out every charlatan who dared question Enja's care. He had seen how Robert had turned again to the drink, though Enja had begged him not to. Her worry had fallen on deaf ears. Robert had fled his dark thoughts into the stupor that encircled his loneliness like a warm cloak. Perhaps the brave king wished to leave of his own accord, James thought, to follow those of his blood who had gone before. His sombre gaze lingered on the familiar face as though he sought to hold its memory one last time.

Suddenly, Robert's eyes flew open, and a transfigured gaze met James from a darkness so deep it sent shivers through even the General's hardened frame. It seemed to him as though another man lay before him, not the one he had followed for so many years. Perhaps it was only his spirit now, speaking to him in a voice no longer his own.

"My beloved companion."

James grasped the cold hand and pressed it, trembling, against his chest. It felt suddenly so unbearably heavy, so foreign, as though the body it belonged to had already slipped beyond life. In that instant, James knew these would be Robert's final words.

"I am a sinner, and the wrongs I have not atoned for in this life I shall answer for in the Kingdom of God."

A vague memory stirred in James of the murder of John Comyn of Badenoch. Robert de Bruce had slain that rival for the crown within the church of Greyfriars near Dumfries in a deed that had roused the Comyn lords against the Scottish king for the rest of his days. Did Robert now seek his God's forgiveness from the brink of death? Had that guilt weighed upon him all his life, pressing to be spoken at last in his dying words?

James held his breath. The face of the dying man grew slack, and life seemed to drain from him as water from a cracked bucket. His pain was gone. The great king lay still beneath a dark red coverlet. James pressed his hand tighter to his chest, as though by sheer will he might ease his sovereign's passage into death.

"Take my embalmed heart to Jerusalem and bury it there where our Lord Jesus Christ met His death," commanded Robert de Bruce, his voice bearing the weight of a final order. "I never reached that holy land myself, but you, James—you will."

His voice was but a faint whisper now, as though it already drifted from a place far beyond this world.

Robert's chest rose and fell a few more times. Deep within, his lungs rattled in a desperate struggle for one last breath. The Scottish king leaned his head back, his eyes flaring wide, and then the harsh breathing ceased. Silence settled over the room. So deep a silence that even the servants' quiet sobs could be heard. Robert's eyes turned still in an instant. James knew at once that the man who had been as a father to him had drawn his final breath.

The great King of the Scots, Robert de Bruce, who had wrested back his people's freedom and power from Edward I, was dead. No mortal soul upon this earth could have stayed his passing.

Chapter 5

Caerlaverock, Scotland, March 1330

Great commotion reigned at Caerlaverock. The day of departure had come, and chaos ruled the courtyard. Hens flapped and cackled in wild alarm, scattering feathers into the air. The three hounds barked at one another for no reason, perhaps stirred by the tumult, for there was no stranger to announce. Even the horses felt the tension that lay over us like an unseen shroud; they pawed at the ground and pranced in place. Children dashed laughing and shrieking through the mire, while men roared their final commands in coarse voices. A few stragglers hurried across the muddy yard to fetch what they had forgotten.

We should have been on the move well before daybreak, yet a pale, diffused light was clawing its way through the morning fog above the dark treetops, and still we lingered. Delays of this kind frayed my every nerve driving me near to despair. To make matters worse, it looked as though we would begin our first stretch beneath a curtain of freezing rain. Though the cold bit hard and the ground lay stiff with frost, we pulled our fur cloaks tight and braced ourselves against the bitter air. Little clouds formed before our mouths as we urged each other to set off. None of these were good omens, and on top of it all, a knot of stomach cramps had plagued me since dawn.

Though the calendar named it spring, dark clouds smothered the sun, and a cold, needling rain sent little rivulets dripping from our boots. I had wrapped myself in a fur cloak to ward off the damp. A soft patter reached my ears as I waited patiently for the packhorses, whose girths were being tightened once more. Twenty-four men rode with us, more than half of them knights. A host of squires, stable lads, and even a cook travelled in our company. Fionna, Mina, and I were the only women among the column. Instead of a maid, it would be only us who accompanied the future nun. That, too, had been my strong-willed daughter's wish; she wanted to bring nothing worldly that had once made her life so comfortable. I wondered what Fionna would say when those delicate hands of hers were tasked with washing the linens.

With my new mare, Lissy, who, after my first spirited ride with her, had proven herself a remarkably gentle mount, I waited for the final signal to depart. It would come from James, upon whose shoulders the command of our company now rested.

My gaze drifted across Caerlaverock courtyard, my home, familiar to me in every stone and shadow. I caught sight of known faces among the smiling maids and a few farmers who had come to bid us farewell. Lachlan McKay would see to the castle and the lands in our absence, steadfast and trustworthy as ever.

One farewell weighed heavily on me that morning. Rachel had come with her husband, Liam McLeod, and his men from the northern reaches of Scotland to bid us goodbye. Despite her three children, she had been determined to see me once more. The past days had swung from bright to bleak, much like the Scottish weather, yet I would not have traded a single hour in which my adoptive daughter and my blood sat together at our family table, perhaps for the last time.

Rachel had changed somewhat through her pregnancies. The once-reserved girl had grown into a mature woman. The burden of her children weighed on her, too, and in this harsh land she often seemed as though she belonged to another world entirely. Her black curls and dark, almond-shaped eyes spoke of her roots in the Orient. Her skin gleamed with the golden bronze of the daughters of Allah, and she reminded me of the time I had been blessed to spend in the East with her mother. Jasemin had placed the newborn Rachel in my arms with full trust. She died soon after from her inner bleeding. Rachel had travelled with me westward, cared for by a wet nurse.

"Safe travels, and may God be with you wherever you roam!" Rachel called from the top step of the great hall's entrance. Most had taken shelter there from the rain and the wind. Now she was waving as well, tears streaming down her cheeks as I blew her one last kiss.

A shiver ran through the column. At the castle gate, James had at last given the signal to depart and was among the first to set off. Close behind him rode the two sons of the Maxwell laird, Alexander and Walter Maxwell, newly knighted only this year. Colin Maxwell had insisted his sons accompany James. The old crusaders were proud to see their descendants take part in such a sacred ceremony.

James, bearer of the royal silver seal, had taken on the role of keeper of the relic. Yet at the very front rode a knight carrying the king's banner. He was an old companion who had volunteered for the duty: Sir Thomas Randolph. His silver-grey mane called to mind the worth of his deeds in the War of Independence. At the victory of Bannockburn, he had been a force to reckon with, commanding one of the four dreaded schiltrons that had spelled death for thousands of Englishmen.

To ride in this procession was a great honour for the warrior who had been so decisive in Robert de Bruce's wars. Few of the old comrades had lived to witness their king's passing, but Sir Thomas Randolph, like my husband, was a living witness to Scotland's battle-scarred history. The proud knight's face bore the ruthlessness of war, as scars cut through his bearded features and two fingers were missing from his left hand. Yet the banner in his right he held as if it were a treasured prize. Behind him, I recognised other familiar faces from days long gone. Sir William Sinclair, Sir William Keith of Galston, Sir Robert Menzies, and Sir Simon Lockhart were but a few I could make out. It was a colourful gathering of nobles from Scotland's ancient lines, assembled to pay honour by following Robert de Bruce's heart. Every gaze was fixed forward, resolute.

A new adventure was stirring, and the promise of a coming feat set our blood thrumming. My stomach felt as though tiny bees were trapped inside, humming without cease. It was enough to drive a sane woman mad. At last, the day of our departure had arrived, and I ought to have been content that everyone had made it into their saddles. Usually, in matters like these, I was calm itself, but today I was more restless and frayed than ever.

James, chief of the province of Dumfries, had resolved to carry the embalmed heart of Robert de Bruce to Jerusalem, just as he had sworn to the dying king in Edinburgh. I confess, I doubted the fate that now led me once more towards a place still vivid in my memory, to a land perilous and unpredictable. The knights returning from the collapsing kingdom of Jerusalem spoke of war and of the Mamluks' brutal assaults upon all Christians. My rightful objections to the danger of such a journey were overruled by a majority of stubborn Scots. Among them stood Liam McLeod, king of the western isles and Rachel's husband. He had fought as a crusader long ago for Jerusalem's liberation, and ought to have known better how perilous James' enterprise truly was.

In recent days, I'd had more than enough chances to throttle Liam, yet for my grandchildren's sake, I restrained myself. I merely cast him a murderous glance from the side that surely left his conscience stinging. I had expected him to stand with me for, to my mind, James' vow to his king to carry his heart into war against the heathens was reckless folly.

But Liam had embraced the venture at once, aflame with eagerness. To carry a relic into a land that threatened the lives of all Christians bordered on madness. It felt as though that place I had escaped as a young warrior by sheer fortune was calling me back more fiercely than ever. I deemed the undertaking nothing short of suicide.

Still, I had agreed to accompany my husband, though only as far as a certain monastery in France. The very thought of it made the bile rise in my stomach once more. It was clear enough, I had not yet come to terms with Fionna's intentions.

Until the very end, she had held fast to her decision to leave her family for a life devoted to God. The double monastery of Fontevraud, where nuns and monks lived under the rule of powerful abbesses, was one of the mightiest abbeys in all Christendom. It was to shape the whole of my daughter's life from this day on. Neither James nor I had been able to sway her stubborn resolve, and at some point, we yielded. To force a spirit like Fionna into marriage would have led only to ruin of the heart.

Suddenly, I felt Fionna's gaze upon me. Her blue eyes rested calmly on my face and she was even smiling. This was a rare sight, for she had been solemn since childhood. Her flawless features and pale hair made her seem almost angelic to me. Perhaps she believed as much of herself.

Since her final decision, she seemed to me as though a great burden had been lifted from her shoulders. She was calm, centred, and at peace within herself. More than once, I wondered whether God truly had a hand in the matter. After all, it had been Pope John XXII himself who granted Fionna's request and, with his blessing, secured her a place in the famed abbey on the Loire. A cleric had brought the scroll to us in Caerlaverock after months of waiting. It contained a single line naming the dowry owed to the convent, a sum not open to negotiation. It was the price required for them to receive our daughter.

Fionna was plainly delighted by the Pope's approval, and the triumphant gleam in her eyes confirmed my suspicion that her Christian tutor, Armand, well connected in Avignon, had tipped the scales in her favour. Had I been younger, I might have rolled my eyes at her air of victory, but now I knew better. Fionna could not have chosen more wisely. Fontevraud Abbey was, in truth, a convent of the highest repute.

While we had awaited confirmation of her place, I had sought information in advance through James' trusted contacts. Fionna was, after all, our only natural daughter, and she would live out her days within those walls. The conversation with Armand, however, proved difficult. He kept his intentions well shrouded, yet he spoke freely of life within the abbey.

"Fionna will be trained to a simple and God-fearing life under the strictest rule," confided the lanky priest, his skin pale and his eyes sunken deep. "She will forget her fancies soon enough and learn obedience. However, if she is placed under the right abbess, she may, with wit and diligence, shape her knowledge into something of worth, even within a convent's walls. Many young women like Fionna are born to the cloister. Give her what your daughter needs most, Lady Enja," he coaxed, almost conspiratorially. His gaze drifted deceptively to the cross at the centre of my brow and lingered there a shade too long. "She will become another woman entirely if she can find herself there, far from home."

By then, I was certain that Fionna would either be shaped into a humble nun at Fontevraud, or flee home screaming. The latter she would forbid herself out of sheer pride. One way or another, I would fetch her back by force of arms if ever she had need of me.

"I shall visit her there once each year. I will keep a watchful eye on my pupil and your daughter." This assurance eased my mistrust of Armand, if only a little. Perhaps he truly wished Fionna well and sought to guide me back to reason.

I exhaled long and steady, then drew breath again. The nervous flutter in my stomach refused to settle. Too much could befall us on the road ahead. Restless, I checked the position of my katana in its back scabbard, then the dagger at my belt. The horse beneath my saddle seemed eager to move after such a long wait. Lissy shifted anxiously in the courtyard, tugging at the reins with her mouth as though urging me to release them at last.

I could only hope we would weather the long journey without harm. Our plan was to take a ship from Berwick to France, and there deliver Fionna to Fontevraud. It would take us at least two months to reach the convent, for our path would be lined with political halts and diplomatic obligations. In truth, our mission made us an official royal delegation of sorts. We would have to accept countless unexpected invitations and bear every delay that came with them.

From the abbey of Fontevraud, James and his crusaders were to continue to Venice as planned. From there, a ship would carry them to Cyprus. On that Aegean island, Richard the Lionheart himself had once prepared his crusades. Its long, fierce history would aid James as he pressed on towards his purpose.

It would be in Muslim waters that our true troubles would begin. The situation in the Byzantine realms was dire. A civil war had broken out there some years ago, and Andronikos II Palaiologos, the emperor of Byzantium, was struggling desperately to hold his realm together. The seas might still be navigable without immediate peril, yet we knew well that this conflict had already strained the flow of trade goods bound for Caerlaverock.

Another peril lay in the state of Jerusalem. The Mamluk conquest of the Christian city had unleashed a wave of violence. The few Templars who had managed to flee to Cairo had been put to death or left to perish in agony from starvation in the prisons. Colin Maxwell and his family had likely been the last to escape that political deadlock unharmed around the year 1300. It was he who warned me then against travelling on to Syria, and with him I finally chose to abandon our original destination. My caravan moved west instead, toward Colin's homeland.

Now, my great love James looked at me with those dark eyes of his. He had turned in his saddle to seek my gaze. Like most of the knights riding with our train, James had thrown a black cloak over his surcoat. It was woven from the wool of Scottish sheep, then dyed and crafted by our women. The natural lanolin gave the fabric a faint sheen, and it had been felted tight to make it strongly proof against the weather. It was a useful garment indeed to fend off the Scottish drizzle that followed us like a persistent shadow.

This man had become the anchor of my life, no matter how fiercely the world raged around me. His face was hardened by war and softened with such tenderness whenever his eyes found mine. James had lost a little weight; the grief for his long-served king and comrade had clung to him like mourning veils. Yet today, some of that heaviness seemed to lift. The prospect of following his lord's sacred call appeared to warm his spirit. Even in the dreich Scottish weather, I could see his smile beneath the fold of his cloak.

Only this morning, I had assured him of my deep love. I smiled and cast him a playful wink. By now I no longer shied away from showing such small tokens of affection openly; after all, we had been married for nearly sixteen years.

Then, once more, my stomach stirred, warning me of the uncertain path ahead. Perhaps fate sought to prepare me for the perilous days awaiting us in the Holy Land. My resolve was still iron-clad. I would return to Scotland as soon as Fionna had been received into the abbey, yet events were racing beyond anyone's grasp. Many nations were locked in battle with the heathen forces pressing in from the East. Meanwhile, France and England waged a bitter feud between their royal houses. Edward III, son of the murdered Edward II, had risen against his mother Isabella and her lover Mortimer, plunging his crown into turmoil. The young ruler's fragile hold on power had sent ripples across to France, the homeland of the Plantagenets from whom he descended.

For Scotland, these conflicts played neatly into our hands. Even the death of Robert de Bruce passed unnoticed by the English throne.

A land without a strong king, so I had learned, soon lost its influence and power, and so it was in Scotland. The void Robert de Bruce left behind bred deep uncertainty within the circle of leaders. All eyes turned to James, who, with Robert's counsellors, had taken up the mantle of Guardian until young David was grown enough to wield the sceptre. Yet at this moment, James placed greater weight on fulfilling his sacred vow than on guiding Scotland with a steady hand. King David was far too young to claim his inheritance. This had been the very heart of the dispute James and I had waged long before our departure.

"Robert asked me on his deathbed to bear his heart to Jerusalem," James' strong voice still echoed in my ear. "It is my sacred duty as a Christian to grant him this last wish!"

"And his people need a strong leader," I had retorted in fury, "especially now, when David, kept in London as a child-king, holds no power. Scotland could slip back into England's hands with frightening ease, just as it was once annexed by Edward I." As I spoke, I had clenched my hand into a fist and thrust it before his face. But James remained unmoved.

"The court lives by Robert's legacy; they would never dare to scheme against David."

"A royal court tearing itself apart, and little David caught in the midst of it!" I countered.

James had been irritated by our sparring, I had felt it keenly enough, yet my concern was far from unfounded. Little David, only five years old, was still wholly in the grip of his advisers. Even Isabella's professed respect for Robert's legacy would not keep her from abusing her power. Her lover, Roger Mortimer, plundered his realm as freely as Edward II had before him, turning barons and magnates alike against him. Young Edward III, England's designated king, was already moving to curb their excesses. At times, James' faith in God's providence was simply more than I could bear.

"Edward I, the Hammer of the Scots, never hesitated to twist the once-good relations between England and Scotland to serve his ends. He turned nobles and knights alike into mere puppets in his reign."

I did not cease reminding James of the political dangers. His father had stood against Edward's designs and had been imprisoned for that very reason. The shrewd lord had seen through the king's game. William Douglas had died in disgrace within the Tower of London, and with him many brave men who had fought for a free Scotland.

"William Wallace was among the first to be condemned as a high traitor to the English crown. Never forget that!"

James' face had darkened, plain as storm clouds. The memory of that hopeless time he had been forced to witness as a young man had driven his pulse sharply upward. I pressed on with hard, unyielding arguments.

His entire family had been grievously harmed in the conflict. The great hero William Wallace had been executed as a high traitor before the eyes of the English people. How could James possibly believe that all would remain as it was now, should he ever return from Jerusalem?

"I will go to the Holy Land, and with me the brave knights who fought at Robert's side," he insisted, stubborn as bedrock, his molars grinding in defiance. "You know full well that Robert never managed to join the Crusade. At the very least, his heart should stand once against the unbelievers. I will carry it against the heathens for him. It was his last and greatest wish, and who would I be to deny him that?"

At some point, I simply surrendered. I had no weapon sharp enough to counter his religious resolve. Only our daughter's wish to devote herself to God had persuaded my husband to delay his departure a little longer. The moment the written invitation from Fontevraud Abbey lay in our hands, he began gathering his men. I had once believed James the only madman among Scotland's knights, but I was swiftly proven wrong. The heroes of bygone days, every last one, came when he called. My resentment lingered even now, on the morning of departure. Perhaps that was what twisted my stomach so tightly.

In truth, it was an impressive company that set out for the Holy Land. Nearly forty horses bore the weight of our great equipment, riders, and squires. Several mules carried the heavy armour, weapons, and chests of coin. James and his brave men were leading a small fortune into an uncertain future, not counting Fionna's dowry, yet it was still but a fraction of the wealth I had once brought him from the Orient with my caravan. Half of Hassan I'Shabbah's estate had reached Caerlaverock through Colin Maxwell's help, securing my standing in Dumfries.

Silently, I looked back at my beloved castle as it faded into the misting rain. It seemed to drift weightless upon the clouds. How easily reality can deceive the eye. A shadow, dark and foreboding, seemed to veil my sight of the days ahead, and it unsettled me. I had always loved to travel, yet today, no spark of joy would rise. Black birds circled above us, shrieking like heralds of death. Even the priest's blessing for a safe journey, spoken over each of us, brought me no comfort. I turned my head forwards again beneath the hood. My mare plodded after the others with a snorting eagerness. This was Lissy's first great journey; at least the dear creature greeted it with delight.

Suddenly the stabbing in my stomach returned, and I pressed my fist hard against my belly until the pain eased. Yet the uneasy feeling—that I had chosen wrongly—would not relent.

Robert's death had weighed heavily on James. The mourning rites had swallowed near an entire year. Whenever a monarch passed, the appointment of royal delegates, naming of new chancellors, and struggle for power and influence quickened like wildfire. Yet Robert, foresighted even in life, had ensured that strong and trustworthy men would guard his legacy. Still, James remained at court until the threat of hostile takeover was safely dispelled. The wait for Fionna's place in the abbey had played neatly into his hands. James was content with himself. He believed he had done everything as it ought to be done.

Robert's son David was far from ready to rule, so the court officials took charge of all decisions until the boy would reach his kingly maturity. They were men James himself had sworn to their duty, and were supported by a strong host, ever watchful of the English crown and steadfast in defending the sovereignty of their young king.

James turned and saw the young knights Alexander and Roderick Maxwell behind him, scarcely past growing faint down upon their chins, yet wearing their surcoats with proud, eager hearts. They were the sons of Colin Maxwell, a former Templar who had fled the Orient with his wife, Salome, and Enja. James' heart quickened. They had come from the very land to which he now set his course.

The charge his dying king had laid upon him filled James with a fierce and humbling pride. As Robert's former confidant, he saw it as an honour beyond measure to bear the embalmed heart into battle. His hand wandered unconsciously to the small silver casket hanging from a chain at his neck. It was smaller than he had first imagined, yet a human heart, drained of blood and water, shrinks until it is but half the size of the living organ. The reasons Enja had put forward again and again to delay their departure had worn him down to the bone. To him, the winter had seemed endless.

Enja had been right, spring was the wiser season for travel, especially with a young woman like Fionna. His delicate daughter would never have endured a journey through the bitter winter. Not that matters were much improved now, for the rain still clung to the company. The clouds had thinned a little, and instead of heavy drops, a fine mist drifted down from the sky.

James cursed under his breath at the ill timing, after more than half a year of waiting. To loosen his stiffened joints, he braced a hand on the saddle's pommel and twisted his upper body around, surveying the riders lined up behind him in a long, patient column. Among them were older faces, men who had ridden beside him for half his life, and younger ones, like the Maxwell brothers. James counted twenty-four riders, and about half as many packhorses. The remaining squires and helpers trudged on foot through the mud.

Their supplies would last for several days, long enough to carry them overland from Dumfries to Berwick-on-the-Tweed. There, warm beds awaited them by the harbour before the company boarded a ship. Jerusalem, he mused, was both a curse and a blessing to the faithful. Many kings, and far more knights still, had answered the Pope's call to fight for faith, glory, and honour. Not all had returned from the Holy Land; some had found only a grave in foreign soil. Men like Colin Maxwell, who had come back, spoke of horrors and atrocities, yet even so, he had entrusted his sons to James' charge.

Perhaps James would not need to travel so far in these unsettled times to hurl Robert's heart against their sworn foes. Rumour claimed the Muslims had already pressed into the lands of the West, yet if that were true, he could not fulfil his vow to lay the relic to rest in Jerusalem. The very thought of journeying so far from Scotland left a tightness in his chest, for it might well prove a voyage without return. At least Enja would accompany him for half the road; he would not be parted from her for so long.

His gaze drifted to Fionna in her warming cloak. The woven wool gleamed a vivid blue the same as her eyes. The young woman was speaking animatedly with her mother on this final journey together, far more than she usually did. She gestured with an elegant, gloved hand, lending weight and, above all, expressive grace to her words.

How alike they were. This was far from the first time he had noticed it. Mother and daughter shared a striking, uncommon beauty. Fionna was almost as tall as Enja, though far more delicate. With a touch of pride, she squared her narrow shoulders and lifted her slight chest. Her pale-blonde hair hung loose beneath her cloak, while her mother always wore hers tightly bound in a knot at the nape of her neck. Their eyes held the same colour, yet Fionna's gaze was gentle, where Enja's could turn so cold it could send a chill through every bone, even in her husband. James' eyes drifted to Enja, sitting almost nonchalantly in the saddle beside her daughter.

Enja was a woman who challenged him as fiercely as she challenged her enemies. Life had left its traces upon the face of the extraordinary warrior. Not only scars, but a few faint worry-lines had, over the years, woven themselves into her once flawless features.

Enja had grown more seasoned, older too, though he would never dare say so aloud. The fierce warrior was still a beautiful woman, now even more so for owning her feelings without fear. The fortress called Enja had gained a few cracks over the years that he had filled with steady, patient love. Not every scar could be mended, yet her spirit bore the calm of a soul at peace. James thanked heaven for granting him such a remarkable woman at his side. She was not only an exceptional fighter, but also a devoted mother and loyal wife.

For a moment, Enja's gaze met his. She smiled with that knowing look of hers, while their daughter explained the world in one of her grand monologues. Warmth stirred in James' chest as he caught Enja rolling her eyes in quiet exasperation. Fionna's tales tended to wander. With affectionate understanding, he blew his wife a kiss and turned his face forwards once more.

Suddenly, a horse appeared beside him. The girl upon it had been riding ahead with the scouts and had let herself drift back. Annoyance flickered through him; he had not heard her approach, yet the clatter of hooves on the pebble-strewn path was plain enough. He must have been too distracted by the sight of Enja.

James paid her no mind at first. She was a warrior he scarcely knew who served under his wife's command. From ahead, he already caught mocking glances; he could not see the men behind him, yet he knew well enough they would be muttering, too. What in God's name did she want from him?

She shot him a cheeky sideways grin, which vexed him no end. She showed not a shred of respect, and he had no intention of treating her like a noble lady. Just as he was about to tell her to get herself back to her place, she spoke.

"Do you truly mean to journey all the way to Jerusalem, my laird?"

The question came so abruptly that James thought he must have misheard her. He let out a dismissive sound and edged his horse away from the warrior girl's shaggy mount. She had ridden far too close for his liking.

"I gave my dying king my word," he told her—then all but cursed himself. It sounded as though he were offering an excuse.

James' voice left no room for doubt. As Lord and Guardian of Scotland, he would not have his purpose questioned by a mere woman such as this.

"It is my duty as a faithful Christian," he added, hoping to impress upon her the weight of his vow. He was, however, more than a little perplexed as to why this woman addressed him at all. Mina was the name his wife had spoken while saddling the horses that morning. She had not been long in Caerlaverock; how long exactly, he could not say.

"Could you not entrust the heart to a knight who would ride to Jerusalem in your stead, my laird?"

James shook his head in disbelief. The woman flung her insolent words at him without a shred of thought. Clearly, she had never heard of a knight's duties or virtues. He wondered what on earth his wife saw in this tactless warrior. For months, Enja had trained the girl in every art of combat, and yet, it seemed she had not learned the respect required of her.

"With respect, you know nothing of honour or dignity."

At last, the young woman saw the anger in his face, and offered a brief bow in apology.

"Forgive me, my lord. I meant no offence …"

James kept his mouth shut. He hoped she would simply ride on, yet the curly-haired lass with the bow on her back stayed stubbornly at his side. She even pulled her lips into a smile that flashed white teeth. In truth, she was a comely sight with those dimples. He steadied himself. After all, she was a woman with no formal learning.

"Where do you come from, Mina? I do not recall you joining us as a child, yet you are trained in arms nonetheless."

James forced his voice into a more conciliatory tone.

Mina's face lit up at once. Her grey eyes shone with sudden happiness, and her brown curls danced about her face like a halo. She was likely one of those souls who found a sliver of good in everything, James reckoned. Just as she did now.

"I hail from Ireland, my laird, at least, that is what they believe. Lady Enja found me as a foundling at the harbour of Galway and brought me to Dunguaire. I was but a child then, and I grew up in the household of the O'Conchobhars. It was a rich upbringing, for I was taught the art of the weapon from an early age. Since I was little, I have wished to be as your lady wife, sire."

She beamed with her whole heart, and James let out a weary sigh. Another of the mad ones. A few young women sought to emulate his wife, and riding beside him now was a particularly vivid specimen of that tribe of warrior maidens; the chatterbox kind. James braced himself for a stream of praises sung in Enja's honour. So be it. At least she no longer questioned his intent.

"Now, I am Lady Enja's weapon-sister," Mina declared with pride. "She is most impressed by my skill with the bow. Did you know, my laird, I can strike a bird at two hundred feet …!"

With that, she yanked her bow from its holster. It was a short hunting bow. James shot her a look of pure disbelief.

"Shall I show you, sire?"

"No!" James cried, louder than he intended, and waved his hand in alarm. He was genuinely fearful for his companions. They, too, had grown nervous, reining in their startled horses. The mad girl's reckless manoeuvres were rousing even his mount to panic. She guided her horse with her knees alone, as though she were on a hunt, as the reins dangled loose over its neck. He had to put an end to this nonsense at once.

"Hold, girl," he snapped, "that's far too dangerous!"

Mina laughed and carried on, as though she took delight in defying orders. With scarcely any effort, she held the bow before her and, in one smooth motion, drew an arrow from the quiver at her saddle. It was swift, the practiced movement of someone who had done it a hundred times over. James found himself both impressed and infuriated in equal measure.

"There is no bird," he growled, cursing in a manner most unworthy of a knight, but before this mad creature, he cared not one whit. At the rate she was going, the fool was liable to shoot one of his knights clean out of the saddle.

"Enough of that," he growled, exasperated. "Save your strength for the road ahead."

But Mina would not relent. Her eyes swept the land and sky without blinking. No bird appeared, yet something else darted across her path, startled by the travellers. Instantly she drew her bow towards it. A single breath later, the string snapped forward and the arrow struck a creature that, moments before, had been hopping cheerfully through the grass. James' heart nearly stopped when he saw that Mina had plucked the hare clean off its feet mid-stride. It was a flawless feat, astonishing. For a moment, he was utterly speechless.

"Ha!" Mina cried in triumph. "Did I not say so from the start?"

She pressed her heels to her horse and swept into a gallop towards the spot where the fallen quarry lay. Leaning deftly from the saddle, she lifted the hare from the ground by the arrow still lodged in it. Holding it high for all to see, she displayed her prize. Such skill earned her due admiration as shrill whistles and clapping rose in a wave. Mina grinned proudly from ear to ear as she drew level again with a rather affronted James. She pulled the arrow free from the hare's body, slid it back into her quiver, and offered the kill to the lord.

Shaking his head, he lifted the dead creature by its ears and hooked it onto his saddle. It would make a fine addition to a stew. *That impudent lass handles horse and bow better than near anyone in her clan,* James thought. *Though heaven knows she still needs to learn some manners.*

"Well earned, Mina."

He did not even dare look towards his wife. His reddened ears were sign enough that, by now, she had fully persuaded him of the girl's training. His praise meant far more to the young warrior than she had ever hoped for. She seemed incapable of stopping herself from grinning at him in delight. Now she even held out her flat hand at chest height, palm open and facing him. Had Enja taught her that as well?

James raised a brow. Hesitantly, he struck his palm against the one she offered. It was the way warriors praised one another. Very well, he mused, perhaps she might yet become one of them.

Chapter 6

France, May 1330

Thus far, the journey had passed with surprising ease. The sea crossing between the English isle and the Flemish Low Countries had spared us storms and any notable misfortune. In the city of Sluys, we had spent twelve days, received with warm hospitality by the Flemish royal house. The deep reverence people held for the name Robert de Bruce, and for James' sacred charge, opened many doors to us. We were welcomed into castles and noble estates, with no need to hurry, and we savoured their generosity. More devout knights joined our company, eager to march with us to the Holy Land. From then on, the white and orange of Flanders also adorned our banner, and our number swelled to more than fifty warriors and an entire company who placed themselves under the command of James Douglas.

From Flanders, we travelled on to Paris, where we were received as guests of the French royal house. On a peaceful mission and bearing the heart of a great king, James succeeded in winning yet more men for his holy cause. We were granted warm beds and treated to the splendours of French cuisine, yet King Philip of Valois IV did not invite us into his grand palace. Whether it was due to a lack of regard or England's refusal to pay homage to the French crown, we could not say. Still, King Philip released twenty of his finest knights to ride under James towards Jerusalem. The powerful monarch had no intention of letting the Scots depart without French steel among them. From that moment, the golden lily also graced the banners of our company.

Our road carried us, with an ever-growing retinue, west of Paris through two French provinces until we reached the lands of the Pays-de-la-Loire. There, in the warm valley of the Loire River, we found ourselves amid an early-summer landscape of chirping birds, blossoming trees, and a true sea of flowers. The scent of lilac and the sweeping green of the fields lifted our spirits. No sooner had we left rain-soaked Scotland behind in Sluys than the weeks of April and May revealed themselves as the finest season for travel.

With Fionna and our considerable baggage, we took the long road from Dumfries to Fontevraud at a gentle pace, sparing both people and beasts. Our stops in the towns granted us brief reprieves from the endless days in the saddle or at sea. Whenever I was able, I spent time with my daughter, who would soon leave us for good. Fionna had always been content in her own company, yet even she understood how precious these final moments with her family were. She was not sorrowful about the farewell ahead; rather, she grew ever more spirited and eager the closer we came to Fontevraud Abbey.

"The Abbaye Royale Notre-Dame de Fontevraud," she informed me with a radiant smile in one of her notorious teaching assaults, "is a royal abbey, and now a mixed monastery."

The rising wind blew strands of her pale hair across her face, and her fair cheeks were flushed with excitement. The sun had scattered a host of freckles across her nose, though she always wrapped a red cloth round her head for shelter from the weather. The golden pin fastening the silken folds gleamed in the falling light. It was the final day of our journey, and the gentle hills of Anjou were guiding us towards the famed abbey of the Benedictine sisters.

"Robert of Arbrissel, the founder," she breathed, her eyes turning dreamy every time she spoke his name, "refused the title of abbot and first led the whole community as magister. He forever went barefoot and wore garments of coarse cloth." She turned her head towards me in open admiration. "Only imagine it, Mother!"

I kept my gaze fixed stubbornly ahead, for I had no wish to picture that man. My imagination refused to stretch so far. Most likely the fellow had merely puffed himself up and he would have bolted the moment my eyes met his.

"The community of Fontevraud drew vast numbers from every walk of life," Fionna went on, "but it was, above all, abandoned wives, harlots, and even lepers who sought refuge with the magister."

Armand had surely filled her head with all this. With such tales he had planted the notion of convent life in her mind and all but steered her towards it. So much knowledge always had a source. The trouble was, anything Fionna heard once took root and stayed, and now, she drew another breath, ready to spill yet more of her needless lore.

"Though there are monks as well, it is said that for more than two centuries only abbesses have stood at the head of the order. Perhaps it is for that very reason that the abbey has grown, these past hundred years, into one of the most powerful in the world. It answers directly to the Pope himself."

In a way, I felt overrun by my daughter, yet the thought that she would now share her knowledge with kindred spirits softened the sting of losing her. I hoped that, in this convent, Fionna would be guided by a nun who could open new realms of learning to her. It was what she longed for, after all.

My gaze wandered across the beautiful landscape. A river murmured to our left along the roadside, and here and there, gnarled old trees with heavy branches cast shadows that made us shiver as we passed beneath them. It was not truly cold for mid-May, yet in the shade and towards evening the air grew brisk. I drew my cloak about me for warmth.

Before us, an impressive host of knights from many lands had gathered. Each man had brought squires and servants who had joined our train with even more packhorses. I reckoned we counted easily two hundred men, and far more beasts besides. James' endeavour, and our journey through fair France, had proved a resounding triumph. Like Christ himself, he drew fervent followers who willingly joined his mission.

"… Henry II of England, Eleanor of Aquitaine, Richard the Lionheart, and Isabella of Angoulême all rest here, in the burial vaults of the Plantagenets."

Fionna's voice reached me as though from a great distance.

"Richard the Lionheart?" I asked in surprise.

Fionna smiled with quiet knowing. "Aye, his mortal remains rest here in Fontevraud," she explained patiently. I had likely missed that part only a moment before.

"During an uprising, Richard was struck by a crossbow bolt. He …"

"He died a few days later of wound-rot," I added, and was met with her startled stare.

"I know a tale or two myself," I remarked with thin lips, savouring the rare flicker of admiration from my daughter. It did not last long, for something else abruptly claimed our attention.

Ahead of us, where ancient oaks opened into two parallel ranks, a wide path led straight towards the entrance of a sprawling abbey. Bathed in a glow like beaten gold, the towers of the convent church, the basilica's great dome, and the mighty outlines of the refectory rose before us. The walls were built of the region's familiar sandstone. No doubt the interiors of those sacred halls were as ornate as they were imposing. In its prime, the abbey had sheltered three thousand nuns. Never had I seen such a labyrinth of interlocking buildings, one added upon another, it seemed, with every wave of growth. The magnificent estate of Fontevraud radiated the self-assurance of generations of powerful abbesses. It eased my heart to know my daughter would be in the hands of strong women. Fontevraud Abbey would teach Fionna confidence and self-command, even though life there was ruled by discipline, prayer, and hard labour.

Here, beneath the abbey's ancient stones, lay buried some of the greatest kings of the Western world. The fertile lands yielded rich dues into the coffers of the Benedictine sisters. Daughters of high nobility, even princesses, found refuge here, whether willingly or not. It was no accident that we had been required to petition the Pope for Fionna's admission. It was a place where my daughter's hunger for knowledge could be well tended, and where I might trust her to be safe.

Our company had been spotted long before we arrived. The dust thrown up by the horses and the men's boots must have been visible for miles. It came as no surprise that nuns and servants were already waiting for us in the abbey courtyard. James, Thomas Randolph, and the delegations of the various realms were received with profound respect. The larger part of our host remained outside the cloister to pitch their tents.

To escape the commotion caused by unloading the pack animals and unstrapping our baggage, we were led straight to the abbess. Her quarters lay in a side wing of the refectory, open to the gaze of visitors. The furnishings of her workrooms, studies, and columned halls were simpler than I had expected. In my daughter's face I could see that she, too, marvelled at their austerity. In that moment it struck me that her naïve, stubborn will would soon be swallowed by these walls. Should I ever be granted the chance to visit, I would likely find a woman quite different from the one she was today.

I shook off my darker thoughts and followed my husband into a chamber nearly suffocated by lavish books beneath dust-laden leather bindings. Such precious volumes, crafted by hand and richly illuminated, were a luxury reserved for cloisters. A vaulted cross-ceiling arched overhead, and along the wall hung deeply gilded statues of saints, the kind borne in church processions. They looked as though they had not been used in years. The room felt cold, though outside the sun shone fiercely and cast its light through a barred window. Dust motes shimmered in the air, stirred into motion as we stepped inside.

Behind a large worktable sat an older nun clad in the typical black habit of the Benedictine sisters. A silver rosary adorned with precious mother-of-pearl told of the wealth entrusted to her care. Otherwise, nothing distinguished her from the other nuns we had met along the way. Yet the way she rose and received us, self-assured and utterly composed, made it plain to all that we stood before the abbess who ruled this house. From the taut expression on Fionna's face, I could tell she understood the gravity of the moment. Here in the abbey of Fontevraud, the course of her life would be decided.

"Abbess Eleanor of Brittany," the stocky, pale woman of seasoned years introduced herself.

She even offered James a faint bow, though in this peaceful setting he looked somewhat out of place in his surcoat and the gleaming breastplate etched with iron. My husband sank gallantly to one knee before her, took her hand, and kissed the ring upon her finger, the sole mark of her high rank.

"Sir James Douglas, son of William Douglas, and a great admirer of your abbey," he introduced himself with courtly grace. "It is our great honour that my daughter, Fionna, has received a personal summons from Pope John XXII. Warm greetings to you, Most Reverend Mother Abbess."

As he had done so many times before, he slipped the small silver casket and its chain over his head in one practiced motion and presented it to the abbess.

"I have brought you the heart of Robert de Bruce, that you may consecrate it and keep it safe within your house until we journey on to the Holy Land."

Almost shyly, she urged James back to his feet and thanked him for coming. "This is a great honour for us. May the consecrated ground of this abbey be a home to you, as are the souls of our departed. May God watch over you and all who are yours."

The eminent woman of God extended her greeting to the rest of the men before her, who had likewise sunk respectfully to one knee. Fionna and I stood a little uncertain beside them. At last, the Abbess addressed us with gentle kindness.

"Lady Fionna Douglas, I presume?"

Fionna merely nodded, her eyes shining with a fever-bright gleam.

"From this day forth, you are simply Fionna, for within our walls all sisters lay aside their titles. Before God, all are equal; there is no distinction."

I saw plainly how Fionna swallowed at those words. Welcome to the world of a cloister, I thought, and I was certain she had imagined her arrival to be quite different.

"And you are the mother, Lady Enja Douglas?"

The Abbess fixed her gaze on me, and at once, I felt as though I were being inspected down to the marrow. This woman stripped a person not only of their title, she also claimed liberties for herself few dared to take, more than any pope or bishop I had yet encountered. And I had known more than a few.

Her face looked like a painting. Sharp brows arched over dark, discerning eyes. A slight ridge along her nose lent her profile a striking authority. Thin lips spoke of firmness and resolve. Her hands were folded before her belly, as though she were utterly at peace with herself and the world.

Her presence stole the breath from us, and we nodded in silence. This formidable woman answered directly to the Pope and held, no doubt, more sway in France than the squabbling kings around her. A mere flick of her ringed hand, and men in every noble house would begin to tremble. She lifted the corners of her mouth like a chaste nun, gentle and benevolent, yet the smile never reached her eyes.

"Welcome, noble ladies. It gladdens me to show you, in the coming days, our famed French hospitality. Though we dwell in a cloister, we have prepared a simple yet wholesome meal. The chambers for the distinguished knights lie in the other wing of the publicly accessible quarters. "However," she continued, her smile fading into a more solemn cast, "troubling news has reached me, and it is my sacred duty to share it with you."

She turned back to James, who had straightened at once, her words setting him on alert. He suddenly wiped his calloused hand across his sweat-dampened face. It had to be a matter of true urgency if, after such a long journey, we were not even permitted to seek our chamber first.

Everyone in the room was instantly alert. When papal messengers hurried to monasteries across all of France, the message came from the Holy Father himself, and with such urgency, it could hardly bode well. Least of all since the abbess revealed it at the very moment of our arrival. She cleared her throat.

"King Alfonso XI of Castile and León has called upon the Pope for aid. Christendom is in peril. Pope John XXII's messengers have gone out to every land of the West, summoning honourable and faithful knights to Castile. Our abbey, too, has received this plea, and I have acted upon it without delay. All our priests now send forth cries for help in their Masses to the Christian flock. Even now, a papal envoy rides towards the King of France."

This was, yet again, proof of how important this nun truly was, despite her modest air. The messenger had come to her first before hastening on to the king. I could not help but be impressed.

"I fear," the Abbess paused a moment, "I fear your stay will be brief."

At the very least, her expression beneath the white wimple was sorrowful. It seemed to pain her to pass this news along, and her regret was no performance, as she continued in a low, grave voice.

"The war against Sultan Muhammad IV of Granada has grown beyond all imagining. The Moors have sailed from the Maghreb with an armada of ships and are striking at the mainland. At the same time, mounted Moorish forces ride out from Granada again and again, pushing into Castile to claim new lands. The King of Spain fears the loss of his domains and calls upon the Christians of the West to come to his aid. Pope John XXII has issued a solemn charge to us that all Christian subjects shall have their sins forgiven by God should they stand as true believers and face the Muslims in open battle."

Breathless, the abbess paused. She held her hands clasped before her chest like a supplicant.

"I must ask you, in the name of the Lord and of our Holy Father, to heed the call of our Pope in Avignon, else the Moors may one day stand before these very cloister gates."

Her voice thinned with fear, and she raised her hands to her face. "Merciful God, shield us from such a fate!"

My heart leapt at once. I knew precisely what was stirring within my husband. James was one of the greatest knights and heroes of Scotland, aye, of all the Western world. This was his calling.

In my mind, I sifted through the possibilities. This papal summons, I reckoned, might be the perfect diversion, enough to halt a journey to Jerusalem. I did not, in that first instant, think of the grave threat posed by the Moors in Aquitaine, but I knew James would answer such a call for aid. Aye, he would likely carry his dead king's heart into battle itself.

We looked to James in tense expectation, for the Abbess' words had drawn a tautness over him. His face, strangely still unmarked by scars, barely shifted. Had even a flicker of hesitation stirred within him, I would have sensed it at once, but there was none. I saw only boundless pride in his features, and the quiet courage that had made him a legend. The formidable knight, sent forth by the dying Robert de Bruce with one final command, inclined his head in solemn assent. All in the room already knew the words he would now speak aloud.

"I shall ride to the aid of the Spanish king, Your Grace. Allow me to take my leave of my family here, and to rest a short while. Then, I will depart with my men for Alfonso XI. It will be an honour to serve Christendom. I will bear the heart of Robert de Bruce with pride into battle against our common foes!"

The room was thick with the tension that had settled over us, brought by an irresistible scent of war, honour, and glory. To me, it carried that dangerous tang of the very stuff men were forged from. My old master Isaak had packed enough of it into his pipe to drift into other realms. The undertaking was madness. like so many that clung to James' life like a shadow.

Truth be told, I could not fault one of them. This was what knights trained for all their lives, what the calluses on their hands were forged through endless blows of the blade to achieve.

Even I felt that fierce thrill after James' words, the kind that surges hot through the blood and keeps a warrior sharp in battle. Suddenly, a tide of old emotions seized me, stronger than they had in many years. Cathal had once told me he had never met a woman like me, who could scent blood and war as though it were carried on the wind. Was he right?

Perhaps I would accompany my husband a while longer, after all. Castile was not so far that I could not yet ride into battle once more. Startled by my thoughts, I furrowed my brow. I would be plunging again into the heart of a blazing mêlée among men, and what, truly, was stopping me?

This time, it was for God, not for a king. Perhaps it was time for me, too, to face the enemy of the Western world, the Muslims, the very men among whom I had been raised. The thought of riding into battle for God and His disciples, of coming to the Spanish king's aid, set my fingers itching. Suddenly, I understood James' resolve far better than I had before we set out. And with Jerusalem now slipping far beyond our reach, this new endeavour gleamed all the brighter.

The Moorish onslaught across Gibraltar onto the mainland threatened the entire balance of power in the West. If we failed to drive the enemy back, Christendom itself would fall, of that, every soul here was convinced. Jerusalem was lost, aye ... but perhaps the West might yet be saved?

Fionna looked first to me, then to her father, despair clouding her eyes. She stood close enough to feel what stirred in our minds. As ever, she had a sixth sense for the worries of others. Her slender hand reached uncertainly for mine. I caught her fingers with firm resolve and guided them to my throat. She would feel the fierce racing of my pulse, of that I was certain. With my other hand I cupped her chin and met her gaze with eyes burning in fierce determination. By that simple gesture alone, I told her how vital this undertaking was.

"Your father and I carry a task given by God Himself: to protect you, and all who stand under the Pope's charge. If our Holy Father calls us to Castile, then we shall follow. For once the Moors have taken Castile, they will surely come for France. We must halt them before Christendom is imperilled. It is our duty, as the faithful, to act. For all that is sacred to us."

Fionna lowered her gaze, likely to hide the fear tightening her features. James cast me a look of clear satisfaction. In this, I was his ally. In war and in love. My only hope now was that this honourable charge might make him forget his original intent: cursed Jerusalem.

Chapter 7

Málaga, Castile, June 1330

The horizon burned as the red fireball of the sun sank slowly towards the sea, which at the line of the world seemed smooth as glass, like a perfect mirror. Yet farther ahead, along the coast, the ocean frothed as though stirred by the fury of Málaga's townsfolk. The wildness of the waves mirrored the horrors of the battle that King Alfonso of Spain had won that very day. With the strength of his soldiers, he had held the harbour city against the Muslim armada. Málaga remained in Iberian hands!

The clash had been brutal, leaving many dead and wounded on both sides. The Castilians had lost good men that day, men who had fought with gallant courage. For now, the motley host of Arabs, Berbers, and Muslims had been driven back towards the sea. The unbelievers had sought to seize the harbour city of Málaga from the water, a vital stronghold for shipping soldiers, arms, and provisions.

The young King Alfonso XI of Castile and León wiped the sweat from his brow. Dark curls clung to his furrowed forehead. His ornate armour was smeared with blood, and his arms hung limp at his sides; he could scarcely have lifted a sword again. Yet, despite the long day of battle, he seemed charged with a restless energy. The shadow of a dark beard lent the nineteen-year-old an older air. The weight of command and the deaths of his countrymen had not passed him by. In these last weeks, he had visibly aged.

When his father, Ferdinand IV, had died in 1312, Alfonso had scarcely completed his first year of life. His grandmother, María de Molina, had prevailed as the chief guardian of the crown, outmanoeuvring the rest of the family. His uncles had lost in the ruthless game of power. The intrigues surrounding the throne had left their mark on the young king's life and had placed his realm in peril.

The Moors had breached the Iberian realms, and the nobility had risen in revolt. Even with the aid of his grandmother, Alfonso had long struggled to bring order to the houses of Castile. Only when he came of age in 1325 was he able, with his loyal soldiers, to crush the rebellious lords without mercy. His epithet, el Justiciero, the Avenger, was well earned in those days. From his earliest youth, Alfonso had been forced to make grave decisions and fight with a hard, unyielding hand. Among his formidable army stood faithful counsellors and battle-worn veterans alike.

Alfonso's black eyes gleamed with murderous fire as he stood upon the rise, staring after the ships retreating in defeat across the sea. His armada had not pursued the Emir of Granada into open waters. The precious fleet remained in the safety of the harbour his soldiers had so fiercely defended. The young king's ears still rang from the thunder of the cannons that had hurled hundreds of iron balls high over his fighting men into the sky. The new weapons, cast of solid iron, did not always find their mark, yet they sowed terror among the enemy ranks. He had ordered twenty-five of these heavy guns to be forged by his royal smiths. A dreadful roar they made when the powder spat the iron shot from the maw of the barrel, and when one struck a ship, a brutal death and devastation were assured for those aboard.

The murderous whistling and thunder of battle refused to fade that day and would surely haunt his enemies' memories. Only slowly did the surge of combat ebb within Alfonso. His hands trembled, and his muscles ached no longer from tension but from sheer exhaustion. Hours had passed since dawn, when the enemy had appeared on the horizon with more than eighteen ships. The Moors had charged upon the harbour city to topple the King of Castile, but they stood no chance against an army so well prepared. When Alfonso ordered iron shot to rain upon the first ships to land, the rest of the armada pulled back. The new weaponry had spared them from a far greater calamity.

Alfonso felt relief yet worry gnawed at him for all that still lay ahead. By day's end, he could no longer count the dead who had fallen beneath the enemy's hand, and on the Moorish side, many lives had also been claimed.

Reluctantly, the young man whose horse bore the crest of the Kings of Castile and León upon its saddlecloth spat onto the ground before him. Red and silver gleamed upon his doublet, though those noble colours were now smeared with a foul mix of blood and mud.

"At dawn tomorrow, we will dare a raid with our ships, Capitán Fernández de Castro!"

Alfonso's voice was loud and hoarse, as though he still stood amidst his soldiers barking orders. The king addressed the far older captain by his full name, a sign that boded ill. Don Pedro had been a close friend of his late father and was a soldier held in deep respect.

"I will teach these heathens a lesson they will not forget!"

The king's words softened when he realised that only a small remnant stood before him now; his captain and three other men from the dwindling command of the Castilian forces.

"Your faith and resolve remain unbroken, *vuestra Majestad*," Don Pedro Fernández de Castro replied in a calming tone. "With wisdom and valour, you have won swift victory this day. Let us not act in haste now."

To steady his words, the veteran soldier, his body still smeared with the blood of battle, raised his hands in a calming gesture. Don Pedro was in his forties, a seasoned and loyal commander of both land companies and ships. Alfonso owed him much, and he valued the counsel of this battle-forged companion.

"The Nasrid dynasty will return with even more Moorish warriors. Next time, it may be thousands, with more ships and sharper arms. Let us not delude ourselves."

Don Pedro drew a long, heavy breath. The constant threat weighed on him like a blade at his nape.

"The enemy no longer comes from Granada alone. Their battle-troops now also reach us by land from Gibraltar. The cannons we've mounted here will be of no use against them. In time, we will no longer be able to hold Málaga, but if we can pull our forces together in the country's heartland, we may yet stand a chance."

Alfonso fell into thought at the well-chosen words. How he longed to hold his ground a little longer and defend his position. Yet his captain's counsel rang true, every bit of it.

"Don Pedro," the king addressed him again by his given name, a familiarity the captain acknowledged with a warm nod. "You have always served me well. You have stood at my side through all. Why do you believe we cannot hold Málaga? We have won a victory today, my friend."

"A victory that was gifted to us, mon Rey Alfonso."

The king fixed his subordinate with a sharp stare, for it was a bold claim. True, the Moors had withdrawn swiftly, yet his own men had fought with iron resolve and won the day. Wisely, Alfonso held his tongue and allowed Don Pedro to speak on.

"The Moors are famed for their cunning in war. What does not strike us today may well descend upon us tomorrow. Those heathen hounds do not seek to break us in one blow, they wear us down. They will keep returning until we finally yield and withdraw. We must not let ourselves be drawn into such a game."

The capitán paused as though weighing his thoughts. Then, he gestured again, his hand sweeping towards the harbour city that lay before their grim-faced company. The rooftops, tiled with shimmering ceramic, gleamed gold in the evening light. The bells of a distant church rang without cease, as if they sought to drown out the excited cries of the people. Soldiers and townsfolk alike were celebrating below, revelling in their victory over the heathens.

"Set a handful of men to feign a continued presence in the harbour city," his captain advised. "Then we can withdraw our regiment inland and buy ourselves time."

Another soldier from his retinue urged his horse closer to his commander, having caught the thread of their conversation.

"I can see to that, Majestad. I was raised here; I know Málaga as well as the inside of my own surcoat. My men will hold the city for as long as humanly possible."

Alfonso looked towards the younger officer. After the brutal fight, all the men bore the same appearance, no matter their rank. Even Alfonso's ornate armour was smeared with filth and blood, making him, for once, simply one among many. The young king felt a surge of gratitude for such valiant companions. These were men respected by the common soldiers, and through them, they lent their strength and loyalty to him as monarch. The king nodded in recognition of such courage.

"Then remain until you can do so no longer, but see yourselves safe in time. Better to put the city to the torch than surrender it whole. Leave those vermin nothing but dead rats in your wake. I am impressed by your courage, Rasques."

The named officer's chest swelled with pride. To the young man, it was an honour beyond measure to serve the King of Castile and León with his very life. He bowed deeply before his sovereign in solemn respect.

Alfonso's soldiers had passed through the very hell of war. Their faces were drawn and their souls tormented, yet they stood unshaken in their resolve to follow their king unto death. The commanders understood that Alfonso could not defend the long Castilian coast with his army alone. His numbers were too few, and the land he was sworn to protect too vast.

However, despite his youth, Alfonso possessed true experience of war. His will was law, and his command would be met with respect by all. Every gaze was fixed upon the king, who now had to choose the course ahead, and Alfonso did not disappoint his loyal officers.

"We ride for Seville!" he declared once more, confidence ringing in his voice. "There, the knights shall gather, all those I have summoned with the support of the Pope in Avignon. Well-trained warriors from every realm of the West, who will join us in our crusade against the Nasrid dynasty. The Pope has promised me thousands of valiant knights who will fight for God and our land. Our Holy Father, John XXII, will not disappoint us."

He saw clearly how new-found confidence lit the faces of those closest to him. They believed in him, and he could not afford to let their hopes fall.

"And once we've taught the Moors their lesson, we'll take Málaga back again."

His heart began to pound with rising excitement. The weight of his words seeped slowly into his awareness. Alfonso might yet become ruler once more over long-lost lands such as Granada and Gibraltar. For now, it was only a dream, but already an idea was taking shape in his mind.

"One day, I shall raise a cathedral in God's honour upon the very ruins of a mosque."

That cry roused his weary fighters into cheers. Hatred for the Muslim occupiers ran deep in his people. For far too long, descendants of those against whom the first crusades to Jerusalem had been waged had ruled the southern realm. With the West in decline, the Muslims had swept in from North Africa to Gibraltar, claiming dominion there. Alfonso saw himself as the saviour of Christendom, the king who would drive the despised heathens from its lands. It was a colossal task, given the sheer multitude of pagan warriors.

The message from a distant kinswoman had stirred fresh confidence in him. Eleonore of Brittany, kin to his Castilian wife, Constance, served as abbess of Fontevraud, his living bridge to Pope John XXII in Avignon. It was through her grace that his plea for aid reached the papal court at all.

It was Eleonore, too, who had sent him another message of the utmost secrecy. James Douglas, the infamous Scottish war-hero, had set his course not for Jerusalem but for Seville. A handful of the most seasoned knights of the West would ride at his side to bolster the Spanish crusade. In this, Alfonso felt hope stirring. With their support, he might yet succeed in driving back the advancing Moors.

Alfonso flashed a victor's smile, his teeth gleaming stark against his dark skin. He cast a daring look at his companions. With him as their captain, they would march through any hell the world could conjure.

The ruler was certain that devout crusaders would—just as they had centuries ago in Jerusalem—drive the unbelievers from his lands. For five long years Alfonso had waged this war against the hosts of the grasping Nasrid dynasty. They had swept into his realm like a plague, and like a plague, they had to be eradicated. He loathed the heathen horde and had fought to reclaim Olvera and Pruna. He had even pushed west of Granada to seize Torre Alháquime. Yet while he carved a name for himself through conquest in the western reaches of the Iberian Peninsula, he suffered losses in the east to the advancing forces of Abu Abdullah Muhammad ibn Ismail, known as Muhammad IV.

By now, this emir had become Alfonso's sworn nemesis. Muhammad IV had ruled Granada and the western reaches of the Iberian Peninsula for many years. Certain of Berber and Arab strength at his back, he had waged a relentless war of positions against the Christians. The sixth sultan of the Nasrid line, he had set his life's purpose upon claiming the Occident, advancing from Iberia like a tide. And he was no easy man to reckon with; not only his foes held that view, but also those closest to him.

The emir's uncle, Muhammad ibn Faraj, was known as his fiercest rival in the struggle for dominance within the Nasrid dynasty. Thus, ibn Faraj, alone among the Muslim adversaries, lent his support to the King of Castile. The old creed held true: the enemy of my enemy is my friend. Yet this jealous uncle remained a perilous ally for Alfonso. For all the hatred he nursed towards his nephew, ibn Faraj was still a Muslim.

The young, ambitious king dreamed of reclaiming Granada's fortresses one day. Cañete, Teba, Ardales, and Turón were each among the finest strongholds ever raised in Castilian lands. All lay under the grip of heathen occupiers.

It was a thorn driven deep not only into the flesh of Castile's ruler but also into that of every loyal soul who followed him.

Alfonso ruled his allies with an iron hand. He chastened the nobility and held the royal house in a grip no other could match. His army was among the strongest of its age, and his weaponry was feared far and wide. In Málaga, he had unleashed the first cannon of his time.

Yet Alfonso's mightiest adversary, Muhammad IV, called upon his ties to the Moroccan rulers. The sultans there, like their brethren in Arabia, hungered to seize the Iberian Peninsula once and for all. Power-hungry Berbers sent their warriors across the Maghreb to bolster his ranks, trusting in nothing but the emir's promise of Castilian lands as their reward.

Alfonso's urgent plea for aid to Pope John in Avignon had been granted at the eleventh hour. One of his staunchest allies, the King of Portugal, had dispatched five hundred knights without delay. Portugal lay beside Gibraltar, the harbour through which the Berbers poured, and was counted by the Muslims, alongside Castile, as their next coveted prize. Portugal would be swallowed whole if the emir gained the upper hand. The rulers of the southern West had every reason to fear for their power and their survival.

Pope John XXII had called upon the kings of France, England, Scotland, and the Holy Roman Empire to aid the threatened southern realms. Every knight of the Occident was commanded to gather in the king's capital, Seville. The Holy Father warned of a peril to Christendom akin to that posed centuries earlier, when Muslim forces threatened Jerusalem. Then, too, the pope had sent his knights to a distant city, hoping to claim that corner of the Ottoman world—strategically, politically, and spiritually—for the Cross. It had thoroughly failed.

Now, the heathens stood before the gates of the western mainland. Pope John had called for a phalanx of steel and deadly precision to confront the barbaric foe. The omens shifted like the tides. A wave set loose long ago was rolling back upon them. Time was running thin for the Pope.

The Emir of Granada, as Alfonso had learned from his rival Muhammad ibn Faraj, was readying himself for a final onslaught against the Occident. For years, his name had been a byword for death and the eradication of Christian culture. King Alfonso would stand against this relentless foe, backed by the knights of every western realm beneath the banner of a Christian alliance. God would stand at his side.

With one last glance, the nineteen-year-old beheld the glow of hundreds of torches his men had lit across the city to meet the rising night. The fires sparked by the enemy's flaming arrows had been quenched, the walls were secured, and the people had crept back from their hiding places. For tonight, the foe had been held at bay, but only God knew how long they could keep this place. Málaga, Alfonso sensed with a stab of intuition, could not be held.

Seville, July 1330

The arrival of the foreign knights defied description. A frenzy of cheers broke out the moment the heavily armoured horses of the northern warriors passed beneath their bright banners into the city. It was a sweltering summer's day, yet James Douglas would not forgo presenting himself to the people of Seville in full armour. He had brought several hundred fighters with him from his journey out of Scotland, and despite the heat, thousands had waited in the Castilian capital to welcome the crusaders.

Petals from the city's lush gardens drifted down upon the men, glowing in every colour before being crushed beneath the hooves of the great war-beasts. The blazing sun lit a vibrant throng that usually moved, unnoticed, in sandy hues between the houses. Women danced in flowing veils, singing and clapping in rhythm. Children shrieked with laughter from their fathers' shoulders. All shone as fiercely as the searing sun itself, raising their voices in welcome for the warriors. To the people of Seville, these men in their heavy armour were the last bulwark against the looming Moorish threat.

King Alfonso welcomed the warriors in person. Many more were expected to join them in the coming days. For months, they had been travelling from every corner of Christendom to answer the Pope's call. Now, the first arrivals rejoiced in the generous hospitality of the Castilian king and his subjects. Naturally, Alfonso invited the most distinguished knights into his palace, as was fitting for guests of high rank.

Once built as a Moorish stronghold, the Alcázar, now a royal palace, became home for a few weeks to the bannerets and richly decorated knights of many noble houses. Vast as the palace grounds were, not every knight could be sheltered beneath the king's roofs. Most of the accompanying company had to sleep in tents pitched just beyond the city's edge.

In the meantime, King Alfonso had not been idle. With shrewd foresight, he had sent his soldiers ahead to Écija, a strategic outpost east of Seville on the road to the Granadan front. Now, he ordered heavy war machinery to be taken there, granting the arriving crusaders a moment's respite. The newly recruited army, commanded by his finest officers, would follow on to Écija a few days later. Coordinating forces of such magnitude was an immense logistical challenge. Here, Alfonso and his leadership showed their full measure of experience. Every detail had been prepared with meticulous care. Only the elite knights of the Christian nations were still missing, and each day, they arrived by the hundreds.

James Douglas, who had become the vanguard by bearing the relic of the fallen King of Scots and, therefore, the leader of all crusading knights, was welcomed on his arrival in Seville with his company and lodged in the royal chambers of the Alcázar. There, the commanding elite of each knightly contingent and their envoys met regularly to weigh the shifting political tides. James saw himself as the chief negotiator for all foreign warriors. History, it seemed, was beginning to repeat itself in those days.

Under the banner of the Christian Church, knights of every hue and tongue had long gathered to fight the shared enemies of Christendom. So it had been at the dawn of the crusading age in the early eleventh century, and so it was now. Even the English contingents, usually bitter foes, came to pay their respects to the Scottish commander.

Every knight who hoped to glimpse Douglas, the war hero of Scotland's fight for independence, greeted the others with easy courtesy and light-hearted banter. All wished, at least once in their lives, to stand before Robert de Bruce's famed commander and ride beneath his banner. It was proof enough of how deeply the hero was revered, especially given that many of these knights were legends in their own right.

For James Douglas, the commotion swirling around him soon grew wearisome. What troubled him far more was the question of whether bearing Robert's embalmed heart into battle against the Moors in Castile would truly suffice to secure the king's salvation. James was a man of profound faith and would not be dissuaded from his sovereign's charge. God ever stood with the Christians, of this he was certain. Could the relic in his keeping lead the West to victory over the Moors? Might it be a mighty instrument to show the world who the true God was?

James had slipped away from the attention of his visitors that day. For three days, he had dwelled within the palace walls, and he had grown weary of meeting the admiring stares of knights who had travelled from far-flung realms. The day, as ever, lay hot and close. Only the many fountains offered a touch of coolness, and the open windows drew in threads of fresh air. The chapel bells were just finishing their toll for None, the ninth hour of prayer.

During the long afternoon lull, the people lay idle, and scarcely a soul dared step from their chamber during the siesta. It was the perfect moment for James to wander a while with his personal guards through the garden nestled within the heart of the complex. The modest patch of green was framed by a colonnade and ended near an arched gateway. He clearly recognised Christian symbols carved into the wooden door, set deep into its veneer. He paused mid-stride, a frown gathering on his brow. His guards also halted, equally taken aback by the chapel's placement. As in a monastic cloister, the house of God stood at the very centre of the palace, not as an adjoining structure, in a mark of profound reverence for the Lord.

Curious, Douglas turned towards the small chapel within the Alcázar, its arches still bearing the unmistakable mark of the Muslim builders of the tenth century. After Castile had reclaimed the palace, it had become what it remained to this day, the seat of the crown and civic power. Alfonso's father, so the young king had told him, had expanded the vast palace further, shaping it into his vision of a new cultural centre meant to embrace the entire city. Alfonso had spoken with pride of Ferdinand's resolve to deepen the historic weaving of cultures that lay at the heart of Seville, strengthening it within these mighty walls.

James marvelled at the delicate round arches, artfully inlaid with coloured sandstone—so unlike the heavy pointed arches and plain stone pillars of his homeland. Inwardly he admired the craftsmanship of the heathen builders, whose devotion to detail had raised such a beautiful structure.

The small chapel commissioned by Alfonso's father lay at the very heart of the palace's bustling life, yet its seclusion made it an oasis of quiet. People in this palace came and went, and voices echoed through the stone walls at every hour. There was scarcely a chamber where James could think or draw near to his God. Here, though, he found peace at last, in the modest grace of a sanctuary that seemed almost plain beside the splendour of the Alcázar. It was a true little treasure.

James slipped through the wooden door and motioned for his guards to remain outside. He wanted silence. One glance was enough to soothe him. The small church was dedicated to the Virgin Mary, his mother's cherished saint. Within a few steps, he reached the front pews. With a weary groan he sank onto a velvet-lined seat, no doubt reserved for the king and his wife. He cared little for that now. James could scarcely believe it; here, at last, he was alone. No other soul shared the sacred ground with him. He stood in the presence of his God and no one else.

His bones ached. The long weeks of travel had left their mark. Enja's healing hands had spared him the worst of the pain while they rode, yet the torment in his knees refused to ease. According to his wife, the years in the saddle and the strain upon his joints were finally demanding their due.

With a contented sigh he stretched out his long legs and folded his arms across his chest. At once, the stabbing ache in his knees eased. Only now did James become aware of the scent of incense and damp stone. His gaze roamed curiously over the richly carved altar, where the mother of Christ was rendered in marble. Then, he closed his eyes, letting his body loosen. Without uttering a sound, he sent a prayer heavenward in the quiet of his mind. As though he were slipping into meditation, he felt the powerful bond with his God take hold of him, drawing him into visions of a life of endless lakes and laden tables, a realm without war or death. Paradise.

James was lost in thought, certain he was safe and alone. He never noticed the moment another presence slipped into the room. She had spotted him and moved towards him with quiet resolve. No sound betrayed her steps. Like a wraith, she closed in from behind.

James blinked in startled confusion when he opened his eyes to find her standing right beside him. How could that be? His guards had been given strict orders to let no one through.

Confused, he found himself staring into a pair of blue eyes.

During the three days I spent as a guest in the splendid Alcázar beside my husband, brief shards of memory kept rising to haunt me. I could not hold them back. The images of Fahrudin's palace, my master's domain, pushed their way from my childhood straight into my mind's eye.

I saw it before me as vividly as if I stood once more at its heart. The splendid gardens with their exotic palms, the rounded gilded domes, and intricately adorned columns. Tiny, colourful tiles were set into white walls, painted wood was inlaid with delicate patterns, and ornate vases were trimmed with leaf-gold. Everything in Fahrudin's palace was of Arabic craft, a mirror of the wealth of the Muslim world. Tapestries, not unlike those in my hall at Caerlaverock, told of the Saracens' triumphs. This memory had not returned by chance.

I encountered the opulent artistry of the Moors everywhere in King Alfonso's palace. The heathen people had given Seville its finest craftsmen, men capable of creating exquisite ceilings, mosaics, and colonnades, and yet the faith of Arabs and Berbers was scorned here. Both religions, however, rested upon the same foundation: a claim to power through divine decree.

Whether it was the Pope or the mullah in Mecca, each called his warriors to fight in the name of faith against the other creed. Had I not embraced Christianity only recently, this quarrel might have meant nothing to me. For James, though, it was the fulfilment of a trial set upon him by God. As guardian of the relic, he had been entrusted with a sacred charge.

Puzzled and unsettled, I wandered through the vast grounds in search of my husband, whom I barely saw anymore. It was long past midday, and the Spaniards had retired to their customary rest after the meal, yet a restlessness had taken hold of me, one I could not name. I passed through colonnades and marble-clad reception halls but found no trace of him.

At night James returned to our chamber only very late, sinking down beside me in utter exhaustion after meetings with Alfonso's senior captains, strategic debates, and an endless line of knights eager to clasp his hand. No doubt he had imagined his stay here would be far less taxing. Seville, and the struggle with the Muslim occupiers most of all, stirred unease in me. This land lay in the grip of fierce conflict, and though our host did all he could with courtly grace, he could not fully mask the danger looming over us, nor could I shake the shadows stirring in my mind.

I no longer knew which frightened me more, the vast host of the Emir of Granada, gathering his forces not far from here, or the memories of my perilous childhood. After so many years free of nightmares, this place had suddenly returned unrest to my nights. Yet I could not say with any certainty what truly stirred my mind.

The night before, I woke with my breath failing me. My body was drenched in sweat, and my hand had flown to my throat, as if trying to tear something away that was choking the life out of me. It felt exactly as it had when the Nubian had once pressed the world into darkness around me in Fahrudin's house. That was how my tormentor had tried to break me. Only my stubbornness and my will to live had kept me from yielding to so powerful a master. In the end, it was my courage that carried me into escape.

Something within me was seeking to warn me. Those morbid dreams were no accident. My friend Moira, the dream-seer, would have urged me to leave this place at once, but I could not. I was trapped in my own darkness, as though my soul had returned to a shadowed place it never wished to face again. The clash with a faith I had known in former days split open once more, like an old wound. It was not my destiny to be here, and this was not my war to fight.

Curiosity and drive, perhaps even a touch of recklessness, had brought me to this place at James' side. His reason for heeding the Pope's call, to free the faithful from the scourge of the Moors, was as old as Christendom itself. The Pope in Avignon felt distant to me, yet the Lord in Heaven was an idea that stirred me. There, somewhere above, dwelt a spiritual power I had called God ever since my baptism.

The thought of riding into battle with my katana drawn stirred me far more. Merely imagining the thrill of a coming fight swept my darkness aside. Perhaps it was not so terrible to stand at the heart of a raging holy war. The tremor of foaming horses, the clash of steel, the roar of a wild horde of battle-ready men; perhaps God did have a task for me here after all.

The echo of the afternoon bell still lingered in my ears when I suddenly caught sight of James near the palace gardens. Lost in thought, he walked alone, his guards keeping a respectful distance as he made his way along a colonnaded passage towards the small chapel.

James paused for a moment, as though caught in thought. He had yet to notice that I was quietly trailing him. Then, he moved again, striding with purpose towards the wooden door. No doubt he sought solace in prayer. His boots rang sharply across the marble floor. He had left his guards, Spanish soldiers from Alfonso's retinue, outside the chapel, as he always did when he wished to withdraw to his God.

Before I could follow my husband through the chapel door, the two men stepped in my way. I stared at the elder of them in disbelief. Did they truly not know who I was?

Hesitantly, he glanced towards the younger man.

"Señora Douglas?" he asked, as though I were scarcely there at all.

The younger man, however, examined me and flinched beneath the chill of my gaze.

"Sí … eh … *es la muerte*!" he stammered, his face draining of all colour. I did not grasp the meaning, only that he seemed seized by a mortal fear. A faint thread of Latin shimmered through his words, the old tongue from which their language had sprung.

A slow anger rose in me as the two men tried to bar my way into the house of God, so I behaved as though they did not exist and stepped through the richly carved wooden door. It scarcely creaked and closed softly behind me. The guards had chosen to let me pass.

I paused for a moment, letting the atmosphere settle around me. No matter where I found myself in this world, churches always had the same effect on me. They stirred my senses awake and drew my soul into harmony.

I saw James at the front, his legs stretched out lazily along the bench. Moving slowly and softly so as not to break the peace, I approached and stopped before him. Only then did he open his eyes, looking up at me in surprise. His mouth parted as if to speak, then closed again. He straightened a little, as though suddenly aware of his relaxed posture. Then, he offered me an uncertain smile.

"What are you doing here?"

I sighed. "I travelled to Seville with you, my love. Do you recall that?"

James let out a soft chuckle at the sarcasm in my voice. "A few days ago," he replied. "My memory is faint."

"It was a wise choice to come here, far from the commotion that follows your name."

It would have overwhelmed me long ago, yet there were few here who knew my face or cared to seek my company. Aside from the two guards outside, hardly anyone showed interest in meeting the wife of James Douglas, not when the great hero himself stood so near.

I settled beside him, trying to match his easy posture, which was not terribly devout, but certainly comfortable. The air in here was pleasantly cool, almost like the palace's wine cellars. The chapel's thick walls let little of the outside heat seep through.

James cleared his throat. He glanced at me from the side, as though unsure I was truly there at all.

"How did you get in here past the guards?"

I gave him a cold smile. I owed him no answer for that. James only grunted, as if piecing the truth together.

"I needed quiet to think," he admitted at last.

I had suspected as much. Hard times lay ahead, and a great weight pressed upon him. My husband would have to lead these foreign legions into war.

"Do you have doubts?"

I had never asked him that before. Even I sometimes doubted whether I truly did what was right. Why should it be any different for him?

Silence lingered for a while, broken only by the soft crackle of candles set upon altars and in carved niches, their warm light settling over everything.

James leaned back again, his eyes closed. Only after a while did he open them, and what he said took me by surprise.

"I am three-and-forty now, and I have won near every battle I have ever fought. Why God has been so generous with me, I cannot say, but I have achieved all I ever hoped to achieve. And I have a strong, beautiful wife at my side."

His gaze drifted to me, and his hand reached for mine. He drew my palm to his lips and pressed a kiss into it, a long, warm kiss. His hot breath sent a shiver racing down my spine.

"Perhaps this will be my final battle, Enja. As a God-fearing Christian, I do not fear death. Sooner or later, each of us must walk the path of the righteous."

I let nothing show of how his words struck me. In that moment, he scarcely seemed aware of me. For all the tenderness of his gesture, his thoughts were far, far away.

“I fear I may go before you, *mo ghra* …”

I had to swallow. His love moved me deeply. He worried for me even beyond the reach of his death.

“That is not ours to decide, James,” I replied, withdrawing my hand. Then I kissed him, lightly at first, then deeper, until our tongues met, and he drew back at last, laying his hand against my heated cheek.

“This is a house of God, Enja!”

Was he serious? Did James truly think God might be watching us?

“To hell with your piety,” I snapped, swinging myself onto his lap with the same resolve I used to mount a horse. He stared at me, startled, about to protest, but I covered his mouth and held his gaze, steady and deliberate. My hand pressed to his chest, pinning him back against the bench. He was caught in my snare.

“God’s grace was upon him, and the people took joy in him,” I murmured, leaning towards his left ear. “Luke 2:52.”

I nipped his earlobe, and he bore the torment with a low, gentle groan. His molars ground audibly, and his rough stubble grazed along my cheek. No doubt the God-fearing James was wrestling his strict upbringing into submission. The struggle did not last. His hands closed around my hips, guiding me in a slow, steady rhythm.

“Your testimonies are my everlasting heritage; they are the delight of my heart,” he breathed softly against my ear, and a shiver ran the length of my spine. At the same time a fierce pull stirred between my thighs. "Psalm 119."

Feverishly, I rifled through Scripture in my mind, searching for any verse that might justify what we were doing. Then, in the last coherent corner of my thoughts, something fitting surfaced. "But the fruit of the Spirit is love, joy, peace, patience, kindness, goodness, faithfulness, gentleness, chastity; against such things there is no law."

With every word I pressed a new kiss to his damp neck. Even here inside, James had begun to sweat. He carried the raw scent of a wild-bred man. At last, I returned my lips to his mouth. Our noses brushed, and the heat of our bodies fanned the fire of my desire.

"I do not know that Scripture ..." he whispered, his voice rough. "You made that one up."

"Galatians 5:22," I moaned against his lips.

James closed his eyes, either to think or to escape the hunger in my gaze. Reflecting on the verses in Galatians was clearly no easy task for him. The proof of his desire pressed unmistakably against my belly. It took him a while to muster an answer to my impudent scrap of Scripture.

"The sweetest joy is found where you least expect it." As he spoke, he held my gaze with unwavering depth.

I paused in the slow, sensual motion of my hips. James' hands slipped around my waist, the heat of his fingers blooming through my whole core. I looked into his eyes—questioning—watching the candlelight flicker in them.

"Where is that from?" I whispered, curiosity threading my voice.

"I just created it!" He laughed softly, his breath brushing hot against my face.

"To hell with—" was all I managed before he sealed my mouth with his.

Then he covered me in heated kisses, his mouth tracing me with tender insistence. His lips wandered slowly down my neck, drawing shivers from my skin. I moved closer in a soft, instinctive rhythm, and the closeness between us deepened until our breath caught and a shared tremor ran through us both.

It was a reckless daring, there in that chapel, in a time fraught with peril for all of Christendom. Yet in that moment, God and the world could be damned; we cared for nothing but each other.

We spared no thought for tomorrow. In that moment there was only James and me. How foolish I would have been not to seize it, to claim my longing and the love that bound us together.

I would never forget that moment. The feel of his heated skin against mine, the sensual wander of his hands, and our surrender, far beyond the reach of reason. Desire cared nothing for age. Physical love was born in the mind, and it swept through every one of my senses. In the end came a happiness so fierce, so consuming, that I let it roll over me completely. No one could ever take that from me.

That shared hour in the sacred quiet seared itself into my memory for all eternity. I would never forget how we'd marvelled, laughing at ourselves, over the decorum we had so thoroughly misplaced, how we'd gathered our discarded clothing with helpless giggles and pulled it back on, and how we'd set about making our retreat, still kissing and grinning like mischief itself. I had gone ahead, pushing back the heavy iron bolt of the wooden door and opening it. As I turned to James, his face met mine, his eyes alight with irrepressible mischief.

Suddenly, his gaze fixed on something behind me. Colour rose up his neck, and his mouth fell slightly open.

I held the door open, meaning to let him pass first. The humid, heavy air outside hit us like a wall. The change in his expression sent a jolt of fear through me. Before I even saw what waited beyond the threshold, my body reacted and my hand flew to the dagger at my belt as I stepped out, blade drawn, and saw her.

It was Mina. Horror was etched plain across her face. No word left her lips to explain why she had come. She had understood at once the state we were in. Perhaps she had been standing there for long enough to hear us, for the guards would never have let her in.

My threatening stance seemed to unnerve her completely. I loosened my grip on the dagger. Mina's face was a tumult of astonishment, fright, shame, and fear all at once.

James wasted no more time. Like a startled creature, he darted past me and fled the chapel, not granting either of us so much as a glance. The guards struggled to keep pace with him.

"She's your problem, Enja," he hissed into my ear as he passed. My husband didn't need to say more for me to know he had little patience for the inquisitive girl.

Of course, Mina had realised what James and I had been doing in the chapel. With a firm grip I seized her arm and pulled her briskly along with me. I confronted her in a small alcove, only after ensuring no one could overhear us. I chose my words to be deliberately sharp.

"What are you doing here, Mina? You should be in the stables, seeing to your duties."

Her face was barely visible. She kept her gaze lowered, hiding behind the curls that bounced around her head. I slid my hand beneath her chin and lifted it, impatient and firm. "What in hell …!"

"Your mare, Lady Enja!" she burst out at last.

A hot stab shot through me. "What's happened to Lissy?"

"She has colic. I went to fetch you, but you weren't in your chamber, and then …"

"It's all right," I hissed. That was reason enough for her to seek me out at any time. She needn't die of shame over my blasphemous behaviour.

I fought for my mare Lissy's life as if she were a sick child. Mina and I took turns massaging her swollen belly, turning and steadying the poor creature and cooling her underside with cold water. At last, I lifted her tail and reached deep into her bowel, drawing out the hard pellets one by one. It was slow, gruelling work, but necessary to save her.

I had no clear notion of what had happened. Perhaps the mare had drunk too little or eaten something that did not agree with her; there was no way to know anymore. The stable boys only stared at us in bewilderment as, by candlelight, we struggled to save our horse. It was the poor creature's last chance. My treatment aimed to empty the bowel so that the trapped, deadly gases might finally escape. If we failed, the young mare would die in agony.

Meanwhile, Mina worked the mare's belly with both hands, just as I had shown her. Nothing changed. I let myself sink slowly into the trampled straw. Lissy had lowered her head to the ground as strange, strained sounds escaped her. From the pale of her gums, the swollen belly, and the trembling, sweat-soaked flanks, I could see how deeply she was suffering.

"I'll put an end to her pain," I panted in despair. My breath was still ragged from our shared struggle.

"No," Mina protested stubbornly, dropping to her knees again as she continued to work the mare's belly.

"Leave it be, Mina. Lissy won't survive the night unless the gases break free."

A quiet resignation hung in the air. Often, such suffering meant a twisted gut, and then all effort was in vain. Had it been nothing more than a simple digestive trouble, our remedies should have taken hold long before now.

By now, Mina had broken into desperate sobs. She loved horses, and the possible loss of my mare struck her as deeply as it did me. She kept running her fists over the mare's belly, refusing to stop.

"Lissy will live," she sobbed. "I just know she will."

Gently, I tried to draw the weeping girl away from the stricken horse, but she pushed my hand aside. Trembling, she sank to the ground and pressed herself—breathless and shaking—against the swollen belly of the fallen creature. Tears streamed down her cheeks.

"She deserves a chance. Everyone deserves a chance," she insisted again, defiantly wiping her face with her sleeve. Dirt mixed with her tears, leaving a streak of anger and stubborn resolve across her skin.

"We did all we could."

My voice softened in reconciliation. Mina reminded me of my attempts, years ago in the East, to save one of Hassan I'Shabbah's young stallions. Her heart was in the right place; she simply possessed an uncanny gift for being in the wrong place at the wrong time.

The creature was not to suffer a moment longer than she must. My hand closed around the dagger at my belt. With a sickly flutter in my stomach, I knelt beside the horse and stroked her nostrils, both in farewell and to soothe her fear.

Suddenly, we both froze, listening. The sound was unmistakable; the trapped gas was releasing from Lissy's belly. Mina leapt to her feet and burst into hysterical laughter.

"She's farting!" she cried out, loud and unfiltered, not thinking for a moment about her coarse choice of words.

Now, the laughter burst out of me, too, freeing and relieving after the strain of the long hours behind us. It was already late, and the stable boys had set oil lamps around us. I felt exhausted, yet profoundly grateful. Lissy might be past the worst. In the coming hours, she would regain her strength.

Mina bounced with excitement and relief. In some ways she reminded me of my old companions Kalay and Winnie. Those two would have howled with laughter over such a momentous fart, and made jokes about it for days.

I gave Mina an approving tap on the shoulder. "Well done."

Then I turned to leave. A strange weariness settled over me, and I longed for nothing but my chamber. To wash and sleep, the very thought stirred a sudden, overwhelming need within me. The girl would stay with the mare; I did not even have to ask. Mina was already smoothing the straw where she meant to lie for the night.

At the doorway I turned once more. Mina was watching me, expectant. Perhaps she thought I would give her further instructions, but there was no need; she knew perfectly well what had to be done.

"I simply wished to tell you that I value your stubbornness. It is a skill that proves exceedingly useful in battle."

Mina looked at me in surprise. She knew how sparingly I dealt out praise, and so she dipped her head in grateful acknowledgment.

"Men seldom appreciate that trait," she replied dryly, a grin tugging at her lips. Her words gave me pause. Perhaps she was not nearly as naïve as I had thought. I would keep my eye on that.

"The right man, yes," I replied, then added quickly, "and I value that quality greatly."

And with that, I stepped through the doorway and could at last withdraw to my chamber.

Chapter 8

Teba, Castile, mid-August 1330

King Alfonso set up a makeshift camp with his allies about two miles upriver from the fortress of Teba. The heat bore down mercilessly, not only on our soldiers; even the Portuguese and Castilians, raised in such scorching climes, suffered beneath the unrelenting sun. Sluggish and worn, beasts and men alike fought for the few patches of shade. Countless sails and strips of canvas had been stretched wherever possible, shielding bare flesh from being roasted like meat over a fire, yet many animals perished all the same. Our stable lads ran themselves ragged all day, hauling cool water from the river for the precious horses. In the local tongue, the source of life was called the Guadalteba. The rivers Grande, Turón, and Guadalteba rose from the water-rich Puerto de los Alazores, a sprawling mountain range between Málaga and Granada. At its widest, the river spanned a full stone's throw; at its narrowest, it tore through gorges and chasms in a wild, foaming rush.

Despite the oppressive heat, I found a certain sweetness in Castile. Flowering shrubs gave way to lush pines, and a sea of succulents draped itself over the rocky hills of Málaga's Andalusian province. Crystal-clear lakes and streams wound through the fertile land, which seemed to slip into a deep summer slumber each year. In such heat, every sign of life held its breath, waiting for the mercy of the next rain.

Not far from us lay the forces of Uthman ibn Abi al-Ula. He was a Berber chieftain in the service of the Sultan of Granada and a wily old fox in the art of war. The warriors under this battle-hungry Berber had pitched their camp with strategic finesse two miles downstream on the far bank of the Guadalteba. It rested safely under the protection of the nearby fortresses of Turón and Ardales, some ten miles from Teba. With the strongholds at his back, Uthman had secured his supply lines, and the river provided ample water for him and his men. From where I stood, it was a clever move indeed.

Each day, the Christians had to drive their livestock to the rivers to drink, which was a perfect chance for Uthman to harry the Spanish lines and launch small raids. It led to regular exchanges of blows, often drawing in foreign knights, yet the clashes never grew beyond scattered skirmishes. I welcomed such diversions over the dullness that threatened to settle in.

King Alfonso had led his host through Écija towards Granada. Their target was the fortress of Teba, where the emir's followers had barricaded themselves. The Muslims were prepared to defend the stronghold by any means, but the King of Castile was in no haste. He waited patiently for the siege engines that would be brought against Teba. Even the thickest walls would, in time, yield to such force. Taking Teba was Alfonso's declared aim, and he would surely have succeeded without difficulty, had there not been another problem at hand.

With unhurried composure, the Emir of Granada's general waited with his troops on the far side of the river, watching for the slightest tactical misstep from his opponent. For now, all remained still. Chieftain Uthman ibn Abi al-Ula had gathered around him a force of some six thousand men in the Castilian heat. Unlike Alfonso, Uthman had his men divert a man-made channel from the Guadalteba to supply the vast Muslim encampment; thus, both men and beasts always had fresh water, without risking their lives each day.

Uthman seemed in no hurry; he was intent on studying his enemy's tactics. The seasoned general knew well that heat and time wore down every man. Alfonso's weakness lay in the supply of water. Diverting a channel from the main river was impossible on the Christian side because of the rocky ground, so the livestock had to be driven to the riverbanks to drink. Time and again, Uthman sent small bands of men to steal our herds from their keepers and make the water carriers' work a torment.

Millions of flies swarmed the bloated carcasses of beasts that had already perished from thirst and heat. To escape the stench, the Iberian troops dragged the bodies away from camp with their horses. Uthman, in turn, had the rotting flesh hurled right back before our rows of tents, just close enough to lure the pestering flies. Those wretched insects crawled into our eyes and robbed us of sleep. It was a test of patience, and that scoundrel Uthman knew exactly how to play it.

The heat, the stench, the poor sanitation of the camp, and the men's frayed nerves, often erupting in shouting matches, took their toll. Everyone waited for a decision or for blessed rain to break the heavy air at last, but neither came.

I had wrapped a length of black cloth around my head to fend off the sun, soaking it again and again in the cool water, just as the Berbers did. It spared me from the scorch of heatstroke, drank up my sweat, and kept the flies at bay. Those vile, buzzing creatures plagued me more than anything else; with the rest, I could make my peace.

Mina had followed my example, wrapping a blue linen cloth around her head. She let the fringes fall cleverly over her brows enough to keep every fly from her eyes, yet not enough to hinder her sight. Clever girl.

She was leading our two horses, along with several other squires, to a shallow bend of the Guadalteba. I watched her with a wary eye. It was a fair distance from camp, and anyone who walked that way was always shielded by a solid escort of our knights and bowmen. Not far from where she now let the horses drink, enemy troops, Berber warriors on their small, nimble mounts, loitered on the far bank, as they so often did. The Berbers were devilishly skilled riders, and fighters to match. They lingered, waiting for the perfect moment to strike, but the river was too broad at that stretch for their arrows to find a sure mark. They showed themselves only to provoke us. Mina was in no danger.

I raised a hand to shield my burning eyes from the searing blaze of the setting sun. The harsh light stung, forcing me to close my lids repeatedly throughout the day just to recover.

Even when sinking low above the horizon, this land's fireball still held a force I felt on my skin and, most of all, in my eyes. A few small clouds drifted across the sun, now glowing a deep orange. The air cooled slightly as evening drew in, and a gentle breeze offered a faint relief to our sweat-soaked bodies. Perhaps tonight the long-awaited rain would come. The hopeful spark stirring in me felt almost too good to trust.

My husband's tent stood a little higher up on a rise, and from there I caught sight of a pale cone of light on the horizon. Our scouts told us that, at a safe distance, this glow marked the Moors' encampments. By their accounts, the structures resembled the tents of Eastern caravans. They said that by day, the whole ground was strewn with bright cloths, streamers, and banners with enough colour to cloak a place that sheltered thousands. The makeshift city must have stretched far inland to hold so many souls. I could not see the full breadth of the enemy dwellings from where I stood, yet the scouts spoke of an impressive host of warriors.

Our enemies, too, must have been crowded far too tightly together. I wondered how the Berbers endured it. The stench, heat, and noise—I imagined it was no less fierce than in our camp. My ears drank in the sounds drifting from the rows of tents behind me. A smith hammered with steady rhythm on a horseshoe, one sharp strike, then a softer one echoing after it. There were whistles and shouting, men jeering, the bright laughter of women, the bleating of countless animals, and all tangled into a dense cacophony. Yet when I focused, I could still trace each sound to its source. Had I walked silently through Alfonso's camp, my steps vanishing into the noise, unnoticed by any ear. One could be invisible.

A thought stirred in my mind that carried the scent of my reckless adventures as a young woman. I gave myself a small shake, as if I could flick my imagination away the way I chased off the flies. Yet the notion clung to me with stubborn teeth. What if I slipped across to the enemy camp? It was but nine miles to their lines. If I let the river carry me downstream for a while, I would reach them faster than any horse could. How I might return … well, I would face that question once it came. My curiosity for the other tent-city had been roused. There were people there whose tongue I spoke. Perhaps I could glean something of their plans, mood, intent, and even their numbers and weapons. Would they attempt to strike us before Alfonso stormed the fortress of

Teba, or merely try to hinder us? How cunning it would be to slip in as a spy beneath the cloak of night and emerge with knowledge that could decide a war!

On our side of the river, King Alfonso's strategists met constantly. Each day, they argued themselves hoarse with the royal advisers over the proper course of action. Alfonso would have preferred to seize Teba the moment the siege engines arrived, but James held back, uncertain of the Berbers' intent. The intelligence they had was far too vague for his liking, so each day brought yet another round of strategy, delaying our advance again.

The officers, knights, even the king himself had spent days debating how they might advance on the fortress, including what part of the host should ride where and which troops were to be placed under whose command. Each day, the same quarrel flared anew: which side would strike first. At times the arguments burned hot, at other times, less so, yet the leaders' wavering left its mark, most of all on the common soldiers.

I, too, was weary of it. What little patience I had left was spent. That evening, I resolved to carry out the reckless plan I had been turning over in my mind. I told no one; I needed no help, and the fewer who knew, the better. That night, I would slip away and cross the Guadalteba. The river was shallow and its current mild. My idea was simple: slide into the water below the horses' watering place and let myself drift across the surface towards the Moors' camp. There, or so I intended,

I would climb out at some quiet, hidden bend, safe from curious eyes.

Darkness would be my ally. What favoured my plan was simple: no one would expect a woman from the enemy camp, least of all a warrior bold enough to slip straight into the midst of the Nasrids. They felt safe among their own, certain that none on our side could ken the tongue of the Arabs.

I had learned Arabic in the East, back when I was still a slave. At first, the pirates had sold me into Persia, where Farsi ruled every tongue, but it was the Arabic of merchants and caravan men I'd been forced to master; the cadence of trade and the breath of desert routes. I had not spoken it in many seasons, yet all I needed was to listen. Like a ghost that had lingered in the chambers of my mind, the language rose again and unfurled itself.

I felt a flicker of delight at my sudden idea. As so often, the danger woven into such a venture did little to dissuade me. What if it went awry and I found myself a hostage of the Berbers? They would hold a costly pledge against Alfonso, yet I would not reveal myself. Who there would know the name Enja of Caerlaverock?

I was curious to see James' face, though he was the last man I meant to let in on my plan. He'd have stopped me in an instant, of that I'd nae doubt, yet the mere thought of what I might uncover set my heart to a quicker beat. It had been long since I'd thrown myself into such perilous adventure. The thrill of it made my hands tremble. That, too, was new.

Our tent lay empty. Mina slept outside by the fire, and the squires were off with the horses. James spent every night at Alfonso's side, smoothing the tempers of agitated knights. It was no easy task to rein in such surging male fervour. I did not envy him.

In the empty tent, I slipped into my black linen trousers and the dark shirt I'd borrowed from James. His scent lingered in the weave, warm and unmistakable. With a belt I gathered the loose cloth tight at my waist and slid my dagger into it—the only weapon I meant to carry. Anything more would have shackled my movement.

Renewed with purpose, I slipped down to the river under the cloak of darkness. The water was pleasantly cool and would temper the heat in my limbs. I had always loved the water; even in pitch blackness I found my way where others felt unease. Like a fish, I belonged there.

James Douglas dragged a weary hand across his face. Alfonso's impatience drained him more than the long hours or the heat. Years of battle had taught him how deadly it was to charge on the back of impulse, yet this young man seemed set on laying bare his entire host, eager to be the first to hurl himself into the fray with his sword already bared. Foolish youth, James muttered inwardly, shaking his head as he had done countless times before the lad that day. He had argued fiercely against launching an early assault; the ground was too uncertain, and they knew too little of the enemy's true strength. But the young Alfonso felt bridled by him, stripped of respect and authority. For James, it was a hellfire ride on burning coals.

The many siege engines had reached Écija only a few days earlier and now stood ready for the haul to Teba. The uncertainty of their arrival gnawed at us all, for without those great hurling weapons there could be no assault on the fortress.

It was not only James who wrestled with uncertainty over their next move. Among the Iberian leaders, confusion spread like wildfire. No one seemed sure who truly stood with the Nasrids. Alfonso fumbled strangely when James pressed him for clarity. He could not say with any certainty where Muhammad ibn Faraj stood, the very man who had so eagerly proclaimed himself Alfonso's ally. Red-faced, the young king was forced to endure James' questions. Ibn Faraj had yet to send a single troop in support, and suspicion towards this supposed rival of the Berber prince Uthman was more than justified.

James was already on his way back from the king's tent, pitched at the heart of the vast camp. To reach his shelter, he turned towards a rise from which he could overlook the river. Below the horses' watering place, the water wound westward, sliding on towards the direction where they believed the enemy to be.

The soldiers on duty had just been relieved, and a few more men than usual lingered about at this hour. It was the second change of the watch, so it had to be an hour before midnight.

James' gaze drifted to the fire where the squires and Mina were spending the night. Her wild mop of curls was easy to spot, the red catching the glow of the embers. He paid her no mind and stepped towards his tent, finding it tied shut. He loosened the leather cord, expecting to see his wife inside, but her bed lay empty.

Enja had not been in their bed at all this night. By now, James' suspicion had hardened into certainty. Uneasy, he stepped out of his tent and questioned the guards. They told him his wife had meant to check on the horses and then take a bath. She had not yet returned. Slowly, worry took root in James' chest. An unfamiliar dread drove a cold point deep into his gut. The war-bred Berbers were forever roaming the riverbank with their horses. A woman bathing there …

He refused to let the thought take shape. With firm resolve he strode over to Mina, who was still sunk in deep sleep, and hauled her upright by the shoulder. Her swollen eyes moved him not in the slightest. If Enja was in danger because of her negligence, he would punish her without mercy.

"Where is Lady Enja, lass? Speak quickly, my patience is wearing thin."

Mina was utterly taken aback. Uncertain, she stared into his face, one half cast in shadow, the other lit by the fire where the flames glinted in his eye. His expression boded nothing good, flashed the thought through the bewildered warrior's mind.

"Is she not in the tent with ye?" she croaked, still thick with sleep as she rubbed her eyes. She pushed herself upright, blinking about in helpless confusion. Her gaze darted from side to side, her whole face a single baffled question that only stoked his rising anger.

"Had she been with me, I would not have woken you."

Wide, innocent eyes fixed on James, just as he lost what little composure he had left. He seized her by the upper arm, hauling the helpless girl to her feet and dragging her all the way down towards the horse trough. Her steps faltered, stumbling as she tried to keep pace with him. At last, he stopped and let her go with rough indifference. She nearly fell where she stood.

"Where did she enter the river? Do not lie to me!"

Good Lord, the warrior woman thought, the man is consumed by pure rage.

"Mmmh," she mumbled aimlessly, scratching her head. Slowly, it dawned on her what Enja's husband meant.

"Had she come to the water here, the squires would've seen her, or the horses would've given her away."

James Douglas did not speak. She could hear only his breath, quick and uneven. He was afraid. She felt it as plainly as a hand on her skin. A suffocating fear, for until now she had known the composed warrior as a man of unshakable nerves. The realisation struck Mina sharply in the chest. Enja had slipped away without a word to anyone. Why would she do such a thing?

Slowly, her thoughts fell back into order. She lifted a finger and pointed towards a spot along the river.

"Down there by the bank stands a tree thick with undergrowth. Perhaps she used that spot to slip into the water?"

It was only a guess, yet Douglas strode at once toward the place she'd pointed out—hidden from the camp's line of sight.

When Mina reached him, breathless and flushed, her suspicion proved true. Footprints marked the ground and the riverbank was churned with muddied earth and flattened grass. It might have been maids or soldiers who'd come to cool themselves here, of course. During the day, the horses had drunk at this very spot, stirring the river's edge into chaos.

There was only one sign that Enja had been here as well—she had laid her black cloak neatly upon a nearby rock. Mina found it and held it up in triumph, but the sight of James' icy face soured any flicker of pride. Enja's husband looked as though he had bitten into a lemon.

Enja had likely wrapped herself in it to slip from the camp unseen. It was a soldier's cloak, plain and familiar. But why in God's name would she have stepped into the water here? Mina scanned the riverbank, yet the lights of the tent city failed to reach that far. The black water murmured to itself, offering no answers, guarding its secrets well.

Mina watched as James Douglas took the cloak from her hand and raised it to his nose. He pressed it to his face and drew in a long breath. Then he tipped back his head and let out a sound of pure despair. To Mina's ears, it was close to a sob, and she had no grasp of what was unfolding before her.

"What has happened, sire?" After a desperate pause in which he gave her no reply, the words burst out of her. "Lady Enja would never take her own life ..."

The very thought of such an outrage robbed her of her voice. No Christian would commit something so shameful, and above all, what cause would that woman have, she who feared nothing?

"She did not take her own life, Mina, but perhaps I should have done so long ago ..."

James Douglas' voice sounded strangely brittle. He had stepped closer to the bank, and now, he stood with his back to her, gazing across the river just as Mina had moments before. The hand holding Enja's cloak hung limp and powerless at his side. His shoulders slumped, as though he had just surrendered something of great worth to him.

Somewhere along the far bank lurked the enemy, waiting for a single misstep from his army. Between them, the river ran black and impenetrable, its current fierce beneath the shroud of night. To Mina, it seemed more menacing than the foes beyond it; the girl could not swim.

"Where is she now?" she asked gently, as though afraid to tear him from his dark thoughts.

James drew a long breath before he turned. "She's likely swum to the far bank and gone to gather intelligence in the enemy's camp. She is a trained assassin, you should ken that by now, Mina."

His voice had taken on an edge of aggression. It was as though he meant to unleash his fury over Enja's recklessness upon her instead. Let him, Mina told herself, so long as Enja still lived.

In truth, the young warrior had never known where her mistress came from. Enja had never been one for idle talk. Her words were few, precise, and always struck true. She wasted none. Beyond that, she guarded the secrets of her past like a locked chest. Only her knowledge of weaponry and the arts of combat and healing had she ever shared freely. Mina was grateful to have such a fierce example to follow. Without Enja, the orphan would likely have ended up in the gutter of some Irish port town.

"Is there something I do not know, something you wish to tell me, girl?"

James' voice dropped into a dark, threatening register. He stepped towards her, a towering shadow looming in her path.

His presence alone was enough to set the hairs on her neck standing upright.

"You two were close from the very beginning, though you came to Caerlaverock only a few years ago."

The words of the mighty man, celebrated by his people like a king, had now taken on a wary, distrustful edge.

"That is true," she admitted, drawing a sharp breath; his very aura unsettled her, despite all her self-assurance.

"I chose, at twelve years old, to leave the castle of Enja's friend, King Cathal, and his wife, Lady Moira, and join Enja's fighting guard in Scotland. It was my own free will," she added, as though she needed to banish any thought that Enja had pushed her into it.

What was meant to sound proud came out pitiful instead. Mina stepped back and felt the brush behind her. James moved in so close she could feel the heat of his breath.

"And you weren't even particularly skilled," he murmured now, never taking his eyes off her. The torchlight cast his face in a ghostly glow. A shiver ran over Mina's skin. Something was vexing him terribly, or was it worry?

Was he truly capable of killing her in his rage? The highest-ranked knight of this host had never liked her—that much she knew. James had both the strength and the authority to do it. Her heart quivered in her chest, rising and falling in frantic waves with her breath. Then his hard, warrior's fist shot forward and closed around her throat.

"Tell me, lass, where you come from, and why Enja guards you so fiercely!"

Mina gasped for air. His fist did not tighten around her throat, yet the threat alone robbed her of breath. She shut her eyes. The link between his question and Enja's disappearance gnawed at her. Her thoughts tumbled over one another in a frantic rush. She had never wondered whether it was a privilege to serve in Enja's ranks. She burned for her mistress and would stand by her, always, but what of her loyalty towards the woman's husband? What did he want of her? They shared no secrets!

The hand clamped around her throat shook her hard, and the sharp crack at her neck made her realise just how swiftly her life could be snuffed out.

"What is it you wish to know, Sire?"

"Where do you come from?"

"From Ireland, Sire. Enja took me in after my little sister died."

Mina remembered only faintly the small body she had cradled until the very end. At some point, Enja had gently lifted the baby from her arms and handed it to an old woman. Late, this much she still carried in her mind, she had woken in the saddle, seated before the fair-haired woman. She had felt the warmth of Enja's chest against her back and, at once, a sense of safety in her presence. At six years old, an orphan with no one to claim her, Enja had simply taken her along on her journey. She had brought her to Dunguaire in the province of Connacht, refusing to leave the child to fate. It had been the castle of her friends Cathal and Moira.

The pressure at her throat eased, yet James' mouth drifted closer to her face. He towered over her by a full head. His eyes glinted darkly, whether from anger or the torchlight she could not tell. She felt his breath clearly when he urged her to go on, his tone polite in form yet twisted with fury.

"I do not know who my parents were, sire," she pleaded, fear tightening her voice, "and I never asked why Lady Enja took me with her back then …" a dangerous silence fell between them. "You must believe me—I had nothing to do with Lady Enja's disappearance!"

Mina's voice trembled. Somehow, she could not shake the sense that James had expected more from her, but what was she to tell him? Then, all at once, an idea struck her. Of course, there was one thing she could say, the only thing she still remembered.

"Let me go, sire, and I'll tell ye about the man on the ship, the one she met back then, in the Irish port town."

His grip on her throat loosened so abruptly that she nearly staggered backward. The brush caught her, and she clutched her neck with one hand, feeling the painful throb beneath her fingers.

"What man?" Douglas rasped, swaying ever so slightly, or was that merely Mina's frightened imagination?

"The man who boarded the longship," Mina hurried on, kneading nervously at the spot his hand had gripped before. She had always held a fierce respect for him, but now she felt true fear. So long as she kept talking, he would hopefully leave her be, so she forced herself to speak.

All she heard in reply was a stifled, weighty breath. Somehow, the mention of it had struck him deeply.

"My memories are only faint … I was but six years old, but …" Mina hesitated, unaware of the weight of what she was about to reveal "…I remember the man with the white hair very clearly. His build was as massive as that of a sellsword, and his face was carved with scars. Not like yours, Sire."

Her anxious gaze swept over James' face, unmarked by even the faintest scar. His eyes seemed to darken, though it might have been nothing more than the restless flicker of the torchlight playing across his features. His hands had curled into tight fists. Mina wet her lips nervously before she continued.

"That day on the ship, the sellsword carried a small child in his arms—a boy."

James Douglas sucked in a sharp breath. A low cry tore from him, as though what he'd heard had wounded him to the bone.

"What did he look like? The boy?"

Mina paused to think. The little one had refused to go to his wet nurse back then and had clung, desperate and trembling, to the leg of that unknown man. Only then had the mercenary lifted the child into his arms.

"The boy had white hair and blue eyes, the colour of ice crystals ..."

James' body trembled. Her words seemed to strike him in some hidden, tender place. Mina felt no guilt; she could only recount what her own eyes had witnessed. Enja had never spoken to her about that day, and in her memory, it lived only as blurred fragments from a distant childhood.

James Douglas uttered a sound like that of a wounded beast. A groan tore from him, and he turned away from her. Then something so strange occurred that the young woman was shaken to the core. The mighty man sank to his knees and began to weep. A cold dread gripped Mina. What had happened back then, what horror still had the power to unmake him so completely?

The warrior did not wait for Douglas—whether out of rage, grief, or some darker impulse—to drive his dagger into her chest. She spun on her heel and fled, racing back towards the tents. She stumbled in the dark, fell, scrambled up again, and kept running. She did not dare look back. Her heart thundered up into her throat, and she thanked the fates when she reached the camp alive.

Some people were peculiar, and the dependence on their choleric masters had already cost more than one servant their life. Mina would have to tell Enja about this strange encounter with James Douglas. Perhaps she could cast light into the darkness and explain what her long-buried memory had truly meant. Whatever it was, it had shaken Enja's husband so deeply that he had forgotten his pride.

My passage through the river was brief. I had already left behind the treacherous crossing where the enemy drove their horses, and at times their troops, through the water. It was a natural ford, and here, the Guadalteba widened. The shallows murmured onward in a gentler flow, so I searched for a place where I might reach the bank without being seen. I let the current carry me until I caught sight of a tree jutting out from the enemy's shore. A storm must have torn it down, the bare branches now hovered above the water like skeletal arms. I let the river sweep me towards it and managed to latch onto its rough bark. From there, I hauled myself along, gripping one branch after the next, until at last, I neared the bank. Bushes reached out over the water, and I split my palms open as I dragged myself up through them.

I moved with care, determined not to betray myself with the splash of water, yet my fear proved needless. They did not guard the entire bank of the Guadalteba, and in the moonlight I could follow the pale glow on the horizon where I guessed their camp to be. On foot it was no great distance now; Berbers, too, kept close to the water. I had to walk a little way east along the bank, for I had drifted too far. The sky here was clearer than almost anywhere. The heat granted us a breathtaking view of thousands of stars strewn across the heavens like tiny diamonds. The hope of rain had vanished with the little clouds that had gathered so promisingly at dusk. Tomorrow would be another harsh day, I thought grimly, but perhaps by then, I would know more.

I covered the distance to the Nasrid camp in swift, quiet strides. My clothing moved easily with me, and my footwear swallowed every sound. In my tent, I had traded my sturdy boots for soft leather socks, bound to my feet with cords of goat gut. It felt almost as though I were running barefoot.

Soon, I caught the familiar clamour of warriors rising from the Berber camp. On this side of the enemy lines, it sounded even louder than in ours, something that surprised me, yet favoured my purpose well enough.

I need only ensure the guards did not see me as I slipped into the camp, for they could not hear me. However, my wet, Western garments would betray me at once. I would have to find myself some unobtrusive Berber clothing.

Slowly, I edged towards one of the many entrances. Each was guarded by four warriors—there would be no slipping through there. The tightly clustered trees that offered shade to the camp's dwellers served me far better. The ground was hilly and strewn with massive boulders. I climbed one and from its peak, drew myself into the canopy. Like in the old days, I swung from tree to tree, unseen and unimagined by anyone below. Pride stirred in me at the skill still in my limbs, and the ease with which I slipped into the enemy camp filled me with fierce confidence, even as my muscles burned, and my fingers roughened from the unfamiliar strain.

The noise drifting from the tent-city grew ever clearer as the hum of voices swelled. Slowly, it dawned on me that these were not heated arguments being shouted so loudly. From my perch among the branches, I had a clear view down onto the bustle of the Berbers below.

That, I realised, was the decisive difference between the two camps. Here, the men did not shout in fury or brawl with one another. They were loud, calling across the tents and structures, but the edge of aggression was dulled. On the contrary, they laughed freely and traded stories. Only the music rose above their easy clamour, weaving a soundscape that drifted towards me, strangely and unsettlingly familiar.

They were familiar melodies, yet they stirred an unfamiliar longing within me. They carried me back to the souks, floating markets, and villages of passing caravans. These were sounds found only in the Orient, played, danced to, and sung for thousands of years.

Before me spread a tent city awash with light. Dwellings of colourful linen and canvas stood everywhere throughout the camp. Despite the late hour, people sat together laughing, while children slept beside them. Goats and dogs wandered freely among the tents. The air carried the scent of cardamom and tea, mingled even with the sweet haze of smoked grass. A fleeting memory of my old master Isaak rose within me, and for a moment I paused, strangely moved.

The ease among the people down there surely stemmed from the fact that their families were with them. The shrewd Berbers had prepared themselves for a long siege. The tension, quarrels, and urge to end the conflict as swiftly as possible did not rule here. In that moment, it became clear to me that they could answer our strategy in an entirely different way. They had time.

My fingers itched to slip into that tent city, alive with memories long buried. I told myself I had no business mingling among the people, yet no matter how sharply reason warned me, curiosity and a reckless delight in my own folly swept every caution aside.

I climbed down carefully from the tree, using the side turned away from the light so I remained in the shadows, hidden from view.

From a nearby washing line, I carefully lifted one of the garments left out to dry. It was a fine kaftan, falling all the way to my ankles. Without overthinking it, I slipped it on over my own water-soaked shirt. A woven cloth belt was attached at the waist. I wrapped it twice around myself and tied the knot at my hip, just as Isaak had once taught me.

A cloth hanging nearby to dry served me as a head covering. A devout Muslim expected a married woman to keep her hair veiled, and as such, I would draw even less notice. The fabric carried a strong scent of lava clay, a kind of soap. At once, my senses were intoxicated by that long-familiar smell, and I stored it deep within my mind. It felt as though I were walking through my own past, like a daydreamer with open eyes moving through a place that had suddenly become achingly familiar. Disguised as I was, I now dared to step among the people.

For a time, I wandered between the tents as though in a trance. Memories stirred and came alive again; I could feel the hot sand beneath my bare feet and I heard the beggar children of Baghdad calling out to me.

Indeed, young people passed by me, yet they called out another name. No one took any notice of me. I was merely a Muslim woman strolling through the camp.

Wherever my gaze fell, it plunged straight into memory. I saw veiled women, dark-haired men bearing fearsome daggers, and slaves forced to serve warriors and nobles of higher rank. Only now did the danger of what I was doing fully return to me. As a child, I had been cast into a house of concubines and bound as chattel. How swiftly freedom could be stripped away, or worse, life itself.

Snatches of many tongues reached my ears. It was idle chatter, light and unburdened. A young couple stealing away for a secret kiss and soldiers trading coarse jests. I never lingered long enough to hear any tale to its end. It was a shared social rhythm, much like the one I knew on the far side of the river.

I decided to follow the music, its melodies settling over the camp like a delicate silk shawl. The notes were the work of skilled Oriental instrumentalists. Music had always reached straight into my soul, and it did so again now.

It did not take long before I found the source of the melody. I must have reached the heart of the makeshift city, for the crowd had grown denser here. Unnoticed, I stood in the shadow of a tent of unusual size. In truth, the dwellings grew markedly larger the closer one came to the centre. A group of musicians had assembled on a deliberately laid bed of sand.

Women in flowing skirts and veils danced with practiced grace to the drawn-out melodies. Pearls and gold gleamed on their hands, at their throats, and even upon their faces. A man sang in a plaintive voice, keeping time with the darbuka—a drum stretched tight with hide—while another musician, clad in traditional Berber dress, a long kaftan bound with a brightly woven sash, played the oud with deft fingers. The people here bore very dark skin, their hair curled and deep black and their eyes the same rich hue. They were a proud folk, if one listened to what they had to say.

The men seated opposite the dancers on cushions and carpets spoke Arabic akin to the tongue I knew from the merchants of Baghdad. One tall Berber among them, sitting beside several men dressed in black like himself, carried a different accent altogether. I guessed he hailed from the

Maghreb. Even so, I struggled to grasp more than a word or two.

Though the air had cooled a little that evening, the heat still hung stubbornly between the tents. How fortunate that the damp clothes beneath my kaftan kept my skin pleasantly cool. Not a breath of wind stirred. It was hotter here than by the river, and among the few trees and palms edging the camp, not a single leaf so much as quivered.

Slaves fanned the men at the centre of the square in frantic motions, palm fronds flashing through the air. The men debated animatedly, their words driven home with vigorous gestures. Once the music fell silent, I could understand perfectly well what their voices carried to me.

"... we're waiting for the supply troops from the north. Provisioning Teba is no longer an issue. We found a gap in their siege and managed to smuggle fruit and bread through."

The voice belonged to a younger man with a neatly trimmed full beard. He was highly agitated, speaking insistently to another who received his words in patient silence. That man was older, a pipe resting between his lips. Only once or twice did he lift a hand with a small flick of the wrist summoning more date wine or food. With the same gesture, he let the music fade, or prompted one man or another to speak. All the while, the elder never ceased drawing on his water pipe, releasing small clouds of smoke into the air at steady intervals. Their sweet scent drifted towards me and conjured a smile of memory upon my face.

Once more, a heated debate flared up. This time, different men were involved, those seated to the old man's right. They were loud and unruly, and their words carried clearly through the air.

Was this possible? Startled, I held my breath. They were speaking of the siege as though seated at a banquet, not amid a war with Alfonso. I had expected such matters to be discussed under canvas and guarded by grim Berber warriors. Instead, beside the musicians, I had stumbled straight into a council of the enemy, yet unlike Alfonso's camp, I saw no quarrelling. It seemed to me that each man offered what he knew, and together they weighed how much trust it deserved. According to its importance, there were more—or fewer—gestures and raised voices.

Suddenly, another man joined the one holding the pipe. It was the tall warrior I had first taken for a leader. He produced a piece of leather and showed it to the old man, then leaned in to whisper something in his ear. The elder waved him off with an arrogant flick of the hand, or was he merely beckoning the musicians to continue?

Indeed, the group struck up their music again, and the old man pointed to the ground with his pipe. Thus far he had not spoken a single word. He communicated only through gestures and glances and I took him to be the most important figure in the camp. Perhaps he was mute?

There was something on the ground before him that I could not make out. He shook his head now, and his black turban bobbed ominously.

The melody now drowned out their voices, and I chafed at not being able to see what lay on the ground before the pipe-smoker, yet I could not creep any closer without arousing suspicion and drawing the men's attention to me.

While the sounds of the Oriental instruments lulled me into a dangerous illusion, my mind worked relentlessly. I even toyed with the thought of knifing one of the Berbers at the edge of the gathering and disguising myself as him to perhaps draw me closer to the truth. But it never came to that. Without warning, the music cut off. The old man's hand shot into the air once more. The suddenness of it made my heart stutter; for a breath, I feared I had been discovered.

But there was another reason. Three Berber warriors burst past my right side and flung themselves to the ground before the old man. They had been running and their chests heaved with heavy breath.

"Greetings to you, Your Highness!" By their dress, they were Berbers from the north. Their voices rang with urgency. "The unbelievers intend to attack tomorrow, Emir!"

The man seated there was none other than the tribal chieftain Uthman ibn Abi al-Ula himself. I flinched as the meaning of their words sank in. Had that been Alfonso's decision this very evening? If so, these men knew more than I did. How had they come by such knowledge?

"We questioned one of the squires who serves us as a spy, honoured Emir," one of the Berbers revealed at that moment, as though answering the question forming in my mind. "The unbelievers will ready themselves for battle tomorrow and begin the assault on Teba."

Silence fell over the torchlit clearing. The younger fighters waited with measured patience for the emir's reply as he slowly rocked his head.

Only then—now for the first time—did I hear Uthman speak. His tone was not loud nor shaped by command, as I had expected. His voice was almost gentle, and though the meaning of his words filled me with bitterness, the authority of the man held me utterly captive.

"We will strike tomorrow. After the Fajr prayer, we shall ready ourselves for the holy struggle against the unbelievers. We will attack Alfonso's host as we have agreed, my brother. Allah will stand with us. He will show His warriors the path to victory. Inshallah …"

How long it had been since I last heard that word. Only a few years ago I had still used it myself. It had slipped from my tongue, like so many things I no longer wished to carry as a Christian. Now, I had certainty. Tomorrow, after the first prayer, just before sunrise. There was little time left, but measured against Alfonso's impatience, time was endless.

Once more, the emir gestured with his hand, and the people rose in silence. The musicians swiftly gathered their instruments, while attendants carried cushions, carpets, and the remnants of food back into the tents. I watched the call to rest from a patch of shadow beneath an olive tree, left untouched by the torchlight. Only after all the key leaders had taken their leave did I dare step from my hiding place. By then, only a handful of people still moved about, and one more or less would, I hoped, go unnoticed. It was only now that I realised there were no children or animals here. This, then, was the heart of the Berber camp. With a few cautious steps, I edged towards the spot where the emir had sat only moments before. Small hollows in the sand marked where the cushions had lain.

Once more, I listened intently to the night. I made myself relax, step by deliberate step, and crossed the sand square bathed in the glow of oil lamps. From this moment on, I would need a ready excuse should I be challenged, yet no one stopped me. Within a few strides I stood exactly where the old man had been seated. And then I saw it.

In the sand was a drawing, made with the neck of the pipe. It was unmistakably the castle of Teba and the river. I had seen this map too many times on a parchment in Alfonso's possession. I could also identify the two camps of the correct nation. But the meaning of the lines and dots drawn around it eluded me. I stared at the drawing like a pupil before a great puzzle. It was a war plan, and those lines and dots had to signify something. Even my knowledge of Latin and Arabic letters was of no use.

I had no time to unravel the riddle then and there, yet I fixed the drawing firmly in my mind and knew I could reproduce it in every detail later. For now, that would have to suffice if I were to make it back to my camp in time. That route was far more perilous, for I would have to travel overland. James would surely be worrying if I stayed away from his tent for too long. Perhaps I should have left him a message? But he had no doubt already found my cloak by the riverbank.

Focused on the task at hand, I had failed to notice my surroundings or the danger that loomed. I had only taken a few steps when a warrior blocked my path. What did he intend?

Startled, I tipped my head back. Only now, at such close range, did I realise how tall he truly was. He was the same man who had already caught my attention during the discussion. His eyes gleamed like the onyx at my throat when light struck it. Chains of gold and gemstones adorned his neck, and the black cloth around his head was fastened with a golden brooch set with precious stones. My pulse leapt in an instant. What was I to expect?

It was a strange encounter. He smiled at me with easy warmth, his white teeth standing out sharply against his dark skin. A curled beard adorned his chin, and his proud gaze appraised me openly, from head to toe.

I made a point of not thinking about the dagger strapped at my waist. It lay beneath my outer gown now, hidden from sight. I wore the garb of a simple maid, I reminded myself, so I must behave like one.

At once, I lowered my gaze, as it was the kind of look that would have betrayed a woman too sure of herself. My mind raced through every option. I could stab him in a favourable moment, swift and final, but could it be done without a sound? Or should I simply pretend I belonged there? What role could I play in an Arab tent city?

"Should you not be hurrying back to your tent, woman? Was the Emir's command not clear enough?"

He addressed me without ceremony in clear proof that he took me for lowly service. Perhaps a maid? If so, there had to be figures of rank within this camp, yet I had seen no women of higher standing.

"Forgive me, my lord," I soothed. "I seem to have lost my way."

I spoke in Arabic and prayed with all my heart that he would accept the lie. My thoughts raced, yet outwardly, I remained calm. I begged whatever gods still listened that he suspected nothing of my spying, and I played the part of utter innocence. It was a hard role for me to wear.

"Which tent do you come from?" He cast a wary glance around. "You do not look like a maid."

That may well have been true; my skin was far too pale, almost glowing beneath the lamplight. Had I truly been a maid, my face would have been scorched by the sun.

"I tend the children of the …" I hesitated. Were there women here—noblewomen even—within this camp? In that moment, I knew I might be on the verge of a grave mistake.

"…dancers," I lied, pressing my hands together so he would not see the strain coursing through me. Throughout our exchange I never took my eyes off him, studying him from beneath half-lowered lids. If he became a problem, he would have to die, yet he merely tipped his head back, amused.

"A teacher?"

Relieved, I followed the path of his thought and nodded. "Yes, a teacher."

His gaze fixed on the inverted cross between my eyes, and he frowned.

"In earlier times, slaves were still tattooed …" he remarked, brushing a calloused finger over the skin above the bridge of my nose. Despite his strength, the touch was strangely gentle.

My hand twitched instinctively towards my belt, seeking the hilt of my dagger beneath the linen of my dress. At the same time, my trained eye registered the khanjar—the curved Arab dagger—hanging at the warrior's belt right before me. Calmly satisfied, I adjusted my tactics. My hand would reach his weapon faster than he could react. The man was as good as dead if he dared lay a hand on me again.

"Have you been in the service of the … dancers for long?" With that, he lowered his hand again.

I let out a careful breath, realising I had been holding it without realising. Something about the way he had stressed that word unsettled me. How was I to get out of this situation? I had no wish to kill the man unless there was no other choice. It would surely draw attention and thwart my escape, so I resolved to shake him off with finesse.

"I must go now," I cut our brief conversation short. "I'm sure I'll …"

"The children will surely already be abed," he cut me off, making a gesture that brooked no contradiction. Something stirred within me. Resentment?

"And as a teacher, you're surely not married. Otherwise, at your age, you would no longer be working."

I smiled at him, meaning to push him back with the weapons of a woman. For I was on the verge of using one, and that, at least, was a craft I had mastered.

"I may no longer be a young woman, but I ask your indulgence if I choose not to linger in conversation with a man at such an hour, longer than need be."

As I did so, I stepped slightly aside, signalling my wish to leave. I was drawn taut as a bowstring, ready to draw my dagger at any moment.

Yet, contrary to my expectations, he remained where he was and even stepped aside to let me pass, just as an honourable knight might have done. Had I wronged him in my judgement?

"I would never stop you. I merely had the vague sense that you are more curious than most of the women here …"

He dismissed me without further questions, neither intrusive nor unkind. That should have been my moment to flee. Instead, I stayed where I was and looked at him. He was entirely right. I was the most curious woman in all the Occident, that is what I would have liked to tell him. Yet I merely held his gaze, unblinking.

He studied my eyes with interest; the blue must have been foreign to him. They betrayed my northern blood. Was he smiling again? The thought struck me suddenly—how old might he be? I judged him to be around five-and-twenty. Perhaps a year or two more.

I had taken in his build in the span of a few heartbeats. He was athletic, though not as heavy-set as my husband. He was leaner, more sinewed. Like most men here, he was dressed entirely in black, even the headscarf wrapped about him with casual ease, yet his jewellery and the belt of a noble sat oddly with the otherwise plain Berber garb. Paired with the curved dagger at his side, he gave the unmistakable impression of a man of rank. Perhaps even the emir's son.

"With whom do I have the pleasure?" I asked the young man, quietly confirming his first suspicion. After all, I had come here to gather information. For that, I was quite content to be called curious.

The Berber, his speech marked by a Maghreb accent, bowed with courtly grace and pressed a hand to his chest.

"My name is Rachid. Rachid ibn Faraj, son of the great tribal chieftain Muhammad ibn Faraj. And what is your name?"

Pride resonated in every word he spoke.

A strange tingling spread across my skin. For a moment, I was tempted to show my surprise and delight. Rachid was the son of Alfonso's ally, but then I remembered I was nothing but a simple teacher, with no knowledge of politics. A Berber would not take kindly to a woman speaking of such matters. In that regard, the men of this people were no different than the Scots.

I was taken aback to see the son of one of Uthman's arch-rivals in this camp. Were the Berbers merely posing as enemies, then, to lull Alfonso into a false sense of security? Would his so-called "allies" suddenly switch sides in the heat of battle and strike our men from within? Might this be the very knowledge Alfonso needed to prevail against the Berbers?

What in the world was happening here?

The young man seemed unsuspecting. He was without doubt one of the most important leaders among the Muslim forces. Might I be able to draw information from him? How far should I go? I found him intriguing. He showed no taste for violence, nor did he look upon me as lesser or base. I had to act quickly.

"I am pleased, noble sir, that chance should have led me to cross your path. My name is …"

Could I give him my name? The likelihood of a Berber unmasking me here in the camp by Teba was, after all, very slight.

"My name is Enja."

Either he gave nothing away, or the name stirred no memory. Rachid was courtesy embodied.

"Should I guide you back, so you can find your tent?" he offered. "Or will you grant me the last night before the battle?"

My heart all but stopped. The warrior was unfailingly courteous and had not so much as crossed a line with a gesture. And yet, he had just voiced an outrageous wish. During my years in the Orient, I had heard of the custom that noble warriors were permitted to take a woman of their choosing on the eve of battle, no matter her rank or tribe. If she were married, her husband was expected to let her go. There would be no consequence, and it would even be counted to his honour should the warrior fall in battle the following day. In such a case, the woman retained the right to refuse. It was one of the few privileges Berber women possessed, yet very few declined the offer of an honourable warrior. Had not Isaac once told me of this very thing?

I opened my mouth, then closed it again. For a moment, words had utterly deserted me.

"You could be my son," I managed to choke out. Inwardly, I could not deny a flicker of pride that this man found me desirable enough to wish to spend his last night with me. "Have all the attractive girls deserted you?"

The man flinched slightly, and I realised I had said something no teacher would say to a high-ranking Berber warrior. Not even a dancer.

That was exactly the sort of thing Enja would have said.

My hand went to my mouth as though in shame, and I turned my head away. Between his eyes, I already saw the furrow of anger forming. I would have to be more careful.

"Forgive me," I babbled in my halting Arabic. "I could not quite grasp why you would choose me of all women."

Now I had no choice but to play along. A refusal would not do; I had already wounded his honour.

The man was hard to rattle. If my blunt manner had not driven him off, then he must have been accustomed to worse. He even smiled, disarmingly so. For now, all was not yet lost.

"You are likely unaware of how attractive you are, especially when you try to hide your intelligence from me."

My hand dropped away from my mouth, and I met his gaze directly. The feigned shame had vanished from my face. "Then you are not offended with me?"

He laughed softly now. "That is precisely what I admire. And now I have you exactly where I want you, Enja."

With that, he made a broad, sweeping gesture, clearly meant to spirit me away towards his tent.

“Grant me the honour of this one night, muaelim.”

I had to swallow the bitter taste gathering in my mouth. The way he used the word teacher—almost like a term of endearment—turned my stomach. Instead, I smiled once more and followed him into the darkness. Away from my path of return and deeper into the tent-city.

Chapter 9

Teba, Castile, on the 25 August 1330

The morning might have been like any other. The sun could have risen as it always did and set again in the evening. In between, it would have set the air shimmering and coaxed birds into song and crickets into their ceaseless chorus, just as on any other day. Today, everything was different. Thousands of men had gathered with their weapons at the place where the fate between East and West would be decided. They followed a conflict born of the age-old struggle between Muslims and Christians.

Had these men looked back, they might have seen that in earlier years in Jerusalem, all religions and sects had, at times, been able to exist side by side in peace. Peoples of vastly different ethnic and religious origins were united in this crucible of society, until the hunger for power no longer permitted such coexistence. Disease and catastrophe sowed discord and brought war to that place—a war of faith carried as far as the western lands and relentlessly pursued by religious leaders. The struggle over the one true God had already claimed millions of lives. It was a disgrace that young men were still being sacrificed in senseless battles to secure the power of others.

If Alfonso were to claim victory on this day, would the slaughter truly end, or would the war merely shift to yet another battlefield?

James Douglas moodily crushed the blade of grass he had placed between his teeth and spat out the remnants. He rode at the head of his squadron, leaving the camp by the Guadalteba behind. The first light of dawn had already risen on the horizon, and not a single cloud dared challenge the dominant sun. It would be another of those scorching days that were the order of the day in Castile during summer. The stillness was broken only by the rhythmic pounding of the horses' hooves on the gravel path, the crunch of stone beneath the soldiers' boots, and the groan of iron wheels straining beneath the weight of their load. It was the same soundscape that had accompanied every one of his marches to war. It was music to James' ears.

Not far from the fortress, some two miles before the castle, he ordered the army to halt. This was a strategic position from which he could survey the Emir's advance from afar. Here, they would wait for the first move, which had to come from the enemy.

Only that morning had James once more personally sworn in all his knights. Thomas Randolph, William Sinclair, William Keith of Galston, Robert Menzies, Robert Maxwell and his brother Walter, and Simon Lockhart, had met his gaze with grim resolve. For years, he had fought alongside these men, and they would have given their right hand to serve him. They had followed him freely on his personal crusade and would fight at his side against the Muslims. Today, James would fulfil his vow to carry the heart of his dead king into the crusade. It would be a talisman of fortune for the brave knights who had joined him, and if they were victorious, he would bear the heart to Jerusalem.

With his chest swelled in pride, the Scottish knight sat astride his heavily armoured horse, letting his gaze sweep once more across the host. Alfonso stood not far from him with his commanders. His white horse was adorned with a gilded barding that set him apart from all other fighters. Most rulers would never make themselves so conspicuous a target, yet Alfonso, despite his young years, was a relentless warrior. He did not shrink from fighting at the front line.

This impressed James deeply. His own king had also ridden in the foremost ranks during the Scottish Wars of Independence, for as long as his health had allowed it. Unconsciously, he reached for his neck and felt the small silver vessel that held the embalmed heart of his sovereign. He had carried it upon his body at all times, and it was with him today. His thoughts lingered with his departed king.

Behind him, his men took up their positions in heavy battle gear. The greater part of the army would march some two miles towards Teba, splitting at a favourable point. James, with the foreign knights, would wait for the enemy ranks that followed. Enja had advanced further towards Teba with a smaller unit. The heavy siege engines had finally arrived there, and this was why Alfonso had chosen to launch his attack.

James' wife would accompany Alfonso's soldiers in the assault on Teba. That way, she would be far from the Nasrids' dangerous cavalry, and James believed her to be reasonably safe. Alfonso, James, and the knights under his command would cut off the Berber host and drive it back to where it had come from.

James would never underestimate Uthman's warriors. The elite riders of the Moorish cavalry were famed for their ferocity, and he had studied their methods of war with meticulous care.

Captain Don Pedro Fernández de Castro was a brave man, James thought. He served directly under King Alfonso and was entrusted with planning wars. He now rode at James' side, his face set in resolute determination. De Castro jerked his mount's head back on the reins, making the horse prance in place. The Spaniard smiled at him with a blend of wild pride and fighting spirit. Black curls escaped from beneath his helmet, which he had left unfastened, likely to grant himself air.

"Are you ready, Sir Douglas?" the Spaniard addressed him in a blend of French, Spanish, and Latin, his eyes resting expectantly on James' face.

"Of course, I am ready, Don Pedro. We have waited weeks for this day!"

James allowed an arrogant smile to flicker across his face, knowing full well that this was merely a courteous formality.

The captain hesitated; there was something weighing on his mind. In his forthright manner, he finally voiced what had occupied his thoughts for days. "You have so bravely offered to risk your life for my king Alfonso, and, thus, for Christendom. Why have you never asked for a reward? A victory here on Iberian soil is worth scarcely half the fortune you would undoubtedly have earned in your own land."

James looked into the face of his fellow warrior.

"It is an honour, Don Pedro!"

As though he had nothing more to add, he turned his horse to rejoin his knights, then he paused once more and turned back towards his brother-in-arms.

"Never forget, my brothers and I are engaged in a holy war. We have sworn before God and my departed king to march against the enemies of Christendom, so that our sins may be forgiven. For this, the Pope has granted us full absolution. That matters to me more than horses, finery, or weapons."

He needed say no more to impress Don Pedro. Once a simple man, Pedro had risen to wealth in Alfonso's host, and his renown was well earned. Sustained by his king's generous pay, Don Pedro had marched through every battle and campaign. Fatherland and crown had been his guiding creed, yet James set the final seal upon it. To give one's life for God also lent the Spanish knight fresh courage for the day ahead.

James, who fought at Alfonso's side without any prospect of reward, had earned the respect of every man in the host. And if he were to die this day, Don Pedro's name would be spoken alongside all the heroes of this battle for all time.

That morning, Mina had saddled my horse, braided her mane, bound her tail, wrapped her legs in linen bands, and presented her to me ready for battle. A single glance was enough to see that Lissy was fit and eager for adventure, ready to ride into the fray at my side. The young warrior stood beside her in silence, holding the reins to pass them to me, yet her expression was uneasy, as though there were something she wished to say. I was just about to ask her what lay behind her strange demeanour when the call to depart rang out and everything turned frantic.

For weeks, the troops had stood at the ready. Everything was in place, with the formations prepared to be called into motion at any moment, yet when hundreds of men, livestock, and wagons began to move, the ground itself seemed to tremble. It was thrilling and at the same time, a chilling sensation, rising from my feet and settling deep in my stomach.

I mounted in haste and looked into Mina's eyes once more, but she lowered her gaze, turned towards her horse, and mounted.

I pushed the thought of the girl aside. Other matters were more important now. My focus rested on the war that lay ahead, nor could I see what might be so urgent that it needed to be discussed before the battle.

Alfonso, impatient and hot-blooded, had decided to launch an assault on the occupied fortress of Teba the evening before. As the opening move, companies under the command of Rodrigo Àlvarez de las Asturias would attack the castle that day with heavy siege equipment. At the same time, James, leading Alfonso's army, would hold the Emir's forces at bay as they hastened to relieve the Muslims trapped within Teba. It was a delicate undertaking, for Alfonso's main host would thus advance against the Emir, leaving only a small contingent to face the fortress.

The Nasrids' strategy was to drive off splinter groups and then destroy them with contingents of swift cavalry. The Emir's fighters were specialists in this, and we had witnessed it more than once. Time and again, knights were drawn into small skirmishes. Several of the enemy attackers would press the isolated group farther away, only to fall upon the separated fighters in overwhelming numbers and cut them down. To counter this tactic, the units had to hold together at all costs. This order was imperative should we come under attack.

James had deliberately assigned me to the assault on Teba, sparing me a direct confrontation with the Berber warriors. Thus, I would once again be kept apart from the heart of the fighting, just as so often before.

But I did not object, for in Rodrigo Álvarez de las Asturias, I had gained an experienced captain at my side who knew how to make up for my lack of experience in storming and besieging a fortress. And Rodrigo was proud to ride with Lady Enja. At least so it seemed, for the caballero kept flashing me a roguish grin from the corner of his mouth. He rode to my right, while to my left, Mina pressed her horse close against my mare. The girl still stared stubbornly straight ahead. Before us rode scouts and heavily armoured knights bearing banners and streaming flags that carried the colours of the House of Castile and León towards the occupied fortress of Teba.

Close behind them rode King Alfonso, proud in his striking suit of armour that gleamed in the sun. Even his helmet was adorned with a circlet symbolising the Crown of Castile. To my mind, such ornament was a hindrance in battle, yet the young king basked in the splendour of royal colours that marked him unmistakably as the ruler.

Behind us, the heavy wagons laden with fire pots, tar, and further weapons rumbled along the stony roads, while men-at-arms and foot soldiers followed in a tightly packed mass.

Bringing up the rear once more was the well-armed cavalry. Somewhere among them, I presumed, rode James with his knights.

A vast cloud of dust rose above our heads, forcing us to continually cough and spit. Even in the early morning, the sun beat down relentlessly, draining man and beast alike. I had bound a scarf over my head to shield myself from the dirt and the heat. It was the one I had stolen from the line during my nocturnal escapade. Made of precious silk, it protected me not only from the sun but also from the soldiers' gazes. Many displayed their curiosity as shamelessly as Rodrigo, who at least knew how to behave. I could not tell whether he feared James or me more. Aside from his cheeky grin, he made no attempt to come any closer.

James had remained with the main army, commanding the foreign knights. We had not even seen one another that morning, for the order to march into battle had been delivered to me by another knight. A faint sense of guilt sat heavy in my stomach, knowing that James had been forced to sleep alone in our tent the night before.

It was already dawn when I finally reached our tent, my clothes drenched through, yet James had not been waiting for me there. That was strange, for I had assumed he would want to hear my account. There was, after all, much to tell from that perilous night in the enemy camp.

The unwelcome attention of Rachid ibn Faraj had placed me in a precarious position after my discovery. Rachid proved anything but a source of useful information. He misread my attempts to draw answers from him as erotic interest. I had to slip free of his advances before they turned intrusive. I outwitted him before we ever reached his tent, much as a teacher might have done.

"Give me a little distance, Rachid. I am a teacher, not a harlot. Let me walk behind you, and I will follow. That way, I can preserve my good name."

The Berber warrior had merely looked at me strangely.

"If I should die tomorrow, Allah will receive you into His heavenly realm!"

"It may also be," I retorted sharply, "that you do not die tomorrow. In that case, my honour would be lost."

Somewhat at a loss over my notion of female honour, he did not argue further. Instead, he allowed me to follow him, and then it was, of course, an easy matter to slip away between the tents. From that moment, I was far superior to him as an assassin. Moving unseen through dwellings and merging with the shadows was a craft I had already mastered in childhood. To the Berber warrior, the muaelim vanished that night as though the earth itself had swallowed her whole.

I could not help but smile faintly at the thought of the expression Rachid must have worn, stunned, as he realised that the tryst he had believed assured was lost to him. Perhaps it would have been easier for him had he known whom he had chosen to cross.

I suddenly felt a gaze upon me, and this time it did not come from Captain Rodrigo, who had turned to exchange a few words with the soldiers behind him. Mina was studying me with an expression that boded no good. She had not spoken a single word all this time, and her face was dark with foreboding, which was utterly unlike her nature. Perhaps she harboured doubts about our task today, or were the men around her growing too brazen?

It was her first great battle, and she was, naturally, on edge. Mina was an excellent archer, yet she sadly lacked the ability to hold her ground against attacks from within her own ranks. Spiteful and envious people were everywhere. Perhaps the lack of acceptance from the other warriors was gnawing at her.

This was something she would have to resolve within herself. I had given her the training she needed, but the courage to put it to use she would have to find herself. I turned my gaze forwards again to escape the disquieting weight of her stare.

Alfonso had, indeed, decided to launch the attack that day, just as I had learned in the enemy camp. The spies had done their work well. As befitted God-fearing Christians, the knights and soldiers received the priests' blessing at dawn so they might ride into battle with God's aid. I hurried to the field with the makeshift wooden cross, expecting to find James there that morning, but he had already ridden out.

A small suspicion stirred in me that he was deliberately avoiding me. James must have been among the very first riders to leave the camp that day. Was he displeased with me? I could hardly blame him.

The massive wooden engines with their throwing arms had been erected around the fortress of Teba days earlier, for Alfonso was no longer willing to lose time. Missile screens against arrows, trenches, and gate-breakers had already been transported into position and were guarded by Castilian troops. Now, it was a matter of bringing the knights and foot soldiers safely to Teba. That task fell to Rodrigo and me. I found it curious that the Emir had not yet moved openly against the siege of Teba. Instead, he had waited in his camp by the river until Alfonso made the first move. Why were the Nasrids so hesitant?

I felt uneasy at the thought of how much knowledge the Emir had amassed. Our enemies had devised something, and I would have liked to share my observation with James. As yet, the riddle surrounding the Nasrid leader allowed me no clear conclusions. Perhaps James or Alfonso had gathered more information in the meantime. The king's sudden change of heart in giving the order to attack troubled me.

My thoughts kept circling back to the drawing in the sand, which had clearly revealed the Emir's war strategy, yet the solution to the riddle stubbornly refused to make itself known to me.

Instead, I forced myself to focus on what lay before me. The main body of Alfonso's army, together with the heavy cavalry, had remained behind our detachment. Alfonso expected the Nasrid onslaught as soon as his host drew close to the fortress of Teba. With the greater part of his army and James' knights, he would shield the besiegers who were to storm the stronghold. James had been ordered to ride successive waves of attack with his force, an art in which his knights were superbly trained. In this way, those assaulting Teba would not be crushed between enemy and fortress. This was the Spanish war strategy; under no circumstances were the formations to be split.

My task was to ensure the supply of the troops who were to ceaselessly rain stones, burning hay bales, and arrows down upon the defenders of the fortress. I could carry this out under the protection of the earthworks and wooden palisades that had been raised around the castle. Though I had never stormed a fortress myself, the art of siege warfare was well known to me. I had learned it from the greatest warlord the Scots had ever known.

When the fortress of Teba suddenly emerged before Mina and me out of the shimmering layers of heat, a shiver of unease ran through me. Like a colossal mass of stone, the stronghold loomed high above our heads atop a steeply rising hill. Its inhabitants stood menacingly upon the walls, staring down at us. The Moors would not surrender this strategically vital fortress to the Christians without a fight. I pressed my lips together. The coming days would decide who would claim dominion over Teba. We were well prepared.

"The Emirate of Granada, also known as the Nasrid Kingdom, was an Islamic realm in the south of Iberia for hundreds of years. It was the last independent Muslim state in the Western world."

King Alfonso's words still buzzed loudly in James' ear like a fly that refused to be driven away. Compared to the Scottish Wars of Independence, which had by now been settled, the history of the Iberian Peninsula resembled a spinning top that whirled ever faster around itself. Muslims against the Portuguese, then Iberians against the Muslims, and then the pattern repeated itself in another part of the mainland. The people of Castile had endured a turbulent past and borne much suffering.

On one of the many evenings the knights had been guests at the Alcázar, the young king had taken the time to explain the history of his land to them. All those present were well acquainted with war, yet the ferocity with which the people of the region and its neighbouring realms defended the Iberian Peninsula inspired genuine respect among the guests.

That evening, James and his companions had learned still more about Alfonso's legacy. After supper, the monarch had led his guests into another chamber of the vast palace complex. At the centre of a plain, circular room stood a single table, bathed in warm light cast by wall lamps. This chamber served as the map room for strategic planning. Here, the movements of the Castilian, Portuguese, and Muslim forces, and more recently those of the many foreign knights, were recorded. Each unit of a hundred men or more was represented by cubes of marble. Within this room, visitors could bear witness to the eventful history of the Iberian Peninsula. There were no chairs or benches, so all gathered around the unusual table.

Upon a parchment of finely scraped goatskin, Alfonso's father had commissioned a map of Iberia and its neighbouring lands. Curious, the Scottish knights leaned in over the table, their heads close together. The depiction of the mainland and its surrounding islands was at least two feet wide and tall enough for all the men to gather around it with ease.

"Around the year 1230, the Almohad Caliphate in the Maghreb ruled over the remaining Muslim territories in the south of Iberia," Alfonso explained, indicating the individual provinces with a golden staff crafted expressly for this purpose. "They roughly corresponded to the Castilian provinces of Granada, Almería, and Málaga."

A murmur of appreciation spread among those present, bringing home just how vast the influence of the Muslims in the Western world already was.

"The ambitious Muhammad ibn al-Ahmar exploited the dynastic strife among the Almohads, rose to power, and established the Nasrid dynasty in these lands. By around

1250, the Emirate of Granada had become the last Muslim polity on the peninsula. Although the sultanate was, in effect, a vassal of the rising Crown of Castile, it nevertheless enjoyed considerable cultural and economic prosperity for more than two centuries."

After a brief pause, Alfonso continued, "During this time, much of the famed Alhambra palace complex was built, upon which my father later had the Alcázar Palace erected. The Nasrids," the young king explained, casting a stern gaze around the room, "were the longest-lasting Muslim dynasty on the Iberian Peninsula."

James recalled that the King of Castile and León accorded a great deal of respect and recognition to those he was, in truth, preparing to fight. They were dangerous adversaries who had already dealt his dynasty painful defeats. James also held Alfonso in high regard for openly acknowledging this.

While Alfonso XI was yet a child, he lived as a ward under the joint regency of his grandmother María de Molina, his great-uncle Infante Juan, and his uncle Infante Pedro. At that time, the three regents agreed to launch a new expedition in the late spring of 1319. This act of war was blessed by Pope John XXII as a crusade, meant to finally drive the infidels from the western lands of Christendom. It had been a dreadful mistake.

"The forces of the Castilian rulers assembled in Córdoba in June 1319 and crossed the border under the command of Infante Pedro. With him came the Grand Masters of the Orders of Santiago, Calatrava, and Alcántara, and the Archbishops of Toledo and Seville. The siege of the city of Granada proved unsuccessful, and our troops were forced to begin their retreat. On the June 25, 1319, in the heat of summer, Pedro led the vanguard, while Juan commanded the rearguard."

At this point, Alfonso hesitated and ran his fingers through the long black curls that fell to his shoulders. He was a handsome man, yet the harsh trials of war had already left unmistakable marks upon his youthful face. His lips were set in a severe line, and his eyes lay deep in their sockets, as though he had not slept properly in a long while. The weight of responsibility and the gravity of the decisions he bore were a heavy burden for one so young.

The king took a few steps across the room before coming to a halt once more in front of his guests.

"At that point, Sultan Ismail chose to strike." His voice had hardened under the weight of the events. "A large force of Moorish elite cavalry, followers of the Volunteers of the Faith, was led by Uthman ibn Abi al-Ula. The Emir left Granada and began to draw the retreating Castilian forces of Infante Juan into skirmishes. Those smaller attacks soon turned into a full-scale assault when the Granadans realised that, in their retreat, the Castilians had lost cohesion and coordination and were no longer able to strike back effectively."

Alfonso had lowered his gaze, as though he still felt shame over what had transpired back then, despite not having been present himself. His voice grew quieter, yet everyone in the map room sensed what had occurred in those days.

"By then, the vanguard was thinking of nothing but flight and reaching the Castilian border. In their panic, many men drowned while attempting to cross the Genil in full armour. This river separates Granada from the province of Seville. The rearguard collapsed for lack of support, and Juan likely fell victim to a stroke or heat exhaustion, bringing about a spectacular Moorish victory. I will spare you the further details, worthy knights."

A deathly silence had fallen among the visitors.

Alfonso's haunting words echoed in James' mind on the morning of the battle. The brave young king had lost almost his entire family to the infidels, much as Robert de Bruce had lost his to the English, yet Robert had never once considered surrender. Alfonso carried something of that same recklessness, and despite his youth, he possessed the rare gift of inspiring those who followed him. The prospect of riding into a holy war for such a charismatic king filled James with fervour.

James and his armoured cavalry had broken camp early that morning. The elite force of some eight hundred men under his command held position roughly two miles before the fortress of Teba. Detached from the main army as a protective screen, they were prepared to suppress any skirmishes with all their strength. Thus, they formed an impenetrable bulwark, shielding the main host from being fractured by smaller attacks. Meanwhile, Alfonso mustered his army behind them before the fortress of Teba.

His knights had formed up in several ranks. The heavily armoured riders bore a multitude of colours upon their shields in a testament to the allied strength of all those who fought together for the Christian God. To left and right, a steep rise and a narrow tributary of the Guadalteba hemmed in any flanking attack. The terrain was ideal, capable of holding even a vast host at bay. Here, the front stretched to roughly half a mile, clear and manageable for the assembled glorious knights and warriors.

From afar, through the shimmering heat, James could make out the towering spires of the fortress that had been held by the Nasrids for centuries. It was the greatest of the ring of strongholds surrounding Granada. Alfonso had reclaimed them all, one by one.

Today, Teba was to fall. By the will of the Pope, Muslim rule was to come to an end.

James would receive the first wave of attack with his well-trained knights. Behind him stood the Spanish king's army, three thousand strong, composed of cavalry and, above all, infantry. Should the knights at the front begin to lose their strength, the main host would advance.

James was sweating beneath his helmet and briefly lifted it from his head to wipe the sweat away with a cloth. His gaze swept across the rolling hills of the parched land. Any enemy would be heralded from afar by clouds of dust. The

Berbers would have to descend the slope before him to strike his front. Against his armoured knights, the warlike Moors would stand no chance.

The anticipation of the coming battle had carried him all the way to Castile. His purpose was clear and the circumstances for fulfilling his vow ideal. The heathens waited within close reach.

All would have been well if only a bitter realisation had not seeped into his mind, something he had never anticipated and that nearly robbed him of his reason. Mina, innocent as she was, had let slip nothing more than a tiny detail that night. She had revealed it without grasping its true significance, but in that instant, James understood with dreadful clarity what had happened to his wife in Ireland twelve years before.

Enja had a child with Ragnar.

That wretched mercenary who she had taken as a lover years ago while spying in Ireland must have been the one who got her with child. Supposedly, she had killed him back then at Dunguaire. James had been standing right beside her when Enja had plunged the knife into the rival's belly. But it must all have been staged. Enja must have healed the bastard afterwards, and all those years, she had let James believe she had been a faithful, loving wife. The Devil take it!

Enja had intended the staged knife wound only to protect her lover from her husband's vengeance. And James had believed her! Out of love, he had forgiven her generously.

James ground his teeth and hurled his helmet into the dirt in a surge of rage. With a clatter, the silver headpiece with its blue plume struck the sandy ground and spun several times upon itself. James glared at it sullenly, as though it were to blame for everything.

Enja must have given birth to the child at the castle of her friend Cathal in Dunguaire. Everyone had known, and not a single word had ever been spoken of it.

She must have handed the child over to Ragnar on his journey back to Iceland. Mina had witnessed that moment as a child. Everything fell into place, forming a coherent picture that suddenly made sense to James. Enja's strange behaviour at Caerlaverock, her many journeys to Ireland, and finally, her constant garb of mourning, as though she were deeply unhappy with something in her life. The foul moods, the bouts of despondency, and the endless apologies. All at once, James had an explanation for so many things.

His world had collapsed. Not a single second had passed since that night without the urge rising in him to strangle his wife, just as he had almost done to Mina, that inglorious would-be warrior. Fire raged within him and hot lava poured in torrents from his heart, mercilessly laying waste to everything he had ever felt for his wife. She had lied to him once again. Betrayed him. Made a fool of him.

"All eight hundred knights, Christian warriors of God, and all sinners before the Lord, await your command, Sire!"

The steady voice of his long-time companion, Sir Thomas Randolph, reached his ear from the right. James started as if roused from a momentary slumber and looked about him. Hundreds of valiant warriors had gathered around him. Their sweat-streaked faces stared at him in expectation. They were waiting for a sign, for his command.

Guilt-ridden, his gaze fixed on the helmet that still lay before him in the sand. With a sharp movement, James turned to Randolph, struggling not to think of Enja. It was a task that cost him dearly. His great day had come, and yet his thoughts were consumed by his marriage. With iron resolve, he clenched his jaw until the muscles stood out beneath his skin. James was a leading figure in this momentous crusade. The men believed in his strength. He had to show it now, even if he felt utterly unready. How fortunate that he had kept out of Enja's way that morning. He would not have been able to restrain himself and would have hurled his suspicions at her. Now was not the time for that.

In a steady voice, he made himself heard by Sir Randolph and his knights. "The messengers have reported troop movements to the west. The Emir's army should appear before long."

His orders were to respond only to forces that attempted to split the ranks of the main army. As a martial phalanx on horseback, his elite warriors were the finest weapon against such tactics. They were all euphoric, aching to draw their swords. It had been a long time since they had been allowed to prove themselves in battle. The scent of war held them all in its thrall. It was intoxicating, far too intoxicating for any knight.

Suddenly, the first plumes of dust rose into the air. A thunderous rumble rolled across the land beneath a flawless sun, yet it was not the sound of an approaching storm. It was the unmistakable sign of an army on the move. On the horizon, James saw what seemed like an entire stretch of land in motion, but it was no land at all, it was the bodies of thousands of horses and warriors. The ground trembled, and the blood in his veins vibrated with it. A jolt ran through the knight. The Nasrids were coming!

Something was wrong.

I had just asked Mina to stay close to me so she would not be needlessly endangered by flying shards and splinters. I scolded myself for my concern; after all, I had trained her in combat and the arts of war just as I had everyone else. Perhaps I had grown softer with age, yet in many ways, Mina was still not ready for a blood-soaked confrontation, and if I could avoid an unnecessary danger, I would do so. The sounds of war made us shudder.

Mina and I arrived before the fortress of Teba at sunrise, together with the Spanish captain. The Castillo de la Estrella, as Rodrigo called it, rose to a height of six hundred yards above sea level with its main keep at sixty-five feet. The massive stronghold sprawled across more than ten acres, making it one of the largest castles in the province of Málaga. Despite the slow-moving infantry and the heavy equipment, the march from the base camp had taken roughly two hours. Now, we stood in the shadow of the protective earthwork that shielded us from attacks launched from the castle.

Numerous arrows were embedded in the wooden palisades that had been erected only days before. The siege engines sheltered behind them were already hurling heavy iron balls at the castle walls without pause. The massive wooden frames creaked and groaned horribly under the strain, and then I heard the whistling of the solid iron projectiles as they cut through the air. A thunderous rumble and crash followed as the walls shuddered beneath the impacts. The entire fortress of Teba seemed to groan under the brutal blows, but this was only the beginning.

Thousands of flaming arrows rained down upon the inhabitants of the fortress. Between assaults, the defenders above had scarcely any time to extinguish the blazing roofs and buildings. Either the missiles or the arrows would finish them. I had no desire to trade places with those up there.

Soon, I would give the signal to the captain of the siege force, Rodrigo Álvarez de las Asturias, to take the fortress with his foot soldiers by way of ladders. First, however, we would grant the siege engines a little more time to complete their destructive work. The battered defenders of the castle would surely surrender before long in the face of such overwhelming force and relentless bombardment. It must have been hell up there.

Despite the deafening din, my thoughts drifted to other realms. The events of that night would not release their hold on me. With a sidelong glance at Mina, I made sure the girl was not watching me. She was staring wide-eyed at the massive wooden frames which, by the leverage of their throwing arms, generated such force as to hurl heavy stones through the air high up towards the fortress. Her face was etched with awe at the calculated destruction wrought by such immense machines.

What truly fascinated me was something else entirely. I had passed the warning on to the king that Muhammad ibn Faraj—uncle to the Emir of Granada—was clearly no ally of Alfonso's, yet the map the Emir had drawn in the sand would not leave my mind. Why could I not discern what the symbols beside it had meant? Two strokes here, six circles higher up. They were not numbers, and yet they carried meaning. The men in the Nasrid camp had debated them at length, crossing things out and scratching them anew.

Only the Arabic letters for north, west, east, and south had been clearly visible on each side of the fortress. The image stood sharply before my mind's eye. What was the solution to the riddle?

"Lady Enja!" Mina called, pulling me back into the present.

At once, I heard the missiles whistle again and men roar in bloodlust. The ground shuddered beneath the impacts.

Buildings were ablaze, as tongues of fierce fire licked out from the walls. Clouds of smoke rose high above the fortress. A murderous screaming carried across the contested ramparts to reach us. Water was a precious commodity in a siege and not to be squandered on extinguishing flames. If they were wise, they would simply let the roofs burn. The stone beneath would endure.

Mina strained her gaze upward towards the wavering walls of the embattled fortress. At that very moment, a hail of arrows came hurtling down upon us, slamming into the wood before us with a loud crack. Startled, she turned to me at once to make sure I had not been hit. The heathens up there were tenacious fighters, I had to admit. They were still capable of striking back with their deadly missiles. As Mina looked at me then, her sense of guilt showed itself once more.

"What is so important, Mina?" I asked absently, my gaze drifting back up towards the fortress. In truth, what was happening up there left me cold. I would much rather have known what those cursed markings in the sand truly meant.

Mina had been circling some matter since morning, burdened by it without speaking. The devil alone knew what was weighing on her simple mind this time. My gaze brushed her face and lingered there. Now I saw it clearly in her eyes. She was afraid. Afraid of me?

"I must confess something to you, my lady," she warned me. Either she had not prepared enough arrows, or she had forgotten my waterskin. A sudden surge of irritation flared within me. Now, please, anything but trivialities.

She raised her voice, for the whistling of the projectiles was swelling once more.

"I had to tell your husband something last night. Something I had not considered important until now."

Now, she had my attention. What could she have told him, and above all, why?

She rolled a stone in her hand, clearly embarrassed. "My lord was most displeased about your nocturnal excursion. He questioned me relentlessly and squeezed me like a lemon."

"What in the devil's name did you tell him?" I snapped at her more sharply than I had intended.

Mina flinched and bit her lip. "About your farewell back then in Ireland, at the harbour of Galway. You know the one."

She hesitated again, fumbling for words, but I said nothing. It was utterly unclear to me what she was driving at. Because of the noise, her face was very close to mine. She had flushed. I had been quite certain that back then she had known nothing of the tragedy surrounding my son Conor. What had transpired between Ragnar and me had never reached anyone's ears. Mina had been so very young.

"When you meant to kill the man with the child … and then you did not. You let him go with the boy."

I stared at Mina, speechless. Things had suddenly taken an ill turn. Something churned deep in my belly.

"You noticed that? You were only six …"

The memory of that poignant moment of farewell still sent a sharp pang through my heart even today. She had watched back then as my son sailed away to Iceland with Ragnar. She could not have known what that had meant to me at the time, nor the pain I still carried.

"I didn't know what any of it meant," Mina reminded me. "I didn't understand it until yesterday. But your husband wanted to know more."

Now my stomach tightened into a knot. Had she given James decisive clues?

"Why did you speak to my husband at all?"

Reason prevailed. Mina did not even know Ragnar's name, let alone the story behind it. Surely James could not have made any sense of her fragmented thoughts.

"He was looking for you and questioned me. He frightened me and threatened me to force secrets from me. I had no idea what he truly wanted from me. Then I told him about Galway. I remember very little of that day. I hope it was nothing terrible!"

My gaze was so piercing that Mina immediately lowered her eyes. The din of the siege raging around us was murderous, yet now only Mina's words echoed in my mind. Why had James put the young woman under such pressure? He could know nothing of Conor. And Mina possessed no more than a handful of childhood memories. I strove to remain composed, but my thoughts were racing. James had never seen Ragnar again, nor did he know of my child's existence.

Only a very few trusted souls knew my secret, and with them it was safely kept. Inwardly, I drew a deep breath.

"Do not worry, Mina. If that is all that troubles your conscience, then I can put your mind at ease. You have said nothing that could bring me into danger."

I smiled at her as I did so. So that was what had been troubling her all along.

"Let us focus on our task today instead. That is what matters now."

Abruptly, I turned and gave Captain Álvarez the long-awaited signal to attack the walls. In the very next moment, some eight hundred brave men surged forward, climbing ladders with wild cries and weapons raised to seize Teba. Many had endured days of impatient waiting and were glad that, at last, the moment had come.

Packed tightly together, hundreds of brave men surged up the steep slope. Roaring and protected only by their shields, they hurled themselves against the walls. The first among them raised ladders, striving to seize the crumbling fortress. The trembling and splintering of wood sent a shiver through me. At the same time, Castilian soldiers battered at the main gate with a ram. High atop the battlements, defenders now appeared, attempting to repel the assault. Fire seemed to rain down from the walls. Burning men ran about like living torches, their screams swallowed by the general roar. Some tried desperately to extinguish their comrades, and without pause, the catapults hurled heavy projectiles into the fortress. The piercing song of those stones set every nerve on edge.

The din had swiftly swelled into a continuous roar, and no one could tell where exactly the sounds of war were coming from. The dreadful melody of death blended with filth, lifeless bodies, and blood into a cacophony of a human abyss. They fought bravely, these Christian soldiers, for their land and their faith.

Suddenly, I could no longer hear any of those sounds. My gaze had fixed itself upon the fortress as it burned and groaned, rearing up into the sky. In my mind, that image overlapped with the outline in the sand of the Berber camp. I was standing almost exactly where the cardinal markings aligned with the perspective, and then, my questions returned.

But this time, I had the answers. Suddenly, everything fell into place. The circles and symbols were nothing more than placeholders. They stood for troops, weapons, and positions. Each mark was assigned a direction of movement and a measure of force, just like in the map room of the Alcázar in Seville, only far simpler and more rudimentary. Even if the Emir did not know the precise numbers, it was clear to me that Alfonso's battle plan had been drawn before my eyes in the sand. Spies had reported the enemy's movements to the Emir in meticulous detail. The devastating extent of the betrayal was now coming sharply into view.

The Emir knew exactly how many men Alfonso had brought with him, and how many foreign knights

James commanded under his banner. And in that instant, something else became clear to me: the Nasrid did not care in the slightest about the Castillo de la Estrella. Alfonso, on the other hand, had sent his troops here to draw Uthman out of reserve. For the sake of a handful of besiegers, he had weakened his army.

What was the Emir's grand design? I recalled that symbols had been placed in the sand to the north, behind the fortress. Again and again, the Emir had pointed to several circles beyond the walls. Perhaps the traitor Muhammad ibn Faraj—the Emir's uncle—was waiting there? It could be the troops of his son, Rachid ibn Faraj, my would-be suitor from the Berber camp. Ibn Faraj would have had to take a wide detour, but such a manoeuvre could be accomplished within a day.

Alfonso would never have expected an attack from the north, with the sheer bulk of Teba Castle rising between them, but that was precisely his mistake. To the south of Teba, Uthman ibn Abi al-Ula could drive a wedge between the knights and Alfonso's main host, or create a diversion just long enough to strike.

Uthman would make certain that Alfonso swallowed the bait, buying ibn Faraj enough time for his wide flanking manoeuvre. So that was the strategy. The Emir had never intended to attack us from the south, where Alfonso had positioned his forces in such numbers. The heathens would come from the other side of Teba, the side turned away from us, perhaps even with two forces, closing in around the massif on which the fortress stood and trapping us there. That was where we were vulnerable.

I had to act. I informed the officer charged with my safety that I was withdrawing. Confusion crossed his face as I moved away from the siege. My firm order to inform Álvarez of my intentions ran counter to his orders to keep watch over me.

My mare was not far away. With a brief gesture, I signalled to Mina that I would break from cover and run for the horses. They had been kept at a safe distance, far enough to avoid the flying debris. Despite the din, the young warrior understood at once and followed me like a shadow, crouched low as we moved through the chaos of the fighting. It did not take long before we reached the animals, already saddled, bridled, and prepared for a possible escape. That saved us a great deal of precious time.

At breakneck speed, we galloped along the rocky path, tearing our way out of the chaos by the same route we had taken that morning towards where I believed Alfonso's army to be. From horseback, I tersely explained to Mina what I had observed in the Berber camp. We hoped we were not already too late to turn the tide of fate.

A surge of fierce excitement swept through the knights under Sir James Douglas. The enemies of the Vatican—aye, of all Christendom—stood arrayed before them in a vast host.

They were the forces of the Emir of Granada, Muhammad XI.

Determination was etched upon James' face. Like his fellow warriors, he was keenly aware of his duty and the sacred nature of his mission. Today, he would fulfil his vow. He took the silver vessel containing the embalmed heart of Robert the Bruce from around his neck and held the chain out before him at arm's length.

"Men!" he shouted hoarsely, and in the heat his voice carried far across to the enemies gathering along the ridge of the hill.

"Knights of the Western world!" he called out once more to the assembled host.

At once, a taut silence fell over the agitated men. Now only the enemy host could be heard, grinding closer step by step. Every man heard James' words, loud and clear. Even the buzzing of bees and the chirring of crickets seemed to cease for a single heartbeat.

"Today is the day on which I will fulfil the vow I made to our dying king."

A roar of jubilation surged through the ranks. Every man present knew the vow that had brought James and his warriors here. Each of his knights would stand with him in battle against the enemies of the Christians.

"Follow me against the warriors of darkness. Slay the occupiers and free the Christians of this land!"

Already the first knights began to chant his name. "Douglas!" James heard, and "Robert de Bruce!"

The horses whinnied nervously, sensing their riders' tension. The smell of blood and death wrapped around them once more. Warrior pride smouldered within their armoured bodies. James Douglas and the knights under his command drew their swords and thrust the blades high into the air. Had the atmosphere not already been so charged, it would have ignited from the heat alone. Shouts from rough male throats spurred one another on.

On the opposing side, several detachments of riders now broke away, clearly intent on hurling themselves straight at the knights under Alfonso. There must have been several hundred of them racing down the slope on their swift horses. James watched closely which path they took. Not one of his knights even considered breaking from their closed formation.

They were dressed like the Berbers depicted on Enja's tapestries along the walls of Caerlaverock, James thought, as he caught sight of the warriors astride their horses. Black cloths were wrapped around head and nose, at their hips gleamed golden curved daggers, and in their hands they carried fearsome half-swords, slightly bent, their blades thickening towards the tip. With seemingly effortless ease, they guided their mounts deftly through the treacherous terrain. Behind them, the riders drew a fine cloud of dust as they thundered towards the waiting fighters.

James raised his hand, and brought it crashing down.

In a tight mass, his knights surged forward. Piercing battle cries tore through the shimmering air. The enemy's answer came in a roaring chorus of "Allahu akbar"—God is great—bellowed from countless throats. At last, the moment had come. With grim satisfaction, James hurled himself into the fray. Thoughts of Enja and her breach of trust were forgotten. Whatever might come to pass, Robert's soul would find its peace.

The terrain was far from ideal for an open battle. Perhaps that was why the Berbers had sent only a smaller detachment. The knights around James repelled the agile attackers with ease. Time and again, the enemy attempted to peel men away from the formation, and James had to exert all his authority to draw his warriors back out of the fierce skirmishes.

Their opponents were seasoned, deadly fighters. Their blows were merciless, and they were very fast, yet the moment James' troops re-formed their ranks, the Berbers withdrew. Strange, he thought. From the corner of his eye, he had been watching the Emir's army. The greater part of it seemed to be holding back. The Emir always sent out only small detachments meant to harry the foreign knights. Why did he not come himself with his full force? What was he waiting for?

Alfonso's army, holding position behind the knights, began to show signs of nervousness. A larger formation bearing the colours of the King of Castile suddenly surged forwards from the rear, riding impetuously past James' left flank. He recognised one of Alfonso's officers on the lead horse, followed by several of his brave companions. At once, several knights moved in to close the gaps.

That was what the enemy warriors had been waiting for. A reckless horde plunged like a wedge from the opposite side into the line of knights, tearing several Castilian fighters away. Immediately, a second group overran the stunned knights and smashed a breach into the Christian shield wall. Smaller combat clusters formed, drifting away from the main body or being lured aside, James could not say for certain. He found himself locked in brutal close combat alongside Thomas Randolph, William Sinclair, Robert Maxwell, and his brother Walter. The advance of the Iberian riders ended in a blood-soaked slaughter.

Sinclair went down, drenched in blood. With a blow that gave full voice to his fury, James smashed the skull of Sinclair's killer with his morning star. He let another feel the edge of his sword. Thomas Randolph covered his back, which James sensed more than saw. Again and again, enemy warriors pressed forward. They possessed a startling ferocity and stamina, James had to concede that without envy. They sensed their moment, driving into the scattered, heavily armoured knights and wearing them down. But the Scottish fighters resisted with grim resolve. No enemy warrior was to break through the living shield of knights. Best of all, Alfonso was not to be drawn into the first clash of swords at all.

Suddenly, James saw something that made the blood freeze in his veins. Amid the knights fighting like berserkers against the swift Berber warriors, a figure appeared. It was someone he did not want to see here. Someone he had not wanted to see all morning, for fear that he might kill her on the spot.

Enja!

His wife stood unbidden amid the ranks of knights who were hurling themselves against the Berbers. She was meant to be accompanying the assault on Teba; that had been agreed with Alfonso. James had believed her far away and safe. What was she doing here now, in the very heart of the fiercest melee?

That woman was his fate and his ruin. She had appeared without warning among his knights, and from a distance he saw how William Keith of Galston managed to stop her at the very last moment. Beside James, Simon Lockhart was thrown from his horse. He fought on stubbornly from the ground, but stood no chance against mounted foes. They drove him down with their swords until he collapsed. James rushed to his aid, but it was already too late. Powerful hands clawed at his feet in the stirrups. He kicked them away in fury.

Enja shouted something he could not make out. Sweat ran into his eyes. James' entire body groaned beneath the weight of his armour. The Berbers were swift and unarmoured, and thus carried greater momentum. By contrast, James' blows were precise, each one claiming lives, yet the skilled riders pressed him hard. No sooner had he dragged one from his horse than another appeared. Again, his gaze swept over his remaining men and then to the woman beside his friend, William. James stared at her, and Enja held his gaze.

Why had she lied to him all these years? How could she have kept the child from him? Bitter bile rose within him, and his fury cost two enemies their lives. He had always loved Enja, and she had repaid him with lies and betrayal. He loved her still, and the pain lodged so deep in his chest drove him to madness.

James did not hear Thomas Randolph's call to fall back to the main body, nor did he see the survivors break free from the mass of enemies. His instincts—his sense for the right moment—had dissolved like mist.

James still felt the blade drive into his unprotected neck into the very place where a helmet would normally have shielded the most vulnerable part of his body. That helmet, he recalled, still lay in the scorching sand, right where he had flung it in his rage.

Hot and searing, the curved dagger sank into his flesh. Warm blood ran down his neck, soaking into his tunic. James' vision blurred. Images from happier days flooded his mind—moments of peace. The face of his daughter, Fionna. A strange calm settled where his heart would normally beat.

The woman among his ranks was gone. She now stood directly before him. Like a spirit, she hovered there, smiling.

Her outline dissolved into a shimmering sea of light. Gratitude closed around his heart, for his wife was with him in the moment of his death.

James felt no more pain when he recognised her face. Gentle voices echoed within his mind. Enja became one of those heavenly beings, seeming as though woven of silk. He knew her by the light in her eyes and that rare smile. She reached out her delicate hand to James and drew him away with her.

Chapter 10

Teba, Castile, 25 August 1330

Mina's and my horses were lathered with sweat when we reached the Castilian troops. The two miles from the besieged fortress of Teba to the front line had felt endless. I had my doubts whether the soldiers would let me pass straight through to the Castilian king, yet it seemed my reputation among the fighters served me well. King Alfonso allowed me through. The urgency of my mission must have been plain to see.

Thus, I told him of my suspicion that the Emir had never intended to attack his army from the south. The Emir's ruse—to draw the Castilian king and James' knights into a feigned engagement in the south while sending the greater force from the north—made sense to him. Still, he would first dispatch scouts to test my theory before finally turning his forces towards Teba.

I had to concede that King Alfonso had mastered the art of commanding respect from his subordinates. I was the wife of one of the most renowned knights in the Western world, yet he treated me as though I were merely one envoy among a hundred. And all the while, I carried news of the utmost importance and had nearly ridden my horse to death to warn him. I could not help but feel a measure of disappointment at such ignorance and vanity, or did the king expect me to have spoken to my husband first? But there was no time left for such a detour, which was why I had turned directly to the king.

For this momentous day, Alfonso had donned his finest armour. He was every inch a ruler, and did not forgo the opportunity to inspire awe in his enemies. Alongside his personal guard, several of his mercenaries had likewise taken it upon themselves to protect the king. It was a striking blend of formidable warriors, grim soldiers, and ruthless protectors. Alfonso could rely on them without hesitation.

Standing beside him, I felt like one of his many soldiers, all of them admiring him as a living legend, yet something about this young king, so successful in his war against the Moors, unsettled me profoundly that day. I could not say what. Perhaps it was simply the weight of too much responsibility pressing down upon his neck.

Beside his white horse stood the magnificent black stallion of his general, Don Pedro. The face of the old warhorse was marked by many scars, and the fingers of his left hand were gone. For that reason, he had wound the reins around his fist, holding his snorting mount firmly in check. Even so, his vigilant gaze swept over me as the senior commanders listened to my account, which I now repeated before the king's soldiers.

"Tell us, Lady Douglas," the king's general interjected suspiciously. "From where does your information come?"

The young king nodded in assent as he leaned upon the pommel of his finely wrought saddle. The gold of the horse's harness gleamed in the sunlight.

In my haste, I had failed to consider that. Now, I was forced to explain myself and reveal a fragment of my story; something I had never intended to tell.

The pause that followed weighed heavily upon me. From far off, muffled by distance, I caught the sounds of battle; proof that the Emir's troops had already begun to draw the king's forces away.

My thoughts raced, fevered and sharp. Mina stiffened at my side; the closeness of the men in command was plainly unsettling to her, yet I had no task to send her away on now. The knights around us regarded us with disdain, their stares grating in every possible way. Even Don Pedro seemed unwilling to credit my words, though he knew the Berbers' manner of war.

"Well then, Your Majesty," I began hesitantly, meeting Alfonso's dark eyes, "as you know, I spent several years in the Orient..."

Alfonso nodded, grave and deliberate. Don Pedro spat into the sand.

"I speak and understand Arabic with ease."

Silence fell again, yet this time I sensed tension coiling through the men's bodies.

"Speak."

King Alfonso demanded that I reveal the source of my information. At last, he stood with me, so I told him and his men that I had slipped into the Berbers' camp the night before, about what I had learned there, and about the image drawn into the sand. At Don Pedro's prompting, I also described the old emir, the pipe held in his hand as he listened to the reports of his scouts.

In time, recognition surfaced in the king's expression, and with it, assent. My account clearly aligned with the intelligence he already possessed, for not only Don Pedro cast Alfonso a knowing glance. One of the royal guards, a cross hanging at his throat, gave a low grunt of approval—much like Cathal would—and nodded. I had seen him before, standing beside James during the troop councils in the king's tent. His name, however, had not stayed with me.

"Your Majesty," I heard him say in a voice used to command. "If what Lady Douglas has observed is true, then her husband and his knights are fighting a lost cause. We should call Sir Douglas back to the main host before he suffers too many losses. We need our best fighters here to secure the assault on the castle."

James. Alfonso had sent him with his eight hundred knights against the Emir's main host, yet it was mounted warriors alone who harried them, making their advance brutal. There could be no talk of gaining ground.

A low unease churned in my belly. Perhaps the heat was partly to blame. It was nearing midday now. At this hour, the Andalusians withdrew into the shade, allowing man and beast alike to rest. It was a sound choice, whenever circumstances allowed. James' men were not fighting the heat alone, they were facing seasoned warriors, forged in the harsh school of Berber warfare. It was wasted effort, for the enemy sought only to draw the army away from the true theatre of battle.

Alfonso wiped the sweat from his brow. Beneath his armour, the moisture must have been streaming in rivulets. At that moment, the monarch of Castile leaned towards Don Pedro and they conferred in low tones about their next move. Urgency hung thick in the air, tugging at my nerves. The Iberians' arrogance was a constant assault on my patience.

At last, Alfonso nodded, casting me a strange look as though I had wounded him. In the end, he sent me off with Don Pedro and the giant to retrieve James' company of knights. I had no intention of tending to the king's casual pride. Far too much time had already been lost. God grant it was not too late.

When I reached the first knights with Mina and the two commanders, I was taken aback. At the very position meant to become the battlefield, most of the fighters had withdrawn into a nearby grove that spared the knights from being encircled. Farther south, scattered skirmishes had flared to life. I could make out the tunics of French and Flemish fighters, and among them, the Berbers' black tunics.

Bodies armoured and unarmoured lay scattered among the carcasses of fallen horses. James must have chosen that moment to order a retreat, for many were riding back on panicked, sweat-lathered mounts. There was no sense in charging at isolated foes; beyond the enemy lines they would achieve nothing. By now, it must have become clear to them that this had been nothing more than a diversion.

Upon our arrival, the Scottish knights closed in around us at once. Some bore minor wounds, yet they held steady in their saddles. None smiled, but they greeted me with courtesy. Heat and hardship had left their mark on them all. Walter Maxwell was among the men I knew personally. He had removed his helm and was wiping blood from his brow. I did not dare ask whether it was his own. The Scottish knight gave me a nod. From his sparse beard, water tinged red dripped steadily.

"Where is James?" I asked without preamble. In this moment, there was no place for titles or formalities. He studied me with grave eyes before turning his head towards the direction where he believed my husband to be.

"Over there, in a skirmish," the young fighter replied, "but it does not look good."

"Take me to him," I demanded, urging my horse past him. "We must end this now and withdraw. It was a trap."

Without looking at him, I drove my spurs into my horse and galloped towards the place Walter Maxwell had indicated. Sand glittered in the air around me. Hooves and struggling bodies had churned up the parched earth and the dust burned my eyes.

A sense of foreboding stayed with me. James had been so careful to ensure that no one strayed from the main field, and now he was caught in a skirmish that had drawn him beyond the army's protection. How reckless, or was it simply the enemy's skill—their ability to pry individual knights loose from the formation, time and again?

Walter shouted something unintelligible after me and followed with his remaining men in my slipstream. He drew up alongside my horse and pointed the way with his outstretched hand. He had likely been startled by my action.

"We have suffered some losses, my lady," he reported, pulling his helmet down with one hand even as we rode at the gallop. His voice rang hollow beneath the metal, and his eyes flashed with battle-hunger through the narrow slits.

"Sir Douglas and some of his men walked into an ambush. Most of them made it out unscathed, except William Sinclair. He is dead."

Knights rode towards us, gesturing frantically to the fighting behind them, their words tumbling over one another in agitation. Among them was Sir William Keith of Galston, a highly decorated leader of the Scottish nobility and son of the Marischal of Scotland. He must have broken his arm because blood flowed freely, and he leaned forward in the saddle, bent by pain.

"William!" I shouted at my husband's trusted companion. "Where is James?"

I hauled my mare to a halt from a full gallop, and she slid back on her hind legs. My whole body snapped taut, and my stomach clenched into a single, hard knot. Damn this heat. I was truly afraid now.

William looked at me in surprise but reacted at once and pointed towards a cloud of dust in the distance. A skirmish was raging there in full force. Four or five horses were involved. One rider, then a second, broke away from the knot and thundered back towards us at a full gallop, but one man fought on relentlessly. He was a seasoned warrior. I stared, transfixed. It was one against two. The lone rider wore the colours of the Douglas clan. It would have been a joy to watch this warrior wield his sword with such daring, how precisely he struck blow after blow, were it not my husband who stood there, without support, holding his enemies at bay. With one hand he guided his sword, with the other he made his horse dance.

My God, it struck me like a blow when I saw his unprotected head. He must have lost his helmet, or someone had knocked it from him …

Suddenly, his gaze met mine. A stab of pain tore through my heart. James was fighting for his life, as he always did, with passion, but something now seemed to unsettle him. The hand that had moments before swung the sword ceased to defend. The horse abruptly halted its movement. As if in single, frozen images, I saw ruin approaching. James suddenly paused in his fight, as though it were already over, but his opponent was still there. He raised his hand, a curved dagger clenched within it, and urged his horse sideways alongside James. James was still looking at me.

I glanced at Galston in confusion, but he too could only stare across, as though equally stunned by what was unfolding.

"Watch out!" I screamed across to my husband, even though I might only have distracted him further. Could he hear me?

"Fall back, James!" Galston shouted. I was on the verge of spurring my horse forward, but in a reaction that was terrifyingly right, Galston seized my mare's reins with his uninjured arm and held her fast. My own arm shot out on instinct, closing around his wrist. With all my strength, I wrenched at it, trying to free my horse. Galston's face was now only inches from mine. He hissed, "Have done with this madness, Lady Enja. James knows what he is about. He will come back."

Overwhelmed by his harsh words, I let go of his arm. I straightened in the saddle once more and looked towards the fateful fight. My blood threatened to freeze in my veins. My voice failed me. It was too late.

I saw it with terrible clarity. The Berber behind James had drawn his dagger from his belt and now, drove the blade into his neck. It was a grave blow, a mortal strike. I knew at once what such a wound would mean.

James sat utterly motionless on his horse, staring at me. My stomach lurched. Blood sprayed and ran down the side of his body. My husband slowly slumped, then fell from his horse. Cheers erupted among the Nasrid fighters, who, like us, had been watching the fight from the other side.

That joy danced upon their souls like the devil in purgatory. The enemy knew that in this moment they had struck down one of the most dangerous knights of Christendom. James Douglas had fallen to the blade of an unbeliever because he had worn no helmet.

My eyes shut in horror, my hand flew to my mouth, and for a moment my thoughts went completely blank. William Keith let out a horrified gurgle, like that of a wounded animal. A sense of helplessness swept through all the knights. James Douglas, long believed to be invincible, had fallen in battle.

Worst was that we could not come to his aid. Several Berbers had already fought their way to the pine grove and, thus, to James' body, and had begun gathering the dead, the living horses, and the weapons. They would claim ransom for the plundered corpses, and as it had always been, wounded knights would be killed on the spot.

William held my hand tightly. He likely feared I would try to ride to James. In my pain, I did not feel his grip. I kept my eyes closed. The agony raging inside me was beyond words. Misery and despair burned a fiery trail deep into my gut. This must be what it felt like when someone tore your heart from your body while you were still alive. I could no longer breathe. The air gathered like a painful blister beneath my breastbone, threatening to steal my consciousness. Heat wavered around me. I was unaware of the turmoil among the knights surrounding us. I swayed, and William supported me as best he could. James' closest friend also had to wrestle with this loss. I heard him groan heavily.

Breathe in. Breathe out. Mina tugged at me as well, trying to pull me into her arms. The young fighter sobbed openly. Hot tears ran down over my hand. Were they mine?

How long I remained there on my horse, I could not later say. My ability to think deserted me for some time. I was alone with my pain. Mina clung to me in desperation. In that moment, she seemed to need comfort even more than I did. At some point, I gently freed myself from her grasp. My mind returned in small fragments. We were both still mounted, and we had to leave this place urgently. Galston was the first to regain his senses. He seized my horse and dragged us along with him.

"Make haste!" he called back to us over his shoulder, his voice trembling. "I will get you to safety. We are withdrawing to the main host."

As if in a trance, I pushed the wailing bundle that was Mina away from me and drove my spurs into my horse. Together with the remaining knights, we withdrew. Galston had been right. On that day, the enemy had held the upper hand. We had uncovered the ruse, but not in time for my husband. His body now lay with those of his comrades in the sands of Andalusia. So, this was the place where James was meant to meet his death. He had fought bravely, and it seemed this death had been his wish.

His final look would haunt me for years, the way he had looked at me in that strange instant of death. I had seen the turmoil and the pain in his eyes. He could have deflected the Berber's strike with ease, had his gaze been fixed on his enemy rather than on me. It seemed to me that he had been ready to die.

Teba Castle had not withstood Alfonso's siege for long. That very day, one of the towers collapsed under a hail of projectiles, tearing open the castle wall. The siege engines had shaken the masonry to its very foundations. Thus, Alfonso's soldiers had little difficulty in retaking the fortress.

Strategically, Teba was a vital stronghold that secured the Andalusian realm. Three days later, the battle ended with the Berbers' withdrawal. Thanks to the secret information I had provided, their stratagem failed. Alfonso sent his entire army north with the knights, thus shielding the attackers who had held their ground before the castle. With his furious host of riders, he slaughtered the Berbers caught off guard behind the massif of Teba. Their deception had been laid bare.

Thereafter, the Nasrid camp was completely plundered, and the Muslims decisively driven back. Alfonso had secured a significant victory for his realm and for all of Christendom. At the same time, he also laid the groundwork for driving the Moors out of Granada. Sadly, it would take decades more before the valleys of the Guadalteba and the Turón were fully freed from enemy rule.

In the wake of Alfonso's successes, Sultan Abu Hasan dispatched Muslim troops from the Maghreb to reclaim Gibraltar. The defence of the trade routes and coastal ports of the Western world was a strategic necessity. The redistribution of goods throughout the Mediterranean lay firmly in Arab hands and was defended by every means available. Not until the fifteenth century would the Iberians reclaim this headland forever, the southernmost stretch of mainland facing the African continent across the strait.

The men who had fought beside Sir James Douglas were in mourning for the man who had battled with Robert de Bruce for the Scottish throne, the brave knight without whom there would have been no free Scotland. His companions—William Keith of Galston, Alexander and Walter Maxwell, Sir Thomas Randolph, and many others—had withdrawn that morning to the hill with the makeshift cross for a time of prayer. Even the victorious King Alfonso did not deny himself attendance at this mass for the many dead. Deeply moved, he knelt beside me. Unlike his bearing towards his enemies, the King of Castile felt humility and solace before his God.

The carved stone cross already stood a little askew, yet the spirit of God was all the stronger as it took hold of us on that mild day. Alfonso and the valiant knights of the West would withdraw from this place before day's end, a ground that had witnessed so much death. Teba would forever remain a place of terror to me that would haunt me all my life. Here, my beloved husband had died, and the feeling of being to blame clung to my soul like resin.

We had broken camp and Alfonso's victorious troops burned the bodies and mourned their fallen comrades. The heat and thousands of flies were ghastly companions. This time, the dead were not the greatest burden the survivors had to contend with.

The priest who held the Mass beneath a cloudless sky found words of comfort and hope, even though we could not lay James' body to rest.

That day, the Muslim envoys brought us the lifeless bodies of William Sinclair and the other brave knights who had fallen in battle, but James was not among them. In vain, I waited for them to return his body to us. The anger over it could not eclipse my grief.

Christians, like Muslims, paid for the bones of their kin. The ghastly stench of boiled remains drifted from the great cauldrons all the way to our hill of devotion. It made me retch, for human flesh carried a scent unlike that of animals. However, it was still better to bring home dry bones than a body left to rot.

Just as I had resigned myself to returning to Scotland empty-handed, we were interrupted amid the Mass by several arrivals. More envoys had ridden into the camp to sell bodies, but this time, the men looked different from the worn-down traders who usually made a fortune from the dead. These men, who were suddenly escorted towards us by the guards, were high-ranking leaders of the Nasrids. I could tell from afar by their glittering daggers and costly horses.

The Berber warriors of noble blood had placed themselves under the protection of the negotiators. Even so, it took courage to enter the enemy camp so openly. There had to be a compelling reason.

My heart stumbled when, among the men mounted on splendidly adorned horses with coloured saddlecloths and gold-embellished breastplates, I recognised a familiar face. It was Rachid ibn Faraj, son of Muhammed ibn Faraj and Alfonso's supposed ally. I felt the young king beside me flinch under the Berber's gaze. He had also recognised him. Without hesitation, Alfonso stepped up beside me and regarded the arrivals suspiciously.

The mounted party caused no small stir in the modest camp. When Rachid reined in his horse before us with his companions, a crowd of curious soldiers and attendants gathered at once. Not a single word was spoken by those who arrived.

My gaze swept over the small group. There were six men in all, their faces grim, leading a horse with a corpse dragging behind it. Heavy boots dangled clearly beneath the horse's belly. The body was wrapped in a costly blanket. Rachid and another man stepped forward. As I recalled, he was one of the advisers from the camp who had sat beside the old Emir.

Rachid's dark gaze settled on me at once, and I held it. Never again would I lower my eyes before this man. Everything was different now. I was no longer a teacher he could draw into his be; I was Lady Enja.

In that moment, he recognised who stood before him. The proud man's face shifted slightly, showing confusion, and then understanding. Was he ashamed now of his suggestive behaviour towards me? No. Why would he be? Rachid smiled, white teeth flashing as he drew back the corners of his mouth.

"My Lady," he greeted me in his finest Anglo-Saxon English. "I presume you are Lady Enja Douglas, wife of Sir James Douglas?"

Alfonso drew a deep breath in, then let it out again. It was an affront not to greet the king first, but the unusual circumstances left no room for courtly manners.

"Your stories have reached our campfires, and I regret not having recognised you sooner. You are not only brave, but beautiful, just as the singers of heroes tell it. It is an honour to behold you, even though the circumstances bring you no joy."

"It is an honour to see you again, Rachid ibn Faraj," I replied firmly and inclined my head. I was uncertain how to conduct myself towards a Berber prince, certainly not as a teacher. Proudly, with my back straight, I waited for Rachid to pay his respects to Alfonso, but he did not so much as glance at him. It was a clear sign of his contempt for the Castilian crown.

The gaze from Rachid's black eyes bored into my blue ones. I remained utterly calm, even folding my arms across my body and taking the time to study him in return. He sat at ease, almost languid in his finely crafted saddle. His turban revealed a symmetrical face with a straight nose. Rachid was fiercely proud, and I had wounded his honour when I dismissed him so lightly. Yet he did not seem angered. Perhaps only now did the full weight of my actions dawn on him. I was the wife of James Douglas. What was he waiting for?

"Why are you here?" I pressed harshly, even though it was perfectly clear to me what he wanted. "If you intend to hand over my husband's body, then do so, but do not be disappointed if we do not invite you for tea."

I had nothing left to lose. James was dead; I had seen him die. Beneath the covering lay, unmistakably, a human body. Rachid had brought his mortal remains into our camp himself.

Suddenly, I tensed. Did they intend to ransom the body for money, or for prisoners? The way Rachid looked at me, perhaps even for me?

Alfonso had had enough of being ignored and cut in, clearly irritated. "What do you want here, Rachid?" The young ruler deliberately withheld his title, just as the Berber had denied him any mark of deference.

But the Berber prince had no intention of paying his respects to Alfonso. On the contrary, in one fluid motion, he slid from his horse and had the animal bearing the corpse brought to him. In only a few steps, he stood before me, and I had to force myself not to retreat a single pace.

This man carried an astonishing air of self-assurance here, in the very midst of his enemies. He held out the rope to me, which I accepted with trembling hands. Despite the composure I showed to the world, I was on the brink of collapsing in tears. With my husband's body before me, his death was undeniable. Another wave of pain and grief swept over me. This time, hundreds of pairs of eyes were fixed upon me. Pull yourself together, Enja!

Thankfully, one of our grooms hurried over and took the horse from me. At least there was someone among those present who was not merely standing frozen, staring at the strange scene unfolding before all eyes, and who removed the corpse from my sight. With that, I managed to reclaim my dignity. I must not break under this.

Suddenly, all my misgivings turned to certainty. The Berber prince Rachid knelt before me as though I were the King of Castile himself. It was a slap in the face to the Iberian ruler beside me, who seethed with rage. I felt strangely ashamed, and yet a certain pride welled up within me, above all at what the noble warrior was about to say.

"I return to you the body of your husband with my greatest respect. He fought like a hero. He faced death as though he feared no hell. He kept his oath to his king and to his God. James Douglas was, to me, a man of honour, regardless of his faith. I hereby pay him my respect and return his mortal remains to you."

A cry of God is great followed, taken up fervently by his companions, and it stole the breath from my lungs. Rachid ibn Faraj was paying profound respect to a fellow warrior. It seemed that something akin to chivalry existed, even among the enemy ranks. James had made a name for himself not only among his friends but also his foes accorded him due honour. Rachid wished to release James' body to me without negotiation.

It touched me deeply. Without thinking, I held out my right hand, open, just as James would have done. The Berber prince lifted his head in surprise, which he had lowered before me. He straightened and clasped my hand. A calloused, warm hand enclosed mine with strength for a few seconds, and then he let go.

Chapter 11

Teba, Castile, 25 August 1330

The days in Scotland were brutally short in November. It was three in the afternoon, and the grey of the day dissolved into a milky mist. The toll of the Greyfriars bells in nearby Dumfries had only just faded when I drew my cloak tighter about me and made for the stables. It was time for my daily round. After the turbulent years of the Scottish Wars of Independence, Caerlaverock had grown quiet. The moated stronghold with its trapezoidal design was the ancestral seat of the Douglas dynasty.

Now, in winter, the thatch upon the roofs was being renewed, and carts laden with freshly bound sheaves kept rattling through the gate. Chickens clucked in a flurry, and children darted straight across my path. One of them slipped and sprawled full-length upon the ground. I was with the child in a heartbeat, hauling it up by the collar out of the filth. Beneath all that grime, it was hard to tell whether it was a boy or a girl. Perhaps one of the smith's?

The child, perhaps four years of age, eyed me fearfully through dirt-caked lashes, and I set it gently back upon its feet. Even so, I could not prevent it from soiling my boots.

It would likely never change, I thought to myself as I wiped down the leather with a cloth I kept tucked into my doublet for just such occasions. With a surge of irritation, I took in the state of the castle yard, which had become a single expanse of mud. The sun had thawed the dirt that had frozen overnight, leaving pools of water everywhere between the rampant tufts of grass. I dreamed of the day I would drain these grounds and lay proper paving stones, but for now, there was far too much work to be done on the buildings to turn our attention to the earth beneath them.

With a surly step, I trudged straight through the evidence of my carelessness and reached the stone wall of the stables. There, I knocked the filth from my heel. At the entrance, warm, steamy air struck me full in the face, carrying with it the scent of fresh dung and urine. The sharp smell did not trouble me, quite the opposite.

Lissy was housed in a small wooden stall at the far end of the dimly lit stable passage. She was helping herself to the fresh hay, richly scented with lavender. I scratched her brown neck and ears, yet she would not be distracted from her well-earned treat. Two weeks earlier, she had returned with me from the long, unsettling ride out of the fierce Spanish sun.

A shiver ran through me. The journey behind us filled me with dread. Nothing remained of my deceased husband but bones boiled bare. Mina and I had set out for Scotland only days after James' remains were handed over in Castile, accompanied by Sir William Keith of Galston, Thomas

Randolph, the surviving Maxwell brother, and a handful of other knights. It had taken us more than three months to return, by land and sea.

Rachid ibn Faraj had not returned James' mortal remains alone. Alongside him, the honourable Berber prince had also found the silver vessel containing the heart of Robert the Bruce. With a disregard for death shown only by proud warriors, Rachid had placed the precious relic into the hands of the Scottish knights. In doing so, the son of Mohammad ibn Faraj proved that remembrance of the dead held equal worth in both faiths. Rachid's gesture was a matter of honour, and it continued to echo within my heart even now, more than three months later.

James' burial took place in the family vault of St Bride's Church in Douglas. It was there that the true seat of the dynasty lay, where the castle had been destroyed by James himself during the War of Independence. The entire village gathered, along with the knights of his banner, the Scottish court, and friends from across the land, to send his soul on its way to the Kingdom of Heaven.

The commemorations lasted three days, and I was given the honour of recounting the story of his violent death to his former companions and to all who wished to hear it. I was uncertain whether the true course of events would ever find its way into the annals of history, for there was much drinking, of course, in honour of the revered James Douglas. Memories would fade in time, as would emotions and pain.

How fortunate that I had carried his bones with me for eighteen weeks before I was forced to take my final leave of him. It had given me time to grieve.

In the small church at Douglas, his parents and his first wife, Elisabeth, already lay buried, and one day, I, too, would find my rest there, if I were ever to find it at all …

I stepped into Lissy's stall and began to check her for ticks. My fingers moved gently over her dark brown, silky coat, and as I twisted the troublesome bloodsuckers from her skin here and there, I soothed her by stroking her mane. Winter would drive these parasites away, but for now, a few still lurked, hidden in the warmth of the hay.

Even as my hands moved with gentle care, my thoughts were far away. The present state of my castle weighed heavily upon me. Too much in Caerlaverock reminded me of my husband, whom I had esteemed and loved as I had scarcely loved another soul. I was a widow now, and by virtue of his morning gift I held the right to dwell in this castle for the rest of my days. My thoughts drifted back to our wedding in St Giles' Cathedral in Edinburgh, and the images alone drew a smile to my lips. They had been brief, tender moments in a time of dreadful battles. Those days had brought death and hunger, but for us, they had been days of hope for a life without war.

On the morning after our wedding, James had presented me with my morning gift: lands, feudal revenues, and Caerlaverock as a permanent home. It was his wedding gift and, at the same time, my safeguard for a future we could not have foreseen. Today, I was grateful to him for his foresight. What he could not have known was that this place would be hollow without my family. My home was as flat and cold as ash. The laughter of others' children now filled the halls of my castle.

By now, I was too old to bear children, and too scarred to be of any allure to a man. My worth to the Kingdom of Scotland had been reduced to my name alone. Lady Douglas. Of what use was that to me?

To my misfortune, after James' death, his son William Archibald had returned from the Western Isles as a newly knighted man. He had not seen his father for eleven years and, upon his return, could do nothing but lay him in the grave. A father who had never once asked after him. A man who had slit his mother's throat with his own hands after her attempt to poison me. There were better family bonds, I had to concede.

William was a handsome young man, upon whom the honour of knighthood had been bestowed at the age of sixteen. It granted him leave to venture out into the world and prove himself a man of honour. It also meant that he laid claim to Caerlaverock. The youth was prone to grandiose words. The name Douglas opened doors for him with ease, yet he lacked the mettle to fill his father's footsteps.

Liam McLeod, King of the Western Isles, was the husband of my adopted daughter Rachel. As the boy's godfather, he had agreed to train the young man as a knight. Unfortunately, his judgement was still in the process of ripening. Perhaps William Archibald also resented me for the fact that James had ordered his mother's death. I could not fault him for that.

Though he had grown up within our family and become a tall, powerful knight, my sympathy for him was limited. On his last visit, he had carried on within my castle as though he were already the new head of the Douglas dynasty, yet he was not even of age, let alone legally empowered to act. He persistently chose to ignore the fact that James had granted me this morning gift, and instead, paraded himself as lord of the castle. In those moments, I no longer knew whether to put this nuisance firmly in his place or simply pack my belongings and leave.

A bitter conflict was inevitable, for I would not take orders from a greenhorn. Upon reaching his majority, William would assume the inheritance of the Douglas lands and trading rights, yet until my death, his authority did not extend to decisions concerning the fate of Caerlaverock.

"You are free to leave," he had declared provocatively before the assembled clan during one of his rare visits. He had planted himself wide-legged in front of me, as though he might need to drive that choice into me by force if required. We both stood before the high table in the great hall. The matter at hand was who among us was to sit in which place. I insisted upon my right to continue occupying the seat of the lady of the castle. My hand was already upon the back of the chair when William sought to drive me from the table with his harsh words.

"You have neither the right to do as you please on my lands," I snapped at him, "nor the courage to send me elsewhere."

I took my seat upon the chair I had always known.

I admit, I was furious and deeply hurt at the time, for he was trampling his father's legacy underfoot. Such words were usually spoken by men and coming from a woman, my voice carried the force of one of Cathal's blasting charges. A deathly silence fell over the crowded great hall. It was filled with the men and women of my clan who had gathered for the evening meal. Their conversations had been lively and loud until my blunt words rang out from the high table.

William's face flushed a deep red. His eyes bulge, and I had expected him to strike me, or at least to attempt it. Instead, he merely clenched his fists. His mouth opened and closed like a fish, yet no words came. At last, the young man, decked out in velvet and brocade, turned away from me and strode out of the hall. Since then, I had not laid eyes on his powdered backside in Caerlaverock. At the time, I gave no further thought to the affronted youth.

Only now did I realise that, lost in thought, I had ended up in the infirmary during my rounds. Once again, my feet had carried me here without conscious intent while my thoughts had wandered off on their own. I cast a stern glance about me. Here, I was in control, for this was still my place of work.

I was in a spacious chamber with two beds for the sick and a simple worktable. A porcelain cup of cold mocha still stood upon it. No one had dared to carry the half-empty beaker back to the kitchen, though I would never drink it once it had gone stale. A wooden chair with a cushion stood neatly before the table. On a shelf, carefully set in order, I recognised the essential tools of a medicus, along with a few dried herbs that spread the scent of chamomile. The room was plainly furnished, yet clean and well kept.

The grey tomcat startled me and pressed against my legs, purring. I lifted him and scratched his shaggy coat. Once again, thick knots and clumps of dirt were tangled in his fur, and I decided to tend to him. I set the animal on my desk, reached for a pair of scissors, and cut the matted knots from his long coat, then I sat on the plain chair where I wrote my reports and shared my cured sausage with him, which I always kept in my drawer. It was a little tough but richly spiced, and he devoured his portion hungrily in just a few bites.

My appetite, too, had stirred, and I bit off a piece of the hard sausage. As I did, my gaze fell upon the old satchel on the shelf beside the worktable, which had been in service for what felt like a century. It was Isaak's medicus bag, which I had taken up after his death. In his lifetime, the medicus would never have allowed me anywhere near that treasured thing, yet I had been chosen in his stead as medicus to Grand Master Hassan I'Shabbah, and whether I liked it or not, I had to use his bag. Airqud fi salam. Rest in peace, my friend.

At least the old piece of leather remained of him, aside from my memories. Had it been up to William, he would gladly have taken even that from me. And he would have held the door with pleasure, if only I would leave. Instead, I had succeeded in showing him out of my castle. Humiliated before the eyes of all the clan members, he would not return here again so quickly. Yet even that brought me no satisfaction; quite the opposite.

Fionna had not been permitted to leave the convent and return home even for her father's burial. The abbess had written to me, saying that her thoughts were with me, yet Fionna's duties lay in Fontevraud. The powerful nun would include James in her prayers.

I wondered how Fionna was faring. The authority of the abbess must have chafed her deeply. She had surely imagined her stay in a convent very differently.

The grey tomcat licked his paws with relish. How clean these creatures were, compared to dogs. All at once, a peculiar thought struck me.

"Isaak," I said with a smile to the grey-furred creature, running my hand over his head. "I will call you Isaak. That way, you will remind me forever of my old master."

As though he had understood me perfectly, the tomcat mewled and demanded another piece of the hard sausage. If

Isaak's soul had indeed been reborn into an animal, I thought, he could have found no finer dwelling than this cat, and I cut another small slice for the hungry tom.

The infirmary was empty, like my soul, a great part of which I had laid to rest in the grave of my dead husband. We had shared an unusual bond, and a deep understanding of one another. He had given me the freedom to be who I was. For that, I loved him. I had made many mistakes in my life, yet he had forgiven me every one of them. All but one, I suspected.

Why had he looked at me like that when he turned his eyes to me for the last time? Why had he not deflected the thrust that drove into his throat?

James had been a seasoned fighter. The knife need not have struck him. A slight turn of his torso, and the blade would have missed its mark.

James' gaze had looked tormented. It was not the look of a man at peace with himself or with his fate. I felt it as he had fixed his eyes upon me from afar. But why?

Had my husband truly known of my son's existence? Perhaps Mina's words had reminded him that, after the English victory at the Battle of Faughart in 1318, I had spent a great deal of time in Ireland. Had James pieced the truth together?

Had he been with me more often, he would have noticed the unwanted pregnancy, but as Robert's right hand in Scotland, he had been consumed with defending the borders.

Thus, I was able to draw a veil of silence over it. I would likely never know what thoughts had occupied him in the end.

Much had changed for me since then. With James's death, the memory of my illegitimate son Conor had become painfully tangible. He was my only surviving son. Even my adopted daughter Rachel now lived far in the north of Scotland with her children and husband, Liam. She no longer needed me. She had become one with the family of her MacLeod clan. I had last seen her at James' funeral. Almost all the chiefs of the vast MacLeod clan had been present. Through the marriage, the Douglas and the MacLeod clans had become inseparable. In this, James had left behind his unmistakable political imprint. To be a grandmother carried with it a faint terror of ageing for me. As beautiful as it was to witness the children of the next generation, they also reminded me of my painful loss.

Conor had turned fourteen that year. I had not seen him for twelve years, and in my dreams, I sometimes beheld a warped blend of a gangly boy and Ragnar. The longing for him would, at times, all but rob me of my senses.

The people around me gave me the sense that they needed me, yet the only thing that would truly bring me happiness was an answer to the question of how Conor was faring. Lately, I often caught myself wishing to sail to Iceland, if only to ask Conor myself. Was he happy with his father? A strange feeling deep within my soul answered that he was not.

Since James was gone, I struggled with being alone. The bed beside me was cold and empty every night. Of course, I could choose a lover, but I would feel as though I were betraying my husband once more. Although I had not always been faithful to him, my love for James reached beyond death.

No, there was no future for me here in Caerlaverock. Everything here reminded me of James. After having such great warriors as James and Ragnar at my side, there would be no other man for me.

Rachid ibn Faraj, the Berber prince, came to my mind all at once. His black eyes had looked deep into my soul, as though they had recognised what set me apart just as Isaak had before him. Despite his few years, the striking Berber prince already possessed the wisdom, sense of honour, and courage of a great warrior. I would never forget the reverence with which he had borne my husband's body to me in Teba.

Ragnar had once confessed to me that I was the very image of his war goddess, whom he so deeply revered. To find someone who so closely resembled one's ideal, he had said, was like finding a needle in a haystack. How right he had been. Were there more of us?

James, Ragnar, and now, Rachid. He had slipped beneath my skin at once, as though the same scent or pull bound us all together. Yet this pagan warrior stood on the wrong side.

As had Ragnar, too. I paused at the strange course my thoughts were taking, but who, after all, decided which side was the right one?

I had always stood for James' cause. I was his wife, and I had turned myself towards his faith. Had I become Rachid's wife, I would be a Muslim today. A sigh escaped my throat. The endless debate over which religion was the true one sent my thoughts spinning in a circle that led nowhere. I forced my mind back to James and finally, to the only lover I had ever known. Ragnar.

After all, I had met three very special people, and with two of them I had shared my bed. One union had brought forth a girl, the other a boy. Fionna I would exclude from the circle of elite warriors, but what of Conor?

By now, the old tomcat had grown bored. He slipped from my hand and leapt down from the table. Settling not far from me, he looked up at me with his great eyes. They were yellow by nature, yet in the dim light, his pupils had widened into large, black orbs.

He looked at me oddly as I let out another audible sigh.

"Where have I ended up, Isaak?" I addressed the creature directly. "And above all, where does my path lead me now?"

But the animal did not answer me. Even so, it felt good to share my thoughts with a soul. Perhaps it truly was that of my old master. Am I growing old and mad? The thought crossed my mind. I did not feel like smiling at it. I was in no such mood.

In truth, I found it hard to step into my sombre inheritance. I still felt young enough, though the shoulder I had strained in a practice bout the week before pinched unpleasantly, and my belly ached from time to time, as if it occasionally remembered having once been grievously abused. And the pulling in my bones! That had to be the cold, I told myself, or was it age, damn it?

Suddenly, the space around me felt too tight within my skin and I sprang to my feet. Startled by my sudden movement, the tomcat flinched and darted beneath the cot as though I had struck him. Stiff from sitting, I hobbled out into the cold. The air wrapped itself around me like an icy cocoon, but at least it was fresh and, save for the goats' exhalations, bearable.

Smoke rose straight up from the chimney stacks into the sky in a good sign that the next day would remain clear and bright. The sun had already slipped behind the castle battlements, and within moments, night would descend upon us. Then, the temperatures would drop by a few more degrees.

Lachlan McKay stood not far from me in the smithy, striking glowing iron with a heavy hammer. James' former foreman had donned a leather apron to shield himself from filth and sparks. He paused in his work when he saw me and called something. Though I could not quite make out Lachlan's words, I waved back at him kindly. It was surely no more than a greeting he had meant to send my way.

The familiar veteran nodded in reply, turned back to the piece of iron he was working on his anvil, and moments later, the steady rhythm of a skilled craftsman rang out again, with one blow loud, and the next softer.

Lachlan kept things in order whenever the lord of the castle was absent. Now, he turned his hand to other tasks, for I was here in his stead. Lachlan had four children with Catriona, Moira's natural daughter. How tall they had all grown by now …

"… or perhaps I am simply old …" I murmured to myself.

Uncertain, I stopped at the steps leading to the great hall, taking in my surroundings with all my senses. A pergola adorned the gate, sheltering visitors from the rain. Garlands of flowers draped the railing that ran up along the steps. Here and there, withered petals lay upon the stones like splashes of colour.

Thoughts of life's transience haunted my mind. In hundreds of years, these stones would still stand, yet I would be gone. As my gaze traced the castle walls, against which the two-storey palace leaned, it came to rest on the smithy where McKay was at work. It brought me an inner peace to know that all I had built here would endure for many years to come, for new generations.

Suddenly, the usually tranquil courtyard burst into life. A group of women came running through the castle gate. They shattered both my inner calm and that of my stronghold, for they were shouting and quarrelling. Two women were being driven before the mob as though animals herded towards the butcher.

I turned towards them and shouted angrily, "Why do you carry such savage quarrelling into my castle?"

In their fervour, the women had not noticed me, not least because I stood in the shadow of the wooden roof. Now, they recognised me and fell silent at once. As lady of the castle, I held absolute power.

They were from the nearest village. Caitlin, the old washerwoman, led the group. She now approached me somewhat hesitantly. Her back was bent from years of hard labour, and her hands were rough from handling water and soap.

"Forgive us, my lady," she stammered awkwardly. Her toothless mouth worked soundlessly. In that moment, it must have dawned on her that she was addressing her lady outside the appointed days for court hearings. Even so, it seemed important enough for her to continue. "There's a dispute here in the village. That one there," she pointed at a middle-aged woman, "quarrelled with her chamber mate and stabbed her in the arm with a knife."

The opposing woman now stepped forwards, her face twisted with pain. She was smaller and far younger. Caitlin and the other women looked at me expectantly. Matters of dispute within the clan had always fallen under the authority of the lord of the castle or, in my case, under mine as lady of the stronghold. If anyone within the clan was proven guilty of murder, execution was inevitable. An attempted murder would, at the very least, end in that person's banishment from our clan.

How fortunate that there were not many such cases, for decisions like those struck at my own heart, too. The temptation to yield to my emotions most often stood in direct opposition to a just verdict.

"Take the woman to the great hall and wait for me there," I ordered Caitlin. "I will examine the victim's wound and follow with her. Only then will I pass my judgement."

I drew the injured woman by her unhurt arm into the infirmary. Tomcat Isaak lay upon my chair.

"Sit on the cot," I ordered her. She wore no head covering, and her long brown hair fell loose down her back. She had evidently already finished her work. She was a simple maid and had to share a room with the other woman, with whom she had fallen into dispute.

"What is your name?" I asked to distract her, for the maid had suddenly grown very afraid.

"Mariann," her thin voice came from where she had taken her seat. I sat beside her and examined her arm more closely in the light of a tallow lamp. The stab wound was quite deep, and I decided to stitch it.

In my bag, I carried prepared needles with pre-threaded sutures for such cases. Catriona always set aside a few in advance for me. Sadly, I could no longer thread the fine silk ties myself; my fingers had grown too unsteady for it.

Mariann's lips began to tremble, as though she were about to cry. To avoid that, I offered her an encouraging smile and reassured her, "It will hurt no more than the knife did. Once I have closed the wound, it will heal well."

With a cloth and a little uisge beatha, I cleansed the bleeding wound and gave her a good swallow to drink. Then, I sought her gaze and waited until she nodded with resolve. It took four stitches, and she clenched her teeth bravely.

"Will you drive Deirdre away, my Lady Douglas?" she suddenly blurted out, looking at me anxiously. "You must know, she meant to strike my child..." she added, her voice growing a little bolder.

Perhaps the alcohol had loosed her tongue. Deirdre was likely the gaunt woman waiting for us in the hall.

"I will hear both sides, and then decide what is to be done."

I wrapped her arm in a clean cloth. I rose more quickly than I intended, and my vision narrowed slightly. My tongue went dry, and I steadied myself by instinct. I drew a deep breath in, and then let it out. My heart thudded hard within my chest. It was surely the strain, I told myself, or the scent of the uisge. The woman, it seemed, had noticed nothing of my weakness.

After a moment and a breath of fresh air, I felt better. I showed her the way out and towards the stairs that led up to the great hall.

We entered the great hall through the side wing, where the group of women was already waiting, whispering in agitation. Two chairs stood before my high table upon a wooden dais. The man-high hearth spat fire, and glowing embers danced like little devils across the stone floor. The scent of burned peat mingled with that of cooked meat drifting in from the kitchens. Hints of thyme and caraway reached my nose.

I did not sit but remained standing before the women. The older Deirdre stared fixedly at the ground, her mouth tightly set. As it emerged, she worked alongside Mariann in the washhouse. In a low voice, the latter repeated her accusations.

"Deirdre threatened me with the knife," she claimed, "and when I resisted, she struck."

"If anyone was brandishing a knife, then it was likely you," her opponent remarked sharply. "After all, it was your knife."

I said nothing but folded my arms across my chest.

Caitlin now stepped forwards and explained in a calm voice, "Mariann has a small daughter and wants Deirdre to find a room of her own, but that costs too much money. The two of them quarrel often. These women's husbands were killed in the war. They are diligent washerwomen whom I do not wish to lose. Could you not simply have Deirdre beaten as punishment, so that I may employ her again?"

Her coarse words sparked approval among the women. Deirdre clearly did not stand high in their favour. But this was not about sympathy or feelings for me, nor did I wish to punish someone who might be innocent. I had the sense that something was not right.

Deirdre suddenly rose to her feet, her eyes fixed on me, then she turned towards the fire, her eyes glinting darkly in the play of the light. She had bound her grey hair into a braid at the back of her head. It was difficult for me to judge her age, but she could not yet have passed the middle of her life. Hard labour had left its mark. Her face was lined and worn.

I had taken my place with my back to the fire. The warmth did me good, and my wildly pounding heart slowly calmed after my moment of weakness. Deirdre seemed familiar to me. I had seen her before, as she now confirmed.

"I have worked in Caitlin's service for many years for the good of the clan and for you, my Lady. I lost my husband to the plague many years ago, God rest his soul. Since then, I have shared a chamber with Mariann. Ever since she had her daughter, there has been constant trouble. The child is a sweet one, but Mariann does not care for her. Instead, she prefers to flirt with men and spend her time in the tavern."

The younger maid had now risen.

"We argued," Mariann admitted softly. "That happens often. But this time, in her fury, Deirdre came at me with a knife. I swear it, so help me God."

The oath did not impress me, but something else was far more interesting. Mariann had claimed that the injury came from a thrust, not a slash. While tending the wound, I had noticed that a pointed blade had penetrated the muscle of the upper arm.

Mariann made a dismissive gesture with her hand. "Deirdre is just jealous. She has no taste for enjoying life and would rather stay in our chamber with my little one. She looks after her while I am away. My zest for life frustrates her. Today, she took the knife from the kitchen table and came at me, just because I told her I was going to the tavern."

Triumphantly, she displayed her bandaged upper arm. I had the knife brought to me and recalled the exact spot where it had pierced Mariann's arm.

I instructed the young maid, who had so vividly described the course of events, to re-enact the scene with me. Reluctantly and somewhat awkwardly, she tried to guide me through the supposed attack with the weapon. It quickly became clear that Mariann had no idea how to handle a knife. In that moment, she gave herself away. She had stabbed herself in the arm, as I demonstrated using my arm, plainly visible to everyone in the hall. Mariann's scheme to portray Deirdre as the culprit and have her cast out of the clan suddenly crumbled like dry bread, and the young maid began to weep.

Tears streamed down her cheeks as she confessed that, in her rage, she had devised this plan and stabbed herself in the arm. In her desperation, she threw herself to the floor before me, clawed at my tunic, and wept with a sound that tore at the heart. Her sudden closeness made me uneasy.

"Have mercy on me," she pleaded through violent sobs. "Show compassion for my child's sake."

In that moment, the gate to my heart slammed shut. In such situations, I had to shield my soul; decisions like these had to be made without the sway of feeling. With this way of seeing the world, I had been able to endure the loss of many friends, companions, and kin throughout my life.

That very evening, Mariann was forced to leave the village with her young daughter. The members of my clan accepted my judgement and returned to their daily lives. Only Deirdre remained standing for a time, lost in thought, pondering the fate of her former chamber mate. Perhaps it was the child she now worried about?

Lachlan McKay was burdened with the hard task of escorting the mother and daughter to the nearest town, Dumfries, so that she might seek new work there. I had cast her out from our clan and from the protection the community had afforded her. Lachlan wore a look of doubt as he lifted the child and Mariann, along with their scant belongings, onto the horse.

"Allow me to pay for lodging for the first nights, my Lady," Lachlan pleaded, "so they are not exposed to the cold."

His face had remained unreadable throughout. He had always been an attractive man, a fine fighter, and a devoted husband to Catriona. Above all, he was loyal to my clan, and even now, with my husband dead, Lachlan would walk through hell for me. I had always held him in high esteem for his loyalty and his honesty.

I looked him straight in the eye. It struck me that the lines on his face made him appear more mature, but not older. Usually, a mischievous smile played about his mouth, yet now it was set tight. His eyelid twitched, as it always did when he was uncertain. Why was he behaving so strangely? As a member of my clan, he was bound to respect his lady's decision. Was it the child? Lachlan had four children, two of them still under ten years of age.

As he made his plea, he tore the cap from his head, and I noted with a start how thin and grey his once thick brown hair had become. It was unusual for him to defy my command.

I hesitated. My decisions were usually irrevocable, but I was no monster, and he was right; the child deserved a chance. She was innocent of her mother's transgressions. If I could not show mercy, then let it at least be granted through my foreman, so I allowed him this small concession and gave him the coins for lodging in Dumfries.

I watched them still as McKay and Mariann rode out of the castle yard with her child. They would reach the county town of Dumfries within two hours. McKay was to find the woman lodging there and return the following day with both horses.

I felt weary. It was a sign that I had, indeed, grown older, for it was not physical exertion that made me feel the weight of my years; it was the great responsibility that had rested upon me since James' death. Where I had once wished to lead the clan and had fought for it with pride, the burden of widowhood now crushed me. Should I truly consider placing the leadership of my clan into the hands of Liam McLeod, William's godfather? A shiver ran through me.

Slowly and deep in thought, I returned to the great hall, which lay empty at this hour. Darkness was drawing near, and most folk had retreated to their houses or chambers. I pulled a large, leather-clad chair towards me and took my place before the fire. It was here that the old medicus Gotfrid had once fallen peacefully asleep. It was a fine place to die, the thought crossed my mind. Startled by my reflection, I shook my head. No, I would not die yet.

But where would I go? What drove me onward?

I missed my husband deeply, especially on nights like this. The fire had collapsed into a small mound and the wood had burned down to charcoal that glowed with a gentle warmth. I had always been one who welcomed the cold, yet in these days, I sought warmth as a moth seeks the light. Still, the fire could not banish the cold and loneliness within my heart. Night's rest, as so often of late, had not yet crept into my soul. Too many thoughts kept me awake, memories and brooding alike.

I must have drifted off at some point, for I was jolted awake when the small side door set into the great gate of the hall creaked open. The iron hinges ought to be oiled, flashed through my mind. I was instantly wide awake, yet I remained seated by the hearth. I had added firewood earlier; the embers would hold for a while longer. Who would come into the hall at such an hour? It had to be midnight!

I turned my head slightly and, in the glow of the orange light, recognised Lachlan. He approached me with a child wrapped in a blanket in his arms. At first, I feared the girl had died, but he raised a finger to his lips, bidding me be silent, and I was relieved to see that the child was merely asleep. Lachlan gently laid the five-year-old upon a cushion and then came over to me.

My head lifted only slightly as he began to speak. I did not bother to rise. My teeth ground against one another, and beneath the blanket, I clenched my fists. A dark foreboding made me brace for the worst. Lachlan dropped to one knee before me and began to speak in a low voice. The report was clearly unpleasant for him, yet he delivered it with the same stoic loyalty with which he had once stormed fortresses for James.

"Mariann handed the little one to me when she had to relieve herself. I turned away out of courtesy. It was roughly at the level of Glencaple. The sea inlet lay directly along our path, and I assume she fell into the water and drowned. I searched for her for hours but found neither her body nor any trace. That is why I returned. I will ride out again tomorrow and search for her once more. I am so sorry, Lady Enja; I have lost Mariann."

He lowered his head with his thinning hair. Did he take me for a fool? Did he truly expect me to believe that McKay—seasoned by every trial and feared by his enemies—had lost a maid to an accident on the short road to Dumfries? Why would he lie for this woman, who had likely taken her own life? Was he afraid for her soul, knowing the Church would not tolerate death by one's own hand, or had he driven her away and taken the child, seeking to deceive me?

For that evening, I let McKay's version of the story stand. For my sake. I would see to the little girl. How Mariann had died would change nothing about that. I rose carefully, my joints cracking terribly as I did. Wearily, I rubbed my hand over my eyes. McKay was still kneeling.

"Rise, Lachlan, and take the child to Deirdre. I will cover his upkeep and education, but the washerwoman shall take the mother's place for him."

The old warrior looked up in surprise and met my gaze. It was far too dark for him to make out my expression. Lachlan was searching for an answer—I could feel it. An answer to a question he had not yet spoken. Why I should believe him.

"God will find a just fate for each of us. If not in this life, then in another. Why should I question the will of our Lord?"

Somehow, I sounded like our priest who read the Mass each day. For the God-fearing McKay, these words were explanation enough for my lack of questions, or even reproach. I turned away from him and climbed the narrow spiral stair to my chamber. It was cold and empty, as it would be on all the nights yet to come.

I wondered whether the walls had drawn me into a dark enchantment. Perhaps the castle itself was now demanding its tribute for my clan's right to live here. Was I ready to pay the price?

That night, I did not fall asleep in exhaustion as I usually did. I sat upon my bed and stared into the hearth fire, the warmth of which failed to reach me. I caught myself wanting to give up, but it did not feel right. The longing to see my son was stronger.

At first, it was only a thought that slowly took shape as an idea. As the embers of the fire faded, a new energy stirred and drew me into its spell. I would leave this place and journey to Iceland. I would walk the path Conor had taken twelve years ago. I wanted to hold him in my arms once more. The mere thought of it stole my breath.

Suddenly, the walls were no longer as cold as they had been hours before. The embers seemed, at last, to warm the room, and I fell asleep with the good feeling that I had finally found my guiding star of the north once more. Rather than lingering in frustration until death claimed me, I was firmly resolved to venture into a new adventure.

Chapter 12

***Ireland, Dunguaire Castle,
Province of Connacht, early May 1331***

How wondrous to be here again in Dunguaire, the stronghold of the provincial king of Connacht. I felt at ease as I had not for a long while. The firmament stretched high above us, dark, clear, and shimmering with distant stars. For this evening, I had chosen one of the rocks as my seat.

Moira and Cathal sat opposite me, pressed close together on a simple wooden bench. They gazed dreamily into the fire, its flames leaping several feet high into the endless night sky. A great wooden cross burned here, at the highest point of Ballycleary, a cliff rising sheer and proud. From this height, the sea lay open before us, all the way out to the narrow waters of the Doorus Strait.

Here, at this picturesque place, the people of Kinvarra and all the surrounding villages had gathered to celebrate Bhelltainn—the Festival of Fire—together with their king. By tradition, the day was observed on the first of May.

With the church ceremony held that morning, the people of Dunguaire had fulfilled their Christian duty, and the pagan rites took command once more. Fire had long been a sacred symbol to the Celts and remained part of the yearly celebrations, even among Ireland's Christian folk. After only a few barrels of uisge beatha, most of those present were already drunk, dancing wildly around the flames. Musicians played over one another in a wild tangle of sound. In truth, so it seemed to me, they were no longer making music, only noise, meant to drive off the evil spirits said to be drawn from the earth by the blazing fire. The louder the din, the fewer spirits would remain, or so the people believed. Celtic traditions still ran deep. At first, I had taken it for an Easter fire, but the Irish had marked the Resurrection of Our Lord weeks earlier, on the second day of April.

Four months earlier, shortly before the New Year festival of Hogmanay, I had arrived in Ireland to visit my friends in Dunguaire. As provincial king of Connacht, Cathal had kindled the fire at midnight with a torch. Moira had guided his hand, holding the flaming staff so the nearly blind king would keep his bearing. For a time after I performed eye surgery two years ago, Cathal had been able to see again, but in recent weeks, his condition had deteriorated rapidly. Now, even my art was powerless. No further intervention was possible.

I assumed he could still sense the glow of the blazing fire yet make out no shapes or outlines, not even people. It shook me to see him thus. My loyal friend and companion, Cathal, was losing his sight entirely. That knowledge alone weighed heavily upon us all, yet he bore his suffering in grim silence.

The great, powerful Cathal was led by the hand by his slight wife like a small child, but fate had decreed it so.

Moira had suffered deeply during the war and the defeat of her people after the Battle of Faughart in 1318. Not only had King Edward de Bruce fallen, along with many valiant warriors, but the dreadful plundering that followed, the spreading sickness in the land, death ever present, and finally the threat to their very existence had worn her down. In her calling as a healer, she had always shared in the suffering of her people, yet despite all this, she fulfilled her duty, stood at her husband's side, and gave her people reassurance, even when it cost her dearly. Her husband's affliction of the eyes had drained her of the last of her strength.

In a moment alone, my old friend had confessed through tears how she truly felt. She had lost weight; dark shadows beneath her eyes bore witness to sleepless nights heavy with worry. Moira and I had met in the small chamber where she prepared her remedies. Dried herbs hung everywhere, along with stores of vegetable matter and animal parts.

With trembling hands, Moira brushed thin strands of her hair—once lustrous and strong as it had fallen over her shoulders—back behind her ear. Her quiet smile did nothing to conceal the fears that haunted her. Her eyes had once held the colour of mature uisge, yet on that day, they were dull and without sheen. Her gaunt shoulders were clearly outlined beneath her dress.

"My thoughts circle death without end, Enja," she said in a thin voice. "I have saved so many from dying, and when I came too late, I comforted them and gave them courage. When Cathal could still see, I was the strong woman at my husband's side. But now, there are days when I fall into a black void. I am fearful, my limbs tremble, and it feels as though I am forever fleeing from the darkness."

Silence lingered between us. I could heal illness or perform procedures, but I had never turned my art to the mind. Outwardly, Moira lacked nothing, save for the marks of age that claim us all in time. What she now described was not new to me, yet I was powerless to help her. I decided simply to listen to my friend.

"I was never one to fear life," Moira went on. "When Cathal went to Ireland, I believed him dead. Even then, I did not falter. I walked my own path."

Tears ran down her cheeks. A little uncertain, I laid my hand upon her arm in comfort and gave it a gentle squeeze. Never had I seen her so desperate. She had always been strong and wise.

"My heart grows so heavy that there are days I can scarcely rise from my bed. At such times, I wish I were with my dead daughter in heaven."

Now, I had to swallow. Sophie had died of a pestilence many years ago. My son Conor had been taken from me at her burial in Dunguaire.

The silence in the chamber was suffocating. I could hear my own heart beating. At the time, I had been so consumed by my son's disappearance that I had failed to see Moira's grief over her daughter's death. I regretted it deeply, yet I had no answer to her fears. Even so, I could clearly see her heart grow lighter the more she spoke. And so, I urged her to go on.

"These days, I find little sleep, or I wake suddenly in the middle of the night, having dreamt of rot and ruin. Then I come here and work."

Moira sniffed and wiped her tears with the hem of her gown. It was made of plain linen; she had always insisted on dressing no finer than the women at court who worked at her side. Her privilege as lady of the castle and wife of the provincial king had never mattered to Moira. She would never have worn fine cloth to her work in any case. Only then did I notice that her skirt was stained with something that looked like dried blood.

"What are those marks?" I asked her curiously.

She cast me an embarrassed glance from the corner of her eye. She was not usually so shy when it came to the craft we both shared.

"I have been working for a long time on a new remedy," she explained hesitantly. "An old midwife who came to me last year because of her aching back gave me a recipe in payment for my services. It was meant to help with women's ailments for which no herb had yet been found, particularly inflammations of the bladder. It is a brew of onions, garlic, wine, and ox gall. I let it rest for nine days in a copper cauldron. The remedy must be prepared in a precise proportion, and then, it proves highly effective against all manner of illnesses."

Now she had my full attention. Was this what Isaac had already discovered? His universal remedy against …

"… everything the body can no longer fight on its own," Moira concluded aloud, as though giving voice to my very thoughts.

That would be a sensation. By now, Moira had recalled her former vigour, and a proud smile stole across her once so beautiful face. The seasoned healer must have laboured long over this preparation, and its success seemed to lift her spirits. The sombre mood had suddenly dispersed. Moira rose to her feet to gather her thoughts.

"I have tested it on many of the sick. It does not help everyone, yet even painful inflammations of the throat or the lungs I have been able to heal with it. My research is not yet complete, but I have managed to dry the healing brew through a special process. In this form, the powder can be transported and divided into small-portioned sachets."

I was certain I saw her eyes glow once more with that beautiful dark orange of rich honey. The light of the oil lamps below was reflected in them, drawing forth a trace of the warmth Moira usually radiated. A look of quiet satisfaction played about her mouth.

"Today, I prepared a fresh brew, and in the process, a little …" she hesitated, looking at me with faint embarrassment, "… a little of the mixture dripped onto my dress."

I did not care in the least whether Moira's dress had grown soiled. Her words rang in my head. Had she truly achieved what had occupied my thoughts for years? If she were right, I could help many people with her powder, including those suffering from wound fever or severe infections. It was a dream for me as a medicus, and a blessing for the afflicted.

The crack of several logs shifting in the fire pulled me back into the present. Thoughts of those strange hours with Moira in her work chamber and the astonishing revelations she had shared still left me somewhat shaken and frustrated, for the work on this new medicine would now have to be set aside.

I was on my way back to my homeland, Iceland, and was using the time at Cathal's castle to bid farewell to those people I had come to cherish over the course of my life.

Beyond the brightly blazing May fire, my gaze caught Cathal as he seemed to stare, transfixed, into the flames. In truth, he was feeling the heat, while the fierce brightness pressed through the absence of his eye's lens. The memories of former years would have to suffice, allowing him to imagine the flames and the laughing faces around him.

Moira held his hand and smiled with serene contentment. Together, they seemed happy, despite all circumstances and the dark hours they had endured. And they had earned that happiness, for Ireland had weathered grievous times and was now on its way into yet another fertile summer.

The English Crown, under Edward II, had bled the Irish provincial kings and their people dry after its victory at the Battle of Faughart in October 1318. As punishment for their defiance, the occupiers ravaged the already suffering land with brutal zeal, leaving behind nothing but hatred and fury among the populace. The Irish nobility, Cathal among them, had been forced to buy back their titles and lands at great cost—possessions that would otherwise have been stripped from them by the Anglo-Norman lords. It had been a bitter, grinding struggle at the court of the English king. Edward made certain the defeated princes felt exactly what he thought of them. Scarred by humiliation and baseness, Cathal returned at last to his province of Connacht. That tribute had demanded dearly of him and of his people.

The past year had been good for harvest on the island. Farmers, fields, and livestock were recovering from the ravages of war. Illness was being contained through better provision of food. People were once more free to celebrate with abandon and look towards the new year in good spirits.

I sat before the burning wooden cross with a cup of uisge in my hand, watching the laughing crowd. I did not drink a single drop, for I did not tolerate the strong spirit, yet I was weary of being spoken to again and again and urged to drink along with them.

Somewhere in the background, I heard Mina's bright laughter. The young Irish men adored the girl with her freckles and cheeky manner. She had accompanied me here from Caerlaverock, and I was not certain she would appear beside me at morning prayer. Perhaps she would spend the night with one of the young men here, who could say? I would not begrudge her if I were to depart for Iceland alone. Mina was a true Irish girl, and she belonged here.

I, however, had begun to feel like a stranger here. When the revellers awoke in the morning with pounding heads, I would already be on my way to nearby Galway. From there, I meant to take the first ship sailing for Iceland after the winter had passed. In the waning year of 1330, it had become clear to me that I no longer wished to remain at Caerlaverock. I needed a new calling, and my deepest longing was to see my son Conor again.

Ever since my decision, I had felt a powerful force within me, drawing me back to my homeland like a magnet. In countless dreams, I imagined what it would be like to meet Conor and to introduce myself to him as his mother.

In the moment I forced myself onto that path, I became another person altogether. My days were once more filled with purpose. With grim determination, I drove myself through my combat drills, which I had allowed to fall somewhat into neglect. I meant to harden my body for the trials that lay ahead. Most often, I trained alone, for there was no one left with whom I could truly test myself.

The young men offered me nothing more than weary smiles when I pressed them to push themselves harder. The warriors with whom I had once fought at the Battle of Bannockburn were dead or broken by age. The young Scots possessed neither the energy nor the will to labour fiercely upon themselves. They boasted of their forebears, yet not one of them had the courage to prove himself in battle.

James's son, William Archibald, was the very embodiment of a generation loud of mouth yet feeble when it came to decisions. James had possessed more courage in his little finger than his illegitimate son carried in his entire body.

My old foreman, Lachlan McKay, had promised to govern Caerlaverock in my stead. Leaving the moated castle in Dumfries had not been easy, yet it was the right decision. My soul sensed the strengthening energy that had taken hold of me, and the force of will that had carried me ever since my fateful choice. Had I remained in my castle any longer, I would have died there after all, slumped in the chair that had already begun to hold me captive. There, I felt the spirits of death circling above my head, and my dark thoughts alone would have sufficed to end my life on the spot.

Now, I sat upon a boulder before the crackling solstice fire, ready for whatever might come. Beneath the din of the celebrating Irish, I cast the last dark spirits from my body. Let them return to hell, from whence they had come. Perhaps the same burden weighed upon Moira's soul. Perhaps she, too, had been haunted by those same dark imaginings.

The longing for my son and my homeland, Iceland, now consumed me so fiercely that I could scarcely endure it. My stay with Cathal had diverted me for a while from my purpose and granted me the time to bid farewell to him and to Moira. Mine was a journey without a certain outcome, almost like the eve of a battle. How often in life had we taken our leave under such uncertainty? For that very reason, saying farewell was especially hard for me.

One surprise still awaited me on that festive night. An old friend who had once brightened my life with her irresistibly sharp wit had come to Dunguaire from her self-chosen solitude to see me one final time. It was Winnie the dwarf, who suddenly stood before me with her family, revealed in the fierce glow of the blazing wooden cross.

In my surprise, I let my cup fall and sprang to my feet. I was left without words and overcome with emotion. Winnie had undertaken a long journey with her husband Padraig and their son Cailean to attend the festival and see me.

For some reason, Winnie wished to speak with me. I had been in Dunguaire so many times, and yet she had never once shown herself. Padraig and she must have something urgent weighing upon them.

The small woman with the bright blue eyes had once fled to Caerlaverock with Kalay, now long deceased, escaping from a travelling circus. Both had been forced to earn their living as street acrobats and had been beaten to the bone.

They accepted my offer to be trained by me and became the finest and bravest warriors at my side. More than once, I owed them my life.

At first, I did not recognise Winnie with her long grey hair, which had once been short and black, but when I had regained my composure, I recognised her unmistakable eyes in that crumpled face. Padraig bowed politely before me, and Winnie was so overcome with joy at our reunion that we simply embraced.

And then something happened that I had never expected. She began to sob uncontrollably, as though she had never been a feared warrior. Such an outpouring of emotion took me by surprise; I had never witnessed anything like it. It would not have taken much for me to begin weeping, too, had so many people not been witness to our meeting. Padraig stood beside her, visibly shaken by the sudden change in his wife. He looked at me in bewilderment, and I could only shrug in response. My heart beat strongly for brave Winnie.

Cailean stood beside Padraig on long, awkward legs, kneading his cap in his hands after removing it for me. He had inherited his mother's blue eyes and her raven-black hair, but beyond that, he bore little resemblance to a dwarf. He was a tall young man, smiling at me with open kindness.

"Cailean is my name, My Lady," he introduced himself politely, and I could almost feel that his mother must have told him much about me.

After gently disentangling the sobbing bundle of a woman from my arms and pressing my kerchief into her hand, I offered the boy my own.

"Lady Enja of Caerlaverock," I said, returning his smile. Quick-witted, he extended his right hand and clasped mine firmly. It was a calloused hand, marked by hard labour and a life of toil. The life of a hermit exacts a heavy toll. I offered Padraig my hand, too, though his expression remained unexpectedly grave.

Could people truly change so completely? With the birth of their only child, Winnie and Padraig seemed to have succeeded in beginning a new life. Winnie, at least, appeared to have shed much of her former boldness since our parting many years ago. The gravity now upon her suited her well.

"Lady Enja," she sighed after several deep breaths. "How wonderful it is to see you once more. It has been ..." she began, hesitated, and glanced up at her son, as though she had to reckon the years. "It has been nearly thirteen years since we last met. They were difficult years, during which I had to survive in isolation with Padraig and Cailean," she explained, accounting for their long absence. "But we chose this seclusion to give our child a chance. He was not meant to be exposed to people's mockery. It is enough that we have spent our lives being a source of amusement because of our stature. Cailean deserves a better life."

To hear such grave words from her moved me deeply. In that moment, Winnie's vulnerability laid itself bare before me. I leaned slightly forward and took her hands in mine. Lowering my voice so that none by the fire might overhear, I promised her, "As long as I live, Cailean shall be protected and trained by Cathal. If you so wish, he may make his life here in Dunguaire. Speak your desire, and I will grant it. I owe you more than one lifetime."

A timid smile stole across Winnie's round face. She clasped my hands, as though she had no wish to let them go.

"I place my son's fate into your hands, Lady Enja. I trust you, and I wish for him to live a normal life, accepted among the ranks of other young men. We have raised him to work, and he will be of great help. Cailean wishes to remain here in Dunguaire."

As his mother spoke, Cailean swallowed several times and twisted the cap in his hands. His parents must have lived a very withdrawn life over the past thirteen years; this might have been the first time he had ever stood among so many people. How strange it must have felt for him.

I looked at him with encouragement and nodded. "I will speak with Cathal and put in a good word for you, Cailean. I am certain the provincial king has need of a strong and capable young man. "Perhaps," and here I met the eyes of both his parents, "he may even learn a worthy trade by which he can earn his own living."

At last, Padraig smiled and looked at his wife with gratitude. I suspected it had been Winnie who had driven this idea and brought them here. Cailean was their only child. It must have been unbearably hard for them to leave him behind, even knowing that, under Cathal's protection, he could hope for a better future. I was deeply moved.

My heart grew suddenly heavy at the sight of the parents, now forced to part from their son. How often had families never seen their child again once they had journeyed to another land. or even to a neighbouring province. I had to swallow the lump rising in my throat. The three of them reminded me of why I longed to see Conor again.

"Tell me about your life in the wilderness," I urged the two of them, hoping to turn our thoughts elsewhere. "Do you not drive one another dreadfully mad out there?"

Now, they smiled, a little abashed, and told me of the small plot of land they tended far out in the Highlands. It was barren and cold, yet there, they had their peace with two head of cattle and ten sheep. Winnie and Padraig would return there.

Winnie stared into the fire beside me as it slowly died down, crackling and hissing as it faded. Little by little, people began to take their leave. Cathal and Moira were among the first to excuse themselves. The drunken ones fell asleep where they stood, while a few others staggered back towards the village, laughing. Up here, silence settled in, and only a handful remained until the fire collapsed into a bed of glowing embers.

Winnie, Padraig, and Cailean remained with me, and we shared stories from our time with Kalay. We laughed together and we mourned together. At some point, I told them of my plans to sail for Iceland. My two old friends met my intention with understanding. Winnie was among the very few who knew of Ragnar and Conor. She had been at Cathal's court with Padraig in the days when I had come to Moira seeking help.

It was an unexpectedly beautiful night, the hours slipping away in the blink of an eye, and at times it felt as though I had never been parted from Winnie and Padraig. Eventually, both the uisge beatha and our stories ran dry, and each of us set off once more on our paths. Cailean took a brave leave of his parents, who would sleep by the fire and depart at first light. The boy trudged the two miles back to Dunguaire behind my horse. It would be his first night, and my last, within those castle walls.

I saw it emerge on the horizon long before it drew near. The wooden ship, with the enormous carved dragon at the prow, looked exactly like the one that had lain in Galway's harbour in the autumn of 1318. For days, I had been waiting for its arrival. I raised my hand to shield my eyes from the glare, yet still, I had to squint. The sun reflected off the water before me, cutting sharply into my light-sensitive eyes. Down by the harbour, a stiff breeze blew full into my face.

Mina and I stood upon the quay of the harbour town of Galway. We had set out on the morning after the festival at Dunguaire. Summer stood at the threshold, and the weather showed us favour. Thus, we arrived in the Irish port town with dry feet. Taking leave of Moira and Cathal had not been easy, for I knew it would likely be the last time we would see one another, yet my chest was filled with thoughts of Conor, and so, in time, I also left my friends in Dunguaire behind, holding them fast within my heart.

Mina still had a pounding head from the drink, yet she had insisted on riding with me. She was a loyal soul, and for that I was grateful.

It was the very same ship as back then, without doubt. The fearsome prow with the dragon's maw gaping wide cleaved the water as the vessel drew ever closer to Galway Harbour, her sails billowed full by the wind. We had been waiting for two weeks now, and I was grateful that Mina had stayed at my side. At least I was not left alone with my restless thoughts.

It was on this very quay that I had first seen Mina as a small child. She had been stranded here as an orphan amid the chaos of war, begging for food. The emaciated girl had suddenly appeared beside my horse as I waited, consumed by rage, for Ragnar—determined to take our son from him. I had learned that he intended to sail to Iceland with Conor, back to his homeland, which had also been mine in childhood. Mina had distracted me then, and reminded me that I was still human capable of feeling and, above all, of motherly love.

A final encounter with my former lover had taken place here in Galway that had ended with Ragnar boarding the ship with Conor in his arms. My decision to let go had been born of love for my child. Conor loved his father, and in that unspeakable moment, I lost not only my child but also my heart. Looking back, I came to realise that I owed this change of heart to Mina. I had taken the little girl with me to Dunguaire, after all, to give her a family.

Here in Galway Harbour, the memories I had suppressed for all those years came rushing back. The cruel farewell to that sweet child's face, and the pale down upon his head. The surging force now drawing me towards Iceland had become a powerful pull, like a whirlpool in raging waters. I could no longer escape it by my will, and its speed almost stole my breath.

Old John was still the undisputed master of the harbour. He had been senile even back then; now, he must have been ancient beyond measure. Yet he still barked his orders in a hoarse voice at the pack of men forever hauling crates, sacks, and live animals aboard ships, or dragging them back onto land. I had chosen to leave my horse behind, unwilling to carry her across to an unknown land. Surely there would be fine riding beasts there, too, that I could purchase. I had brought silver enough for that.

Mina seemed a little uneasy, yet I could not tell whether it was the motion of the sea or the new land we were about to travel to. Either way, she was excited and brimming with memories, which she shared with me in a lively stream of words.

With a sullen gaze, I watched Old John, who was still redistributing the goods with remarkable precision. His left hand rested upon a staff, while the other pointed the way. Even back then, I had been fascinated by the efficiency of the Irish harbour. The old man knew exactly what he was doing.

"Should we sell our horses to the harbour master to cover the passage fee?" I heard Mina ask uncertainly. We had left our valuable horses behind in Dunguaire and were riding two Irish ponies we had intended to part with.

"Let us see what Old John will offer for our horses. I have no desire to pay more for the passage than need be."

I did not recall the harbour master as a man of honour. I could not have known that Old John would surprise me. Old John seemed not in the least impressed to see me back in the harbour; he greeted me as though I were an old friend.

"My Lady Douglas," he called out to me, as though I had been gone no more than ten days rather than twelve years. "What a joy it is to see you again!"

As he did so, he gave a bow that seemed remarkably graceful for a man of his years. There was still a great deal of vigour left in him.

"And if my rusted memory does not deceive me," he added, "this young lady must be Mina, the one who once made herself at home in my warehouse long ago. Welcome back to Galway Harbour!"

He swept out his right arm and let it circle from the town all the way to his warehouse, as though he were king of this place. And in truth, he most certainly was.

I would not have credited the good man with such a memory. How many people must he have seen pass through this place?

"I have not forgotten you, Lady Enja," the old man hastened to say, having clearly noticed my surprise and my mistrust. "Your fight with the dark-haired assassin, and later with your heart, will remain with me always. And despite your loss, you were generous to little Mina, and have plainly raised her well. How could I ever forget such things?"

I did not consider taking in a street child to be any great deed. Even so, I was touched by his kind words.

"Perhaps you might name us a fair price for the voyage to Iceland, good Master John? In return, we would leave our riding horses to you, if they are worth the pennies, in your reckoning."

Old John hesitated for a moment, weighing my offer. As he did, he appraised the two Irish ponies with a practised eye, animals the worth of which would scarcely cover the cost of the passage. Inwardly, I braced myself for a hard bargain, but I was soon proven wrong.

“I will gladly take the two riding horses as the fee for one person wishing to sail for Iceland aboard this ship.”

A dark foreboding spread within me, and I had already drawn breath to hurl my finest lines at Old John with phrases I had learned from traders in the Orient. I would not yield so easily, but he forestalled me.

“For your passage, Lady Enja, the exchange of the two horses will not suffice. But do not trouble yourself. The voyage was paid for long ago by the man you now follow.”

I let the air leave my lungs with a groan. The meaning of his words struck me like a bolt of lightning from a clear sky.

Ragnar! How had he known that I would head towards Iceland? How could he have been so certain?

Keep your composure, I admonished myself, and swallowed my anger. Was my life truly so predictable, or had Ragnar merely been wildly speculating?

He had truly managed to unsettle me. In my mind, I counted to three. I would not allow myself to falter before this old man. My clear-headed composure returned. At that time, Ragnar had been a man of means; he could easily have paid the fare from his considerable wages earned as a gallowglass. He had spoken to me often of his homeland and had planted the very idea of a journey to Iceland within me. Now, that seed had taken root. I had cut my anchor in Scotland and set my course for new shores. Perhaps I had simply underestimated how well he knew me.

With newly found resolve, I straightened my shoulders and replied to the seasoned harbour master, "I accept your offer. In doing so, I am not indebted to you, but to our friend who awaits me in Iceland. I shall settle that matter with him when I meet him there."

Old John gave a knowing nod, a disturbingly satisfied grin spreading across his face, and had us dismount from the horses. Our baggage was not great in quantity. Everything we could carry lay in the saddlebags, which we slung over our shoulders. Weapons, silver, and provisions were taken aboard the Nordic ship by dockhands and sailors. I left it to Old John to settle the fare for Mina and myself with the captain.

We spent the night aboard the ship in our berths; thus, we spared ourselves both the cost of a room at the Galway Inn and the din that the sailors and labourers raised in the taproom well into the night. It was a quiet night, carried on softly lapping waves that brushed against the hull in the harbour. Without the loud revelry of the crew enjoying themselves in the town, we found our blessed sleep.

The captain was not the one I remembered, yet this bearded seafarer, clad in a warm fur vest and woollen trousers, struck me as reliable all the same. Dark hair jutted from his head in every direction, and his beard was longer than the hair upon his scalp. Weathered by wind and storm, he was a stern fellow with little humour. But he clearly understood his ship.

With practised hands, the sailors freed the sail from the yard the following morning, and the captain slowly guided us out of the narrow strait. His great hands rested upon the helm as he manoeuvred us past rocks and shoals. He did not even require the aid of his mate, who was occupied with securing the cargo. This seafarer would bring us without trouble to the island that had once been my homeland.

"The voyage should take eight days, if the weather—and Odin—grant us their favour," I heard the captain grumble into his beard as we cast off from Galway.

Everyone called him Rollo, and since he understood Gaelic, we could speak with him a little. I resolved to learn as much as I could about this land in the far north, and above all, where I might find Ragnar and my son.

The farewell stirred old memories. Within me arose the sense that I would never return to Scotland or Ireland again. The realisation set my heart fluttering like the sails high above me. I felt a little cold, though it was a warm summer's day. The chill, however, was surely born of the uncertainty with which I had embarked upon this adventure. Would this be the final journey of my life? Did I wish to remain there, or should my bones be carried back to Caerlaverock? Once more came the thought of death. It pursued me, and I hastily shook it off.

Old John had watched me with a blend of pride and concern, as though he knew precisely what drove me towards Iceland. Mina rubbed her eyes several times as Ireland's northern coast shrank to a thin line in the grey of the horizon, only to vanish altogether. She stood beside me the entire time, staring sullenly at the receding shore.

Brave girl, I thought. She had done everything to please me, time and again pushing beyond her limits. I could think of nothing better than to draw the young woman into my arms, and she nestled gratefully against my breast as the sails filled and the ship creaked, gathering speed.

For a long while, the image of Old John waving remained before my eyes. The gulls shrieked their farewells, swooping low over our sails in hope of a scrap of food, yet even those troublesome companions of the seas fell away at last the farther we drew from the mainland and pressed on into the boundless vastness of the open sea.

The sails fluttered in the rising westerly wind. The prow ploughed through the water, setting the dragon with its gaping jaws dancing, just as I had seen it for so long in my dreams.

To travel into an unknown land as a woman without male companions was a perilous undertaking, yet I felt no fear, for my purpose was clear. All that I was, and all that I was capable of, I carried with me on this journey into the unknown. It was my path. Some might walk beside me, but none could walk it in my stead. I was a warrior, and I would see my son Conor again. Nothing and no one would stop me.

We reached Iceland ten days later. A storm had driven us somewhat off course, but Rollo proved equal to it. The voyage, however, took a harsh toll on my stomach, and Mina had to give me a few of my small pills. She refrained from taking any herself, for they induced sleep. Clearly, the little warrior had no intention of letting me rest unguarded.

I slept through most of our time at sea, overcome by the strength of its effect. I began to dream with unusual intensity of the green Highlands and the rugged mountains with their moss-covered rocks. I attributed it to a side effect of my medicine that thoughts of Caerlaverock drew me so powerfully back into the past.

Mina and I were grateful, after those long days at sea, to feel solid ground beneath our feet once more. I no longer cared what the place was called that Rollo made for so long as we were spared the need to balance upon swaying planks. From my conversations with the taciturn seafarer, I had learned little of the island, much to my frustration. Only this had become clear: Iceland had been brought under the Christian mission. Its people lived chiefly from fishing and kept goats and sheep. Without doubt, life there was demanding.

In truth, the captain guided the ship through every turbulence to a safe landing place. To call it a harbour would be generous, for the few people who received us on that side of the world had built nothing more than a simple wooden jetty into the water from which the ships were unloaded.

The sight that awaited us as we steered towards Iceland struck me to the core. From my childhood memories, I had always pictured this land as rich in colour, with lush green, turquoise waters and an azure sky shaping the image I had carried within me. But in truth, it was grey and bare. The trees stood black, as though scorched by fire, and the clouds above mirrored waters that were neither blue nor green. Iceland bore no resemblance to what I had expected, and it was bitterly cold, with the wind cutting hard.

The mountains rose in conical shapes, repeatedly broken by bizarre forms and colours. The sky merged into a milky cloud that gathered over the island. A diffuse, wavering air hung about the land, so dark it seemed as though it had been blackened with soot.

Even the sea here had turned black, as though it were the very antechamber of hell. My expectations of this land had been so much higher, but now, for the first time, I began to doubt my mission.

Mina followed me hesitantly onto the jetty that was overgrown with damp algae. Children bundled thickly in furs gathered around us curiously, repeatedly pointing towards a church that rose in the distance like a foreign body from the bizarre line of mountains. How could it be otherwise; it, too, was built of black stone.

One of the older children seized my arm excitedly and spoke to me in the local tongue. Irritated, I shook the insistent boy off. The intent behind his gesture unsettled me, though his face was flushed with eagerness. Again and again, he uttered a word I could scarcely translate. During my time with Ragnar, the language of the Icelanders had grown faintly familiar to me once more, yet I could not speak it.

"Christ!" they shouted over one another. "Christ!"

Of course, I understood. They were speaking of the marking upon my brow. An inverted cross, the sign of my bondage. It had become my mark of recognition, and now it seemed to stir the tempers of the island's people.

"Pay it no mind, My Lady Douglas," explained Rollo, usually so sparing with words, as he climbed down from the ship behind us. "The cross symbolises the Church of the Christians, who forced a new religion upon the people here through their priests. Thus, the belief in a single, all-encompassing God came to our island."

The captain had already begun to bring the goods ashore with his mate, and some of the older boys helped him with the task. It was the mission of all clergymen who travelled out into the world to spread the word of God. Here, on this island, they had also left their mark.

"Why do the people take issue with the cross upon my brow?" I asked warily. I was somewhat irritated, no doubt a consequence of the hardships of the journey. Once, a priest had explained to me that the inverted cross was a Christian symbol. One who was crucified upside down understood the power of the sign; no disciple had deemed himself worthy to die in the same manner as Jesus. It was a mark of humility. For me, however, it had become a personal emblem of rebellion and power.

"Not all Icelanders agree with the monks' mission," the captain remarked gruffly. "Especially when it comes to pacifying the tribes."

His sceptical gaze lingered on the church, which, from a distance, appeared so peaceful. His eyes looked weary. Like Mina, he had slept little on this journey, but we had no horses as yet, and I instructed Mina to see to it. She went off with the mate to one of the fenced meadows to choose suitable animals.

Meanwhile, Rollo's words would not leave me. It had not occurred to me that a faith other than the Word of the Lord might be practised in Iceland, and yet, I had wrestled with the Christian faith for a long time. Had I not once believed in many different gods myself? My memories had faded.

"Have the people of this island not converted to Christianity?" I asked the seasoned skipper, who had already turned his attention back to his ship. With practised hands, he fastened the ropes to the wooden posts set along the pier for that very purpose.

He paused briefly, studied me with a measuring gaze, and then replied, "Religion and power are two things fiercely contested on this island. Stay on this side, close to the monks, and nothing will happen to you."

With that, he seemed to have said all he intended to say, and I turned away in frustration. At least his mate managed to procure two riding animals for us at little cost, much like those bred back in Scotland. They were small horses, which Mina led behind her. Their colour was peculiar, almost milky white, with a dark stripe running through their manes and down their tails. To my eye, they appeared sturdy and well-suited to the land. No doubt these horses had once been brought here by the first settlers and had since adapted perfectly to wind and weather.

I drew my cloak tighter around me. A cold wind whistled near the sea, chilling my body to the bone. I took a pelt from one of the saddlebags and draped it over my shoulders. I also pulled a cap over my head to cover my ears. For a summer's day, this weather was a rather miserable welcome.

Weary and spent from the long journey, we set off towards the church with our newly acquired horses. It looked welcoming enough to offer us, perhaps, a warm bed for the night. The thought of sleeping at last without the ceaseless roll of the sea beneath us lifted my spirits. When I looked into Mina's face, I saw that she had grown thin in just those few days. She had taken little more than water. The poor child had worried greatly over me. It was time for a proper meal that did not consist of salted herring. My stomach growled in unmistakable agreement.

The priest could scarcely trust his eyes. The women who came into his church were strange to behold. Brother Cornelius had seen a great many things in this region, yet these two strangers left a most singular impression.

He clutched the rosary at his leather belt and crossed himself, steeling his soul for the encounter with the tall warrior woman and her companion. They came in peace, the younger woman told him in simple Gaelic, the tongue of traders. Even so, he was grateful for the scapular resting over his tunic. That consecrated cloth would shield him from the fires of hell. Cornelius's hands had turned cold, and a trickle of icy sweat ran down his spine. Not even the presence of the region's clan chiefs had ever filled him with such dread as did the sight of this woman.

The warrior bearing the mark of the inverted cross upon her brow carried something deeply unsettling about her. Her aura reminded him of a predator. She was at least as dangerous as a she-wolf guarding her young. The gaze of her crystal-clear blue eyes did not leave him for a single moment as she advanced towards him down the aisle of the small church. The younger woman, who also wore a surcoat of arms, appeared far less threatening.

The tall woman wore black boots and fine cloth beneath a leather fighting coat. She had not troubled herself to lay aside her weapons, as custom would have it. Nor had she removed the cloak of warm wolf's fur. Only her cap had been taken off, in deference to the Lord. Silvery-white hair had come loose in wild strands from the knot at the back of her head.

When she dropped to her knees before the altar and crossed herself, a great weight fell from Cornelius's heart. Despite her martial bearing, she appeared at least to be Christian. The younger woman crossed herself, too. Unlike the leader, she kept glancing at him repeatedly, as though afraid of doing something wrong.

With a low groan, the woman straightened again, as though her very bones ached. Slowly, she turned and surveyed the simple church. At last, her intent gaze settled upon Cornelius, and his pulse leapt once more. Thus far, the mysterious stranger had not spoken a single word.

"My name is Lady Enja of Caerlaverock," she introduced herself politely.

Cornelius was taken aback by the fact that she conducted her speech in Latin. In a place like this, at the very edge of the world, such a thing was highly unusual. What could someone like her possibly want here?

"We have come a long way from Ireland and are in search of lodging. Would you be so kind as to provide a warm meal and a chamber for myself and my companion? We shall show our gratitude in a fitting manner." As she spoke, she tapped the purse at her belt.

Indeed, the monk surmised that she must hail from a wealthy house, judging by the confidence with which she carried herself. The silver brooch upon her cloak, the finely wrought belt, and her costly garments all suggested a person of consequence. It took Cornelius a moment to recover both his voice and his manners.

"Forgive my astonishment, My Lady. My name is Brother Cornelius, and I was unaware that such an esteemed visitor was to be expected within our humble walls. Nor do I know what brings you to us." His curiosity was plainly evident. "But, of course, I can offer a chamber for you and your companion. Nor shall there be any lack of a warm meal."

His fellow brothers would surely not object to sharing their meagre meal with the two women, even though food on the island was scarce. Hunger and cold ruled here. Cornelius depended on the few shipments the Norwegian king permitted. Were the Icelanders not such skilled fishermen, there would be little more each day than what the fields and the northern motherland could provide.

For a moment, he believed the woman must have lost her way. In the next, he thought he discerned a certain sense of purpose in her eyes. She was searching for something—or someone—of that he was certain.

Cornelius was in the prime of his years, and carried out his duties faithfully, in keeping with his vows. For sixteen years now, at his request, he had served this small parish. Born here, he was on good terms with the local people. Iceland had been under Christian mission for more than three hundred years, yet it's natives remained a warlike folk, scarcely restrained by a distant king. And the influence of old rites and traditions was impossible to overlook. Even Cornelius was obliged to tolerate and respect the visible signs of pagan ritual.

"Tell me," he began cautiously, "what draws you to this harsh land? You appear educated and well-placed. Surely you have travelled from far away. If it is something you seek here, then you will find nothing in Iceland but filth, blood, vengeance, and superstition."

Frustration rang clearly in his words, and the woman's face showed surprise. One brow arched upward. Only then did it dawn on him that he had voiced the truth bluntly and without grace. The harshness of life here had rubbed off on his manners. She was surely not pleased by what he had said.

"Pray, forgive my bluntness," he attempted by way of explanation. "I have lived in this land for too long now. I am no longer accustomed to the company of ladies."

She answered his submissive attempt to soften his words with nothing more than a cool smile.

It became clear to him that she had little patience for pleasantries. Before him stood an unusual woman who had passed the middle of her life, yet the body beneath her surcoat was that of a finely trained warrior. Her air of self-assurance taught Cornelius fear outright. He sensed the arrogance she directed at him. Her full lips had briefly tightened, her dark brows drawing together just beneath the black cross upon her brow, as though she were displeased. Her gaze remained fixed upon him.

"Well then, it seems we have come to the right place. The person we are seeking fits this world precisely."

Her voice carried a chill that matched the glint in her eyes. In the blink of an eye, it became clear to Cornelius that Lady Enja would bring no small amount of trouble with her.

Chapter 13

Iceland, May 1331

The wind whistled straight through our clothes, as though we had made no true attempt to guard ourselves against it. What, then, must winter be like in this land, if even spring came so cold and unforgiving?

"Scotland is at least as unforgiving in spring," Mina continued the thread of my thoughts. She fared no better than I did, her face buried deep in a scarf of grey wool. What was meant as comfort left me with a quiet ache of longing. No doubt Mina, too, felt a touch of homesickness for Caerlaverock. And yet our great adventure drove us onward.

I drew my fur cloak tighter and surveyed the land from my horse's back. The bizarre rock formations of the surrounding mountains had given way to flatter hills dusted with patches of green moss. Fascinating as the black hue of the sandy ground was, it struck me as sombre and dramatic. Foul-smelling pools and smoking vents felt like harbingers of hell. These were glowing mountains that spat fire and growled. Streams of molten heat poured from some, devouring everything in their path as they crept towards the valleys below. This place radiated a violence as ancient as the earth itself. The landscape was shaped by raw power rising from deep within the ground, endlessly forging new rivers, mountains, and lakes. Gigantic fountains of water erupted from subterranean springs. In no other land did air, water, fire, and earth lie so closely bound. Here in Iceland, they still seemed locked in contest with one another.

At first glance, the land seemed uninhabitable, yet upon a second look, it revealed something utterly fascinating. Where the earth was not gnawed raw by fire or buried beneath scree and sulphur, colourful plants ran wild, as though sprung from a fairy realm. Moss and flowers of vivid pink stood out like splashes of paint. Everywhere we saw animals akin to our deer and small foxes, though cloaked in dark fur. Along the shore we discovered strange birds with orange beaks. They could not fly, yet they were skilful divers.

The land was, thankfully, blessed with a remarkable abundance of fish in its seas, rivers, and lakes. During our voyage by ship, we had watched countless whales and seals and vast shoals of fish. In the sky, gulls and swallows had taken turns, darting through the air in strange formations. On land, I noticed a few barren farmsteads, scattered far apart. Only rarely did I see sheep and ponies penned within small stone enclosures, enduring the forces of nature and chewing their hay. Time and again, we came upon simple wooden huts or byres marked by the stone walls that traced the boundaries of their holdings. These were the only signs that human life existed here.

The route described by Cornelius led us along the western coast and past vast mountain ranges that reared up in the heart of the great island. No pass crossed them, for these mountains were in constant motion, ceaselessly spewing fire from their glowing throats. We kept to the only path of note, worn just enough to follow, as the priest had described. It took several days, and we quickly learned that nights were better spent in caves or abandoned byres than on open grassland, or worse still, upon the shore. On this side of the island, the weather turned harsher still. Storms lashed over us, bringing driving rain and even hail. We did not let it deter us but stood fast against the hostile elements.

The farther Mina and I rode north, the more the hostile climate seemed to ease its grip. Yet even here, the vegetation left much to be desired. Only a handful of shrubs and trees dared withstand the harsh conditions. For a farmer, it must have been a hard fate indeed to secure enough fodder for the long and brutal winter.

Now, after almost six days, the tracks grew ever rockier and more uneven in a sign that these paths were seldom used. Our two ponies trudged on uncomplaining through wind and weather, as though nothing could halt them. Nor could it halt me. I felt myself already close to my son, and that belief gave me the strength to keep moving, even as Mina shook from head to toe like a drenched dog. I had no mind to heed her discomfort now; my goal lay within reach.

"The village you seek, my lady," Cornelius' words still echoed in my ears, "lies in the north of the island. The people there still cling to the ancient ways of the Vikings who first settled this land. We men of God are not welcome among them." At that, Cornelius had sighed. "They continue to worship the Norse gods Odin, Thor, and Loki."

He had not let us ride out the next morning without a warning.

"The clan leader of the Nordic province is called Arnulf Johansson. He is a dangerous man who seized power through violence. You will likely find your Ragnar, the man you are searching for, there, if he still lives. In the ceaseless conflicts, many ambitious men have already tested themselves against Johansson. They all lost." The priest's voice carried a clear note of clear frustration.

I felt compassion for him, for he had grown weary of the ceaseless outbreaks of violence and the turning away from Christian norms. The harsh conditions of life caused even the God-fearing to doubt.

"Give Arnulf my regards. Tell him that God will be waiting for him on this side, and so will I."

Cornelius walked alongside my horse as though he could scarcely believe that I was truly setting out.

"Do you hear?" he had shouted up.

I had heard him well enough, yet I stared straight ahead.

"Give Arnulf the Papar's regards. That is what they call us men of God here on the island."

I glanced back at him once more and raised my hand in farewell. Lines of worry were etched upon his brow, and the wind billowed his habit.

"I shall show him the love of God, dear Cornelius!" I had called through the cutting wind, urging my horse into a faster pace to deliver the poor man from his fate.

At last, he stopped, breathing hard, and waved after us in helpless farewell. "Go with God …" I heard him call.

By then, we were already too far away to catch any further words.

I cast a grim glance at Mina, who followed behind me on her horse. The warrior, usually so full of life, had grown alarmingly quiet since our departure from Galway. Perhaps my resolve had made her realise that there was no road leading back. Mina had sworn her loyalty to me; she was devoted and true. With firm conviction, she had chosen this journey, yet now, I sensed her hesitation, fear of the unknown, and doubts about my mission. Mina was young, with her whole life still before her.

I, on the other hand, had nothing left to lose. For a long time, I had not felt it, yet a part of my soul was missing. There gaped a hollow where love had once made its home. With James's death, I understood that it had to be filled. I felt the love for a son I had never been allowed to keep.

Iceland was not only the homeland of my forefathers, but Conor's, too. This time, I would not retreat. This time, everything would be different. Cornelius had seen Ragnar and the boy upon their arrival many years ago. They had stayed under his roof. He clearly remembered the child with the mismatched eyes, one as blue as mine, and the other flecked with brown, a whim of nature. By that sign, I would recognise Conor even now.

From Cornelius, I also knew that Ragnar had intended to return to the village of Akureyri, the place of his birth. I suspected it was the very village where I had grown up with my family. Akureyri stirred something strange within my memory, its name echoing in my mind. Might I find someone of my family there still?

Uncertainty gnawed at me. According to the holy man, Akureyri lay sheltered within a sea inlet known as Eyjafjörður, a long, drawn-out fjord that stilled the water's surface until it lay as calm as a lake. Vaguely, the image of my farewell to the village of my childhood rose before my inner eye—how my father and mother had sent me away. I remembered my sister, Jalla, clinging to our father's leg as they waved to me for the last time. Thousands of people, or maybe only a handful, had lined the paths and the shores of the bay. The drumming of the musicians still echoed in my mind, the rhythm lingering within me like an ever-present pulse.

Tam-tam, tara-tam.

Our ship had moved through the water as if guided by ghostly hands. Its sails must have been set, yet it glided soundlessly across the waves. No noise reached my ears, as though they had been stopped by unseen fingers. We had been bound for the active mountain Hekla where, at the age of six, I was to be sacrificed to the Norse gods to appease their wrath. The volcano lay on the southern side of the island. The village must have sent a ship there to carry the offerings to the foot of the mountain.

When the great wooden vessel carrying my mother and me had sailed out into the open sea, it was caught by a storm. It danced upon the waves, and we were given over to the relentless play of the forces of nature.

My memory failed at the very moment we were dragged beneath the surface by the pull of the sinking ship. My mother had bound me to herself so as not to lose me, and she truly managed to swim with me back to the surface. There, I came to myself again as she untied me. My mother knew she would die, for in the icy sea there was no salvation. With her last strength, she placed me upon a floating wooden crate before the waters drew her body down into the endlessly deep abyss.

My hand reached for the black onyx at my throat without conscious thought, set in silver and hanging from a leather cord. Since childhood, I had worn it as the sole clue to my origin. It was the symbol of my clan, as Ragnar had revealed to me, and the mark of a clan leader. Svartur, he had called the stone. Ragnar suspected that my father had been the chieftain of the village. By tradition, he would have been required to sacrifice one of his daughters to honour the gods. What I had not understood then has since become painfully clear. The sinking of the ship had taken my mother's life, but it had spared me a far darker fate.

Since my arrival in Iceland, I had felt a strange power emanating from the stone like a second pulse racing through my body. Perhaps it was only my imagination, yet just as the onyx lay in my hand, I, too, seemed to merge with the raw, untamed land. Here I felt welcomed and sheltered, as though I had returned to my mother's womb. When I closed my eyes, I sensed the spell of this uncanny island working upon me. The trembling of the ground and the humming of the air were like a thousand bees swarming all around. This island spoke, just as it had to our forefathers, through the mouths of ancient souls. And I surrendered to it with all my senses. I understood its peculiar language. Images and thoughts dissolved into a single wild dance. Tam-tam, tara-tam.

We were just crossing the crest of a mountain ridge when Mina's call tore me from my thoughts. Excitedly, she pointed towards several distant shapes that looked like a cluster of huts. There, far off, a settlement had suddenly emerged in the clear light of the sun. Today, the weather had finally eased, and we felt the first warming rays of spring upon our skin.

The roofs were overgrown with grass and moss, making them hard to discern from a distance, yet we saw smoke rising, and I fancied I caught the scent of burning peat upon the air. Vaguely, I could also make out people going about their work.

Had we already reached Akureyri? Cornelius had estimated our journey to last a week, so it was possible. Moreover, the cluster of houses matched the description of the place the man of God had given before our departure. Beyond the huts, a bay took shape, where the villagers' boats rocked gently upon the water.

Mina reined in her pony, and I checked mine to take in the beauty of the moment. All the while, I struggled to master my rising excitement. Had I reached my destination? Would I finally find Conor down there? Everything looked so peaceful that I dared to hope he had lived a happy life here with his father.

My heart leapt in strange spirals, and butterflies danced in my belly. I had last felt this when James had kissed me for the very first time. I drew a deep breath and listened, yet all I caught was a distant waterfall roaring through one of the many rocky crevices. Water, like fire, was a constant companion on this island.

Mina and I exchanged a glance that held both joy and excitement. We gathered the reins and urged our horses closer. Now, I also noticed movement on a hill not far from us. Children were playing there, but they suddenly froze mid-motion. Startled by our presence, they ran screaming towards the village. Good. The sooner our arrival was announced, the quicker I would learn who held authority here. I could not have known that we were already awaited.

Arnulf Johansson merely gave a grim nod when the children informed him of the arrival of the two women. The powerful warrior betrayed no sign of whether the visit pleased him. So, Ragnar Sigurdsson had been right after all. Conor's mother had returned, and she had not come in peace, so Ragnar had assured him. She had come to reclaim her son.

The clan leader of the village of Akureyri knew no fear, least of all of a woman. And yet, he had seen the respect in Ragnar's eyes whenever he spoke of Enja. Even after many years and an ice-cold attempt on his life, the war-scarred giant still spoke of that warrior as though she were a force of nature. She seemed to be something extraordinary, and now, she was coming, just as Ragnar had foreseen.

Arnulf's wife, by contrast, visibly flinched at the news. She knew all too well that her sister, Enja, was the daughter of the former leader. Their father, Leif Eriksson, had once ruled as chieftain from the very seat Arnulf now occupied, and had eaten at the same table.

Enja's family, and the greater part of the villagers, had perished in the devastating volcanic eruption of the year 1300, choked by ash and days of unbroken darkness. Some of the villagers had managed to flee into a cave in time and endure until the sun finally pierced the clouds once more.

Arnulf had been among the young men who had managed to take refuge in that shelter with a handful of children. Like him, his wife had survived the catastrophe as a little girl. Thunder had rolled again and again, the ground had trembled, and the earth had shaken. They lived on berries and small wild animals he had caught in traps. When the days began to clear, they set out for the place where the huts of Akureyri had once stood. Lava and scree had levelled the dwellings to the ground. Only a few had survived the eruption, the darkness that followed, and the cold. They had realised that the village's only great ship was missing. Some of the inhabitants had clearly fled with it into the open sea. In time, they, too, had returned. Enja's father had not been among them.

As a strong young man, it had been easy enough for Arnulf to take the helm as clan leader in those days. Together with the survivors, he began rebuilding the village for the roughly eighty people comprising men, women, and children. They had unearthed what remnants they could, so long as they had not been consumed by the molten heat and founded a new village community.

To legitimise his rule, Arnulf had married Enja's sister Jalla a few years later; she had been twenty-one at the time. Through that union he had claimed the seat of the forefathers, leaving no doubt as to his ambitions. Conflicts with other clans, and even within the village itself, he crushed with brutal severity. He was a formidable warrior, a fact he proved in countless single combats.

In time, even the last of the traditionalists fell silent, those who had wished to see a different leader seated upon the carved wooden chair on which he had just taken his place for the evening meal.

Jalla now looked at him with fear in her eyes. Her sister had returned and would demand her rightful place. Jalla was forty-three by then, yet she had lived her entire life in fear of her husband and his power. But she also feared her sister and the conflict her appearance would unleash. Jalla had always longed for calm and peace. The looming escalation robbed her of sleep.

"Promise me you will not kill her, Arnulf," she whispered to him now, so softly that no one else in the room could hear.

The clan leader was angered by her interference in his affairs. His face twisted as though he had tasted something bitter. She was likely afraid that someone might overhear her plea.

"She is my sister," she whimpered, "the only survivor of my family. I will tell her that she must leave, go back to where she came from. She will believe me when I tell her that Conor is safe."

A faint tremor in her voice betrayed how difficult it was for her to make such a request of her husband.

Arnulf growled like a bear with an itchy hide. His coarse, rugged face was crowned by a thick, flowing beard, and his red-blond hair was bound into a braid. He had thrown a cloak over his shoulders, stitched together from various scraps of fur. His feet were shod in wrapped fur shoes, and his trousers were woven from the rough wool the women spun from sheep fleeces. Arnulf looked like the Vikings of his ancestors' tales, and he was proud to uphold their traditions. Thus, he resisted the priest's attempts to impose a new faith. Cornelius had no place here.

"If Ragnar is right in his prophecy, Enja will refuse to leave without Conor. You know exactly what that means."

Arnulf needed to say nothing more to bring tears to Jalla's eyes, yet that was no great feat. Since the miscarriage of her only daughter, she had become a bundle of raw nerves. Arnulf pursed his lips in disapproval; his woman seemed fragile to him now, with her tearful manner and constant fear.

Ever since Ragnar had returned with Enja's child, she had cared for the boy. He had become like a son to her, and although she knew neither her sister nor her motives, she feared for the fragile balance of her family life. Arnulf had declared Conor to be his own son. That would not sit well with Enja.

Jalla's face tightened, the corners of her mouth twitching. She was clearly locked in a terrible struggle of conscience. Even to Arnulf it had become apparent how deeply she feared the coming encounter.

"No," she gasped in desperation, a nervous hiccup breaking her words. "No, not that. I will not let Conor go with her. Enja will have to understand …"

She got no further. Arnulf had already risen and was striding towards the exit of the great hall. The clan leader's seat was a vast longhouse with room for more than a hundred people. Plain wooden benches and fur cushions were scattered throughout. Only his table bore fixed benches for his innermost circle of warriors. They were all battle-hardened men at his side, wild fighters, resolved to anything. Without being summoned, four of his retinue rose and followed him as his bodyguard.

"Let the woman go to the dogs," the powerful chieftain muttered to himself as he left the hall.

With a simple hand gesture, Arnulf readied his bodyguard outside the house for the arrival of the stranger, to whom he intended to make it clear—here and now—that Conor was no longer her child. The young man was now, officially, his son.

Conor was another pillar of the power he had built within this clan. Arnulf had come from a simple fisherman's family. Now, he was the husband of the clan leader's daughter, and his foster son carried that bloodline. No. A woman like Enja would not take that from him now.

With self-assured poise, he straightened before the entrance to the longhouse. With his imposing height and compact build, he cut a fearsome figure, and Arnulf knew it well.

Should Enja demand her son's return, he had already decided he would eliminate her. First, he needed to learn what she truly knew and what demands she intended to make. After that, he would either kill her or send her back to Ireland on a ship. The choice would be Enja's. Perhaps he would even pretend to let her leave, only to have her killed later, for Jalla's sake.

"Let us see what this woman thinks she can accomplish," he said to Thor, who had taken his place beside him. At a single gesture, his bodyguard would dispose of Enja. This woman, Arnulf was convinced, could pose no problem whatsoever for a clan leader. Thor merely nodded with quiet understanding.

Arnulf's gaze settled upon the village's main square, where the well stood from which the women drew their water. Now, the place lay swept bare. Even the children, who usually tumbled in the dirt of the fields, had been pulled indoors by their mothers. Many of the villagers peered cautiously from behind their tents and wooden huts. They sensed that something threatening was about to unfold.

Slowly, more henchmen took up their positions. The quick-witted and powerful men lined up beside him and folded their arms. Like an impenetrable wall, they formed a shield around their leader—a cuirass of muscle and steel. In Arnulf's mind, that should be more than enough to drive off even such an extraordinary warrior on the spot.

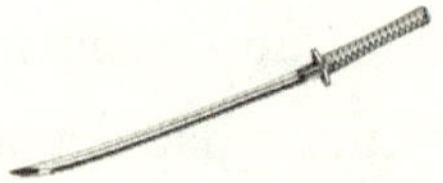

An uncanny stillness lay over the place as we rode into the village along the black gravel path. The noisy children who had announced our arrival from afar were gone. It was as though the people of Akureyri were holding their breath.

Even I felt a flicker of unease as our two horses trudged into the settlement Cornelius had described. Tents made of animal hides, simple stone huts with grass-covered roofs, and only a few wooden buildings bore witness to how the early seafarers had settled this land. The Icelanders had no right to independent trade. Since the Norwegian king allowed only scant supplies of food to reach them, they relied on the pelts of wild animals and the raw materials gained from whaling. They lived chiefly on fish, sheep, goats, and horses, as well as chickens, and geese. And yet, this village gave the impression that nothing was lacking.

I saw piles of stacked hides and the frames used for skinning animals. A small forge, its chimney still smoking, must have been in use until quite recently, yet it stood abandoned, as though the entire village had fallen into a strange slumber. Only now and then did a hen cluck or a sheep bleat. The inhabitants had all withdrawn in fear.

Mina sat bolt upright in the saddle. Her face was pale and solemn. Her childlike expression had vanished as she stared straight ahead, tense and tight-lipped. When she sensed my sideways glance, she attempted a smile, but it did not quite take shape. I would have liked to give her a measure of confidence, yet at that moment I, too, felt uncertain. What awaited us?

At the centre of the settlement stood a well of black stone and a half-filled bucket of water set aside in haste. The tracks in the dirt spoke of the lives of many people who had all vanished. It was a strange welcome indeed.

Before a great longhouse stood a stout warrior, legs braced wide, his arms folded across his chest. His authority stood out unmistakably from the other men he had gathered around him. At his shoulder, an ornate silver brooch fastened his pitch-black cloak as it billowed in the wind. Various weapons were thrust into his leather belt. The grim fighters flanking him completed the picture; the look on their faces boded no good. Then, suddenly, more men emerged from the longhouse, leaving no doubt as to what they thought of my arrival.

My stomach felt as though I had swallowed a brick, and my hands were damp upon the reins. I was not one to feel fear, so why did this moment unsettle me so deeply? Before me stood some fourteen men who looked as though hell itself had spat them out, and at their centre loomed their leader, Arnulf.

I did not feel fear but the immediacy of the threat, and I cursed my naivety. Cornelius, and even the taciturn shipmaster Rollo, had warned me.

They had been waiting for me. Arnulf, so I identified the man with the silver brooch, had, for reasons unknown to me, known that I would come.

With a brief tug on the leather reins, I brought the pony to a halt. Mina stopped her horse directly beside me. With a keen glance, I made sure that Ragnar was not among the crowd. The men remained calculatingly calm, and Arnulf appeared to be giving me a thorough appraisal. Then, he spat, and placed his hand upon the hilt of the dagger at his belt. It was a gesture of threat, nothing more.

For Mina, that alone seemed enough to set her nerves on edge. The girl shifted restlessly in the saddle.

"You know who I am?" I asked bluntly in the local tongue to shatter the nerve-racking silence. "You have been expecting me."

Arnulf merely nodded. "Ragnar always warned us about you, Enja. He said you would appear here one day, searching for your son. But he is not here. Conor has fled with Ragnar, that mangy dog."

The clan leader growled menacingly as he spoke. Why did I have the feeling that he was lying to me? Was it the greasy grin, or the strange emphasis when he spoke Ragnar's name? I did not believe him. Did he truly think he could be rid of me more quickly this way?

"Then I trust you will not object if I avail myself of your hospitality," I said politely as I swung down from the saddle. Mina followed my lead. Her face had taken on the colour of milk. I saw clearly how her hands trembled as she took the reins from me. She would tend to the horses.

"We have ridden a long way to see Conor, and I will not leave without making certain that he is well, Arnulf."

The tension was now almost tangible. I gave no sign of the relief I felt at knowing Conor was still alive. By now, I was berating myself as a fool for riding into Akureyri unprepared. The hope of seeing my son had clouded my instincts as a warrior. I had stirred a hornets' nest, and the creatures were buzzing around my head, just like my thoughts.

All the warning signs were there. Still, I ignored the obvious and walked towards Arnulf with steady steps. Attack was the best defence. The leader had to feel secure in his clear numerical superiority.

Anger was etched across Arnulf's face. It was not a pleasing countenance. Straggling strands of hair stuck out in every direction, though his head hair was braided, as if he slept with it still bound. His dark beard was ragged and uneven. His eyes sat deep in their sockets and his nose was broad and pitted with heavy pores. Arnulf's mouth was pressed into a narrow slit.

He stepped towards me in a threatening manner and planted his hands on his hips. "You are not welcome here, Enja."

That much was clear to me. "I will not leave before I have seen Conor, Arnulf. Do not think for a moment that I travelled this far only to turn around at your door."

My voice cooled by several degrees, and courtesy was no longer on the table.

Arnulf now stood directly before me. I squared myself against him, met his gaze without flinching, and set my coldest expression to underscore my words. No, I did not fear him.

With a sideways step, I tried to slip past him into the great longhouse. His arm shot out to block me. I halted at once. Only a few inches now separated me from his face, which I fixed with an angry stare.

"Do not dare lay a hand on me, Arnulf!"

So close to my goal, I would not turn back. Perhaps he sensed my resolve, for he suddenly yielded and drew his arm away. A faint flush crept into his face, as though he were ashamed to deny a guest her right to hospitality.

With clenched fists, I strode past him into the great house that served the people of Akureyri as their gathering place. Here, anyone could find food or shelter for guests. I was aware of that, and it was precisely why I meant to enter straight into the lion's den.

Inside, I paused briefly to let my eyes adjust to the darkness. I made out several fires burning in wrought-iron braziers, casting not only light but also warmth. The longhouse was nearly as vast as the great hall of Caerlaverock, though its ceiling hung lower. An intricate framework of wooden beams supported the thatched roof. There were no windows. The rear of the hall was partitioned with animal hides, where the clan leader likely lived with his family. At the centre stood a large table, with space for at least twenty men seated on two long benches. Elsewhere in the hall lay only fur-covered seats stuffed with straw. The floor was hard-packed, dried earth. The air carried the mingled scents of smoke, metal, and men's sweat.

The first woman I caught sight of was a maid with a broom. She had been cleaning when I burst in. The poor kitchen girl looked up in fright and fled into the partitioned space at the back. I paid her no heed and seated myself on a bench at the table. I pulled a cushion beneath me, my body aching from the long hours in the saddle. Once, I would not have felt such riding, but today, I was sore.

Behind me, I heard Arnulf enter. He must have exchanged a few words with his men outside the house. I caught the hiss of his hurried whispers and felt the draught as the leather door covering was pulled aside. I did not need to turn to know that

Arnulf was moving towards the table. His footsteps thudded heavily against the hard floor. With a snort, he dropped into the seat opposite me, and even the table shuddered slightly.

He instructed the maid to bring food and some mead diluted with water. As it still contained alcohol, I was tempted to wave it away. I refrained, however, unwilling to provoke my host further. Even so, I would not touch a drop of it, and instead welcomed the stew the maid set before me upon the greasy wooden table. The fragrant blend of meat and fish had clearly been simmering in the cauldron all day. It stood off to one side above a hearth, together with several barrels of the honey wine. Everything here was simple, yet the food tasted excellent.

Just as I dipped my spoon into the bowl, Mina entered. With ill humour, she informed me that she had stabled the horses in a wooden shed and given them some hay. Judging by her sullen expression, no one had offered her any help.

At the scent of the food her mood visibly brightened. She sat down beside me and eagerly set upon the stew that was brought to her at once.

Arnulf had said nothing the entire time. The leader merely glared darkly at me, then at Mina. That, too, was a way of driving guests away.

"Where is Ragnar?" I finally continued the sparse exchange, slipping a heaped spoonful into my mouth. My clipped sentences were owed to my limited command of the language. Mina kept eating in silence, for she did not understand the foreign sounds at all.

"I do not know," my counterpart replied, leaning back with deliberate ease. "I have not seen him for months. Who knows where he is roaming."

In my mind, the face of the man who had fathered Conor during our brief affair took shape. My son may not have been born of love, yet I had never once regretted bringing him into this world.

Ragnar had abducted the boy from Cathal's stronghold of Dunguaire when he was just one year old. I managed to confront him at the harbour of Galway before he set sail for Iceland, but there, on the quay, I quickly realised that the child felt no bond with me as his mother. As painful as it was, I had been forced to let him go with his father to Iceland.

I had pushed Ragnar from my thoughts. I had first met the mercenary in a monastery in Ireland, and he had first told me of my homeland. With his help, I relearned the language of my country, and he awakened in me the notion of returning here one day. Without him, I would not be here now. Without him, I would not have Conor. In that sense, Ragnar had shaped my fate.

"If Ragnar and Conor are travelling alone, someone must have seen them. The island is not so vast that their whereabouts could have escaped your notice."

I underscored my words with a touch of expression and gesture to make myself understood. Arnulf's gaze lingered on my face for a moment before he replied.

"The caves and coves of Iceland are many. He could be hiding anywhere."

"Why would he hide?" I asked in return.

Arnulf made a dismissive gesture with his hand. "We had a quarrel."

I would get nowhere like this. Arnulf would never tell me the truth. Tomorrow, I would have to search on my own. Someone must surely have seen Ragnar. He stood out wherever he went, even among the outlaws of the island.

Just as I was about to press him further, one of the hides stretched between floor and ceiling stirred at the rear of the hall. From behind it stepped a youth of perhaps fifteen years. A woman followed him, clearly trying to hold him back. I flinched at first, suspecting an ambush. My hand twitched towards the dagger at my hip.

But I let them fall again when I recognised who stood before me. In that instant, I was paralysed. Everything around me faded away. All my senses focused on the young man with two differently coloured eyes. The moment he rounded the table and came to a halt in front of me, I recognised my little Conor in that unfamiliar face. I leapt to my feet. It was my son!

He stood before me, eye to eye, uncertain and ... curious?

I began to tremble with excitement. Helplessly, I raised my arms, unable to utter a word. Conor's eyes shone like a star rising in the sky. He was tall for his age. His fair hair was bound in a braid at the back of his head. His features were balanced, almost noble, and still so young. One eye, crystal blue, the other flecked with brown, flashed at me with joy.

Conor said something, yet I did not understand him. For a moment, my power of speech deserted me. There were no words for what I wished to say. I longed to draw him into my arms, but we were too much strangers for that. The emotions that overwhelmed me were beyond description, joy, pride, and relief foremost among them. I forgot where I was, the danger hanging in the air, the clan leader's anger at Conor's appearance—everything was swept away.

"Conor," I croaked, struggling to find words. The room seemed to spin around me. I fought to steady myself. What happened next nearly broke my heart. My son threw himself against my chest.

"Mother ..."

I could no longer hold back my tears. With them came the anger and frustration that had built up within me over the years in which I had missed him so deeply. I held him tightly against me.

Despite my blurred vision, I suddenly became aware of the woman who had appeared behind him. She had called out to Conor earlier, but now, she stood behind him in fear;

I could see it plainly. She had dark-blond hair and blue eyes, yet I saw no resemblance to Conor. Now, she tugged at him, clearly urging him to come back to her.

In her fear, she all but screamed at him. Conor tore himself from my embrace and shot her a defiant look. Only then did I finally break free of my paralysis and become aware once more of the tension filling the room.

Fired up by the rapid turn of events, Arnulf leapt from his bench. Now he roared at the boy, ordering him back to where he had come from.

Conor shot me a warning look, which I misread. I turned towards Arnulf, who was coming around the table brandishing his fists in the air. His face was twisted with rage, flushed a deep red.

Mina had risen with him and tried to place herself between his fists and me. The brave warrior truly meant to stop him, to keep him from lunging at me. It was courageous, but unnecessary.

I had stepped aside, reaching for Conor. Instead, the blond woman was there at once, placing herself protectively in front of him. My hand closed on empty air.

Slowly but surely, I grasped what was unfolding before me. I seized the woman by the shoulders and shook her.

"That is my son, and I am taking him with me now!" I screamed at her, carried by the upheaval that had seized everyone in that moment. Another gasping cry from Mina tore my attention away. The warrior woman had been caught in a crushing hold by Arnulf. She must have seen something that drove her to that shrill warning. It was likely another attacker, for I felt a blow strike the back of my head, sending me reeling down onto my knees. I had not guarded my back. Damn it.

My disregard for every danger and warning now exacted its price. Behind me, Arnulf's henchmen had forced their way into the room. One of them caught me from behind. After the second vicious blow to my temple, I lost consciousness.

Chapter 14

Iceland, May 1331

When I awakened, a thunderous ache hammered through my skull. Perhaps that pain hauled me back into the present. My field of vision was narrow and warped, while hellish sparks flickered and shimmered before my eyes. Before my mind fully cleared, realisation seeped into my awareness, slowly and relentlessly like water dripping from stone. I was in a perilous position. My hands and feet were bound tightly with rope.

I stood upright, yet I was utterly immobile. The binding was expertly done, tight enough to almost steal the breath from my lungs. I shook myself and strained against the ropes, but they did not yield. As though emerging from a fog, my thoughts began to clear. My hands, feet, and head were all still where they belonged, and yet, I found myself in a decidedly dire predicament.

Arnulf's men had bound me upright to a post. With every painful throb in my head, fresh understanding surfaced of what must have happened. I dared a cautious glance to the left and saw that Mina, like me, was tied to a post. I heard the girl sob softly. At least we were alive. Arnulf had not meant to kill us outright. Something had stayed his hand.

Bringing my vision into focus was maddeningly difficult, as though I were out of step with time itself. Enja, focus, damn you, I ordered myself.

With iron resolve, I fixed my gaze on the crowd gathered before me. By now, I could make out individual faces. Arnulf had planted himself before them and was addressing his clan in forceful, swaggering words. Fortunately, I understood enough of what he was barking in that domineering tone.

"… and therefore, I will not permit anyone other than my son Conor to take the throne as clan leader after my death. Whoever takes issue with this decree stands against me, and whoever stands against me will die."

The full weight of his words had not yet reached me in that moment. I would gladly have slipped back into unconsciousness for a while longer. I felt utterly unable to do anything to free myself from my dire predicament. Before me, the faces of Conor, Arnulf, and Arnulf's wife swam and shifted once more. Pain flooded the images that kept forcing their way into my awareness. Again and again, I squeezed my eyelids shut, trying to hold on to what I had seen.

Mina finally tore me back into the present with her unparalleled screaming. She shrieked as though impaled. Despite the pounding in my head, I turned towards her and saw tongues of fire licking at her feet. One glance downward was enough to tell me that flames were burning beneath mine, too. They meant to burn us alive.

As if someone had hurled a bucket of water over my head, the truth struck me all at once. With this fire sacrifice, Arnulf meant to be rid of Mina and me once and for all. It would also serve as a spectacle for the villagers. And only then did I recognise Conor's horrified face in the crowd. He was meant to watch as his own mother was burned alive.

"Stop!" I shouted, summoning my last remaining strength. "Stop!"

I coughed, my voice rasping like a file, and with every word the searing pain surged back into my skull.

"Let Mina go. She has nothing to do with this matter!"

My cries went unheard, and the wind made the flames lick higher beneath our feet. Logs crackled and spat. With every hiss, Mina screamed again. It sounded as though she were losing her mind. Her face was utterly contorted with panic.

I looked sternly over at her; she was no more than five yards away from me.

"Mina, look at me!" I shouted, not knowing what else to do. "Look at me, I said!"

She heard me through the smoke and the noise of the burning wood. She turned her head towards me. Tears ran down her chalk-white cheeks. She stared at me with a mouth twisted into a scream and breathed heavily. I could see it in her chest, which rose and fell violently.

"If we die, then we die as warriors!"

She listened to me intently. Her gaze did not leave me.

"We will die here together," I shouted to her, "hand in hand, but we will go with our heads held high. No matter how great the pain, we will endure it. Do you hear me, Mina?"

She nodded absently. Her mouth twitched once more, but she had stopped screaming.

"I am proud of you, Mina. I always will be. Just follow me, I will go first."

The heat became unbearable as smoke stung my eyes and made me cough. Strangely, it was my own voice that comforted me, as though I were not calming Mina at all, but myself.

Through the billowing smoke, I looked over at Conor once more, frozen in shock. His eyes were wide open, and fear made him tremble. It was a barbaric decision, Arnulf forcing him to watch his own mother burn.

Strangely, the dark-blonde woman was holding my terrified son tight against her breast. Her gaze was just as rigid, and tears streamed down her cheeks. Tears for me?

Just as I was about to take my leave of this world with a prayer, I felt a trembling run through the stake. I clearly sensed movement beneath my feet, and suddenly, the logs beneath us seemed to tip away of their own accord. Like fire-arrows, the burning pieces shot towards the gawking crowd. Struck by sparks and glowing fragments of wood, unrest broke out among the spectators. Everyone tried to flee. My senses must have been playing one last cruel trick on me.

At that very moment, I felt someone sever the ropes from behind. My arms dropped limply, and I pitched forward, having lost all support. Strong hands dragged me away from the pyre.

My eyes burned and streamed terribly, yet I stumbled forward without will of my own. My head pounded with pain as I followed the direction in which the strong hand was pulling me. There stood a horse. Someone helped me into the saddle. I felt it more than I saw it. I kept my eyes tightly shut. Blindly, I reached for the reins, and my feet found the stirrups all by themselves. In the same moment, the animal sprang forward, and I instinctively clung to the saddle. I still could not see anything, neither the direction in which we were riding nor who my rescuer was. I could hear the horse carrying the groaning Mina galloping directly behind me, and the villagers, who were now shouting and raging because they had been robbed of their sacrificial ceremony. Even Arnulf's voice rose above them. He was shouting the loudest and the angriest.

With one hand, I rubbed my eyes. An irritating cough tore at my lungs. Amid the gallop, I became aware of a hand holding a water flask moving towards me. I knew that hand all too well. It bore skin markings over the third and fourth fingers, Celtic symbols of power and fortune.

I grabbed the waterskin and choked on the cool liquid during the wild ride, then I poured a little more over my face. Coughing wracked me, but the drops of water cooled my head and overheated body. My lungs burned and water dripped from my hair, but at last the heat left my face, and the pain subsided.

Mina had escaped far less lightly. One side of her hair was completely burned away. She had come perilously close to suffering severe burns. Her skin was reddened, and our rescuer had also given her a water flask to combat the heat. Her eyes were inflamed, and her eyebrows and lashes were gone. I would examine her more closely once we were safe.

I shook my hair like a dog after a bath, and my vision became clearer. My face was probably as discoloured as Mina's, and my eyes burned like hell. At last, I was able to look at my rescuer riding so nimbly beside me. Ragnar Sigurdsson. It was the first time I was glad to see his face again.

His face had never been particularly handsome. The scars that marked it spoke volumes about the hard life he had lived, but now, he was grinning at me, his mouth twisted from an old sword cut. I had never been so grateful for his mockery that I bore gladly.

He looked changed. A bald head had replaced his hair, but in return he had grown a full beard. The silver strands of beard concealed the striking scars well and made his features appear softer. I thought he had lost none of his attractiveness. On the contrary, age suited him well.

A crushing weight lifted from Ragnar's chest. He had managed to pull Enja and her companion out of that hell. That monster Arnulf had meant to burn them as an example before the villagers, all to show Jalla and Conor that Enja was mortal and no threat to him.

News spread very quickly on this island. Priest Cornelius had informed him of the arrival of Conor's mother. Word of her coming had reached even the outlaws' hideout, and Ragnar had returned to Akureyri just in time. In the village, the former mercenary still had friends from the time when he had arrived in Iceland with Conor.

The young man Ragnar had brought back from Ireland was, in the eyes of the village elders, the rightful clan leader. He was Enja's son, and thus, the grandson of the former chieftain, Leif Eriksson. To secure his power, Arnulf needed only to remove Ragnar, who could cost him both his foster son and his claim to recognition. But he had not succeeded in that so far, no more than he had managed to burn Enja on the pyre.

The former mercenary ground his teeth so hard that his jaw muscles stood out visibly. It was unthinkable what might have happened had he not learned of Enja's arrival in the village. In this way, he had been able to rush to her aid and prevent the vile murder. Ragnar could understand quite well what Enja was going through at that moment. To have been betrayed and almost killed still lodged in him also, like a thorn deep in his flesh.

Since his flight from Akureyri, Ragnar had lived with the outlaws. They shared his fate, for like him, they had been cast out of the clan because they had opposed Arnulf and his hunger for power. Since then, they had lived in the forests and caves outside human society. These people without possessions had never asked him what he had to do with Arnulf. No one told the others where he came from. They helped one another and procured meat and grain.

Ragnar had a trading relationship with the churchman Cornelius. He bartered game meat for honey, and rare herbs for mead. The monk's message reached him just as he was on his way to meet him. They had come together on one of the secret trade routes used by outlaws.

The poor priest had been at the end of his nerves when he had sought out Ragnar. He had met Enja upon her arrival and knew that she intended to ride to Akureyri to meet her son. The holy man had warned her, but she had brushed everything aside. Enja had no idea what kind of hornets' nest she was about to stir up. How fortunate that Cornelius had alerted him immediately. For years, Ragnar and his men had been on hand whenever Arnulf threatened the church. Without him, Cornelius would no longer have been on the island, or worse still, no longer alive.

Unlike most of Iceland's inhabitants, Arnulf still believed in the Norse gods and saw his faith threatened by Cornelius. Ragnar and the islanders who had converted always protected the small church community whenever Arnulf tried to burn it out and drive the priest away. Who would have thought that Ragnar—the cold-blooded mercenary—would one day become the protector of a Christian congregation?

Bitterness crept into his soul at the thought that here in Iceland, with all his accumulated spoils and lofty plans, he had become entangled in a conflict that had nearly cost him his life. Of all people, it was now a priest who helped him to survive as an outlaw. Whenever one of the men fell ill, Cornelius aided him with his medical knowledge. Without him, he and his companions would already have perished miserably. Damn Arnulf.

The woman riding beside him said not a word. She stared grimly ahead, as though wrestling with her thoughts. Enja must have been deeply angered by the situation she found herself I, as she always was whenever she made a mistake. At the sight of her, he remembered the time they had shared, a time that would remain with him forever. This woman had seared her mark into his soul with her fire, right beside the scar on his belly where she had once slashed him open with a dagger. And yet, he could not help but love this warrior. She was his fate, his kindred soul.

When Ragnar saw Enja again in the village, his heart had almost burst. He had hidden himself in one of the stone houses that belonged to a friendly family. From there, he was able to follow what was happening to Enja. How she rode up to the main house of Akureyri as if she were King Lionheart himself. Proudly, she had sat astride the small horse and was not intimidated by Arnulf's hostile demeanour, neither by him nor his henchmen. When she passed him with her head held high and walked into the longhouse, he had been compelled to pay her deep respect.

Before Arnulf had the two women bound to the pyres the following morning, Ragnar had coordinated the preparations for their rescue with his accomplices. Some of the villagers had helped him discreetly fasten chains to the framework that held the logs together. Arnulf had wasted no time inspecting it.

When the logs were burning, Ragnar's men simply made the harnessed horses, which were standing inconspicuously in the marketplace, break backwards. With ease, the animals tore apart the substructure of the hastily erected pyres. The burning logs and sparks flew towards the spectators and triggered a panic. The stakes with the women were carried away from the embers by the force of the movement. In the general confusion, Ragnar's accomplices freed the two of them from their bonds. The rescue had succeeded without further injury.

'We must dismount and hide in the undergrowth,' he hissed to the two warrior women, who were still clinging to their saddles. Shock and relief must have settled deep into their limbs.

"Arnulf and his henchmen will not dare to follow us into the forest. The clan leader has made too many enemies to risk coming here."

Enja said nothing; she merely nodded. The girl who had come here with her looked at the mercenary with wide eyes from beneath a layer of black soot. Burns marked her face, and her hair was badly singed. She was still in shock, no doubt. Ragnar would not have been surprised if the Lord Himself had had a hand in this escape. They had made it out by the narrowest of margins. Angrily, he pressed his lips together. Damn it ...

On foot with the horses on long leads, they plunged into the thicket of a deciduous forest. A path became visible, along which the three of them struggled forward with their ponies. Branches and bushes blocked the way and had to be bent aside. Had Ragnar not charged so purposefully straight into the undergrowth, the two women would probably have turned back. Just as it seemed there was no way forward, a broader path suddenly opened.

The trail was lost to their pursuers. They would not dare enter this thicket. Ragnar, however, pressed on at a determined pace, ever deeper into the sheltering forest. At last, they stopped and listened back into the darkness behind them. No betraying sound reached their ears. With quiet satisfaction, the small group realised that no one followed them. They had shaken off their pursuers.

Ragnar had decided not to ride back to his forest camp, where he lived with his companions. He would stay here with the women, at least for one night, to cover their tracks. He knew she had not come because of him, but because of her son. He accepted that, even though the sight of her still set his blood racing. He only had to see her, and her immense presence caught him like the wind catches a feather.

With Enja at his side, he could take his son back from Arnulf's grasp. She possessed the courage and legitimacy to unseat Arnulf from the throne. Enja was the daughter of Leif Eriksson. By the law of the elders, she could claim Arnulf's place. If Ragnar were to marry Enja, he would become clan leader. It was time for things to change. For far too long had the boy been exposed to the violence of that tyrant. Conor was his son.

The former mercenary motioned for the two women to rest in the small clearing. Enja was visibly exhausted. A crust of blood covered the back of her head. She was probably suffering from severe headaches, but she did not let it show.

"We can ride on, Ragnar. I'm fine," but scarcely had she spoken the words when she fell to her knees in the soft moss and let her head sink into her hands. Her face was blackened with soot.

"It's safe here, *mo ghra*," Ragnar told her. "Arnulf's men won't follow us into the thicket. It's treacherous, especially at night when you don't know the ground.'

Enja's companion looked at him strangely, perhaps because he had used a Gaelic term of endearment. Enja had not even noticed. She turned onto her back, drew up her legs, and placed her hands over her eyes. Ragnar had never seen her so utterly worn down. She was injured and vulnerable; the iron-hard warrior was gone. Of course, she was still beautiful, but now she radiated a maturity that she had lacked as a young woman. She stood above things, and Ragnar wondered whether she had been happy in her life to preserve that radiance. A sharp pain went through his heart. She had chosen her husband James and instead driven a knife into his ribs. That had been thirteen years ago.

Ragnar gazed at this woman with quiet affection and could scarcely tear his eyes away from her. Their love affair lay far in the past, yet he had never been able to forget her. Their passion had lasted only a few days, but it had sunk beneath his skin and never left his thoughts.

Ragnar had firmly expected that she would come to Iceland one day. It was only a matter of time. Presumably her husband had died, and she had set out on the journey. That was how he had judged her. He had been prepared. Just like Arnulf, that damned toad!

He should never have made the mistake of telling Arnulf about Enja. Back then, he had stood at Arnulf's side and trusted him. The warriors of Akureyri had held together, defending the village against rival tribes. Conor was meant to grow up in safety. Then, Arnulf had suddenly raised himself to chieftain and with that, the tide had turned.

Ragnar's son, the young Conor, was the rightful successor to the old clan leader. Arnulf had played a dangerous game and demonstrated his power.

The young woman with the scorched hair sat apathetically on her knees beside Enja. The girl troubled him. She had narrowly escaped death in an edge-of-the-abyss experience Ragnar himself had faced many times in his life and survived. It was a bond he shared with Enja. Like him, she had stared again and again into death's ghastly maw and spat in its eye. Her courage, her pride—Enja still possessed everything that made her so compelling. She was the perfect warrior.

"What is your name?" he asked the girl softly as he sat beside her. Half of her hair had been burned down to the scalp. The colour of her strands was no longer recognisable, for the pitiful remainder stuck out from her head like straw. With compassion, he handed her a filled waterskin so she could wash herself. Wordlessly, the girl took the leather vessel and drank from it. Then, she began to use it to cleanse her charred head.

'Her name is Mina. She is the orphaned girl I found back then at Galway Harbour. I took her home with me.'

Enja regarded him appraisingly from the side. She had turned her head towards him. "In place of Conor."

As she spoke, she studied him intently. Her reddened eyes no longer held their former sharpness, yet they seemed to look straight into the depths of his dark soul.

"Was it so terrible to part from a son you had not seen for such a long time?" Ragnar asked, although he knew the answer. As he straightened himself to stand beside Enja in the moss, he was aware that he was playing with fire. "I truly believed I could protect him and secure his position as leader. I was wrong."

His admission of his fallibility impressed Enja. Contrary to his expectation, she did not reproach him.

"How did you know that I would come, Ragnar?" she asked him.

Soot still smudged her beautiful face in places, yet her eyes remained fixed on him, unblinking.

"Priest Cornelius ..." he began by way of explanation, before her brusque hand gesture made him stop.

'I did not mean your spy in Iceland. I meant the harbour master in Galway. How did you know that I would take the ship to Iceland from there?'

Ragnar sat down beside her with a sigh. He would, at last, have to tell her what he had always known about her. Slightly embarrassed, he picked up a branch and turned it in his fingers. His gaze was fixed straight ahead.

Birds chirped, and crickets sang almost without pause. A gentle breeze brushed through the leaves of the deciduous trees, setting them rustling. The ferns bent slightly, but otherwise, there was no trace here of the cold wind's bite. The dense canopy above the treetops allowed little chill to reach the clearing. The mood was almost peaceful.

"I saw it in your eyes, Enja. Every time I told you about Iceland, your eyes had that gleam. There was a deep longing to be seen there, a natural curiosity for the place of your ancestors. You were born here, Enja, in this village, which is now ruled by a tyrant. A damned bastard who married your sister and passed our son off as his own."

Only with his final words did he turn his head towards Enja. The shock was plain on her face. 'My sister, Jalla?'

Ragnar nodded. She had not known. Enja's face had turned pale and she had to swallow several times. He gave her a little time to absorb the news before he began with further explanations.

'Your sister was the only one of your family to survive. She was fifteen years old when the disaster struck. Some of the children and youths fled into a cave during the volcanic eruption. For weeks, the land lay shrouded in darkness. The animals perished, and the cold was bitter. The small group survived on fish, plants, and whatever little they could still find. Survivors from the ships eventually discovered them and built a new village. That is how a handful from our clan endured. They formed the core of today's settlement. Now, they all live in fear of Arnulf, who has seized leadership, though it does not belong to him by blood.'

"Why did you not take Conor back from him?" There was a slight reproach in Enja's voice.

Ragnar shook his head wearily. 'I tried more than once, you must believe me.'

She did not ask any further questions and likely sensed that he had risked his life to save his son. An oppressive silence settled between them, then he sighed.

'I knew that Jalla cares for Conor like a mother. She loves him deeply, for he is the only thing left to her of her family. I have ...' He hesitated for a moment and drew his gaze towards Enja, who still lay quietly beside him. With one hand, in an unconscious gesture, she squeezed the water from the strands of her hair.

"I told Jalla what happened between us. That Conor is your son. Your sister was unable to have children herself. She nearly did not survive her first and only childbirth. Perhaps that is why she clings so tightly to Conor. When you finally appeared, it must have been a shock for her. Conor knew that I am his father, and that one day his mother would come to see him. He recognised you at once in the longhouse, Jalla could not prevent the meeting..."

Enja listened to him in silence. He could clearly see how she had to process the new information. Slowly, she raised her upper body and supported herself on her arms. Thoughtfully, she ran a hand through her white-blond hair, which now, despite the soot stains, shone more silverly than it had when he first saw her. With her fingers, she distractedly combed the strands and gathered them together at the nape of her neck. Then, she drove the finger-long dagger from its decorated sheath through the knot to secure it. How often had he pulled that dagger from there and felt her fine, soft hair against his face? He would never forget her scent.

Slowly, she rose to her feet with a groan. Her balance had not yet fully returned. The blood had been washed from her head, but she would feel the blow for days to come. With effort, she forced herself to focus, and lifted a sceptical gaze to his face.

"How did you get us out of there?"

Proud of his idea, Ragnar explained the plan he had devised for the rescue. Enja listened, fascinated. Their gazes met. For a fleeting instant, he thought he saw again that admiration she had once held for him, but then, she lowered her lashes, unwilling to betray herself.

"You had help?"

'Yes, but they were hiding among the villagers. Not everyone agrees with Arnulf as leader, not even the council of elders, yet they cling to tradition and are unwilling to rise against him. His strength lies in the fear he sows within his clan. He cowes people through violence. It takes courage to stand against him.'

"Not a good environment for Conor," Enja added bitterly.

Over the next hours, Ragnar's gaze returned again and again to her pale face. Meanwhile, she had tended to the horses and fitted them with hobbles. Now, she sat beside Mina, one arm wrapped around the girl who was still in shock, yet her thoughts were elsewhere, her eyes fixed on some point in the middle of the clearing. Had she forgiven him for trying to abduct her back then at Dunguaire? She was not one to hold grudges, but she had not forgotten it either.

Their gazes met again. He noticed that blood was still running from her head wound down her neck. She did not seem to notice.

"Are you still angry with me about my attempt to abduct you at Dunguaire"

Ragnar wanted to know after all. His bad conscience had always plagued him. She tilted her head, and her neck vertebrae cracked. As she did so, her eyes softened. She was probably remembering the desperate duel the two of them had fought in the castle forge.

"Well, at least I didn't feel the slightest remorse when I drove your own dagger into your belly."

"Into the only place where no organs would be fatally injured."

Enja looked up in surprise when he reminded her of the deliberately placed thrust. She had not believed that Ragnar knew this detail.

"Who told you that?" Her voice sounded suspicious.

Ragnar grinned with quiet delight. Even after all this time, he could still surprise Enja.

"A healer told me. What was her name again …?"

'Moira …' came tonelessly from Enja's mouth. It took no more than three seconds before she let out a hoarse laugh and shook her head in disbelief. As far as Ragnar knew, a deep friendship bound her to Moira.

"Let me look at the wound at the back of your head. It may need stitching, and Mina looks as though she is not yet able to do it …"

Once again, Ragnar had managed to surprise me. I had thought I knew every facet of him. This caring side was new to me. Perhaps the responsibility for our son had changed him deeply. I found myself liking this quality in him; it made him more human.

At first. I had believed my wound was only a tear, but it would not stop bleeding. More gently than I remembered his hands to be, Ragnar washed away the crust at the back of my head. I could feel a solid swelling where a blow had struck me. It was a laceration, and we left it as it was, without stitching it. Strangely, the blow to my temple had caused nothing more than an ugly bruise.

Using a little chamomile soaked in water, that was growing wild in the clearing, Ragnar carefully dabbed at the wound. My headache slowly began to ease. As long as I did not move my head, everything was bearable.

Poor Mina. The girl was trapped in the memory of what had happened. She was not yet able to process the terrible experiences. At her age, I had already killed people to not become a victim myself. Death had been part of my survival back then, and I still remembered well the Grand Vizier whose throat I had slit in his sleep. It had been my first murder, but Hassan had helped me at the time to escape the melancholy it brought.

She would learn soon enough. If Mina wished to become a warrior, today's ordeal would carry her forward. As harsh as it sounded, if she could not accept the possibility of her own death, she had no place bearing a weapon. Even so, I spoke to her again and again, to make sure she knew she was not alone.

I had suffered a concussion from the hard blow to the back of my head and had to vomit several more times. The headaches did the rest, keeping me from sleeping at all. Ragnar waited patiently until both of us felt better. He procured a rabbit, fish, and wild carrots for us. I wondered why he had been excluded from the community of the villagers in the first place. Had Arnulf driven him out by force?

In time, Mina found her voice again, but she avoided speaking about what had happened in the village. The girl ate and drank, keeping herself to the barest necessities of words.

That evening, we had sought out a water source to water the horses. Mina had distanced herself from the two of us, as if she wanted to give us space.

Ragnar explained that we would stay by the small stream for the night. I unpacked blankets and furs that were strapped behind the horses' saddles. The damp was slowly creeping into our limbs, and I wanted at least some source of warmth.

Ragnar skilfully made fire with a flint, striking it against another stone. Small pieces of tinder served as kindling, and before long, a serviceable fire was burning, giving off warmth.

Without many words, Ragnar set about preparing the hare on a spit for our supper. He handled the task with more skill than I had expected. Later, he wrapped the carrots in a piece of hare's pelt and buried them in the embers to cook. Soon, an irresistible scent of roasting meat reached my nose. Only then did I realise how ravenous I was. The pain in my head ebbed, and hunger struck all at once. My empty stomach growled as if some beast were trapped inside me.

With relief, I noticed that Mina was taking a few bites. Once the first hunger had been satisfied, I began a conversation with her. She sat opposite the two of us and stared into the fire without interest.

"Mina," I said carefully, after rinsing my fingers in the stream. 'Let's talk about what happened today.'

Mina was in the process of using a stick to retrieve another carrot from the fire, but she paused. In the glow of the flames, I could see that she was eyeing me suspiciously. Her singed hair looked dreadful. We would have to cut it so that it could grow back evenly. Otherwise, the fire had left no lasting damage on her skin, only on her soul.

'I need to know whether you wish to keep fighting or return to Cornelius. You can wait for us there. I will not fault you if you choose to turn back at this point. Being burned alive is not among my favoured ways to die either, but we survived because we chose to survive. That is all that matters. It is your will that shapes your life. God has set a different path for us than dying quietly at home in our beds. If you do not believe in your fate, you will never find trust in yourself. You are strong, Mina. I can feel it. You must find that strength and turn it against your enemies.'

Mina looked at me seriously across the fire. Her bright eyes, which usually shone so lively and cheerful, were strangely dull. The ordeal showed plainly on her. She let the carrot sink down.

'I have sworn my loyalty to you, Lady Enja,' she replied firmly. 'I have always admired you. Your courage and your deeds were known far beyond all borders. It was always my wish to ride at your side and, if need be, to die for you. Perhaps I was not prepared for what happened today, but because of your words, there among the flames, I suddenly no longer feared death …'

Mina faltered as the memories flooded back again. "I am aware that you spared me from something worse."

She broke off to clear her throat. It sounded as though she were fighting back tears. She began to peel away the hardened hide of the burned pelt, exposing the carrot beneath.

Ragnar had remained silent. He added a few more branches that we had gathered in the forest. He had no fear of being discovered. None of Arnulf's men dared to enter the thicket at night. This was Ragnar's home.

After a few minutes of reflection, Mina finally began to speak. 'I will continue to accompany you, Lady Enja. My mission is not yet complete. It was destined for me to meet you, and God has chosen me to stand at your side. It is my wish to continue supporting you, and if I must die in doing so, then so be it.'

I looked for a long time at the young girl who was slowly becoming a woman. Her lips trembled, but her voice was steady. The expression on her battered face appeared determined. Her freckles had vanished, as if they had been burned away. Perhaps, the thought struck me, she might yet become a passable warrior. This year, she would turn eighteen.

'It is always doubt in ourselves and our abilities that stands in our way. Do not become a slave to your fears. When we fall, we must rise again and keep fighting with our heads held high. That is what we were born for.'

Mina seemed to sense my joy at her loyalty. She drew the corners of her mouth into a cautious smile and nodded. She would make it, I was certain. God was with us all.

Turning once more towards Ragnar, I began to sort through the thoughts circling in my mind. My resolve to wrest Conor from the clan leader's grasp remained unbroken.

"How was Arnulf able to separate you from Conor?"

That thought had been burning at me all along. A man like Ragnar would not allow what was his to be taken from him so easily.

He did not answer me at once. He finished his last bite and wiped his mouth with his sleeve. He tossed the bone into the fire, which flared up once more and hissed as the remaining fat evaporated in the embers.

'When I returned to Akureyri in 1318 with Conor and his nurse, Arnulf welcomed me into the village. As a former clan member, he took me in, as he had all who returned over the years. I trusted him. He was of our clan and related to me through his father, but when he learned that Conor was the grandson of the old clan leader, and thus the rightful heir to the throne, the relationship suddenly grew strained. Arnulf had married your sister, Jalla, and with that, he had already begun reaching for power. He carried himself like a clan leader and led the village men whenever our territory had to be defended. I held back. My bloodline did not make me clan leader, and you …' Ragnar paused meaningfully, '… you did not wish to marry me.'

I could not help but smile a little as he once again made his disappointment clear.

'It was enough for me,' he said slowly, to underscore the weight of his words, 'that Conor would become one.'

A strange pause arose. It made no sense to me. Ragnar was not the kind of man who submitted to anyone, and yet suddenly he did so of his own free will. Once again, we exchanged looks that required no words, and I began to understand. His son and his son's future had become more important to him.

'You handed Conor over to that Arnulf willingly?' I asked in disbelief.

Ragnar shook his head in anger. "Of course not! You know me, Enja, I would never do that. That swine had his sights set on the position of clan leader. The council of elders did not see him as the tribal chief who deserved the throne of Enja's and Jalla's father. They spoke of bloodlines that must not be broken, and the Svartur was still missing, the Stone of Power, which could only be passed to the legitimate successor. Arnulf wanted my son within his family to reinforce his claim. As long as Conor was still too young, he would assume rule on his behalf …"

'Our son,' I corrected him angrily, earning an irritated glance in return, but he did not correct himself.

"I was mostly at odds with Arnulf. You can imagine that we were rarely of the same opinion. He was not yet a recognised leader of our village when I returned with Conor.

Although he presented himself as such, the council of elders had not appointed him as chief. Conor was in the care of Jalla, who had looked after him since I arrived in Akureyri. My wet nurse and your sister replaced a mother for Conor."

Ragnar paused briefly, making sure I was not about to go for his throat, but his return to Iceland lay far in the past. I was utterly calm, yet the calmer I remained, the angrier he seemed to grow.

"I believed myself safe within the village community. Together with Arnulf, I trained capable fighters and hunters. Unfortunately, most of them stood behind Arnulf unconditionally as the new clan leader. He promised enough meat and fish for everyone. No one was to go hungry anymore. In fact, he often went hunting with the young warriors and even poached in neighbouring provinces."

Ragnar paused and examined his fingernails. My impatience grew. The male games of power and veiled threats were not unfamiliar to me from Scotland.

"I always held back during those hunts, and Arnulf formed a kind of wolf pack with the young fighters. Perhaps he even told them that I would lay claim to the throne, especially with Conor as my son."

Ragnar took the blade of his knife and began cleaning his nails with its tip in the glow of the fire. Night had fallen over us. I tossed a few more branches onto the flames. At once, it flared up again, crackling greedily into the darkness of the night.

"One day, while we were out hunting, an arrow struck me in the back. At first, I thought we were being attacked by enemies, but the only enemy I had at that moment was Arnulf. The missile had hit me just beside the spine. When I turned around in anger, I saw Thor, one of his closest fighters, drawing his bow with another arrow."

Ragnar froze mid-movement and looked at me. I could clearly see in his gaze how that moment of realisation still unsettled him to this day. A certain hardness settled over his features; the cold fury of betrayal.

"Arnulf tried to murder me from behind to remove me from his path. The young warriors were obedient to him and watched without reaction. I fell from my horse and rolled to snap the shaft. It was clear that they intended to finish me off. Arnulf drove his horse towards me to trample me to death. Somehow, I managed to save myself from the deadly hooves. Finally, Arnulf dismounted to deliver the final blow."

Here he made a meaningful pause. Betrayal within one's own ranks cut deep, but had he not disposed of his enemies in much the same way himself?

"I managed to escape," he continued, "by throwing myself into the nearest river. Arnulf probably did not expect me to survive such an injury, but that," and as he said this he gave me a crooked grin, "is what others before him had believed, too."

A log cracked sharply, scattering embers and ash across our legs, and we hastily beat away the burning fragments.

"I drifted downstream for a while," he went on, and my respect for him grew. In truth, he had already survived several attempts on his life. Like a cat, he had nine lives.

'Again and again, I fought my way back to the surface, until my strength finally failed me. When I awoke, I found myself in the care of the outlaws. They had dragged me from the water, removed the arrowhead, and nursed me back to health. But one realisation struck me harder than the pain in my bones.'

And now he paused for a few seconds, during which he stared motionless into the fire. "In that moment, I knew I had lost Conor. Arnulf would never have let me return to Akureyri without flaying me alive ..."

Ragnar had turned his face away from me and fallen silent, but when I glanced at him from the side, I saw his jaw muscles grinding. I had always known him as a fighter who did not surrender easily, yet most of the warriors stood with Arnulf. Even if a few villagers still supported him, they would never rise against Arnulf. Ragnar would have needed to muster a small army to take his son back from the clan leader's grasp.

I felt just as desperate as he did. It had grown completely dark by the small stream. The moon shone brightly on the glittering waves, which reflected the light. Crickets chirped without pause, and in the distance, I could hear water rushing. It was surely a natural cataract.

I remained silent beside Ragnar, who was leaning against a tree. One leg was drawn up, and at last, he had put away the knife with which he had been cleaning his nails.

When Ragnar had been so severely wounded by Arnulf, Conor must still have been a child. He surely had not understood why his father did not return from one day to the next.

Conor's face rose before my inner eye, his beautiful, even features and mismatched eyes. My son was innocent of everything; he was nothing more than a pawn in a game of power. We had to free him from Arnulf's grip before it was too late. If Conor were to come of age, he would become clan leader and drive Arnulf from the throne. That was certainly not in Arnulf's interest. He would kill our son before allowing that to happen.

"Conor must not stay there, Ragnar. He recognised me as his mother, so Jalla must have told him the truth. I do not know my sister, but she seems to be afraid of her husband. Perhaps she is the weak point in Arnulf's plans?"

Ragnar agreed, yet he saw little chance of reaching our son through Jalla.

"Arnulf hardly ever lets the two of them out of his sight. Whenever they are allowed outside, his men are always with them."

There were only three of us. The friends Ragnar still had in the village could offer no more than passive help. No one dared rise against Arnulf; the fear of his well-trained fighters was too great. My hope began to fade, and with it, the joy of reunion. Unconsciously, my hand reached for the onyx at my throat. It comforted me whenever doubt crept in. And with that touch, I remembered my mother's final words.

You are the chosen one. The gods will stand by you.

I will never forget the moment she placed the onyx stone into my hands, her fingers trembling with cold in a desperate gesture of love. The stone was the mark of my clan, the proof of my bloodline. Perhaps the time had come to claim my inheritance. Akureyri was my father's village, and I would see to it myself.

As always, when I was about to make a decision, my heart pounded louder, and my breathing quickened. This did not escape Ragnar, who watched me with a mixture of interest and suspicion.

'I am certain of what I must do, Ragnar,' I finally told him.

The gaze from his water-clear eyes remained fixed on me.

'That much is clear to me, Enja. And I will help you.'

A strange excitement seized me. Goosebumps spread across my back. I had felt this before a fight on many occasions, but never had a single thought triggered such a sensation. It was the indescribable pleasure of fighting once more alongside my former lover.

Chapter 15

Iceland, June 1331

More than once, when Ragnar watched Enja, he glimpsed the woman she truly was. Not the warrior nor the leader of a clan, but a woman with needs and a yearning for love. Just as now, as she lay motionless beside him, asleep.

With his gaze, he traced the contours of her body. He could see nothing. Enja lay wrapped deep within her blanket, yet every single detail of her naked form was etched into his mind. It was a body with little softness, her muscles honed by relentless combat training. Her belly was hard, her arms sinewed yet powerful, and her back—marked by the inked dragon—was more finely defined than that of many a man. To Ragnar, she was the most beautiful woman he had ever known. She was his soul's twin, one of those rare beings one encounters but once in a lifetime.

It had been love at first sight, and she had gone straight beneath his skin. Enja had never shown fear of him, nor contempt for what he had done. From the very first moment, he had been lost to her.

Ragnar had tried to force her to go with him to Iceland, but a woman like Enja was not swayed by such demands; she had stood against him. More than that, she had humiliated him and very nearly killed him. At the time, he could not fathom why she would not return with him to his homeland, Iceland. Now he knew that love was stronger than blood.

Driven solely by revenge for her rejection, he had taken their shared son from her in Dunguaire. This woman, who had taught him feelings he had never known before, was meant to suffer the same despair that consumed him. It was a selfish love that had driven him to such an act of desperation, and his vile plan had worked. When he had left Enja alone in Galway Harbour, he had seen a woman utterly broken.

His sense of triumph had not lasted long. Little Conor began to win his heart. In time, love for his child ignited within Ragnar; selfless, unconditional love.

Ragnar swallowed at the thought. A small child had taught the feared, steel-hard warrior gentleness and remorse. From that moment, his thoughts were no longer shaped by vengeance, but by concern for Conor. His decision to take the little boy back to his homeland now seemed reckless. He had wanted to gift his son the land of his forefathers, and instead, everything had been taken from him, as though fate itself had conspired against him. Arnulf had nearly killed Ragnar. His weapons, his wealth, and his son were in the hands of the powerful clan leader who had proclaimed himself such.

And now, Enja had returned, to him, and to Conor. This time, she would stay, for after her husband's death, she had resolved to claim the legacy of her homeland. She had come at the right moment. Ragnar needed this woman in his life now more than ever before.

Sleepily, Enja lifted her head and looked at him through glassy eyes. With one hand, she brushed away the soot that still burned from the smoke in her eyes. Then she chose to drift back into sleep.

They had made their camp by the stream. Mina had gone a short way back down the path they had taken, keeping watch from there. Ragnar had been lying awake for some time, as he always did when dawn approached. He had never needed much sleep, he admitted to himself. The woman beside him had claimed him forever since the moment he had first laid eyes on her.

Here in Iceland, summer days began early, barely three hours after midnight. The nights were cool. A diffuse light lay over the land at this hour of morning. The fire beside them had long since burned out.

Ragnar watched Enja with quiet curiosity; she was usually awake at first light. This time, she seemed worn to the bone.

"How is your head, *mo ghra.*?"

She murmured something unintelligible beneath the blanket and turned onto her side, as though trying to escape his unwelcome attention.

"There is a way to cast Arnulf from the throne, Enja."

At once, he felt the tension in her body beneath the pelt. She turned back again, now alert, and faced him. In the faint gleam of light along the horizon, he saw her eyes open.

Her lids were swollen, and it still took effort for her to focus.

"We have no chance of fighting an entire village, but tradition allows a rightful claimant to challenge the ruling clan leader. You must face Arnulf in a king's combat to reclaim your clan honour," Ragnar murmured softly. "As the daughter of his predecessor, you carry the true bloodline, and have the right to challenge him. He will have no choice. He must convene the clan elders. If they sanction the duel, you must fight him without weapons, with only a staff and bare hands and feet. One foot will be bound with a rope, its end fixed to a stake driven into the earth. Thus, the opponents are held at a constant distance from one another. This has been done for centuries, so that not the strongest, but the most skilful, is given a chance."

Enja turned her head away from him and looked into the grey-stained sky.

"Do you truly believe I could defeat him?"

Ragnar considered for a moment, uncertain. "I know him and how he fights. I can show you where his weaknesses lie. If you are still as strong as you were in the forge at Dunguaire, your chances are good."

Enja allowed herself a narrow smile. She had once defeated him narrowly under very different circumstances. Tilting her head, she asked, "Would you show me the duel as our forefathers fought it?"

Ragnar hesitated for a moment. Once, in Ireland, he had told Enja of the traditional king's combats. When no heir was declared, rivals were forced to face one another under strict rules. Would Enja emerge victorious from such a fight? She would need great skill to overcome Arnulf, who was younger and far stronger. The manner of combat was brutal and draining; the ropes allowed little space for ordinary fighting movements. Ragnar had his doubts, but he did not voice them.

"I will teach you everything you need to know." For once, he did not have to lie. "You cannot rely on the advantage of your swift sword, but you are far more experienced, and lighter, than Arnulf. He has known this traditional form of combat for a long time. We have practised it since childhood."

Enja propped herself up on one elbow and rested her head in her hand. His candid words did not impress her. She was hardened; he had to grant her that. Her face remained still, save for her mouth, which curved in a faintly mocking line. To this day, the respect he felt for this woman was without bounds.

"Where are your two short swords, anyway? The only weapon you're carrying is a rusty dagger."

Her question threw him off balance. More than that, Ragnar bristled at her remark. He let out a sound of contempt and cursed under his breath. His blue eyes narrowed to slits. In moments like these, he was at his most dangerous.

The short swords, forged especially for him by a master weaponsmith, had been the most precious possessions he had ever acquired. They had also been his hallmark, for he had always worn them crossed upon his back.

"Arnulf has them," he ground out through clenched teeth. "He has taken everything from me, including my lands and my son. Just as he took everything from you when he captured you both in Akureyri."

Enja swallowed. No warrior ever surrendered their weapons willingly, they both knew that from bitter experience.

Now, anger showed on her face, too. A sharp crease formed above her nose. "Then he has my silver too, the silver I brought here," she said in a grave, hollow voice.

Ragnar felt a strange restlessness take hold of him. They had both lost everything they possessed and had barely escaped with their lives. They had to act if they were to change their fate.

"Let us begin the preparations. We have little time to make you fit for combat. By tradition, the challenge must be issued before the solstice. After that, no reigning clan leader may be challenged until the next turning of the times." Ragnar seemed to weigh his thoughts. "Arnulf will not expect you to choose the traditional path. The surprise will strike him hard."

Enja pushed the blanket aside and moved to rise. She paused briefly, pressing a hand to her head, then she let out a hard laugh and replied, "I do not know what hour it is, but it must be early morning. My aching head will not dictate how long I am to sleep. Let us begin."

A dry, guttural laugh escaped Ragnar. He shared her outlook and let himself be distracted by the way she stretched and flexed her finely trained body.

Enja and Ragnar understood one another at once, as though they had never been apart. They shared the same thoughts and intentions, and she seemed to trust him. She appeared a woman at peace with herself. Perhaps he should strive for that as well.

The training was brutal. Again and again, Ragnar's staff whistled down onto mine, crashing with savage force. My arms trembled from the strain of holding the weapon up in defence. The impact of each blow reverberated through every vertebra of my spine. Worst were the headaches. Time and again I pressed my fingers into the hollows at the base of my skull, rubbed my temples, and dragged air deep into my lungs. It did nothing. The pain throbbed mercilessly. I gave up for the day. By morning, a savage ache would join the headaches, my muscles screaming in protest.

The pleasure of grinding me into the ground was written plainly across Ragnar's face. I let him have it. His drills were meant to prepare me for a brutal duel and they challenged even me. Ragnar was determined to ready me for what might be my final great fight. I accepted the challenge, my teeth clenched tight.

Breathing hard, I sank down where I had just been standing. I could not take another step. We had chosen a rocky plateau that commanded a clear view over the rolling land. Far in the distance, the peak of Jökulfjall rose against the sky, a volcanic range streaked with white patches of glacier, sullied by ash and sooty air. Massive granite colossi repeatedly cut through the green like warts upon the skin in stark witness to the island's violent eruptions. The volcanoes had hurled vast stones from their lava throats as if spitting out bothersome cherry pits.

The day remained overcast, and occasionally a raindrop fell, yet I was sweating as I had not in a long while. Sweat streamed down my face in rivulets, stinging my eyes. Since my youth, I had trained my body and kept my muscles honed, but these unfamiliar staff drills laid bare my limits.

Ragnar sat beside me and handed me his water skin. His face, too, was slick with sweat. The drills also taxed him, I noted with a trace of satisfaction. Even this steel-hardened mercenary wrestled with age, though I had to admit, the years had treated him well. His beard gleamed silver where it had once been black. His crystal-blue eyes shone almost grey in the diffuse light, while only his lashes remained dark. His presence was still imposing and his aura unmistakably dangerous. Ragnar held an attraction for me that proved fatal to my concentration.

Our affair from many years ago had never released its hold on me. I had never spoken of it to another soul. Ragnar awakened a desire in me unlike anything I had ever felt with another man. We did not even need to touch to sense its force; the air between us felt electrically charged. I felt it at once when we saw one another again after so long. His open interest, his looks, and his murmured endearments, as though we had never fought, hated, driven one another away, or even drawn blood.

Perhaps this ebb and flow was simply part of love's game. I thought back to my marriage to James. There, too, had been those waves between anger and happiness, but on a reasonable plane. James had tried to assert his will without ever humiliating me. Ragnar, by contrast, would do anything to be at my side, and would gladly follow me into every heaven and every hell. An intoxicating man.

I had always wondered what love truly was. It came in so many possible forms that I was no longer certain a single, true love even existed. Why should a woman not be able to love two men? James had been dead for more than a year now. Why, then, did I behave like a chaste virgin towards a man with whom I had done things that made my cheeks burn with shame at the mere thought of them?

I poured cool water from a leather vessel over my face and let a little of it run into my mouth, keeping my eyes closed as

I did so. The liquid worked wonders. Slowly, the headaches eased, and my skin cooled. What I would give now for a bath in a stream or a lake …

A shadow fell across my face, and I opened my eyes. Ragnar stood before me, his hand held out to mine. He must have risen without my noticing. Now, he studied me intently and said, almost casually, "Your wish can be granted."

Had I spoken my thoughts aloud? He seemed to sense what I needed now to ease the aching in my muscles. It had been my routine back in Ireland. Ragnar had not forgotten.

With unerring certainty, he led me down from the plateau along a path strewn with moss and stones. A scattering of ferns and broad-leafed shrubs lined the way, barely recognisable as a trail. We were drawn ever deeper into the barren landscape, lashed by cold winds. I had expected a lake, or perhaps a hot spring, but instead, we crossed jagged rock and moss-covered hollows. Only when I heard it did Ragnar's destination become clear. At first, there was nothing more than a distant trickle, but the sound grew heavier and deeper until there was no doubt: Ragnar was leading me to a waterfall.

It took some time before we fought our way through the jagged terrain to reach the river. In the end, we climbed a steep rock path, clearly hewn into the stone by our forebears. The man-carved steps stood out plainly. By then, the roar drowned every spoken word, and I followed Ragnar in silence, my curiosity growing with each step.

When I stood before it, I was struck by its sheer scale. Though I had seen no river, water thundered down here in a breadth of at least fifteen feet. The spectacle rose perhaps ten men high, broken again and again by smaller ledges where the water gathered, only to plunge further downward. There were many waterfalls of this kind on the island, most of them nameless. What set this one apart was the basin at our feet, where the roaring water crashed down with deafening force. Over centuries, it had carved itself deep into the earth. Somewhere down there, it must have flowed away underground.

Sheer rock faces along the edges barred any leap into the cool water. Only directly beside the falling torrents was it safe. At one point, a natural opening offered us access, allowing an entry into the pool.

The basin seemed to churn, glowing in daylight with an unreal green that reminded me of seaweed. For a moment, I thought I caught the scent of sulphur, though it might have been my imagination. After all, the island was studded with black volcanoes. In places like this, the smell could be overwhelmingly sharp.

"It's a former volcanic vent, plunging deep into the earth. The water is not as cold as you might think; it is warmed from below. There must be a hot spring down there. Here at the edge, the falling water is pleasantly cool," he said.

Once again, Ragnar had guessed my thoughts; the way he watched me was almost unsettling. Hesitantly, I looked from the rim down into the dark centre. The pool was nearly circular, with a diameter I judged to be about thirty feet, barely twice the width of the waterfall.

How deep might the crater be, I wondered. My curiosity about deep waters made my hands move instinctively to my clothing. Only when I had already pulled my tunic over my head did I notice that Ragnar, too, had undressed.

Completely naked, he stood beside me, poised to leap beside the roaring torrent. Almost graceful for such a large man, he plunged into the water, gliding a few yards beneath the green-fringed surface before bursting back up, spluttering. He wiped a hand over his wet beard as he emerged. Droplets gleamed like pearls upon his scalp.

In one swift motion, I freed my hair, decisively pulled down my trousers, and plunged in after him. Pleasantly warm water received me like an embrace. Instead of surfacing again, I let myself glide down into the throat of the basin, which seemed mysterious to me. The temperature was, indeed, gentle and appeared to rise the deeper I sank. A sharp taste pierced my senses, tearing me from my reverie. It was a warning not to venture further, even though the darkness drew me in with magnetic force. I strained to peer downward, trying to make out something—anything—but my view was clouded by particles drifting all around me, as though soot hung suspended in the water.

Disappointed, I fought my way back to the surface with powerful kicks. Ragnar stared at me as though I had lost all sense. He could not fathom where I had vanished to. This time, I flashed him a cheeky grin.

"Did you wait for me?"

His gaze narrowed, his lips pressing into a tight line.

"Don't do anything foolish, Enja. Nature here is treacherous. It is in constant motion, and if I believed in hell, I would be certain it lies somewhere on this island. I know you are not afraid of it, but it is no more afraid of you."

With only a few strokes, he swam over to me. The dark look faded, replaced by concern. His fear for me was genuine.

"I know how at ease you are in the water, Enja, but here, the enemy waits deep below. Many islanders have died in treacherous hot springs or suffocated in the vapours. Stay here, where I can see you. Please," he added. A word I had not often heard from him.

There was something in his voice I did not yet know. It was concern. The Ragnar I remembered had been a stranger to such a feeling. The extent of how much he had changed crossed my mind. Now, his head was directly before me in the water, his eyes fixed on me like a serpent on its prey. He hesitated, as though a question stood between us that he had not yet dared to voice. His behaviour unsettled me.

Ragnar had never asked anyone for permission; he had always taken what he desired, sometimes for coin, sometimes by threat. The life-hungry warrior had seized everything he could, body and soul. His directness and passion fascinated me. Treacherous thoughts of heated kisses drifted through my mind like veils of mist. I felt the warmth rise to my face.

Triumph flared in his eyes as he recognised my traitorous thoughts. His face was so close to mine that I felt his breath from his slightly parted lips brush my skin. In a hungry motion, he crushed his mouth against mine. One hand gripped my nape, the other my backside, as his large, muscular body pressed against me like a starving man.

My hands clawed into his shoulders. The pain seemed only to drive him into greater frenzy. Ragnar's urgency sent my pulse racing. His tongue was uncompromising as it sought and found what it desired. Ragnar loved as he fought, relentlessly, until the final breath.

Like an annoying fly, I shook off my feeble attempts to complete my year of mourning in chastity. His honed body wrapped around me without mercy. He dragged me almost beneath the surface, for we no longer offered any resistance. Then, he released me and drew breath. We gasped for air. The ferocity of our passion and the surging waters around us had nearly drowned us.

At last, Ragnar reacted and pulled me by the hand to where the water came crashing down from above. It was pleasantly cool.

If I had believed Ragnar meant to hurry back the way we had come, I was mistaken. He turned sharply to the right, straight into the wall of water, and simply pulled me after him. I held my breath and followed blindly. There it was again, my trust in his strength. I felt it often when I was near him. It was a kind of primal faith in the right choice. Ragnar would not disappoint me. He was a good protector.

The wall of water was not wide. The cataract poured its cold mass over us once, briefly and with force, and then we were through. Beyond it, a small cave awaited us, shaped by the water over the course of centuries. It was wet and refreshing, and we stood ankle-deep in a shallow pool, but the heat in our bodies did not care.

Ragnar pressed me against the rock face with both hands, cupping my head and holding me fast. Behind us, the water roared, its thunder pounding in my skull. My stomach fluttered. His sex pressed hard and hot against my belly in compelling proof that he felt it just as fiercely.

Ragnar's thumbs traced over my lips. His gaze had turned dark and hungry, drilling into mine with fierce intensity. At once, my knees went weak, and inwardly, I was grateful that, in the cave's dim light, I perceived his heated look only in fragments. From this moment, there was nothing left but raw desire.

He did not waste time kissing me, caressing me, or further stoking my already seething body. Ragnar's powerful arms lifted me, sliding beneath my hips. My legs closed around his waist and drew him hard against me as he entered me. A groan tore from him, as though in pain in a pleasure-laced torment that only drove me on. The noise we made was swallowed by the thunder of the waterfall. Even the cry of release dissolved into the roaring surge around us.

It was indescribable. Everything was still there, the desire, the longing, and the love, as though I had never been gone.

Ragnar had longed for this with all his being. For so many years, he had waited for the woman of his dreams, clinging to the hope of a reunion. The knowledge that Enja returned his feelings robbed him of reason. He had never meant to press her, had intended to wait and see whether he would need to court her anew, but such thoughts had proven futile.

Her body had betrayed her. Her mind was not yet ready, but every muscle in her body had pleaded for his touch. Lying beside her through the night had already been an ordeal but bathing with her beneath the waterfall had demanded every shred of his self-control not to take her then and there. Enja, naked in the water, was the dream of his sleepless nights, and there had been many of those in recent years. Hardly a night had passed in which he had not thought of her.

Now, he held her in his arms. Her naked skin against his body felt as hot as lava. She breathed heavily from their exertions of love. Her head rested on his shoulder, and her wet hair fell across his face and dripped down his back. A surge of happiness spread through him. Ragnar had once been unable to deal with such emotions. Instead of loving her, he had wanted to force her to go with him. He had been ready to use violence because that was what he had been taught.

Enja sighed and straightened. With one hand, she brushed the wet strands from her face and looked at him with a hint of uncertainty.

"We should see to Mina. She is surely worrying about where we have been for so long."

Ragnar nodded with understanding and turned towards the exit. With sure steps, he moved into the falling water, and paused briefly beneath the cascade to rinse himself off. Then he stepped out and set about dressing.

Enja, too, was out of the water within seconds. She stood beside Ragnar as she dressed. She had just slipped into her trousers when he snatched her tunic from the ground. She looked at him questioningly with her light-coloured eyes, one finely arched brow lifting. Only a few faint lines around her eyes betrayed Enja's age. She did not know what he intended, but she let him have his way.

Ragnar searched for the right hold on the fabric to pull the garment over her head. She answered his attempts to help her dress with a laugh. Still, she lifted her arms slightly to find the sleeves. Even as he drew the tunic down over her, his mouth was back on her lips. Ragnar had not yet had his fill of her, and his body made his readiness unmistakably clear.

However, this time he was interrupted by a strange sound. Enja had heard it as well and pulled away from Ragnar at once. It sounded like the cry of a fox, a high, wailing howl.

They listened and heard it again. This time it was closer. With narrowed eyes, they stared in the same direction until the cry grew clearer. It was Mina. She was calling for help. Panic rang in her voice, and it sounded as though she was coming fast towards them.

Nothing held them back now. Armed only with their staves, the two fighters charged off back towards the hill with the rocky plateau, and beyond it still.

Even from afar, Ragnar could make out Mina in her billowing fighting skirt, running for her life and the men behind her clearly intent on finishing her off. There were at least six pursuers closing in on her.

Enja now roared with all the force in her lungs, drawing the men's attention to the threat she posed. Ragnar joined in at full voice. Perhaps it would make them break off from Mina, if only to buy her a few desperate seconds. Mina staggered, stumbled, and hauled herself upright once more. The young woman was at the very end of her strength.

As Enja and Ragnar came into the attackers' line of sight, the group behind Mina ground to an abrupt halt. Almost reverently, the pursuers remained at a cautious distance and lowered their weapons.

Ragnar and Enja halted in mid-stride. Mina stumbled the final steps rather than ran them, then collapsed to her knees before Enja, utterly spent. Her breath whistled harshly through her lungs. She was no longer able to utter a single word.

The men said nothing, catching their breath instead. They were poorly clad, with trousers and jackets patched again and again and ropes serving as belts. Their feet were wrapped in bound scraps of leather. On closer inspection, their weapons were no better. Wooden clubs and rusted knives were slipped out of sight. The expressions on the dirty, bearded men were wary, uncertain.

"Are these your women, Ragnar?" asked one of the men who had been running at the very front.

Ragnar laid a possessive hand around Enja's shoulder as she regarded him warily.

"They are my women, Erik. Quite right," he said, pride resonating in his voice. "This is Enja of Caerlaverock. She is the mother of my son, and she has come to reclaim Conor from Arnulf's claws."

Mina hauled herself upright and looked back and forth between Ragnar and the men.

"They tried to rape me," she croaked hoarsely. "Those bastards almost had me."

"Mina belongs with us," Ragnar called out in a stern voice. "You will treat her with respect, or you will have a problem with me."

As he spoke, he pointed his forefinger at his own chest. The men clad in rags nodded eagerly. They understood that threat all too well.

Ragnar turned to Enja.

"These men are outlaws. They were cast out of the village because they stood against Arnulf. They helped me when I had an arrow wound in my back. Erik gave me food and drink, even though they themselves had nothing. I am indebted to them for as long as I live."

Erik merely grunted in uncertainty and scratched his nose in embarrassment. "Forgive our behaviour, my lady. Had we known … we thought she was one of them …" he clearly struggled to put into words his pursuit of Mina.

"Enough," Enja said calmly. "You look as though you have not seen a woman, or even a wash, in quite some time. Mina is forbidden to you, and at the next opportunity, I will personally teach you some manners, brothers."

Her gaze remained fixed on Erik, who looked distinctly uncomfortable in his own skin. Beneath her stare, the men found it hard to keep their composure. Ragnar only just managed to suppress a grin.

"What are you doing here, anyway?" he asked impatiently. "Should you not be waiting for me?"

Now another man spoke up. "Erik said the waiting was taking too long. We wanted to see where you were, Ragnar."

“Idiots …” but he did not sound angry. “Let us hunt something to eat. I am hungry, and I am certain the women here are as well.”

Suddenly, the group sprang into motion. Glad to be doing something after the fiasco, each man threw himself onto the trail of small game. For the hunt, they carried short bows slung across their backs, simple wooden weapons with homemade arrows. They had vanished behind the hills before anyone could count to three.

Chapter 16

Iceland, Akureyri, 13 June 1331

My great day had come. The sun stood high in the sky, blazing at midday as though it meant to drive me on to hasten Arnulf's swift end. It was one of those rare summer days here in Iceland. Ragnar assured me it was a good omen.

The trees rustled in the light breeze as though carrying the news from leaf to leaf. We walked along the well-worn path we had taken to the village many weeks before. To the right lay the rise where children had once been playing, their voices announcing Mina and me to the village.

This time, neither girls nor boys came to welcome us.

I was on my way to Akureyri to challenge the clan leader. Tension settled over the small group accompanying me like a coarse, scratchy blanket. Mina, Ragnar, and the outlaws meant to give me protection. Who could know what Arnulf might do if Ragnar and I marched into the village square alone?

My battle companions' nervous glances spoke volumes. Again and again, Mina sought reassurance that my spirits were steady, and I tried to appear so, yet what I intended to do was far more dangerous than charging into battle with all my weapons drawn.

With her hair cut short, Mina might have passed for a boy were it not for her finely arched brows and full lips. The style suited her well; it set off her eyes to greater effect. She smiled a little shyly when she caught me watching her with pride. I had been doing so more often of late, for she pleased me more with each passing day. As a warrior, she had to forget her looks. What mattered were courage, skill, and the will to survive.

I carried nothing with me but the staff with which I had tested myself against Ragnar in training over the past days. I had endured hard hours with him, filled with pain and bruises. Each blow from the wooden staff left vicious marks. At last, my sparring partner called a halt and nodded in satisfaction.

"Your skill is sound," Ragnar had said, plain and spare. "May fortune stand at your side, and with it, victory."

Given my aching limbs, I did not see the prognosis quite so favourably. I rolled my shoulders to keep my muscles loose and glanced over at Ragnar, who was marching beside me.

He stared stubbornly straight ahead, as though nothing could deter him from our purpose. In truth, he had shown himself to be far more emotional over the past days, which was quite unusual for a man otherwise so hardened.

Perhaps this fight also marked a turning point in his life. Long before, when we were still together in Ireland, he had told me of his dream. One day, he wished to return to Iceland and rule "his clan" with me at his side. Back then, I had not understood what he meant. Now I was her to bring that vision to life together with Ragnar.

Had this always been our destiny? Had God traced these strange turns of my life long ago, and was I merely playing the role He had assigned?

At times, the coincidences in my life seemed far too banal to have been devised by God, and so it was with this moment, being at this place at the end of the world, challenging the rule of the clan exactly one day before the solstice, just as tradition decreed.

My gaze fell upon the men in rags who marched proudly behind me. They had found hope in Ragnar and me of being welcomed back into the village community. Since they had been declared outlaws for daring to criticise Arnulf, they had endured a life of poverty and constant fear. Stripped of all rights, they were at the mercy of anyone who stood above them.

Like his companions in fate, Erik had become a victim of his own courage, for he had stood against Arnulf when the latter rose to claim leadership of the clan. Had Ragnar foreseen what Arnulf was plotting, he would have withdrawn into the forest at once with Conor and the outlaws. I had heard this assurance from Ragnar more than once in recent days. I believed in the sincerity of his intent, but it did nothing to change our present situation.

I had grown close to the men who lived their shadowed existence in the forests of this region. They were a motley band of strong-willed characters, bound by one thing alone, that each had been banished from the village of Akureyri by Arnulf. They had been forced to leave behind their families, friends, and belongings, banding together to survive in the wilderness.

During a long night by the fire with nothing but the open sky above our heads, Ragnar had explained to his followers why I had appeared so suddenly. He laid out in detail why Arnulf feared me and what we were planning. My lover left nothing unsaid. Even my knife attack was mentioned, earning me a few words of approval. With each sentence, my story grew more vivid. Silence settled over that gentle night, which were so brief in Iceland at this time of year.

The outlaws were astonished to learn there was another claimant entitled to challenge for the throne. As proof, I showed them the black onyx at my throat. One by one, they touched the dark Svartur with reverence. Still warm from my skin, it was the mark of my noble lineage. Every one of the dispossessed pledged us his ai without a moment's hesitation.

Over the past days, they had helped Mina, Ragnar, and me with the intense preparations for my fight. They sought out suitable wood for the fighting staves and provided us with food, drink, and fire. Most remarkable of all, however, was that they had built an excellent fighting arena in a clearing in the forest. It mirrored the one in the village. It was the best idea imaginable, for it allowed me to grow accustomed to the space and study the limits of my movement.

I had made good use of the short time leading up to the fourteenth day of the Solstice Moon to learn the proper staff technique from Ragnar. In some ways, the training reminded me of my education among the Assassins. In the beginning, I had trained not with a sword but with a bamboo staff. The instruction in the Assassins' halls had been painful, yet largely without mortal risk. Ragnar, by contrast, showed me for the first time how to kill a man with such a staff. As was customary in a traditional duel, he had also bound my foot in a loop, meant to prevent me from leaping aside to evade dangerous blows or circling my opponent. Beyond that, I learned several new—and highly effective—thrusting and choking techniques with the long wooden staff, which otherwise appeared so harmless.

We had been marching towards the village for several hours now. The guards would surely notice us soon. Tension made itself felt as a tingling along my back. I usually associated that sensation, the way the fine hairs on my skin rose, with the onset of battle. This time, I did not face the enemy on horseback, katana in hand. I was advancing with a handful of men clad in rags, armed with rusted knives and wooden staves, towards a village defended by seasoned warriors wielding sharp swords. Never had the odds been so unevenly stacked, and yet, as always, I was filled with the greatest confidence.

My fists clenched instinctively as the village drew closer beneath our resolute strides. My hands were swollen and scratched. The rough wood of the staves had torn my skin open during the intense combat training, leaving it bloodied. It did not trouble me, for today I meant to win. Even when Ragnar looked at me with doubt, I was certain I would defeat Arnulf.

I drew my hope from the many hours of hard labour that lay behind me. Time and again, Ragnar had pushed me to my limits. Day after day, I had faced him head-on, gritted, ferocious, and unyielding. Each encounter became a savage struggle to the very edge. He had granted me nothing.

One moment remained etched in my memory. I had tightened my grip around the staff, made slick with sweat and blood, expecting an attack. Like a caged animal, Ragnar had glared at me furiously.

"Watch your rope, Enja," he hissed threateningly, as though he were Arnulf himself. "If your opponent gets hold of it, he can throw you down as he pleases."

I knew his warning words by heart. Even so, he caught me off guard once again. He hooked one leg around mine and threw me off balance. No, I had not fallen, but Arnulf would have exploited the situation without mercy. I was reminded of that more than once.

"Don't step so far forward, your rope leaves you no room to manoeuvre! Arnulf could evade your thrust with ease that way. Leave yourself some slack!"

Out of breath, he kept shouting corrections at me—demanding, furious, and worried all at once. A perfectionist was not easily satisfied; I felt that in my bones after only a few days. How often had I bitten my lip and endured the ordeal. I wanted it over at last. It was one of the most decisive moments of my life, and it could not be botched. The outcome of the fight would determine what became of me and my family.

Lost in my thoughts, I had likely been walking faster and faster. Mina, who followed close behind me, was struggling to keep pace. She had wrestled hard with herself, yet she wished to accompany me on my mission. What she had endured, I was certain, had hardened her and deepened her faith in herself.

I heard her heavy breathing draw closer. With a few quicker strides, she caught up to me. Mina had been silent for quite some time. Fear for our future had robbed her of words. Then, utterly unprepared, she suddenly blurted out a question I had not allowed myself to face.

"What will happen if you do not win the fight, Lady Enja?"

In my mind, I did not allow for that possibility.

"I will settle this confrontation in my favour today, Mina." I poured all the confidence I possessed into my words. "I am doing this for my son. That is my greatest motivation, and my thoughts of him will carry me to victory."

She trudged on silently behind me, so I added a few words I wished to pass on to her. After all, she would need them for the future.

"You should make it a habit never to question the outcome of your fight. In doing so, you also cast doubt upon yourself."

"Forgive me …," it slipped from her. "But the possibility remains …"

"Then run," I hissed angrily and came to an abrupt halt before her. She nearly collided with me in her momentum. She looked up at me in shock. "Run as fast as your feet can carry you, or face the enemy and fight like a warrior."

I saw clearly how she swallowed and struggled for words. The force of my words had come without warning.

"Then I will fight," she choked out quickly. "I will not run."

"In the event of defeat, I will not be there to witness it, Mina. I will be dead."

No, I thought to myself, that would not happen; I would win. My gaze rested hard upon her sweat-dampened face.

Her face flushed red, as it always did when she felt ashamed. She drew a few deep breaths in and out. Then she forced the words out, as though gagging on them like a fat toad, "You will not die, Lady Enja!"

A deep snort shook her body. It sounded a little like a sob, yet her blue eyes fixed bravely on my face, and she clenched her fists with resolve. There was a note of conviction in her voice that I liked. With one hand on Mina's shoulder, I made sure she was listening to me.

"My son will be there as a spectator when I fight. Keep an eye on him."

"I will, My Lady. I will protect him with my life." Mina nodded earnestly. Once more, a deep, trembling breath rose from her lungs, yet with every passing minute, her expression grew more resolute.

I looked past her now and studied the men who had halted with us. They regarded us with awkward expressions. Perhaps they had harboured similar thoughts and had now become witnesses to our exchange. Their faces gave no hint as to whether, like Mina, I had convinced them of my success.

Ragnar's new companions had treated us with respect. They had never troubled Mina again—quite the opposite. From time to time, the band brought her flowers they found while hunting, or particularly beautiful bird feathers. They wriggled like eels for the chance to exchange a few words with the young girl. I had their respect. But did I also have their trust?

We set off again. Up ahead, Ragnar had been waiting for us impatiently. He could hardly contain his eagerness to challenge Arnulf. Time and again, he scanned left and right with sharp attention. Armed guards might intercept us early on our way to the village. What would they do if they discovered us?

That question was answered swiftly. Two guards barred our path as we rounded the bend beyond which the first houses came into view. The village stretched like a long ribbon along the shore of the fjord. For a single heartbeat, I thought seasoned warriors lay in wait to ambush us and end any challenge before it began, but it was only two young lads.

To show our peaceful intent, we raised our hands and remained still. They recognised Ragnar and stood watchfully ahead of us on the path, lances ready. Ragnar exchanged a few words with them loudly in their own tongue. They listened uncertainly, I could see it in their expressions.

That was the first test of our cause. Would they clear the way? During the brief exchange, my body had tensed like a cat poised to spring, ready at any moment to sweep aside the two armed guards together with Ragnar and our following. Yet they made no move to stop us, as I had feared. On the contrary, they stepped back with respect and guided us towards the direction from which sharp barking and children' cries could be heard. This time, many people were gathered in the village, which was very different from our first visit to Akureyri.

A horn sounded from the centre of the village, long drawn out and piercing. The note froze not only us but also the villagers. The two guards who had taken Ragnar between them called out loudly. I did not fully understand their words, yet it sounded like an all-clear. Even so, the tension was unmistakable. A tingling again crept along my back in an infallible sign of trouble to come.

We did not slow our pace, and entered the village road that ran straight through the rows of houses. Something stirred at the great longhouse, the clan leader's seat. Directly ahead of us, a broad, heavyset man stepped outside, followed by several of his warriors. His reddish-blond hair fell in curls to his shoulders. The woollen cloak, fastened with an ornately worked silver brooch, stirred lightly in the wind. I recognised the stocky figure with the full beard at once. It was Arnulf. His beard had been trimmed, giving him a somewhat more civilised appearance, but even so, he reminded me of the Norsemen who had settled in Dunguaire as traders. The four men at Arnulf's side were likely his personal guard, for they did not take their eyes off him—or us. In an instant, we found ourselves in a highly threatening situation. They had drawn their massive swords. I was certain they would attack without hesitation.

Without pausing for even a second, we walked past the curious villagers who had stepped out of their dwellings. We only had to keep our nerve, I told myself. Without hesitation, our group headed straight for Arnulf and his men. Some of those present recognised Ragnar and even greeted him warmly. The former villager did not seem unpopular here, which I could not say of Arnulf.

Some of the men and women we passed started following us warily. A whole crowd gathered, eventually coming to a halt behind us and before Arnulf.

The clan leader stood firm on powerful legs planted solidly on the ground. Beside him stood his wooden throne. With his muscular arms folded across his chest, he waited for us before the entrance to the longhouse. The warriors at his side took up their positions.

Mina stumbled slightly over the last few steps but regained her footing. I could clearly hear her breath, hissing as she drew it through her mouth. She was afraid, yet she stood firm beside me, like a tree rooted in the ground.

Children eyed us with curiosity. Like their parents, they were dressed in coarse wool. The faded colours spoke of the age of the fabric, the grime on their faces of scant cleanliness. Despite the warmth, the women wore scarves to shield themselves from the wind that swept ceaselessly across the island. A stooped old man sat beside the entrance of a house, watching us.

We had gone unnoticed by no one. It was clear to all who was marching into the village. Ragnar and Enja, Arnulf's adversaries.

Ragnar finally came to a halt before Arnulf, towering a full head above him. His build was still muscular and in prime condition.

I could not help but think that beside Ragnar, Arnulf looked like an ox with a thick neck. Arnulf's baleful gaze was not fixed on Ragnar, but on me. Rage burned within it, for I had dared to return here after escaping the pyre. Now, Conor's parents stood before him. Would this prove to be the downfall of the self-proclaimed clan leader?

I positioned myself confidently beside Ragnar. I left the speaking to him, even though my Icelandic had improved considerably.

The atmosphere on the square was charged, almost hostile. Ragnar had certainly already drawn Arnulf's wrath, but my escape from the pyre truly rankled the clan leader. The villagers behind us edged forward just far enough to catch every word of the exchange.

Someone else joined this confrontation—someone who made me flinch in my taut stance. Conor and Jalla pushed out of the longhouse behind the burly leader and pressed themselves against the wall at his back. Through the gaps between the men, I could see my sister's eyes, wide with fear.

Her eyes were a darker blue than mine. Perhaps it was my father's colour? I could no longer recall his face. Even Jalla's dark blond hair I could not associate with any other member of my family. I would never have taken this woman for my sister.

Conor craned his neck to see me, and I sought his gaze. There it was, a moment of distant appraisal. I stood so close to him yet could speak only with my eyes. How I longed to speak with him in confidence, but like this, he was beyond my reach, save for our shared glance. For that fleeting moment, we found one another.

Conor's face was striking. One eye was a beautiful, crystal-clear blue framed by black lashes. The other bore strange brown flecks that altered its original hue. Perhaps it was an inheritance from my ancestors?

Conor still bore the soft features of a boy, yet the gravity in his face made him seem older. He did not smile. I merely gave him a brief nod as a sign that I had come for him. His mother was ready to fight for him.

Conor was my son. I had every right to claim him as mine. One day, he would become the rightful clan leader. Arnulf, too, sought that end through his role as foster father—but only as a pretext. Conor would be nothing more than his puppet. Unless Ragnar and I finally succeeded in bringing Arnulf down.

Jalla pressed the boy against her chest. At the end of this month, on the 29th of June, he would turn fifteen. Conor already stood slightly taller than Jalla. He would grow more yet—I could see it in the unevenness of his limbs. Perhaps one day he would be as tall as Ragnar, or taller still …

It was Arnulf who spoke first, yet he did not sound as confident as he wished to appear, despite his blustering words and threatening gestures.

"What do you two want here in this village? You have no right to be here. I have outlawed every one of you. Crawl back to the hole you came from and take your ragged rabble with you. If the two of you believe we fear you, you are sorely mistaken."

Nothing happened. No one moved, and our group held its ground. The warriors stared at one another stoically, yet not a single man yielded so much as an inch.

Ragnar's body straightened as he addressed Arnulf and the villagers.

"My name is Ragnar Sigurdsson, and I was born and raised in Akureyri. This is my wife, Enja Leifsdottir, daughter of Leif Eriksson. At the age of six, she was meant to be sacrificed to the gods by her father, the clan leader, but the ship sank on the way. The gods had greater plans for her."

My face twitched slightly. Ragnar had made me his wife without so much as a word. Presumably, he wished to leave Arnulf no room to question our bond or our parenthood. I would have to speak to him about it later; his self-assured manner irritated me more than a little.

Calm yourself, Ragnar's glance seemed to say as he briefly studied me, before continuing to speak before the people and the enraged Arnulf.

"We are the parents of Conor Ragnarsson, whom Arnulf took in against my will to secure his claim to the throne as Conor's guardian until he comes of age."

The people behind us grew uneasy. Only now did they seem to grasp how serious this matter was to us. We were risking our lives.

"My wife, Enja ..." Ragnar continued, casting a sidelong glance at me. Did the corner of his mouth twitch? I must have been mistaken; he possessed no such sense of humour. "My wife, Enja, as the daughter of the last clan leader, lays claim to his throne for herself and for her son, Conor. I stand beside them both as husband and father. Leif was killed in the devastating volcanic eruption of the year 1300. His daughter is owed the honour of inheriting his legacy, and as the eldest, she is bound by duty to take his place."

That was news to me, yet the villagers nodded in approval. This custom, it seemed, was familiar to them. Ragnar was not finished yet.

"Enja is bound to take her place within this hierarchy and may challenge anyone who dares to oppose her to single combat."

At least two hundred pairs of eyes stared at me expectantly. I seized that moment to remind the villagers of my lineage.

"My mother accompanied me on the ship before it sank," I added to Ragnar's address, haltingly, in the language of my ancestors. "In her final moment, she entrusted the Svartur to me."

With one hand, I tore the chain from my neck and held the black stone high, plainly visible to all. For a moment, a deathly silence fell over the square. The Icelandic word for black made many of the elders freeze where they stood. Some were likely seeing it again for the first time, for no onyx stone hung at Arnulf's neck. No other such piece existed.

Only a few seconds later, scattered voices broke the silence with calls for justice and shouts hailing Leif, my father, the former clan leader. I could clearly read astonishment and admiration on the villagers' faces. Only Arnulf had expected my return, even though Ragnar had proclaimed it time and again.

Ragnar looked at me with pride, then turned to Arnulf and addressed him directly. Everyone could sense that the clan leader was ill at ease. He kept shifting his weight from one leg to the other, and his already sour expression darkened further.

"I hereby call upon our Council of Elders. In the name of our gods and in accordance with the ancient traditions of our people. Should Arnulf refuse to step down of his own accord, Enja holds the ancestral right to challenge him to single combat in the arena. The rightful successor demands justice."

Had the situation not been so grave, Arnulf's reaction to Ragnar's demand might have been amusing. His face changed colour twice before he could give vent to his anger. His mouth opened and closed like a fish gasping for air. At last, he gathered himself enough to bellow aloud, "I secured my rightful place on the throne by marrying Leif's second daughter, Jalla! I also took Conor in as my son. One day, he will become the clan leader, regardless of who held the position of chief before him. I have led this office for many years for the good of all. I will not step aside for someone who appears here after a long absence and dares to lay claim to this seat."

Arnulf's bellow broke into a hoarse croak as the blood surged violently into his neck. A wave of fury swept over his supporters, too, who hurled threatening gestures in our direction. One of them even drew the flat of his hand across his throat.

"I will see to it that you do not leave this place alive. I will not relinquish my position willingly. Your husband will have to kill me, or I will have you all put to the sword."

At these words, Arnulf's face twisted into a devilish grimace. The emphasis he placed on the word *husband* made it clear to me what was passing through his mind at that moment. Arnulf did not expect—at all—that a woman would be the one to challenge him.

Before the entire village, he had sworn to kill not only his challenger, but all of us. We were facing a man who knew no honour. For a moment, I lost my composure.

Arnulf seemed to notice it, for his eyes flashed with triumph.

Ragnar recognised my inner conflict, and I felt his strong hand settle on my shoulder. With the strength he radiated and his quiet confidence, he steadied me when I threatened to falter. To calm myself, I briefly closed my eyes and drew a deep breath. Then, he spoke again.

"People of Akureyri, hear me!" Ragnar called out. "Your clan leader Arnulf shapes the fate of every one of you, but when it comes to who is the leader, it is the Council of Elders who must decide. Arnulf cannot appoint himself, nor can he deny another their rightful claim. This, as our tradition decrees, must be judged by the wise."

Without waiting for any reaction, he added, "As a woman, Enja holds the right to appoint a champion to fight in her stead. She waives that right and will step forward herself. If Arnulf is as brave as he claims to be, then surely, he can face a woman! However, if he is afraid, he is welcome to send a champion in his place ..."

Arnulf's masculine pride was deeply wounded. In his boundless rage, he nearly lunged at Ragnar. His men hurriedly restrained him to prevent something worse. At that moment, several people stepped forward from among the villagers. Ragnar had called upon the Council of Elders.

Those who now revealed themselves were all very aged inhabitants. A council as old as humankind itself, I thought. Since time immemorial, it had been the elders who were called upon to decide. They had gathered the greatest measure of wisdom and life experience. Here, too, in this Icelandic village, their word carried weight. A strong leader might guide Akureyri through harsh times, but its course was set by the elders.

The wise elders gathered bravely before Arnulf, who displayed his fury at the affront without restraint. His fists clenched as though he might strike one of them down at any moment. His rage seemed directed mostly at Ragnar, who had just turned towards me with quiet satisfaction. The tension was like a live explosive. One careless spark, and the men would erupt. I did not take my eyes off a single soul around us.

"You will have your duel, *mo ghra*," Ragnar murmured to me at that moment. "And then, I will take you as my wife before our God."

In that moment, his promise sounded like a desperate attempt to give me certainty. He might almost have succeeded, had Arnulf not suddenly lunged at me in his rage. Perhaps, in his eyes, I was the weakest link in the chain, but I evaded him with ease. His fists struck nothing but air.

The bodyguard sprang into motion, as though someone had ignited the vibrating, spark-charged air with a detonator. Base rage and frustration sent fists flying and a brawl erupted between our followers and Arnulf's men. I had just driven a kick into the raging Arnulf's belly when a sharp whistle cut through the chaos. And then another, just as piercing.

To my astonishment, the whistle came from the old man I had first seen sitting hunched over on his chair. He now stood beside the six elders, holding his hand before his mouth like a funnel.

"Stop!" he commanded in a rough voice. "At once!"

Indeed, his word carried such weight that the brawlers broke apart. "My name is Gudmundur Gunnarsson. I am the oldest in this village and leader of the Council of Elders. It is our duty to examine Ragnar's claim. If Enja's lineage is confirmed, we must decide whether she may challenge Arnulf to single combat. If not, she and Ragnar must leave this place."

The old man's voice was hoarse, yet loud and clear. Five men and one woman had gathered around what appeared to be the council's leader. All bore grey hair, their faces weathered by wind and storm. The speaker clearly held the greatest authority among them.

The fighters stood still, breathing heavily as they listened to the old man's words. It took some time before they truly withdrew, for their fury did not dissipate as quickly as it had flared. An absolute hush settled over the people gathered. Only the sheep and goats bleating and the groans of those who had taken a blow could be heard. It was deeply unsettling.

At last, Arnulf's men broke away from us, cursing under their breath. We gathered ourselves, ready to receive the decision of the Council of Elders. With a simple gesture, the wise ones motioned for us to step back a little, easing the tension between the opposing side. Excitement sent blood surging through my veins. Arnulf, meanwhile, resumed his seat upon the wooden throne before the longhouse. Jalla had sunk to the ground beside it, frighteningly pale.

I had lost sight of her in the turmoil, but Conor had knelt beside her and was holding her hand. Jalla's lips trembled with fear. She had every reason for it; someone close to her would lose their life today.

Nervously, I bit my lip. My gaze shifted from my sister to Arnulf, then to Ragnar, and finally to Mina, whose eyebrow was bleeding. The warrior had fought bravely alongside the outlaws against Arnulf's assault. She shot me a defiant look and wiped the blood running down her cheek with her sleeve. I nodded to her in appreciation. At last, my eyes settled on the elders, who had gathered to deliberate. My future now hung upon their decision.

The only woman on the Council of Elders stepped towards me and demanded the chain I had hastily tucked into my belt to free my hands. Reluctantly, I handed over the symbol of my lineage.

The old woman bared her gap-toothed smile.

"Trust me," she murmured. "This stone is as old as our people. It always finds its way into the right hands."

It felt like an assurance that they would make the right decision. Relieved, I looked into her face. Her skin was weathered, lined with deep furrows, yet there were surprisingly many laugh lines at the corners of her eyes.

"You are the very image of your mother, Enja. Your lineage is beyond dispute."

I nodded hesitantly, and she turned back to the men deliberating over my fate, carrying the precious token with her. The old woman's acknowledgement filled me with confidence. Right was on my side.

Arnulf had withdrawn with his men in mounting agitation, likely to discuss strategies in case he should lose the fight. Or in case I were the one to come off worse.

I resolved to accept the council's decision, whatever it might be. With sudden satisfaction, I realised that my trust in these villagers was greater than I had been willing to admit after our first encounter. That they had once stood by and accepted my death by fire without resistance had left me with the impression of a weak community that sanctioned every decision of its power-hungry leader. As weak as my sister Jalla, who submitted herself to her husband's will. My disapproving gaze lingered on the shaken woman.

The elders had gathered a short distance away. Each voiced their opinion, and Gudmundur listened patiently to every word spoken. It felt like an eternity, but now, the wise ones—those permitted to decide the fate of the village—spoke.

They turned to face us. Like a fortress, the frail men and the woman had positioned themselves between the two opposing sides, conferring with their backs to us. Now, Gudmundur raised his voice to announce the outcome of their deliberation. The old man straightened to his full height once more and addressed us first. We watched him, tense with anticipation.

"The Council of Elders of Akureyri has reached a decision. Enja's stone is genuine; it is the family stone of the

Svinfellingars, a lineage that has produced clan leaders for generations. Leif Eriksson was one."

The old man paused between his sentences, as though granting his listeners time to absorb his words. He showed great skill in holding the people spellbound.

"Enja is the firstborn daughter of Leif Eriksson, whom I still knew personally as clan leader. I remember both girls, Enja and Jalla, very clearly. I was present on the day when Leif's elder daughter, Enja, boarded the ship with her mother. The vessel was meant to carry them to the volcano, Hekla."

That memory made the fine hairs on my back rise, but Gudmundur seemed not to notice my turmoil and continued with his speech.

"Jalla Leifsdottir is the second-born. Her bloodline must yield to that of her sister. Enja is entitled to challenge the rival for the throne."

That decision stirred movement among the people who had been frozen by tension. A murmur rose, edging on dismay, as though they were suddenly worried for me. Yet, they did not know me at all, nor had any notion of what I was capable of. My heart hammered hard in my chest. Unconsciously, I pressed my fist against it. I would accept the decision!

"Let me kill Arnulf in single combat, as your forefathers once did. As my father would have done," I cried out to Gudmundur, who had just turned towards Arnulf. "I have waited a long time for this moment. Let me restore my family's honour!"

The wise elders glanced at one another uneasily, and I realised that things would not unfold as I had imagined. Arnulf had been seized by a grim resolve. His face reflected the arrogance of a seasoned fighter. He was certain he would win a duel against me. The hesitation of the Council of Elders brought us all to a standstill.

"Thus far, the traditional laws of our people have determined who holds which rights," Gudmundur continued, wiping his mouth with a trembling hand, "but there exists another statute, and it does not permit a man to fight a woman. Only those of the same sex may face one another in single combat. In this case, the two sisters must fight each other."

I felt Ragnar's gaze upon me from the side. I had to swallow. A blow to my face would not have shamed me as deeply as the council's ruling. All my hopes of finally measuring myself against Arnulf in combat were in vain. In my life, I had won most of my fights. I had worked hard for that—and now, I was once again confronted with that loathed feeling of powerlessness. I lowered my gaze, unwilling to reveal my despair.

Silence settled over those present like a heavy blanket. I watched Jalla from beneath lowered lids, as she seemed to harbour the same thought as I did, her hand rising in shock to cover her mouth. I was meant to fight my own sister?

As though we were holding a silent exchange across the distance, she shook her head. She would never fight against me, and I would not fight against her. We both knew she was no match for me. For one cruel moment, I considered whether I should withdraw, perhaps for her sake.

"These two women are sisters!" I heard Conor's voice, loud and clear, for the first time that day. The boy who had stood so dutifully beside Jalla until now had risen, and he turned towards the Council of Elders. "They are both my kin. You cannot allow this!"

His voice reminded me once more of why I had come. It was the voice of an adult, hoarse and rough. At nearly fifteen, Conor stood on the threshold of manhood, and I, as his mother, had been allowed only a single year with him. Twelve months in my entire life. My hands trembled with emotion. This day still seemed to hold more bitter surprises in store for me.

The villagers argued heatedly among themselves. Isolated shouts and Arnulf's furious curses rose above the uproar. Gudmundur raised his hands in a calming gesture, as though about to speak, but he did not get the chance. Suddenly, something happened that nobody had anticipated.

Ragnar stepped past me towards the elder, and sank to his knees before him. His hand lay flat against his chest—like a noble knight—and my heart leapt.

"Gudmundur, hear me!"

The noise fell away at once. Ragnar was impossible to overlook as he knelt there before the assembled elders. His words rang out loud and clear, audible to all.

"I am Enja's husband. Tradition decrees that she may appoint a champion to take her place in the arena. If the Council of Elders consents, I will face Arnulf, man against man. As it is written. May the gods decide who shall emerge victorious, and thus, the rightful heir to the throne."

I could barely breathe. Ragnar was offering himself to fight Arnulf in my place!

Chapter 17

Iceland, Akureyri, June 1331

A northern fulmar sang in the distance, black-headed gulls squabbled with raucous cries over a fish, and a lone gyrfalcon wheeled high across the cloudless sky. Akureyri's mood had utterly changed. Where fear and silence had reigned before, the people were finding hope once more.

Surrounded by his bodyguard, Arnulf had felt secure. Now, it was precisely the one opponent he had not expected since his banishment who had challenged him. The reunion with his former companion—who had taken Leif's eldest daughter to his side—was wholly unanticipated. Long ago, they had crossed blades in this very arena during their training bouts. The memory of it weighed heavily on him.

Arnulf had taken the lead of the crowd, which followed him slowly up the rise. From there, a breathtaking view opened across the bay of Eyjafjörður. The long, narrow inlet stretched deep into the heart of the land. At its farthest end lay the small village, home to some eight hundred souls.

Unlike most Icelanders, the people here had not converted to the Christian faith. Three centuries earlier, missionaries had granted them this freedom on the condition that they worship their gods only in silence. Thus, Akureyri had remained faithful to the old beliefs. Shamans and wise elders were held in high esteem and served as the attendants of the Norse gods.

The Elders' Council's decision to pit Ragnar against Arnulf was a vital element of their Icelandic culture. Only the strongest prevailed and rose to lead the village. Unconditional obedience was required to cement this structure of power. Arnulf had seized the office after the destruction of the village. Through threats, banishment, and even attempts at murder, he had eliminated his rivals.

Yet he was bound to submit to the Council's ruling. They determined who might lay claim to leadership and which children held the right to the throne. Each year, until the day of the midsummer solstice in June, a rival with a legitimate claim could challenge the reigning leader.

After that, Arnulf remained leader for another year. For more than twenty years, he had ruled with brutal severity. Ragnar, as a potential rival, he had driven from the community through an attempted murder. Conor he used as a foster son to legitimise his rule until the boy came of age. It was an exceptionally shrewd move—yet only so long as he was feared by his wife Jalla and the villagers alike.

Today, everything was different. The villagers denied him their unconditional allegiance. The Council of Elders had placed a rival squarely before him, which he had always feared in secret, for Ragnar, older and seasoned by every tide, was deemed invincible. His enemies feared him, and Arnulf, too, had long avoided direct confrontation. His cowardly attempt on Ragnar's life years ago had failed, and now, the gods had granted his adversary another chance.

Arnulf allowed his bodyguards to lead him into the oval. He was uneasy. The signs of the times spoke against him. Had he demanded too much of the gods?

The clan leader, risen to dubious renown, placed the cloak, the brooch, and the chain of silver coins into the hands of one of the attendants, who carried the insignia of power to the wise council. Arnulf knew all too well that at the end of the fight, Gudmundur would present them to the victor.

Arnulf would defeat Ragnar today, of that he was utterly certain. He was younger than the mercenary, even if the man was—he had to admit—tough as leather.

Slowly, as though he had all the time in the world, he tied his reddish-blond hair back into a knot. His arrogant gaze swept over his opponent on the far side of the arena, yet the man did not deign to grant him a glance.

Ragnar stared upward, straight into the sun. It stood high in the firmament—higher than it rarely did in Iceland. It was the day of the solstice, and it was the day when his and Enja's fate might also turn. It was the day of reckoning.

Ragnar felt the wind as a light, fresh breeze cooling his heated temper. With his hand raised to shield his eyes, he surveyed Akureyri's fighting arena . Before him lay an oval enclosed by simple wooden palisades. Fresh rushes covered the ground to soften the fighters' falls. Here, as a boy, he had fought with the men and youths of his village. They had taught him how to bring down enemies, wield a sword, and endure a fistfight. In Akureyri, men trained from childhood in what it meant to be a man. He had also trained on this ground many times with Conor, before Arnulf had taken the boy into his household.

Of all the battles he had ever faced, this was the most important. It was not merely a struggle of life and death, but it would also bring honour to his family. Ragnar would either die or leave the field as the victor. It was a strange notion, yet it did not fill him with fear. Quite the opposite.

A single glance into Enja's eyes, sharp as they studied him, filled him with pride. The knowledge that he was fighting for this beloved woman and for his son gave him confidence. It was reason enough to risk his life. For the first time, he saw a higher purpose in killing his enemy. It would benefit everyone in the village, and most of all, his son. In Akureyri, law and order would once more uphold the community. Ragnar smiled at Enja with quiet confidence.

She remained solemn and returned his gesture with a nod. Her face was pale, and strands of her bound hair gleamed silver in the sunlight. Her searching gaze was fixed on the distance, as though she were seeing something hidden from all others.

This woman, who had lived in Ragnar's thoughts almost daily for fifteen years, seemed unsettled to him. And yet, she had never once in her life wavered over a decision. Did she not believe in him? Did she doubt the outcome of the fight?

Earlier, Enja had checked the fit of his surcoat and tightened the leather thongs of his boots. It was a tender yet vital gesture. Before the gathering on this ground, she had taken him into her arms once more and, for the first time, confessed in deeply moving words how much she loved him. She would do everything within her power to give Conor, him, and all the people of Akureyri the safety they needed.

After all the years of anxious waiting, his heart was drifting among the clouds. After everything they had done to one another, he had finally reached his goal. Enja was at his side at last.

He knew that against the younger Arnulf he possessed only one decisive advantage: he had to draw upon his experience. Over the course of his life as a warrior, he had acquired thousands of tricks. With one of his stratagems, he would show Arnulf what he was still capable of. Ragnar was in high spirits.

It was a beautiful summer's day. The sky was cloudless at the height of noon. Were this not the day of decision, I could have enjoyed it. Like gentle kisses, the rays of the blazing light warmed my cheeks. In the distance, I could make out the surface of the sea, glittering like molten gold in the bay of Eyjafjörður. Not a single wave broke the shimmering skin. The water lay smooth as glass. The few specks upon it were surely waterfowl; never had I seen them so numerous, not even in the Scottish Highlands. How often had I bathed in the sea to refresh myself.

The rise lay some hundred feet above sea level. It was covered with grass and low scrub, the green scattered with countless lava stones. Sheep grazed in the distance, untroubled by the presence of people. The wind, stronger up here, cooled overheated minds. White and orange wildflowers streaked the meadows like splashes of paint. Almost by chance, blue lupines thrust their heads up through the grass.

I forced myself to turn my gaze to the events unfolding before my eyes in the man-made arena. The two men prepared for their final fight. Ragnar with the routine of a seasoned mercenary who had practiced this a thousand times before, and with the certainty of victory. Arnulf with a grimness that revealed much of the fury stirred in him by the elders' decision.

From the secure position of clan leader, Arnulf had not expected a decisive duel against Ragnar until yesterday's proclamation. He stood almost a full head shorter than my companion yet was powerfully built and markedly younger. His thick neck had flushed red in a sign of his agitation, which had by now seized everyone in the clan.

Except me. I felt strangely hollow and disappointed, as though I were in the wrong place. How I longed to stand where Ragnar stood now, to wield my staff in his stead. That had been denied me. All I could do was utter a prayer for a favourable outcome.

Opposite us, Jalla had taken her place with Conor. She was closely guarded by Arnulf's loyalists and unable to make contact with me. Grim faces among the opposing ranks made it clear that this was not desired, either.

The feelings that swept over me in those days made me realise how deeply I had missed my son. The thoughts that haunted me in the solitude of the Icelandic wilderness were almost entirely memories from my past. James filled a great part of my heart, but not all of it. Slowly, it was allowing space for a new love.

The moments in which I had been happy with that singular man were etched deep into my soul, yet so many other things now mattered to me. Conor and Ragnar were matters of the heart, and with them, my life began to reorder itself. The pain of losing my husband grew more bearable with each passing day.

But it was nothing compared to the anguish I felt as I now looked into my son's face. Conor was torn between his loyalty to Jalla and to me.

His gaze kept drifting back to me and lingering on my face. His features were still youthful, yet they would soon take on the sharper lines of a grown man. Perhaps in a few weeks, a beard would sprout where tender child's skin still lay. I ached to take him into my arms, to stroke his cheeks and offer him comfort. Conor was a tragic figure in an ugly struggle for power and rule. He was a pawn over whom the two men now contended.

The opponents took their positions. Ragnar stood to my left, with Arnulf facing him on my right. Attendants fastened each man's weaker leg at the ankle with a rope of about five feet long, which, in turn, was tied to a stone. This left both fighters with little room to close the distance. What struck me was that Ragnar allowed his right leg to be bound. He was right-handed, yet equally adept with both hands. He had always surprised his opponents by wielding both short swords with the same mastery. Was he planning to attack Arnulf on his weaker side? If Ragnar handled his staff with his left hand, his rival's unguarded flank would open to him, but the reverse was also true. I could not quite tell whether it was a good idea, but the decision now lay in his hands. I trusted him.

When I had confessed my love to him before the fight, tears had stood in his eyes. I wanted him to enter the battle with a good feeling of being loved and valued. I had also confronted him about why he had introduced me as his wife. In response, he had merely grinned crookedly and said that in Iceland, every man referred to the woman with whom he shared his bed as his wife.

What was I to say? I pressed a finger to his chest and murmured softly so only he could hear me, "If that was already our wedding, then I will just as swiftly have myself divorced before these Norse gods. One single night of physical love as a wedding is not enough for me."

That made him laugh, and he promised me an official wedding in the Christian rite if he were to win.

"Nothing else is acceptable," I whispered to him and kissed him, pouring all my love and hope into it.

I had learned from my mistakes. James had died willingly back then, fighting against the Moors. He had offered no resistance to his opponent. Something had weighed heavily upon him in Teba. I suspected that, through Mina, he had learned of Conor's existence. Once more, I saw his tormented face before me, his eyes empty. I had never been given the chance to speak with him again, to cleanse my guilt before him and before God. Never again would I send a man into battle without assuring him of my unwavering trust. Today, nothing would stand between Ragnar and me.

The unrest in the arena pulled me back from my thoughts. The villagers were genuinely taken with Ragnar and with the idea of having me as their leader. They recognised that we stood for a different kind of society. They needed help in developing the village. With Arnulf, they saw only a return to an old system of power, threats, and death.

Again and again, encouraging shouts rang out from the crowd; more supporters stood on our side than on Arnulf's.

This did not escape the reigning clan leader, for he kept scanning the crowd with lips drawn tight.

Both wore padded leather vests with apron-like skirts. They reduced injury, yet left head, limbs, and knees exposed to blows. They offered no protection against heavier strikes. In the end, any blow could mean death.

Several times as they waited, the two fighters checked the position of the rope, which still lay slack upon the rushes. In the staff fight, they would advance until it drew taut. This limitation of reach had its dangers. As I had discovered in my training, the rope prevented wide, sweeping movements. Thus, the fighters were left with circular motions of the staffs through the air, blows, or thrusts straight ahead.

Thrusts with the blunt, sawn-off end were the attack of choice when it needed to be swift. Vulnerable areas such as the face, belly, or lower body were more readily exposed to direct contact with the staff. More than once, I had launched a powerful, sweeping turn of the wood toward my opponent's head, only to feel the painful impact of the staff's tip in my gut far too early. This technique had to be learned, and I held deep respect for what now awaited Ragnar.

Opposite me, Gudmundur had taken his seat on the padded rim of the oval, settling onto the chair prepared for him. To signal the imminent start of the fight, he raised a horn fashioned from a cow's skull, which hung from a leather thong around his neck. The rest of the Council of Elders had stationed themselves along either side of the oval as judges.

Silence fell over all present. Even the ceaseless chirping of the crickets seemed to miss a beat, as though the insects were watching the course of events with wary eyes. At last, the horn sounded.

The opponents did not circle one another, for the rope made that impossible. They advanced with caution, their bodies lowered. The two men reminded me of stags poised for battle, each anxiously careful not to tangle antlers in the fight. Each had to find the weakness in the other.

Tense and utterly focused, Ragnar stared at his rival. The hand holding the staff was raised, ready to react in a flash.

Arnulf stood before him like a bull poised to charge, and I had the unerring sense that he would strike first. The muscles of his back tightened and, indeed, he lunged forward, thrusting the end of the staff towards Ragnar's head.

Ragnar had been prepared for the attack and deftly sidestepped to the left. As he did so, he knocked the dangerously whistling staff away from his neck with his hand and, in the same motion, thrust his weapon into Arnulf's chest from the left. The rushes on the ground squealed and flew up. Ragnar's movement was so swift that most recognised the hit only by the clan leader's strangled grunt of pain.

Arnulf recoiled at once. Rage and suppressed pain made the veins in his neck stand out. For a moment, his opponent was immobilised, and Ragnar exploited it without mercy. With a powerful sweeping motion, he sent his staff whistling through the air once more towards Arnulf. The end crashed down on his right shoulder. The leather padding absorbed little of the blow. Crying out in pain, Arnulf clutched his right upper arm with his free left hand. A strike like that drove straight into the bones. Perhaps his collarbone—or even his shoulder—was broken. It would not have surprised me.

But Arnulf only staggered slightly and hurried back towards the stone to gain distance. Ragnar's expression did not change.

My gaze fell upon the people behind the wooden barriers. Breathless, Jalla pressed her hand to her mouth. In horror, she watched as her husband absorbed Ragnar's heavy blow. Perhaps she truly feared for the life of this man—or perhaps she feared what would happen if he died.

In any case, my sister—alongside Conor—was the one who stood to lose the most. No matter who won today, she would lose either a sister or a husband. I would not survive this day with Ragnar should he lose, for Arnulf would have me killed as his rival. A shiver ran through me as I thought of it. Normally, I always believed in victory when I faced a challenge. But today, I was not the one fighting. What if Ragnar failed? What would happen to us in defeat? To Mina and the loyal companions who had followed us here?

These thoughts might have been Mina's. I had always driven the question of "what if" out of her. Until now, it had always worked, but today, I was a bundle of nerves. I assessed our situation to regain control of myself. We had all arrived with only simple weapons. Without my katana, I felt uneasy and exposed. Casually, I studied the bodyguards' equipment. They carried swords and knives; some even had axes tucked into their belts. And they outnumbered us. One stood strategically to the right, close to Jalla and Conor, never taking his eyes off them. I could not shake the feeling that he was positioned there deliberately. Perhaps he was their watcher.

Movement stirred again before me. Arnulf had evidently recovered somewhat, for he began to whirl his staff in a circle around his left hand. On the one hand, it displayed his skill; on the other, it was meant to draw his opponent's eye. Ragnar watched him with narrowed eyes. He did not appear impressed in the slightest. The sun was beginning to glare, slanting into his face, and sweat ran into his eyes.

Arnulf attacked again. In a deadly circular sweep, he cut the wooden weapon through the air at the height of Ragnar's neck. He came close to striking true, but Ragnar ducked aside and drove his fist into the heavy man's face. The staff followed, meant to strike the chest once more.

The punch—a powerful upper hook—would have knocked me flat. Arnulf, by contrast, scarcely reacted and absorbed the blow with ease.

Ragnar had not expected such resilience; he had clearly been trying to buy himself time. With his next staff strike, he came dangerously close to his opponent's body. The rope drew taut. Then, Arnulf did something no one had anticipated. In a split second, he switched the staff from one hand to the other, then simply caught Ragnar's weapon out of the air with his left. With decisive force, he tore the wood from his stunned opponent and tossed it casually behind him. Ragnar's only weapon was gone!

A shocked cry rose from the crowd. Everyone—except me—shared a single thought: this was Ragnar's end. I could clearly sense that they believed his chances of victory had dropped to nothing.

Horror was quite literally carved into Jalla's even features. All the blood had drained from her face. Conor had clawed his hands into the wooden barrier that separated him from the field. For him, it must have been unbearable to watch his father die. His young soul could not yet know that it was far from over. How I longed to give them courage now and spare them what they were about to witness.

Ragnar was a fighter in every fibre of his being. He would go on even without a staff. Even blind, even with only one leg, he would still be a formidable opponent, but he became truly dangerous to anyone who underestimated him.

And indeed, Arnulf already believed himself victorious. With a triumphant grin, he bared his filthy teeth. His mocking expression grated on my nerves, even though I had to admit that his surprise had succeeded.

"Tha mi a' creidsinn annad, Ragnar!"—I believe in you!—I shouted in encouragement, this time in Gaelic so no one could understand me.

"Seall dha dè as urrainn dhut!"—show him what you can do!

Not for a single second did Ragnar let his gaze stray toward me. He was far too focused on what now had to come, yet a crooked grin flickered across his face, showing me that he had heard me perfectly well. He would give everything. Arnulf now believed himself safe. That was his mistake. One should never underestimate one's enemy.

Arnulf's men, too, had taken the loss of Ragnar's staff as an early end for the challenger. With satisfaction, they folded their arms across their chests and exchanged filthy jests. Jalla's guard had relaxed slightly and was chatting with the man beside him.

I did not take my eyes off the men. They were up to something. That was why I was the first to notice the knife the bodyguard must have been holding all along. Now it protruded carelessly from behind his folded arm. What did he intend to do with it?

My attention was drawn back to the movement of the two opponents. Arnulf now had the upper hand. With his staff, he could batter Ragnar as he pleased. He had taken the weapon back into his left hand to spare his injured shoulder. Now, confident of victory, he charged at Ragnar with his arm raised. With precise blows, he struck or thrust at will, seeking to finish him. Despite his age, Ragnar evaded him with skill. Whether the attack came from above or was aimed at his midsection, the wood struck only empty air.

Suddenly, there was a crash. The staff had found its mark: Ragnar's thigh. As always in combat, his leg was bent, the muscles taut and braced against the blow. Even so, a sizeable bruise would form. Ragnar retreated a little and shifted his weight onto his other foot. He must have felt the strike keenly. Distance from one's opponent always meant safety.

Arnulf was sweating. Strands of hair clung to his head. With his sleeve, he wiped the damp from his cheeks.

Ragnar, by contrast, seemed only just to have warmed up. His chest rose and fell, betraying how heavily he was breathing from the exertion. His speed had served him well so far. And once again, I recognised his excellent conditioning. Ragnar had trained for this all his life.

The bull-like Arnulf possessed great strength, yet his legs lacked agility, and his powerful attacks drained him of energy. He would not endure this struggle for long. I remembered how this way of fighting had demanded everything of me as well—how cramps and pain had raged through my muscles for days afterwards. The two men hold their ground with courage and absorbed heavy blows, yet Arnulf no longer used his right shoulder, and Ragnar was clearly limping.

Inhuman pain raged through Ragnar's leg. Arnulf's blow had not broken the bone, but it had badly injured the muscle in his thigh. Throbbing waves of agony surged through his leg in rhythm with every heartbeat. He clenched his teeth. Now, it was truly beginning. His adrenaline allowed him to push the pain aside. He still had every chance. The staff in Arnulf's hands had to disappear—that was Ragnar's goal, for what the brute had demonstrated so deftly, Ragnar could do just as well. That was his plan.

Once he had breathed through the worst of the pain, Ragnar returned to his fighting stance. He drew his injured right foot back slightly and raised both arms, fists clenched. Without a weapon, he focused entirely on his opponent's next strike.

Arnulf believed himself safe behind the protection of his staff. He went at Ragnar at once; victory was already his. Murderous intent glittered in his eyes. Once more, the blow came from above. He aimed for Ragnar's left shoulder.

Ragnar saw the wood coming before it struck. Arnulf's grip and the arc of his swing betrayed his intent. Ragnar's response was instant. With a step of his uninjured foot, he shifted to the right, altering his stance. His left fist shot forward and caught the weapon before it could unleash its force. With his right, he smashed another hook into the same spot on Arnulf's chin.

That blow landed true; Ragnar felt it reverberate through the bones of his hand. The man has a chin like an anvil, flashed through his mind. Wincing with pain, he drew his hand back and pressed it against his chest.

But now the hook to the chin took effect. The counter-punch used as defence had been a vicious surprise. Meanwhile, Ragnar had secured the staff and turned away from his opponent with it. The leverage and diversion left a stunned Arnulf behind. Suddenly, he was without a weapon, clutching his aching chin. With a step back into the safe zone, Ragnar kept his reeling opponent at bay until he grasped the new situation.

Arnulf roared in fury. He must have realised what this meant. Now Ragnar held the staff, and he was helplessly exposed to his attacks. So swiftly had the tide turned. But Ragnar had no time to revel in it. He had to bring this fight to an end, for only Arnulf's death would bring him closer to his goals: to lay the throne at Enja's feet, reclaim his son, and free the clan.

Once more, Ragnar pulled himself together, steadied his racing breath, and focused on the fight. Slowly, he moved back towards the centre, towards Arnulf. His opponent also lumbered forward, his face flushed red with rage and exertion. Red hair stuck wet with sweat to his face. The ropes drew taut again.

Enja watched Ragnar's movements closely. She had already urged him on, and she knew what reserves of strength he was capable of. His wife had filled him with pride even before the fight, for she believed in him completely. In him, his victory, and their love.

Now it was Ragnar who showed Arnulf how deadly a simple wooden staff could be. Left and right, his blows whistled towards the unprotected body of the bull-like opponent. The carefully placed strikes mostly found their mark. The mercenary made Arnulf feel with brutal clarity that he was now the lesser man.

Once more, Ragnar struck Arnulf's injured shoulder, and he roared. Hit with searing pain, he recoiled, clutching his wounded arm in a rigid grip. In that moment, he was completely exposed. Ragnar seized the chance and drove the end of the weapon into his stomach. Arnulf folded forward, straight onto Ragnar's knee, which he jerked upward, smashing it into the pain-twisted face. The clan leader collapsed before him. In that instant, Ragnar knew he had won.

How often had he experienced such moments, when a grievously struck opponent crumpled to the ground. Now, he had the only chance that remained to him in a fight of life and death. Ragnar did not hesitate for a second. He raised the staff to smash the skull of the man crouched before him. It would be Arnulf's certain death.

Ragnar was wholly focused on the final act and only dimly registered that a scuffle had suddenly broken out beyond the arena around Jalla and Conor. But then an aggressive shout from Thor reached him after all.

It was unmistakably the voice of the bodyguard whose arrow in his back had nearly cost Ragnar his life. He hated this man, who had carried out his leader's orders so unquestioningly. Thor shouted something into the crowd that sounded like a threat.

In disbelief, Ragnar turned towards the direction from which the voice had come. There, he saw Thor standing with Jalla. The warrior had wrapped his muscular arm around her throat, nearly cutting off her breath. Enja's sister had clawed both hands into his forearm and screamed in panic. In his other hand, Thor held a knife. He threatened to stab the poor woman at any moment.

In disbelief, Ragnar looked toward Conor. One of the other bodyguards was holding him fast with brutal force. His boy struggled fiercely, but against the strength of a full-grown man, he stood no chance.

Ragnar drew in a sharp breath. Arnulf's bodyguard had clearly been ordered to intervene should their leader fall at a disadvantage. He would not be able to kill his opponent today, as tradition demanded. With their treacherous plan, they now held the situation in their grasp and could keep not only him, but all the other villagers, in check.

"Drop the staff, Ragnar!" Thor shouted at him. He must have repeated it several times already, for Jalla was hysterically urging him to kill Arnulf, crying that her own life meant nothing to her.

Then, Ragnar looked to the spokesman of the Elders, who had stepped forward at once.

"This is against the rules!" Gudmundur shouted hoarsely, shaking with rage, and the others joined him in loud agreement.

"You are breaking our traditions! Any further rule by Arnulf is hereby excluded." As he spoke, he clenched his fists and thrust them threateningly toward Arnulf, who was just then struggling to his feet again, gasping for breath.

Ragnar tightened his grip on the staff. The danger to Jalla and Conor was grave. He could still kill Arnulf, but suddenly, Arnulf growled menacingly. He had freed himself by loosening the noose around his foot.

In horror, Ragnar saw Arnulf hurl himself in fury at the old man who had stepped closer to them on the fighting ground. Gudmundur had struck him from behind with his courageous defiance, so his voice had to be silenced. Ragnar's rope kept him from intervening, and he was forced to watch, utterly unable to intervene.

With only a few brutal punches, Arnulf brought the old man down. He stood no chance against the raging man's strength and collapsed, bleeding and motionless. All eyes were fixed in horror on the dreadful scene.

That was why no one noticed the person who was taking advantage of the chaos. Enja had moved to the opposite side of the arena. Advancing behind the spectators, she drew closer to what was unfolding. Ragnar was the first to realise it, for his gaze had sought her where she had stood all along. The place was empty, and he immediately knew why. Hastily, he looked to the other side of the oval, where Jalla cried out once more in terror.

Enja appeared beside her sister and drove her fist into Thor's temple. The startled bodyguard reflexively lowered the hand holding the knife, as well as the other arm with which he had been gripping Jalla. He staggered sideways, and Enja followed with a precise kick to his knee. All could hear the crack of bones shattering beneath her boot. A short roar tore from Thor's throat. Ragnar clearly saw the knife lodged in the man's chest. Enja had neutralised the bodyguard with his own weapon.

Suddenly, Arnulf surged back to life. Furious at having lost his man to Enja, he advanced on Ragnar, whose leg was still bound in the noose. Arnulf, by contrast, could move freely. Ragnar raised the staff defensively. But it was no longer a threat to Arnulf, for he now held an axe in his hand, thrown to him by one of his men. It all happened in the blink of an eye.

Now Ragnar found himself in a dire situation. He could barely grasp the speed at which everything was unfolding. First, the old man, grievously injured by Arnulf. Then, Thor, stabbed by Enja. Now, it was his turn.

Hastily, he tried to free the noose from his leg. In the background, he heard people screaming. Ragnar's men now seemed to be attacking the bodyguards. Enja and Mina were likely among them, but he had no eyes for that now.

He saw only Arnulf, aiming at him with the axe in his hand. His opponent was truly pulling out every stop. He would not even need to come closer. Ragnar was utterly at the mercy of his enemy's thrown weapon. Was this his death sentence? Would he die unworthily with an axe buried in his chest? He knew only one man who could catch an axe in mid-air, and that was Cathal, his former comrade. It was impossible!

Arnulf drew back. Ragnar's fate seemed sealed. The fatal blow was about to strike him. Even he would not be able to evade a precisely thrown axe. But it did not come to that.

Suddenly, Ragnar felt someone throw themselves in front of him. A person he had not expected. A slender body that had reacted just in time. It was Conor, hurling himself against his chest and wrapping his arms around him.

Ragnar felt the impact strike the boy's body as though it were his own. The force of the weapon shook him as violently as if he himself had been hit. Conor groaned and sagged in his arms. "Conor," Ragnar stammered in horror and dreadful clarity. "Conor, what have you done?"

A thousandfold rip of pain tore through the father of the child he loved so deeply that he would have done anything for him. Ragnar's voice failed him. Slowly, he sank to his knees, drawing the boy's lifeless body down with him. Gently, he laid him on his side and saw the blade of the axe embedded in his back. It was lodged halfway in, directly beneath the shoulder blades. Blood gushed from the gaping wound.

As a former mercenary, he knew this wound was deep and fatal. Internal organs were likely already damaged. A sense of utter helplessness spread through him, along with an all-consuming pain, as though someone were tearing his heart from his chest. His son—the one he had fought for these past years, the one for whom dying would have been worth it—was now breathing out his life. Tears welled in his eyes. His vision blurred as he realised that Conor was still conscious. The brave boy's mismatched eyes looked up at him, his lips shaping words, but no sound came from his mouth.

"Why did you do this?" Ragnar whispered, stunned. His rough hands cradled the pale face with tenderness. Tears fell onto Conor's cheeks and mingled with his blood. "Your life was worth so much more ..."

Words and composure slipped from him. His son had given his life for him. Conor was so young. The axe had been meant for his blackened soul, and God knew, he had deserved it. Ragnar's chest tightened. He held the boy's motionless body pressed against him, as though he might breathe life into him once more. In his shock and through a veil of tears, he did not notice what was happening on the other side of the arena.

There, Enja and her companions fought bravely to overpower the bodyguards. She had not yet realised that her son was dead. Poorly armed outlaws waged an unequal battle, yet they seized the weapons of their enemies.

Arnulf recognised his hopeless situation the moment the axe throw had failed. Conor had sacrificed himself for his father, and Ragnar had survived. His men were, even now, being overpowered by the villagers. He had no options left. He cast a frantic glance around. Escape! That was all he could think.

Like a mangy dog, he slunk away while his fighters risked their lives for him, and Ragnar clutched his dying son. At last, the brave men and women around Enja made short work of it once they had gained the upper hand. The few fighters who remained surrendered when Enja assured them that no punishment would befall them if they swore loyalty to her. For she was now the new clan leader, whether Arnulf was dead or not.

From among the group, Jalla was the first to realise that something was wrong with Conor. She climbed over the wooden barrier and threw herself in horror upon the boy's lifeless body. Ragnar let her have him and released his hold. In deep grief, she began to sob and wail. Her pain was genuine; she had loved him as her own son. Ragnar watched the scene with clenched resolve. His heart had frozen. He felt nothing at all. A shout tore him from his shock.

"Arnulf!" Enja shouted from the crowd. "He's trying to flee!"

From the edge of the fighting ground, she pointed with her finger towards a path that would lead the clan leader into a forest. There, he could hide well. Enja had understood what was happening, but from her position and amid the press of the crowd, she had still not discovered Conor's lifeless body.

Ragnar rose to his feet, wracked with pain.

Jalla's cheeks were flushed with tears and her chest heaved, yet she resolutely drew a knife from her belt.

"Here," she choked out between two sobs, "finish that pig."

Ragnar's gaze met Jalla's. Her eyes were swollen, and her mouth twitched dangerously, yet her expression held a deadly resolve.

"Avenge your son."

No one needed to tell Ragnar that. With a single cut, he finally severed the rope from his foot. Now he was free and could pursue the fleeing man. Ragnar knew he would not return until Arnulf was dead.

"Arnulf is already dead. He just doesn't know it yet."

The threat in his voice left no doubt, Jalla's husband was doomed to die. She only nodded and kissed the bloodless face of the boy on the ground.

Then, Ragnar was gone.

Chapter 18

Iceland, Akureyri, June 1331

Fortune and sorrow are bound as one. Without suffering, we would never know happiness, and without joy, pain would be without end.

Old Sigrun, who, as clan elder, buried the dead Gudmundur alongside the villagers, had spoken with wisdom. Her words honoured a man who, to his final breath, had upheld the ancient traditions of their forebears. Arnulf had struck the old man brutally upon the head when he had dared to stand against the breach of law in the struggle for the throne. For his belief in what law still meant, Gudmundur paid with his life, succumbing to his wounds in the night that followed.

The dead of Akureyri were laid out in a cave where, for thousands of years, lifeless bodies wrapped in linen had been left behind. The tides and the hand of nature reclaimed, piece by piece, what life had once bestowed upon them. Their souls would join those of the others and dwell in peace in the world beyond.

Mount Helgafjell had been Gudmundur's declared destination in the world beyond, so the wise woman Sigrun told us. It was an imagined place in the Nordic faith, where he was to be reunited with his family for all eternity. For the burial rite, Sigrun placed his few possessions at his feet and spoke words I did not understand. Incense candles thickened the air. Vaguely, their scent reminded me of myrrh.

Mina and I stood beside Sigrun, who had just delivered the funeral speech. She had braided her long grey hair into a single plait. As a mark of her rank, a circlet of silver rested upon her brow and a chain of wildflowers adorned her neck. In mourning, her eyes were rimmed in black with coal. As the eldest among the wise, she now spoke for the council and was, at the same time, the shaman of the tribe. Sigrun looked at me expectantly with her black eyes, framed by deep-set lines. As clan leader, it was now my duty to give those present the sign that the ceremony was complete.

I crossed myself in the name of my Lord Jesus. "May God receive Gudmundur in the world beyond," I said, speaking from my own faith. "For me, there is but one afterlife for all who die. One heaven, and one hell. You were a brave man, Gudmundur. Go in peace."

With those solemn words, I turned once more toward the exit, accessible only at low tide. The sea murmured softly against the rocks. As everywhere in this bay, the waters here were restrained. That evening, a mood of peace prevailed, a deceptive peace that had not reached my heart. The burial of the dead was a duty I was bound to attend as leader, yet my heart lay heavy with worry.

The past days had been among the worst of my life. As though God had decreed a particularly cruel punishment for me, the dreadful scenes surrounding Conor replayed again and again before my mind's eye. I knew that such reflections plagued people after deep wounds of the soul. It was a torment that churned through my insides like a blunt knife.

In that moment, my thoughts surged up once more, and with them my guilt. I could not comprehend why I had not recognised the danger to Conor sooner, especially when I had already eliminated the most dangerous man from Arnulf's band.

During the decisive clash, I had realised what the brute intended, just as Ragnar was about to deliver the final blow to kill his opponent. At that moment of reckoning, the powerful fighter had seized my sister brutally and clamped his hand around her throat. A second bodyguard had grabbed Conor, who stood beside Jalla. A knife had flashed in Thor's hand, and he had pressed it to Jalla's throat while Conor fought fiercely against the other man.

"Hold, Ragnar!" Thor had shouted. "Let Arnulf go, or Jalla will die!"

The blood had drained from my face. Whether from shock or rage, I could no longer tell. It was a breach of all rules and, above all, cowardly. Ragnar would never have delivered a killing blow with his wooden staff. He would never have endangered my sister's life. Under no circumstances. Jalla had cried out bravely and struggled beneath the bodyguard's rough grip, yet she could do nothing against him. She had been helpless.

But I was not!

Without hesitation, without a single thought, I had slipped through the crowd from behind towards the two hostages. Thor continued to bellow at the mass of people, and Arnulf's voice had briefly been heard, too, but I paid no heed to their shouts. I focused entirely on what I now had to do.

The two bodyguards had felt secure among their own and had not expected an attack. Erik and his companions had already broken away from the crowd. They noticed at once as I crept up on Thor; thus, we were able to catch them off guard from both sides.

The bodyguard who had held Conor in a crushing grip was taken completely by surprise when I suddenly appeared at his side. A single punch to the temple knocked him unconscious. He likely felt nothing of the pain from my kick to his knee before his leg buckled sideways. All of it unfolded in a matter of seconds. Conor immediately dropped away, slipping out of the danger zone. Within the next breath, I turned on Thor. He stared at me in stunned disbelief as I appeared before him so abruptly. In his desperation, he shoved Jalla towards me to gain a moment's space. I had anticipated that. With little effort, I ducked swiftly past the knife in his hand, seized his arm, and twisted it into a simple joint lock. Using the momentum, I drove the blade into his heart. It was a trick taught by my old master, Shi Fu. Both men were neutralised in seconds.

Thor's knife had not been a sharp Scottish dagger, yet it was enough to end his life. My gaze swept to my sister as she hauled herself up from the ground. With a firm grip beneath her arm and a glance into her face, I made certain she was unharmed. Jalla nodded, signalling that she was not injured. In that instant, her eyes slid past me, and something compelled her to rush forward. I turned back towards the fighters who still depended on my aid.

My allies had fallen upon the remaining bodyguards at the same moment I struck Thor. We were all so deeply entangled in the chaos of battle that the tragedy unfolding in the arena went unnoticed at first.

Arnulf's men had finally come to their senses and heeded my command to surrender to me. I reminded them that I was now their leader. Until that very moment, everyone had believed that Ragnar had defeated Arnulf once and for all.

Only once the turmoil among the warriors had subsided did I turn towards Ragnar. Sweat had carved rivulets down my brow, and I had to wipe my eyes with my sleeve.

My wandering gaze had snagged on the man who had just hurled an axe—Arnulf. I could not believe my eyes. What I saw stole the breath from my lungs. For a tormenting moment, my pulse ceased. I would never forget that instant for as long as I lived. The image of my motionless son on the ground, my sister clutching him to her, seared itself forever into my memory. My heart drove cold blood through my veins, and my lungs forgot how to breathe, the air thinning around me. Black spots danced before my eyes. It was like a grotesque nightmare.

The sight of my blood-soaked son in the centre of the arena plunged me into a kind of stunned paralysis. The haft of an axe jutted from his back. Beside him, his desperate father had fallen to his knees. Ragnar's face was grey as ash. Jalla held Conor's lifeless body in her arms, sobbing.

Cries of horror rang out. All had understood who had hurled the axe at Conor, and they cursed aloud the man who had so cravenly sought to save his own life. Arnulf had just hauled himself upright and turned clumsily about. At once, he realised that his men had surrendered. From them, he would receive no aid. His plan had failed.

He glanced about wildly, like a beast driven into a corner. There was only one direction in which he could flee, towards the place where no spectators remained, for all had rushed to aid Erik's men. It was the villagers' one chance to rid themselves of Arnulf once and for all. They recognised the moment for what it was. In that instant, they cried out loudly for his death.

The voices around me blurred into a cacophony of shouts and lamentation. The men and women—Arnulf included—no longer mattered to me. Suddenly, I felt trapped in another world, sunk into a sea of soft wool. Shock drove my movements as though in a trance. Slowly, step by step, I placed one foot before the other. My limbs scarcely obeyed me. All the while, I screamed at Ragnar again and again to kill Arnulf at last. It did not sound like my voice. Only dimly did I register Ragnar's response. At last, he stirred, and looked after the fleeing Arnulf.

The cruel realisation of what had happened seeped slowly into my mind. Like molten lava, the certainty scorched a trail of devastation through my soul. My son lay dying in Jalla's arms, and I had to be with him now.

Jalla had recognised it, too. She drew a dagger from her belt and handed it to Ragnar. He broke free from his paralysis and tore the axe from Conor's back. With a feral roar, he went after Arnulf to finish him once and for all. With astonishing speed, as though he were still the warrior of twenty, he chased after the fleeing man.

I dragged myself towards Conor, as though every step had to be fought for. Blood streamed down his body. So much blood.

Wordlessly, I dropped to my knees beside him. Jalla's shoulders shook, her dark hair soaked with tears. Her soundless sobbing was little more than a whimper. With a trembling hand, I grasped her shoulder so that she would release Conor.

How often had I faced such brutality in my life? Yet never had it been my own child lying before me in that state. My emotions were shut down. I had not known I was capable of such practiced detachment, but my mind had simply taken over, unyielding. I had to save my boy. The strain I endured in that moment was nothing like the stress of a battlefield with hundreds of enemies around me. It was worse. This was my son's life.

Arnulf was doomed to die. The thought hammered through Ragnar's mind again and again as blind hatred surged through his veins. This man bore the guilt of his son's death.

Ragnar had been pursuing Arnulf for an hour. His swollen thigh throbbed and ached in time with his steps. His rival had at least one shattered shoulder, and despite his head start, his strength would fail him eventually. The terrain was well known to Ragnar. For years, he and his companions had struggled to survive in this harsh wilderness. He knew every river, rise, and hiding place, thanks to Arnulf, who had condemned him to that life.

Arnulf—the name drove Ragnar onward. In his mind, he envisioned strangling him with his bare hands, watching him draw his final breath before death claimed him, seeing him soil himself in terror.

The dreadful moment flickered through Ragnar's mind once more. No person should ever have to witness their own child die. Conor had thrown himself bravely in front of him to shield him from certain death, and with an ugly sound, Arnulf's weapon had driven deep into the boy's slender back.

Without a second thought, Ragnar had torn the axe from his son's lifeless body. Jalla's knife was not enough to kill Arnulf with certainty. He followed close behind the murderer as he fled the arena.

Arnulf had to be close. His fist clenched around the haft of the weapon, its blade still slick with his son's blood. With every agonising step, his rage burned ever hotter. Ragnar cursed, groaned, and sweated, yet he did not stop. He would never stop. He had to kill Arnulf, even if it was the last thing he ever did.

The tracks in the fresh grass were unmistakable. Arnulf was a heavy man, leaving deep impressions in the wet earth. Even on dry ground, the blades of grass lay visibly crushed. The man was running for his life. Not even the river he had waded through slowed Ragnar. The broken branches on the far bank clearly marked where Arnulf had hauled himself from the water.

Like a growling bear, Ragnar followed his trail. His gaze raced across the landscape unfolding before him. To Ragnar's left, the sea lay still; Arnulf could not be there. To the right, rose a steep incline of rocky formations, and climbing it would cost the wounded Arnulf too much time and strength.

Ahead, towards the south, stretched only gentle green hills where sheep grazed. Had he taken that path, his pursuer would have seen him from far away.

Ragnar was no more than a mile behind the fugitive, he sensed it instinctively. Likely less, he thought grimly, if Arnulf was even half as exhausted as his rival. He kneaded his thigh, which burned as though set aflame. On the stony path, the lead could not have amounted to more than a few minutes.

Ragnar chose the rocky high path. From above, he would have a clearer view of the surroundings. Deep down, he suspected Arnulf had fled that way for the very same reason; the countless granite stones offered solid cover.

Ragnar's legs were weary. First, the march to Akureyri that morning, then, the gruelling duel, and now, the pursuit. Yet he possessed a far stronger motive than the fleeing man ahead of him. He had his son to avenge, and that drove him on without mercy.

His thighs trembled with exertion, his feet, trapped in leather shoes, were raw from sweat and damp, and his lungs whistled with every breath. Ragnar ignored the pain. An unseen force lashed him onwards. He had now reached the path that ran along the base of the steep slope. Shepherds must have worn it into the ground, for it was clearly defined. Black gravel lay scattered across the way and great boulders lined the path like sentinels before a vast entrance.

Ragnar was just passing another of those monoliths when he heard it. Something massive whistled past his ear at great speed and grazed his shoulder. It was a stone, large enough to kill him on the spot. Instinctively, he threw himself aside, ignoring the blood spilling from the gash at his collarbone. His battle instinct had awakened. Ragnar cursed himself for not having considered this possibility. His exhaustion had made him careless.

Arnulf had thrown the stone from above. He had likely hidden atop the boulder, lying in wait for him. Ragnar pressed his back against the smooth granite face of the monolith, shielding himself against another attack.

Step by step, he edged backwards along the oval stone. Straining, he stared upwards. There had to be a ledge up there where Arnulf had found footing. From that vantage point, Ragnar's presence would not have gone unnoticed.

Ragnar weighed his options. He had the axe, Arnulf only stones. Another rock came flying, this time missing its target entirely. From his hiding place above, Arnulf could likely no longer make him out clearly. The arc of the throw betrayed the attacker's position. The element of surprise was gone, and up there, Arnulf was trapped. How many stones did he have left?

Ragnar stepped forward boldly. He was certain he could now evade any further throws, and indeed, from this angle he could make out his rival higher up. The granite boulder rose perhaps five men high into the sky. Arnulf crouched atop the massive rock, staring down at him. He must have brought a handful of large stones into his hiding place, but now, only one remained. He held it ready in his hand. Arnulf had realised he was trapped. He rose to his feet and appeared to wait for Ragnar.

Ragnar drew a deep breath, then let it out. He would have to bring his opponent down from up there. A few steps more, and he spotted a jagged notch in the stone. It was a fissure in the otherwise smooth monolith, cast forth by one of the many volcanoes. Arnulf must have climbed up here.

Ragnar did the same now. If that bulky man with an injured shoulder had managed to climb up, then he would manage it twice over. He shoved the axe into his belt to free both hands, then he hauled himself up the boulder. His muscles burned, his shoulder struck by the stone throbbed with pain, and the climb demanded Ragnar's last reserves of strength, yet it would be a pleasure to finish off that cursed man up there. For Conor and for Enja, once and for all.

Ragnar's keen gaze remained fixed on Arnulf throughout the entire ascent. Arnulf's face twisted increasingly into a mask of panic. In the grip of his fear of death, he had lost all composure. The former clan leader now stood alone.

Two more pull-ups with bloodied fingers, and Ragnar reached the plateau of the granite stone. Over time, the weather had laid a thin layer of moss across its surface. Breathing heavily, the warrior stopped at a cautious distance from Arnulf. He struggled to keep his balance on the uneven ground. Weakness surged through his legs, setting them trembling. Blood and sweat ran into his eyes, which he wiped away begrudgingly with his sleeve.

Ragnar drew his axe from his belt and stalked toward his greatest foe. Rats driven into a corner were dangerous.

"Don't you dare jump, Arnulf. You would rob me of the pleasure of splitting your skull with my axe, the very same weapon that killed my son."

Ragnar's voice dripped with hatred. Just so had he once stood on the battlefield, mocking his enemies. As a mercenary, he had killed for the basest of reasons; for coin, glory, or simply sport, but now he had a declared purpose. He would execute his son's murderer.

"I did not mean to kill Conor," Arnulf croaked hoarsely. He sensed what awaited him. "It was a terrible accident!"

Ragnar stepped forward once more, and Arnulf slid farther back. He was already standing at the point farthest away from Ragnar.

"He was my son, too!" he cried desperately.

Seemingly resigned, he raised the hand holding the stone, as though he meant to surrender. His left arm hung limply at his side. It dawned on Ragnar that it must have taken enormous effort to climb up here with an injured shoulder, but he banished the thought in an instant, for the seemingly helpless clan leader was drawing back for one final blow.

Arnulf hurled the stone at him with desperate force. At the same instant, Ragnar hurled the axe. Then, the unthinkable happened.

Axe and stone collided in mid-air.

A harsh clang froze both rivals in place. The axe struck the stone, which rolled heavily and harmlessly to Ragnar's feet. The axe, however, carried on a little farther towards Arnulf because of its greater weight. Like a wayward missile, the weapon slammed blade-first into the ground before him and spun several times on its axis. It whistled past Arnulf's feet as it did so. The hunted man saw his chance, bent down to snatch the axe, and stepped back in the process. With one hand, he caught the weapon by the haft and yanked it up with a triumphant grin.

It was the final step of his life.

The sloping stone became his undoing. With the weapon in his hand, Arnulf plunged into the depths. A scream of terror accompanied his fall before it cut off abruptly as another ugly sound rose from below.

God's judgement, Ragnar thought without emotion.

Long after silence had fallen, he stood, breathing heavily. He heard nothing, saw nothing, and felt as though he were numb and incapable of forming a clear thought. Arnulf was dead, but that did not bring Conor back to life.

Suddenly, unimaginable pain lashed through him, through his head, his entire body, and his soul. Ragnar was utterly spent. He did not feel the tears running down his cheeks.

They streamed down uncontrollably, beyond his power to stop them.

Slowly and in agony, he finally descended the rock once more. Arnulf's unnaturally twisted corpse lay on the path. He must have died instantly. The axe lay not far from him. With a deep sigh, Ragnar looked toward the sun, caught at a point on the horizon. From there, it would slide straight down and vanish almost imperceptibly. Evening must already have advanced far.

But Ragnar Sigurdsson would not rest until he had returned to the village. With the axe, he would sever the dead man's head from his body and bring the grisly remains to the people of Akureyri as proof of his vengeance. Surely Enja, as the new clan leader, would place the head of Conor's murderer upon a stake, as a warning to all who might dare challenge her right to the throne.

Groaning, I straightened up. It was long past supper, yet I had felt no hunger. My body, soul, and mind were utterly hollowed out. In the past hours, I had neither slept nor eaten. Like an agitated tiger, I had paced back and forth before my son's sickbed. Again and again, I turned over the questions that were circling in my mind.

Had I examined all his organs? Had I overlooked something? Were there still tears, internal bleeding, or foreign objects lodged in Conor's flesh?

But I had done everything humanly possible, everything within my power. Conor's motionless body lay upon his bed, pale and without any sign that he would survive such a grave wound.

When I pulled him from Jalla's arms on the fighting ground, I first thought he was dead, until I noticed a faint breath. So slight that I felt it only when I held my eye close to his nostril. My pulse surged. I screamed hysterically at the people around me to bring my physician's bag, which Arnulf had taken from me upon my arrival in Akureyri. With long strides and my bleeding son in my arms, I ran to the longhouse, where I had enough space to treat him. The villagers followed in panic, then hurried to gather my instruments with all haste.

Fortune favoured me in that moment. Jalla knew where my bag had been hidden, and the women prepared clean cloths exactly as I instructed them.

Conor was still alive! Never had I sent so many prayers to my God as in that moment, but it was only a matter of time how long Conor would survive with such blood loss. I therefore decided to operate on him at once to examine his internal organs. If he was still alive at that point, then no vital organs could have been damaged. So went my theory.

With one sweep of my arm, I sent cups and plates clattering loudly from the table where Arnulf and his companions had once sat. Helpers stepped in to turn Conor onto his stomach. Only dimly did I register that a few of Arnulf's men were silently lending their hands. One stoked the fire in the hearth to heat my instruments.

Fortunately, Jalla returned shortly after with my bag, breathing hard. Wordlessly, she handed me the instruments I asked for: scalpel, forceps, and suturing kit. Meanwhile, Mina carried torches in from outside.

When I began the operation, the room fell deathly silent. Conor's life hung by a silken thread, and I held it in my hands. In the depths of my being, I hoped he would neither awaken during my work nor slip into death. My lips moved of their own accord as I murmured prayers again and again.

The axe had shattered Conor's shoulder blade and pierced two ribs, yet the force had not been sufficient to drive deeper into the body. That was what spared his internal organs. Conor had been incredibly lucky. A large scar would remain across his back, marking him for the rest of his life.

If he survived, a dreadful fear seeped into my very gut.

I focused on my work. In the next step, I covered the wound with linen cloths that had been soaked in arnica and nettle brew. They protected the injury and, I hoped, would encourage healing.

Conor was a young man. His recovery could progress swiftly if the dangerous wound fever did not yet claim him. That was what I feared most.

With Jalla's help, I shaped a mixture of clay and healing mud that hardened like stone after a while. We laid my still-unconscious son into it and spread the remainder across his chest and shoulders. Thus, we sealed the cocoon of soft clay around his body and left the mixture to dry. Conor would have to lie within it for at least four weeks.

I had done everything I could. Now, only hope for healing remained. What followed were agonising hours of waiting, during which I paced restlessly back and forth through the longhouse.

At this late hour, a suffocating stillness had settled over Akureyri. The uncertainty surrounding Conor's life gnawed at the people's nerves, much like Iceland's barely setting sun. The events of the past hours had drained all strength, and weariness had crept in. Only my mind kept me awake. It must already have been past midnight.

Sigrun, the shaman and village elder, performed all manner of smoke offerings and danced in place with a plaintive voice. Without pause, she paid homage to the gods and pleaded for my son's life. Others merely sat or slept. Not even the bitter scents of the smouldering herbs could keep them awake.

I followed Sigrun's example and begged my God for forgiveness for my sins. I implored Him to spare my son, clinging to the hope that his death could not be His will. Then, in turn, I cursed blasphemously, sank down in frustration, and pounded my fists into the dried clay floor. Anyone who saw me must have thought I was possessed by the devil.

Perhaps I was. At some point, I collapsed inward, utterly spent. Jalla, who kept unshakable vigil at Conor's bed, eventually handed me a cup filled with a sharp liquid. I smelled it. It was unmistakably alcohol. She studied me oddly over the rim of the cup. My sister could not know that I could not tolerate the stuff, but this time, I did not care. I only wanted the demons driving me mad to vanish from my mind. With a trembling hand, I took the clay cup from her and raised it to my lips, ready to surrender myself to this devil's brew, should it choose to claim me.

At that moment, I heard a commotion outside the entrance of the longhouse. Instinctively, I drew my katana from the sheath on my back, which Jalla had returned to me alongside my old leather bag from Arnulf's weapons store.

The grip around the tsuka—the hilt of the katana—felt so familiar that a sense of safety flooded through me. Whatever was happening out there, I was prepared. With this weapon, I felt invincible.

Angry male voices rang out. Despite my grief and exhaustion, I had to act. With fierce resolve, I pressed the dangerous alcoholic drink back into Jalla's hand, squared my shoulders, and pulled aside the animal hides covering the entrance to the longhouse. Outside, a horrifying sight awaited me.

Ragnar stood bleeding and utterly spent before the people of Akureyri, holding aloft the skull with Arnulf's twisted visage by its long hair. The stump was still wet with blood. Ragnar had returned in the middle of the night to prove to me that he had avenged his son and slain my rival.

Now, there were no doubts left; my family's position was secure. A great sense of relief washed over me, despite my fears for Conor.

The people around me recognised the head of the dead leader and erupted into exuberant cheers. Mina, who had run out of the tent beside me, simply joined in. She did not understand a single word of what was being shouted around her, yet her face lit up completely. A mad, almost absurd joy surged within me. The people here seemed happy, as though a great burden had been lifted from them.

Ragnar recognised me in front of the longhouse and staggered towards me, shuffling weakly. I had not seen him so utterly drained in a long time. He must have fought until the very end. For us. For his clan. Feelings surged within me, emotions I usually kept tightly reined. I swallowed the lump in my throat with effort. I could barely bring myself to embrace him here.

With a final exertion of strength, he laid Arnulf's head before me. In a rasping voice, he told what had happened, loud enough for all to hear. Then, with bloodstained hands, he drew the insignia of the clan leader from his torn tunic and handed them to Sigrun.

I slid the katana back into its holster, for there was no danger, except that I might lose my heart to Ragnar forever.

Sigrun draped the shimmering chain over my shoulders. I had to bend down towards her, for the old woman was not tall. The intricately worked silver brooch, meant for a cloak, she fastened instead to my weapons tunic, for lack of one. All the while, she murmured words I had never heard before. It was likely the enthronement in Icelandic. Like everything this people did, the ceremony was austere, simple, and practical.

Sigrun stepped back and bowed weakly. Many of the men around me now called out my name. The women joined in, cheering, "Enja Leifsdottir, wife of Ragnar Sigurdsson and clan leader of Akureyri!"

At last, the noise ebbed, and I stepped forward. The excitement had given me one more solid surge of strength. Despite my exhaustion, I was filled with pride, and I tried to appear confident and charismatic to the people before me.

"People of Akureyri!"

I had to clear my throat. It had been a long time since I had spoken to people who placed their trust in me. I searched my memory for my knowledge of the Icelandic tongue.

"I scarcely knew my father, my mother died for me, and here I stand as the rightful clan leader of Akureyri. Once, I was meant to be sacrificed to your gods to halt the eruption of Hekla. My father fell victim to that power. The gods did not will my death, they helped me find my way back across great distances to my land, and now I am here, as your leader."

With one hand, I wiped a tear from my eye.

"I follow a different faith from you, yet I understand what drives you and why you believe in the Norse gods. One day, I will show you how powerful my Lord is—our God, in whom we believe," and as I spoke, I looked into Ragnar's eyes, who had stepped proudly to my side. He did not look away from me even once, "…and how merciful He can be."

I fervently hoped Ragnar would not make any emotional gesture. I would not have survived it in that moment.

"My son is fighting for his life in this house. I have tended to him as well as I am able. Now, I place his fate in the hands of my God."

My voice trembled slightly now after all, and I struggled to keep my composure. Ragnar flinched. Only now did he grasp that Conor was not yet dead. The last time he had seen him, he had lain lifeless in Jalla's arms. His face suddenly bore an expression that tightened my throat. Hope, love, his entire heart lay within it. He drew in a sharp breath, and for a moment his eyelids fluttered.

"But I hold it in high regard that you, too, call upon your gods for their aid," I added with effort.

My voice grew ever quieter. Ragnar's hand closed around my shoulder after all, and he pulled me against him. A kiss upon my temple burst the knot that had lodged so stubbornly in my throat. Damn it.

"So help me God," I whispered, barely audible. Then I lowered my head to Ragnar's shoulder and wiped countless tears from my eyes.

Only twenty-four hours later, the fever set in. At times, Conor woke, and I was able to speak with him. For the first time, I had the chance to exchange words with my son, now standing on the threshold of death. What a cruel fate.

Conor was an intelligent boy with a profound knowledge of animals and weapons. How could it be otherwise with Ragnar as his father? He possessed a natural curiosity, and I never tired of telling him my stories from the Orient. It made the hours bearable in which he drifted between clarity and delirium. Again and again, I wiped the sweat from his brow and cooled his calves with cold compresses. I did everything to lower the fever that threatened to consume him from within.

It was a race against time, yet Conor was a tough lad. Yellow fluid seeped from his wound, a sign of the foul humours spreading through his body and draining his strength. It became ever clearer to me that he would not live much longer. We were fighting an unseen enemy. In desperation, Jalla and I flushed his festering wound very carefully, so as not to endanger the healing of the bones. No effort was too great for us.

In those days, I grew deeply humble. Ragnar, too, had realised that the hours with Conor were merely borrowed. His death seemed inevitable. Never had I sent so many prayers to the Lord God, who now seemed to have abandoned me. Even Ragnar had grown very quiet. I promised the Lord in heaven things I had never promised in my life before. I clung to every smallest shred of hope. It did not grow better.

Why I suddenly believed in God with such fervour was unclear to me, but never had I longed so desperately to heal a human being with my worldly medical skill and God's aid. I would have promised my soul to the devil, if only it would have helped.

At some point, Conor's frail body refused all nourishment, a certain sign of his approaching death. God gave me no reprieve. Ragnar and I had sinned too greatly, and this was our punishment.

It was Conor's birthday, the twenty-ninth of June, when Mina made a decisive discovery. On that day, Conor had turned fifteen. A day he no longer experienced in full consciousness.

Mina had been searching my leather bag for pain-relieving pills. In doing so, she had come upon a filled leather pouch. It was the small sachet of foul-smelling powder that Moira had given me as a parting gift in Dunguaire. Thoughtfully, Mina handed me the medicine my old friend had been so proud of.

I grimaced in disgust as I held the contents beneath my nose. It smelled exactly like what I had found aboard the ship to Scotland in Isaak's wonder chest. Back then, I had given a brew of it to the gravely ill Cathal, and it had not taken long before the fever subsided. After that, he had recovered completely, as if by a miracle.

I stared at Mina in disbelief. I had not thought of this medicine, which Moira swore by, in all this time. Almost greedily, I grabbed the pouch and shook it. Suddenly, an overwhelmingly vivid memory rose before my eyes, as if Isaak himself stood there in the flesh, grinning with his gap-toothed smile and pointing at the little bag with his weasel-like eyes.

"This is the medicine that cures even severe fever," he had slurred, a little tipsy from his date wine. "No other physician before me has discovered it. You only have to find the right dosage," he hiccupped twice in between, "so that it can truly unfold its power."

Years later, I had discovered the precise dosage encoded on the bottom of the leather pouch. Isaak had filled the container as a travel portion and revealed the dosage in his scrawled handwriting. I had told Moira the story a thousand times. The clever healer would not rest until she had tracked down the recipe. She had been utterly obsessed with finding the correct preparation … a remedy for all that the body cannot fight on its own, she had explained to me. Her strange words resurfaced in my mind.

Could it be? I did not speak it aloud. Excitedly, I tilted the pouch and looked at its bottom. There it was indeed, written in clear numerals: 642. Moira could write Arabic numbers, but not letters. I had taught her this to make the dosing of medicines easier. Instead of naming the herbs, she simply stitched a dried piece of the plant onto parchment or leather. Even Catriona, her daughter, had thus been able to roll my pills and prepare a brew. It was our little arithmetic of medicine.

Moira could not have known how grateful I was for her foresight. If it was the same active substance Isaak had once used, then it might truly help Conor. Why this medicine conquered so many feverish illnesses had remained a mystery to me, yet it triggered something within the body that aided it in lowering the excessive heat. Perhaps one day, I would discover how it worked, now that I held the remedy in my hands. But in that moment, it no longer mattered.

Work with your mind, not with your heart. Isaak had drilled that into me time and again.

A jolt ran through my body. Suddenly, I knew that God had guided me not to drink the cup of alcohol, and that He had sent Mina to place the pouch in my hands. God was there, and He had heard my prayers. Now it was for me to act upon His signs.

Swiftly, I explained to Mina what I needed: a bowl, measuring spoons, and hot water. The girl ran off at once to gather the items. Jalla followed close behind, grateful to have something to do.

My sister had felt her husband's death as a relief. At first, I had worried that she might harbour anger—or even hatred—towards Ragnar and me, but the opposite was true. She was grateful to have been freed from her marriage. She did not speak much about it, yet she sought closeness with me and cared for Conor as though he were her own child. She would likely need time to process what she had endured. Women burdened with terrible memories sometimes needed years to do so, and some never managed it at all.

My feelings toward her remained restrained. Knowing that we shared the same parents was not enough to forge a bond between us. We had been separated for too long. To me, she was a woman like any other. The only thing that bound us was our love for Conor. I felt responsible for Jalla, and I would take care of her. More than that, I could not manage at this time. Perhaps, one day, a sense of closeness would grow between us. Time, they said, healed many wounds.

Jalla entered with Mina through the drawn-back leather hides, their cheeks flushed. They set a bowl of warm water and several spoons for measuring the powder on a small table beside the sickbed.

I took the leather pouch, opened it, and measured out six medium-sized spoonfuls. The spoon was made of wood and roughly the same size as the one Isaak had used. My fingers trembled slightly. As I stirred the brew, I looked at the child sweating beneath the sheets. Sunken eye sockets and a face far too pale told me that death was already waiting inside his body. The thought that Conor might leave me forever tore my heart apart; that he would never come to know me, and I would never come to know him.

With all my strength, I forced that thought aside. If I did not believe in the medicine's power, then who else would?

I turned to my son to administer the brew. He had fallen into a deep sleep from which he would likely not awaken without help. Expectantly, the two women who had kept vigil with me at his bedside over the past days looked at me. They were counting on me, and on Moira's remedy.

Surrendered to my fate, I simply nodded.

From the other side, Jalla lifted Conor's head and pried his mouth open with her fingers. I fed him spoonful after spoonful until the bowl was empty, pausing in between to make sure he swallowed. It took a long while to get the liquid into him. Then there was nothing left to do but wait. That was one of the hardest trials for me.

Chapter 19

Iceland, Akureyri, September 1331

Love transcended all boundaries. It made no distinction between rich and poor; it knew neither good nor evil. It simply existed, and I savoured the moment in which I could surrender to that incredible sensation. After all that I had seen, endured, and suffered in my life, I took quiet joy in my astonishingly tranquil existence and in everything that had grown dear to me.

Among these blessings was a husband who had transformed from an emotionless, ruthless mercenary into a passable man of soul. Admittedly, Ragnar liked to drive me hard with the sword, yet I was still equal to his physical severity. That I was the leader of the clan, he accepted without prejudice. His conduct towards other men who failed to respect him—or me—often erupted in fits of rage, but I had dealt with such behaviour before. When matters came to a head, my word was law.

At times we engaged in heated debates, yet I would miss them were he not Ragnar. Both James and Ragnar were prone to grandiosity, yet despite this trait, Ragnar had survived to this day. And I would do anything to ensure that he continued to do so.

Slowly, I climbed the rise towards the arena. It was the stage of many traditions and lay not far from the village. It was the place where Arnulf and Ragnar had last crossed blades, and where Conor had nearly died.

At that moment, two men were practising the art of swordsmanship. I paused briefly to catch my breath and glance up towards them.

The sun hung low above our heads, and I blinked against the glare. Shading my eyes with one hand, I watched the two men as they took turns attacking each other with wooden swords. Strike, step, strike, step. That was how my old master, Shi Fu, had taught me. Not only the technique had to be right, but also the rhythm. The sound of wood pieces colliding carried down to me. Even from here, I could already tell that one of the two was the more seasoned fighter.

I smiled and looked down at the samurai sword I held in my hand. Like my katana, the rare weapon was exquisitely crafted, with a leather-wrapped hilt and a silver collar. The blade mirrored the sun's rays as they shone from a cloudless blue sky on that autumn day.

It had once been the sword of Rabia, the daughter of Hassan I'Shabbah. Like me, she had been trained as an assassin in the Orient, and she had died by my hand. I had given her katana to Ragnar back then, with the promise that one day, Conor would be made familiar with this weapon.

My grip on that beautiful piece tightened, and I pressed it against my chest. A slight dizziness washed over me as the memory of that moment returned—one that had deeply shaken me at the time. I had been forced to let my little son Conor go with his father. In hindsight, I was grateful for that decision, as difficult as it had been. It gave me the strength to leave everything behind and, after nearly thirty-nine years, sail back to my homeland. I have never regretted it.

Let go of the past and embrace the present, for it is the only moment we truly possess.

That was it. That was my calling and my daily practice in learning how to face loss and hardship.

Once my heartbeat had settled, I continued up the path that led me to the two fighters. It was a beautiful autumn day; wild grasses and herbs sprawled everywhere tousled by the wind that seemed to blow endlessly across this island. My body had long since adapted to the harshness of the land. This was Iceland, my home. It was like me: fierce at the core, cool on the surface, and shaped by the forces of nature.

My lungs pumped air through me. Physical exertion had always been part of my life. A day without wielding a weapon was a day lost to me. The strength I poured into my daily training preserved the suppleness of a warrior.

Only now did the two men notice me and stop striking at one another with their harmless wooden replicas. One of them was Ragnar, who—as he so often did on such occasions—had removed his tunic. His powerful upper body, covered in countless scars, gleamed with sweat.

When he looked at me, his light blue eyes sparkled with the exhilaration he always felt when facing an opponent. His crooked smile made my heart leap even higher. I handed him the cloth that hung over one of the wooden posts so he could dry himself. My husband accepted it gratefully and wiped his face and chest. Then, with curiosity, his gaze shifted to the weapon in my hand.

The light tunic of the young man who had joined Ragnar clung to his chest, while beads of sweat ran from his tousled hair. His cheeks were flushed from the exertion, yet his face shone with delight.

It was my son, Conor, who restored the peace I had always sought. This child, long believed lost, made me whole again. He healed my soul as though it had been an open wound that had finally closed. Conor was the part that had been missing from my dazzling life.

Conor had, indeed, recovered from his severe injury. Just a few hours after taking the first six spoonfuls of Moira's miracle remedy, the devastating fever had subsided, after four more, it had vanished completely, and with the final two spoonfuls, hope for a full recovery was firmly restored. My son began to eat again and regained his strength swiftly. As a young man still growing, his bones healed more readily than those of a grown adult. Only the scar upon his back would forever remind him of how bravely he had accepted death to save his father as a proud testament to his courage.

Grateful for every day I was allowed to spend with the two men, I had followed father and son to the training ground with the earnest intention of finally giving him his birthday gift today.

"Have you decided to test yourself against me and my sword?" Conor joked, his boyish face twisting into a mischievous grin.

I tilted my head slightly and regarded him coolly. "Until you show your mother the respect she deserves, I will most certainly not cross blades with you."

At once, his lightness vanished, and he turned serious. Ragnar laughed aloud.

"You still have much to learn, my son. With a sword in her hand, your mother has taught the fiercest knights to fear her. Choose your words carefully!"

To soften my words, I gave Conor a conciliatory tap on his slender shoulder.

"At your age, I began training with my katana, and it took an entire lifetime to turn this weapon into the deadliest instrument I have ever held." Then I handed my son Rabia's sword.

I could clearly see recognition flash in Ragnar's eyes. In Galway Harbour, he had watched his companion at the time, Rabia, die beneath my sword, and he had taken her weapon with him to Iceland. In Arnulf's weapons storehouse, there had been not only Ragnar's katana and mine, but also this samurai sword from the previous millennium.

The curiously unadorned Asian weapon was a work of the finest craftsmanship, forged by a true master of his art. Had I not already possessed my katana in this perfect design, I would have kept Rabia's legacy for myself.

Hesitantly, Conor took hold of the extraordinary sword by its hilt and studied it with genuine curiosity. He tested the blade with his hand and promptly cut himself. Startled, he brought the bleeding finger to his lips. It made me smile.

"When we parted many years ago, I asked your father to teach you the proper handling of this sword. At the time, I could not have known that I would ever see you again." I swallowed the feelings rising within me. "I have decided to teach you the samurai technique myself. At fifteen, you are old enough to handle a sharp weapon. You will learn respect because, from now on, every mistake will be painfully felt."

Conor's mismatched eyes sparkled in the low-hanging sun. Whether from joy or excitement, I could not tell, but he thanked me profusely, and Ragnar cast me a loving glance. To him, wielding a katana would have felt like chopping wood with a scalpel. From now on, I would take Conor under my wing. He had no idea how rigorous my instruction would be. To train with such a sharp weapon demanded the strictest discipline.

I was just about to turn away when Conor's surprised exclamation stopped me.

"Do you want to start with me right away, Mother?" he asked. "I'm already warmed up, and Father is tired …"

For that impertinence, the cheeky lad earned a scolding from Ragnar.

"I'll show you who's tired here …" he growled menacingly.

"We begin tomorrow at sunrise," I decreed.

Conor looked at me in disbelief. "So early?"

"Yes," I replied evenly. "That way we'll arrive at the service in good time."

Only now did it slowly dawn on him what he had committed himself to, but he recovered quickly. "I will be here on time, Mother."

For a brief moment, he was once more the serious young man I had met months ago, anxious and careful not to offend. Since Arnulf's death, Conor had gained a measure of confidence, and he would need it, for he was a talented fighter. To be truly good, one needed courage and skill. Courage, he already possessed.

The church in Akureyri had been built by all the villagers together, using the wood of the native birch trees. I had driven the construction forwards once Conor had recovered. It had been my vow to God. Admittedly, it was made in one of my weakest hours, somewhere between cursing and prayer, when I gave that promise. I would build a church in the pagan village to the glory of God. I would bring my faith closer to the people and praise the Lord. Even now, I flinched slightly as I recalled the promise I had made.

The five of us stood before the structure, which still smelled of fresh wood and even bore a bell in its gable. On this Sunday morning, it now rang the faithful from their beds, Ragnar, Conor, Mina, Jalla, me, and the rest of the village community. Only a few days had passed since its completion. The dark red paint had just dried and was meant to help protect the walls from the forces of nature.

Only hesitantly did the Lord's message spread within my clan. For the baptism of the first converts, I had enlisted Priest Cornelius' help, who was also celebrating Mass that morning.

Delighted to gather the last sheep of this island under his care, he had supported me in fulfilling my vow. The plans for the construction of the church had come from his own hand. Cornelius had even brought the church bell himself for the consecration a few weeks earlier. He remained as a guest for several days to persuade more of the mistrustful villagers of the Christian faith. Conor and Jalla were the first to receive the sacrament of baptism from Brother Cornelius. Erik and his friends followed. The former outlaws had since become loyal followers and ardent champions of the new era I had ushered in.

Sigrun had died before the church was completed. She had been the fiercest critic of Christianity in Akureyri. It was now only a matter of time before I would convert all the inhabitants to my faith. The gift God had granted me in the life of my son could never be measured against this, yet I felt as though I had settled my debt.

One after another, our small group passed through the plain doorway into the interior. No window illuminated the enclosed space, only numerous oil lamps made from fish tallow cast their light upon the simple furnishings. At the far end stood a modest wooden altar with a carved cross. No images, no symbols, and no statues adorned the house of God, yet the people streamed inside all the same. Gradually, the room filled. Lacking shingles, we had covered the roof with straw alone. Flower garlands hung from the wooden pillars that supported the roof structure. Diligent women—foremost among them my sister Jalla—had tended to this simple adornment; thus, the air no longer smelled of wood and fish tallow, but of yarrow and heather. It would take a long time yet before all the inhabitants would attend service regularly, but as their leader, I was content with the progress we had made so far.

Conor stood beside me with his head bowed, his hands folded in reverence. His fingers were bloodied from the first exercises with the new weapon. That morning, filled with pride, I had shown him the first steps and the correct stance with the katana. Conor possessed a natural talent and a rare joy of movement, I could see it at once, but the path to becoming a skilled fighter was still a long one. I would walk it with him as a strict mistress of the blade.

Suddenly, I felt a hand gently slip into my right one. It was Conor's, seeking closeness. It was a small gesture, yet it meant the world to me. We looked at each other and shared a moment of gratitude and love, spoken only through our eyes. In all those years, Conor had missed me just as deeply as I had missed him, and he admired his parents greatly. We will find each other again, I promised him. We were only just beginning.

Cornelius concluded his sermon with a communal prayer. The faithful went down on their knees and murmured the Lord's Prayer. High and low voices, sometimes hushed, sometimes resolute, prayed together.

"Amen," all those present said together.

"Inshallah …" I murmured softly. God would hear it, and He would understand.

Afterword

The description of the Battle of Teba was difficult for me. Too many differing versions of the attack on the castle in Castile circulate through the historical records. I have read a great deal about it, yet to this day, I am not certain how James Douglas died exactly. Of course, he was killed by his enemies in battle, but in what manner? Opinions on this differ greatly.

John Barbour's account, written nearly two hundred years later, struck me as overly exaggerated. He claims that the famous Scottish knight, surrounded by his enemies, hurled the silver casket containing the embalmed heart of Robert de Bruce at his foes. Given the earlier veneration of saints, one could easily view this gesture as heroic, but for my novel, I found it too heavy-handed. Instead, I allowed myself to create a highly personal interpretation of James's death. The tragic bond with my fictional character Enja and her illegitimate child mattered more to me than adhering to the scant and uncertain historical circumstances.

The Pope's message to Christendom must have reached James Douglas when he was already in the Netherlands, for King Alfonso XI had informed him of his crusade against the Moors while Douglas was in Sluys. The Scottish general remained there for twelve days and, in his role as clan chief, held court. The deep veneration of James Douglas as a hero and the reverence shown towards the embalmed heart of the deceased King of Scots appear in every historical account. It is certain that James had already decided to travel to Castile upon his arrival on the European mainland. This would also explain why so many knights chose to follow him.

The use of cannons during this period gave me some pause. It was only by chance, while writing, that I realised cast-iron gun barrels did not come into use as weapons of war until a later time. That prompted me to research whether King Alfonso IX, who was known even then for his advanced military technology, might have had access to such means. And I did, in fact, find evidence of it.

The origins of gunpowder and firearms lie in China. The earliest known reference to the formula for gunpowder appears in a Chinese text dating from the year 1044. The Mongols, who ruled China at the time, may have employed primitive firearms as early as 1241 at the Battle of the Sajó in Hungary. It is certain that they used cannons during their invasion attempts of Japan in 1274 and 1281. From early forms of cast tubes, they fired projectiles or fire arrows using gunpowder.

The new technology first spread to the Islamic world, and from the middle of the thirteenth century onwards, projectiles filled with gunpowder were launched there from catapults. An Andalusian botanist, who died in Damascus in 1248, referred to the saltpetre used in the production of gunpowder as "Chinese snow." In Persia, it was known as "Chinese salt."

Along the Silk Road, not only goods but also knowledge was carried. It is therefore unsurprising that this technology eventually reached Europe. Early, though still uncertain, indications point to the use of primitive cannons in 1284 during the defence of Forlì in Italy; others refer to Brabant in 1311 and the siege of Metz in 1324. However, the first reliable evidence of their manufacture appears as early as 1326, in an authorisation by the city council of Florence to cast "metal cannons" for the defence of the city. An illustration in the Milemete manuscript from England, dated 1327, also unmistakably depicts a cannon.

The first recorded use of cannons refers to the siege of Cividale in Friuli in the year 1331. From that point onward, reports of this new weapon begin to multiply in European sources. In France, these heavy weapons were mentioned for the first time in 1338. The English, with near certainty, employed them for the first time in a field battle at Crécy in 1346.

Alfonso XI may, therefore, already have made use of some of the earliest cannons.

With this fifth volume of the Highlanderess saga, the story of my heroine Enja comes to an end. I have told everything I wished to tell, and thanks to Aufbau Verlag, who decided to continue the German-language series, and Leap Publishing, it has been made accessible to readers all over the world.

I am deeply grateful for this wonderful opportunity to close a wide circle and untie many of the knots that formed over the course of the series. Many of my readers repeatedly ask how much of my own personality resides within the heroine Enja, and I must admit, it's more than I had been willing to acknowledge. Perhaps it is the fate of every author to weave personal experiences into a book. Love, death, illness, and fear are ever-present in every century and the subject of countless works. Even in our enlightened age, these emotions and struggles remain profoundly relevant.

The courage for life, the motivation, and—admittedly at times—the turbulent determination of my heroine reflect today's ideas of a successful personality. Enja is my heroine, an energetic woman of strength and self-belief, determined to realise her dreams. I hope my readers find these very qualities as inspiration for their own paths in life. As hard as Enja had to fight against the daily challenges of life in the Middle Ages, all possibilities should stand open to us and our children today. We need only recognise them as opportunities, believe in them, desire them, and work tirelessly to achieve them.

I cannot conclude this series without thanking those who have accompanied me since 2021 on the long journey to the end of this volume. Among them are Drs Franziska and Malte Heidemann, who supported me with their remarkable expertise in medieval history and medicine throughout every book. With them, there were always intense yet warm-hearted discussions about the almost superhuman qualities of my heroine Enja. By this last volume, the character had clearly grown dear to them, for the editorial review contained surprisingly few suggested changes.

I am deeply grateful to Dr Heidemann for her suggestion that Robert the Bruce may have suffered from psoriasis and ultimately died after many years without treatment. I would never have imagined that a person could die from this condition, certainly not when measured against the effective treatments available today, but at that time, this chronic inflammatory skin disease was unknown and untreatable. In the end, the patient would die of organ failure caused by an unchecked autoimmune reaction. There is a strong likelihood that Robert the Bruce died from this illness, as many sources also report. For a long time, scholars had named leprosy as a possible cause of death, but this has since been disproven through analyses of the skull.

Of course, I would also like to thank Constanze Bichlmaier, my editor at Aufbau Verlag. I owe her the fluent and coherent writing style of my texts. With her firm yet always warm manner, she managed to turn my initial shock at seeing pages cut into gracious acceptance. By now, I avoid overly detailed descriptions that would never make it past her desk. Her critical eye surely spared some readers from gruesome details. Nevertheless, it has not escaped anyone how harsh and merciless the living conditions were in Enja's time. Hunger, labour, illness, and death shaped life in the Middle Ages. I will not even begin to speak of justice and fairness.

Last but not least, I wish to thank the one person who has accompanied, supported, and encouraged me in my writing from the very beginning: my husband. After almost five years and more than 2,500 pages of historical exploration, he is still by my side, and he stands there with pride.

At this point, I would also like to thank my readers, who have accompanied me and my Enja so faithfully over all these years. To all those out there who have been inspired by my heroine, or simply carried away to another time, do not let anyone take your dreams from you; we need only have the courage to make them real.

If you wish to learn more about me and Enja, then join the worldwide clan. Immerse yourself in the thrilling rise of the Highlanderess Enja across the globe.

Yours, Eva Fellner

www.highlanderess.com/clan

IMPRINT

The Highlanderess—Enja's Battle
Eva Fellner
First edition: February 2026
ISBN: 978-3-949109-49-2

LEAP PUBLISHING

 Leap Advancement Germany GmbH • Colonnaden 5 • D-20354 Hamburg. Registered at Hamburg Court HRB 158497

www.ingramcontent.com/pod-product-compliance
Lightning Source LLC
LaVergne TN
LVHW041052080826
845145LV00007B/1539